Praise for
Blood W

"*Pariah* is a fine example interesting take on the stanc.... .u....sy tropes. A complex tale featuring adult themes and intriguing, relatable characters, it's a promising beginning to the *Blood Wizard Chronicles* series."
-C.S. Marks, author of *The Elfhunter Trilogy* and *The Alterra Histories*

"Readers who expect serialized cliffhangers in each chapter, popularized by authors like Dan Brown, may be disappointed. Instead Jay Erickson builds every moment to an intense conclusion, using graphical landscapes that are vivid and provide the backdrop to a powerful dialogue that drives the story. The emotional and psychological depth given to the characters shows that Jay Erickson is laying the groundwork for a growing future with each interaction."
-Brad Mitchell, PhD, MA, MS, Med. Associate Professor of Psychology and author of *Surviving Psychology*

"*Pariah* has many aspects that make a great fantasy tale. Author Jay Erickson captivates you with the emotions of the characters and once he has you, he doesn't let you go. There is love, hate, fear, joy, revenge, and justice, with a cohesive writing style that keeps you riveted page after page. There is so much happening, that you are left stunted, wondering how it all will end. I could not put it down!"
-Joe Strohmeyer, author of the upcoming series, *Triad of Evil-Mystal*

"Remarkably well done! An epic fantasy adventure masterpiece! The end will leave you begging for more. An excellent launching point for the *Blood Wizard Chronicles*. I am looking forward to Ashyn Rune's next adventure!"
-Jason Bigart, film director, *The Empty Throne* and the web series *Apotheosis*.

Praise for
Jay Erickson

"Absolutely phenomenal! Jay Erickson's unique ability to transport his readers into the world he has created within the pages of his book is extraordinary. I couldn't put it down!"
-Hope Norton, award winning artist, 1st place winner at the Artist League of Sandhills Annual Art Exhibit for *Mehndi Beta*

"Jay Erickson likes to grab you from the first chapter and never let go!"
-Taurean Seneca Gray, screen writer, *Befriended*

Praise from the fans

"*Pariah* had a grip on my imagination from the very beginning. It was a page turner until the very end.
-Marty Carmichael, Steelworker, IN.

"*Pariah* keeps you on the edge of your seat with riveting action scenes and in depth character development. Author Jay Erickson manages to insert real world issues into a fantastical environment in subtle and often informative ways. It was a book I never wanted to put down . . ."
-G.E. Law Enforcement, IL.

Praise for
A Blood Wizard Chronicles Novella: Stormwind

"*Stormwind* is an intense, character-driven melodrama that never ceases to be entertaining. It's heroes are immediately likeable and the action is vivid, but it has just enough substance to make the reader think. Plus, it has so many plot twists both M. Night Shyamalan and Christopher Nolan are jealous!"
-Nathan Marchand, author of *Pandora's Box*, and co-creator of *Children of the Wells*

The Blood Wizard Chronicles

BOOK I

PARIAH

JAY ERICKSON

HALSBREN
PUBLISHING, LLC

BLOOD WIZARD CHRONICLES: PARIAH

Edited by Katherine LaSelle
Cover design and layout by Jay Erickson.
Character art by Hope Norton.
Photography by Roy Ferrer
Additional art royalty free by FreeVector.Com
Headpiece template, royalty free for commercial use, by Retro Vector

Published By: Halsbren Publishing LLC. *La Porte, IN. 46350*

ISBN 978-1-942958-05-5

Made in the United States of America.

DEDICATION

This dedication goes to my father, James Erickson. My first and truest fan. Thank you for all your support over the years.

-Jay Erickson
Author

THE ✦ EAST

Dire Plateau

Mystic City Ruins

Jaës

Oganis

Highfolk

Eratat Lake

Broken Teeth Mountains

R. Koba

R. Adnama

Buckner

Tilliatemma

Fermänia

Dakoria

Czynsk

Shalis-Fey

Bremingham

Ire Ocean

Sprigen

Vesuvian Range

Ghomelaneum

Gnomesgate

Jay Erickson
2014

KULDARR

TABLE OF CONTENTS

PARIAH

TOME I:

The world of Kuldarr consists of many things that are dark and evil, but none as perverse, none as foul as that of the wizard. Rumors whisper quietly that these magical conjurors once ruled over all species with an iron fist. Back before the Fifth Era . . . Before the forgotten times . . .

They were tyrants, one and all, who wielded their immense power through the gifts of magic. All of them knew how to wield not only the magic of **Creation**, the blessed gift of the Maker, they also know that of **Destruction**, magic which is obscure, taboo, and above all else, evil beyond reproach.

It was through these magical abilities that they conquered and enslaved all the species of our world. They used people as tools for their twisted experiments, as playthings, and as labor to erect their vast stretching empires.

Our world was a foul one then, a dark one. It is no small wonder why all of its history has been marked as lost, be it burned, destroyed, or torn asunder from thy initial manuscripts. Such evil things not need plague one's thoughts now. We were different people then. Lost sheep in need of a shepherd; Praise the Maker.

Yet it is important to recognize that such dark things still do exist. Even today in the Sixth Era, the Era of Enlightenment, wizards, enslavers of life, desecrators of crops, and the destroyers of kingdoms, are real. They *do* exist. Though their numbers are merely a pathetic shadow of what they once had been, the fact remains; wizards are indeed very real.

So heed this warning friend, should you come across one of their monolithic towers steer clear of that great evil.

For if you do encounter a wizard in this world today, rare though they be, then may the Maker have mercy on your soul. For the wielder of **Destruction** shall show you none.

-From the Writings of a Devout Jasian Purist

PRELUDE

B lood oozed from over a dozen cuts in her flesh, tiny blooms of magenta, like rose buds against a smooth copper landscape. It was an irritant, but still she did not relinquish her pursuit. She was too close. Her quarry was not far from her now.

Sweat soaked her raven chin-length hair and her tanned muscles ached from the strain of overuse. The chase had been ongoing for over three days, ever since one of the hunters had spotted him in their domain. It was a creature of great evil, a skewer of the balance of things.

Her lungs burned as she continued to regulate her breathing. Her fingertips and toes were raw from scaling rocky crags and ancient stonework from long-dead races that were scattered intermittently throughout her people's woods. She grabbed at another outcropping, feeling the burn tingle underneath her flesh and up her arms. She didn't have time for pain.

Suddenly a rustling sound came from her left. She had been pursuing alone for little more than a day and there was no one with which she expected contact with, yet. She paid attention to the sound. It could just be a young doe fleeing her presence, or perhaps even a predator. These woods weren't the most forgiving. Things greater than wolves lurked in the dark shadows of the Shalis-Fey.

Still moving forward, she drew a javelin from the deerhide quiver across her bare back. It made not a whisper as she brought it around. The haft was well balanced, and the deerskin smooth and oiled so her weapons could slide free. There was no glint of sunlight against the steel blade for it was deeply coated in a black ichor. The poison, skillfully crafted by the druids, was made using the root extract of a strychnos flower. This prevented the usually gleaming metal from reflecting light and giving away her position. It was also a neurotoxin. Whatever she stabbed with it would begin to become paralyzed almost immediately, offering her a greater advantage in combat. As a hunter she had spent countless months developing a resistance to the paralytic. She was virtually immune now should she accidentally knick herself.

She had only moved about another two hundred feet when she caught another ruffle roughly twenty feet to her left, deep within a line of tall bushes. It was definitely following her. She looked down at the tracks ahead. The skewer of balance had taken a direct route, and had done little to mask his passing. She doubted the creature had doubled back now just to try and get the jump on her.

The huntress slowed her forward momentum and took careful aim to her left, preparing to launch her projectile should her pursuant decide to attempt to flank her.

Suddenly her midnight-colored eyes caught a flash of movement between the large thick oaks of the region. She studied the area, waiting for another sign. It was then that she realized its sudden foreignness to her. She had never been in this part of the forest before. In her lengthy winters, she had thought she had known every inch of these woods. She slowed to a stop.

Still wary of the new threat, she began to take in the tall vine-covered monoliths of stone, mingled with the sentinels of wood that protected the ancient forest. Only crags and fissures of rock often dotted the massive forest, with a few smatterings of ancient stonework relics scattered about, reliefs and totems of long forgotten peoples. They were generally never taller than her height and perhaps half that more.

These were statues, massive and gargantuan in comparison to what she had known. Each one of the goliaths stood over twenty feet tall. They were human-looking enough, though worn from centuries, possibly millennia of neglect. Their faces were long shorn away from wind, rain, and decay, but she could still make out that they were standing in a variety of poses. These stances seemed very important. She also could tell that they were all representative of men, and yet they all were wearing robes. She studied the figures with their hands outstretched in weird postures. Most of the fingers were worn away or broken off, but she still understood the concept. It was magic. They were all frozen likenesses of humanoid men in the acts of casting spells.

The sight of these human statues in her woods caused her involuntarily to run her free hand over the high tip arch of her pointed ear, momentarily lost in thought. Her ears were long and tall, coming to their apex at a height slightly surpassing the crown of her skull.

This was an area of high magic. It seemed fitting, she thought disgustedly, that the evil creature she pursued would run through these parts. Though she didn't loathe magic, she didn't care for it either. Not amongst her own, at least.

Humans wielding magic, however, had always been . . . troublesome, even unpredictable. You never knew what they were going to do from one moment to the next. Elves, on the other hand, always had a propensity and patience for magic that the short-lived humans seemed to lack. And had magic not had its uses among her own kind, she would claim that it too was a skewer of balance. As it was, magic walked a very fine line in her eyes.

Standing in the shadow of the stone behemoths, it also dawned on her how utterly alone she was. The branch of hunters that she commanded were all dead. Indeed the one she pursued had not only killed her eight, but had also already managed to slay six Councilors and over two dozen more hunters. He was just one beast and yet he triumphed versus the many. What had she really thought she could do alone against the likes of this one? Armed with nothing more than a few poison-tipped javelins and a short spear, she was only one Elf against his powerful wrath.

Yet the dead burned fierce behind her large dark eyes. She had watched each one die in this pursuit, had their blood slick in her hands and against her very flesh as she had tried to staunch the flow from some of the grievous wounds this monster had made. If she broke her pursuit now, the evil would win. The death of all those Elves would be for nothing. That thought galvanized her need to continue, even against a fear she felt growing within her.

She accepted that fear, but refused allow it into her heart. She would not let it slow her; it wouldn't cripple her. Her mind worked against the fear and soon she rationalized that though he was powerful, he fled. That made him vulnerable. It made him mortal. And that meant he had limits on what his power could do. Limits were his weakness and weakness meant he could be killed.

She took that as a good omen from the spirits. They watched out for her. They strengthened her resolve so that she may be the one to triumph over this blasphemous creature yet. To have reliefs of her victory etched into the walls of her people's history.

A twig snapped behind her. Her keen Elven ears picking up the sound easily. Her pursuer had grown bold.

She determined that the one who stepped on it had weight, and judging from the lack of a following crunch, it walked on two legs, and not four. That ruled out a wolf. She waited a moment, feeling the presence grow behind her. She felt the warmth of another being wash over her back, but she did not move. She held. Just as she felt the creature's presence reach its climax, she reacted.

The Elf dived into a half roll, expertly maneuvering between an oak sentinel and one of the monstrous human effigies. She felt the dirt and sharp lines of grass draw across the bare flesh of her shoulder as she rounded through her roll. As she did, she pivoted on that shoulder so that when she came up she was facing the opposite direction of her movement, bringing her javelin to bear in line with her potential assailer.

Her pursuer was clearly unprepared for the speed of the Elf, and had little time to avoid the soaring projectile that she had released.

The blade cut through the air and her pursuer just narrowly avoided its piercing tip as he fell backward to the ground. Hand over hand he flipped until he landed on his feet and one hand, crouched low to the earth like a wild beast. His own short spear was drawn.

"By the spirits!" he hissed. "Brodea, it's just me!"

With shocked recognition she realized that she had almost skewered a fellow Elf. Quickly she recovered and moved over to the defensive man. "What were you thinking sneaking up on me, Ambit?" she whispered back. "I almost killed you."

"The sneaking wasn't meant to be upon you, Brodea, but to elude alerting the Unbalancer to our presence. Similar to what you, yourself are doing," he commented dryly.

Brodea shook her head. "It still doesn't change the fact that I almost impaled you."

Though he did not smile with his face, Brodea did not miss the smile in his amber colored eyes. "Perhaps," he whispered back. "I thought you would have realized it was me approaching though, and not the Unbalancer. You have known my heat for countless winters," he said quietly, raising himself to his full height.

Brodea nodded, silently berating herself.

"I should have," she confessed, but then looked around at the alien surroundings. "But this place seems to have me . . . disconcerted."

Ambit looked around as well, nodding, his dirty brown shoulder-length hair swaying gently in the idle winds that danced through the tree line. "True enough."

Brodea studied his bare chest. It was a well-muscled and tanned frame adorned in the ritual paintings of his patronage. Though no outsider could recognize the distinction of markings from one Elf to another, each set of body markings were distinctive to the very family line they either descended from or were life-mated into. Brodea knew the swirling patterns of Ambit's familial body paint well. She bore the very same across her abdomen and breasts.

Ambit approached her, his eyes never leaving his surroundings. "I heard about your branch," he told her quietly. "I couldn't stand the thought of you hunting the Unbalancer alone, so at risk, while carrying our blessing," he finished, closing the gap and putting a well-callused hand against her abdomen.

Brodea put her hand over his, and smiled lightly at the man to whom she had given herself. "This is our calling," she whispered back. "It is the spirits who will protect me, and ours."

"Still. . ." he countered, but Brodea placed a finger over his mouth.

"We've a job to maintain balance in this world. As a Councilor, I cannot shirk that responsibility ever, not even a little," she told him passionately.

Ambit nodded. He understood her. Brodea smiled. He always understood her. "If you're here, where is Vooken?" she asked.

"Perhaps an hour behind us," he replied. "He brings two more branches, and a host of druids. This Unbalancer doesn't have long. I'm sorry Brodea, but I ran fast and hard to your side; I could not wait."

She nodded, and turned back towards the towering monoliths that surrounded them. "I am glad you are here. I did not wish to face this skewer alone. I had been fretting over that very thing when you came to me. Surely the spirits must favor us, for responding to my needs so quickly."

"Surely," Ambit returned.

The two spared little more words as Ambit let Brodea resume her trail on their prey. They had scarcely pursued for more than an hour when Brodea held up her hand, signaling to stop. Her dark eyes looked into Ambit's amber ones. "The trail ends," she mouthed, and instantly Ambit was alert.

Brodea drew her short spear and Ambit did the same. They examined all around them looking for traces of their quarry but all they could see were another set of those human effigies surrounding them. These were even taller than the previous works. In fact, Brodea realized that they stood amidst a semi-circular clearing. The trees in this particular area had all but disappeared, leaving only the stone monoliths to stand vigil over them.

Brodea carefully moved forward. Vines snaked themselves across the earth and connected with the massive silent figures looming above her. She stepped over the thick flora, her bare feet grazing over the lush and moist green moss that blanketed the surface. Her foot slipped a little, ripping up some of the olive morass.

She knew that her footing on this terrain would be slick and she would need to be extra careful. It wouldn't do to have to fight the Unbalancer on this ground, only to slip and break her leg. Frankly it would be insulting.

As she entered the center of the semicircle of ominous statues, Brodea noticed that the moss-strewn ground she walked on was smooth. Too smooth to be natural landscape, she thought. Cautiously she crouched down and rubbed away some of the verdant green lichen. She was aware of Ambit studying her curiously. Yet Brodea was more alarmed with what she found than she was concerned with Ambit.

Underneath the mire and muck she was surprised to find crafted masonry. She knew immediately from the rate of decay around the area that it was beyond centuries old. Even then, it held up to all the rich forest and nature could throw at it. Her fingers traced along the thin seams of the fine brickwork. It was firm and sturdy, showing no signs of deterioration that may result in a cave-in or sinkhole.

As she looked to the silent sentinels of stone once more, Brodea realized what it was that they were standing on. It was the top of an archaic temple. As she looked around she could see signs of where there were rises and peaks in the earth that had caused the temple to shift and eventually sink long before. Brodea couldn't even guess at how many millennia such a natural event may have taken, or if it had even been natural at all.

Quickly she stood and waved Ambit over. Ever alert, he obeyed, but his eyes never left any of his surroundings. When he was mere feet away, Brodea stopped him with a warm hand on his chest. "Fear not retaliation at the moment, Ambit," she said calmly. "We have the Unbalancer cornered."

Ambit arched a brown eyebrow. "How can you be certain?"

Brodea smiled an immaculate white smile and pointed to the stonework beneath them. It took only a moment for Ambit to understand. "He has gone to ground," he said with an equal smile.

"No doubt he thinks the subterranean halls of this nature-defiling temple will break our trail, and he'll find an exit elsewhere," Brodea returned.

A scowl came across Ambit's face as he realized Brodea was right. "Then there is still a chance for him to elude us."

"Not if we pursue quickly," Brodea countered. "This Unbalancer seeks to disrupt us using the machinations of ancient men. I will offer him no quarter."

Ambit's frown hardly lessened at her remark. "There's bound to be limitless tunnels beneath there, with no way of truly knowing where he went. We should wait on Vooken and his branches. They shan't be but a score of minutes behind us by now. Likely the druids will even be able to draw him out."

To Ambit's surprise, it was Brodea's turn to glare. "I have pursued this Skewer of Balance for days. I have lost my branch to this monster! I do not intend on letting him escape whilst we twiddle our thumbs and wait!"

Ambit grimaced. "Surely you can see my reasoning?" he asked his life-mate.

Brodea nodded, but it took away none of her icy demeanor. "And surely you can understand mine. He has killed our brethren, Ambit. Fellow Hym we called kin. I cannot brooch the thought of him escaping when we have him cornered now!"

Ambit did understand. One of the hunters killed had been a cousin. It was rare enough for them to have offspring as it was, so to lose a true family member was hard to accept. He didn't like it though. It felt reckless, even for Brodea. Additionally, he had more than just her to think about. She bore something dear to him inside of her as well.

"Brodea . . ." he tried.

"I will not be reasoned with on this," she replied tartly.

And that was that, Ambit understood. Brodea was determined, and she would go in without him if that were the case. He had seen that look many times before over the centuries. In the past he may have let her, but now it was different. He looked to her abdomen; it wasn't even protruding yet. He couldn't let her go alone. So in the end it was he that reluctantly nodded. Brodea smiled at him, but it did little to quell the knot he felt swell deep within his gut.

"Fine," he conceded. "Let us at least leave Vooken something to prove this is where we have entered. I don't want them passing us completely."

Brodea nodded. It did make sense. She looked to what she had travelled with over the last three days. It had been light, and for the most part she was virtually naked. Only a strip of tightly linked leather covered her breasts, and equally a deerskin leather skirt covered her lower loins. It was the standard garb of a female Councilor on extended hunts, in order to travel as lightly as possible.

Other than her waterskin and small hip pouch of deer jerky, all she had upon her was her quiver of javelins and spear. She looked to Ambit, and sadly he bore even less than she. Ambit, being a hunter and not a Councilor, had on little more than a loincloth and a coarse leather quiver lacking many javelins. Brodea noted that he had indeed rushed to her side. He didn't even have rations, only a waterskin.

Normally they had a certain kind of bark, dubbed 'blood bark'. This bark exuded a reddish secretion when pressed firmly upon an object and they could generally mark where they were going for other of her kin to follow. Because it looked so much like blood, most outsiders would never even recognize the trail being made by the Elf until it was too late. As it stood, Brodea had lost her blood bark two days prior when the fifth member of her branch had died in her arms. Poor Shenalia. She had been a mother too, though her daughter was full-grown.

Instinctively she put her hand against her abdomen. The skewer would suffer, she told herself. But it did little to change the fact that they were under-equipped. Since she didn't want to be defenseless heading down into the temple, losing the quiver wasn't an option. Leaving their food stuffs also seemed unwise, and any scavenger beast might come by and eat it before Vooken even arrived. So in the end there real was no choice.

Pride was not their way and so with little humility, Brodea reached up and undid the latches of her leather stripping. Soon it fell away exposing her fair sized chest. Ambit said nothing as she took the leather-binding strap and hung it unceremoniously on the foot of one of the vigilant monoliths.

"Does that work?" Brodea asked.

Ambit nodded. "I think it will."

"Good," Brodea replied. "I just hope we don't have to run fast. Lack of security makes full sprints . . . cumbersome," She quipped to her life-mate. Ambit merely chuckled.

It didn't take long for Brodea to find the entrance of the temple. Indeed the Unbalancer was hasty in his retreat, not even attempting to re-cover the portal with the vines and foliage that he had roughly moved aside. Brodea took it as a further sign of good fortune from the spirits. But she could see that it made Ambit all the more wary.

Ambit knew the Unbalancer was no fool and to take him as such would be equally as foolhardy on their part. To not even hide his comings either meant confidence or a trap, in Ambit's eyes. Brodea, however, did not seem to be hearing any of it. Ambit studied his life-mate's sudden overbearing determination and wondered briefly if she recognized the danger, or if this driving vengeance at the loss of her branch had temporarily blinded her? Perhaps the spirits had been watching her after all, he reasoned. If he had not been there to protect her she may have very well walked to her death. He was glad then that they delivered him so expediently to her side.

Their initial descent into the temple started easily enough, with only vines and mold growing partway into the entrance of the large subterranean structure. It wasn't until they were firmly underground that the situation had changed significantly.

The hallways were cluttered with heavy oak roots from the trees far above that had managed to puncture through the stone cut ceilings some fifteen feet above them. And though the stairways were wide, they were also very steep, and the residual scree made by the shattered remnants of the roofing above made the climb downward slow and treacherous.

Water dripped and ran in the distance, causing an eerie echo to resound throughout the entire structure. Wind howled through the perforated stone channels creating an ever-present moan as they descended into near darkness.

What alarmed Ambit the most however, were not the alien sounds or the dangerous footing, but the fact that it never seemed to get completely dark.

Ambit knew that there was no light source to illuminate their path in any way, but for some reason, there always seemed to be a small pale blue iridescent light cast into the near darkness. It had no discernible origin, either. Not from the floor, or walls, or even ceiling above them. It was just there. It was just enough to see in front of them, but never showing enough of where they were truly going. The light seemed to be directing them, and that thought was not comforting. Ambit felt the knot in his gut tighten. He was about to object, but a single stolen glance from Brodea told him there was no turning back now.

Ambit was wished he could stanch tracking their prey, or prepare for the inevitable conflict, but there was little he could truly do. There was no trail to follow on the broken ground, and there was no strategy to truly make when neither of them had any ability to see past the half a dozen feet in front of them. Ambit couldn't even study the temple walls and architecture because there wasn't enough light to give them any substantial definition. It was like walking into a hazy, incomplete dream, he thought. Or nightmare, maybe?

They journeyed deeper and deeper into the temple for several more minutes and with each passing moment the duo was sure that the Unbalancer was going to appear and strike them down. But it didn't happen.

Brodea, now as bare-chested as Ambit, began to notice a growing chill as they got closer to what she reasoned to be the center of the ancient structure.

It started out small, and she had figured it was just from being enclosed and underground. But now as they descended deeper and deeper into the complex she began to think that it was more. Her nipples stood erect and hard underneath the persistent cold, and she began to feel numbness in her fingertips. She looked to Ambit, staring into his eyes, their color no longer discernible in the pallid azure light. She saw his breath coming out in small white plumes.

It had never been that cold in the Shalis-Fey, even in winter.

The shaft of her spear began to grow cold, and just when she feared that she wouldn't be able to hold it from the biting frost anymore, the shadowy compound suddenly opened up before them.

They entered a large spherical room, larger than any Brodea had ever seen before. It could easily fit their entire tribe within comfortably. She looked towards the ceiling and was amazed that she could see nothing. It travelled so far from the light that it disappeared into blackness. How far had they descended? She wondered.

A strong cerulean glow emitted from the middle of the room. There stood an obelisk that dwarfed all the statues she had seen prior. It was like a pyramid, except that the four sides were long and flat and travelled up forty or fifty feet into the chamber. Though it was tall, it wasn't wide, she realized. It was perhaps two, maybe three Elves wide, standing side by side, shoulder to shoulder. Only seven feet up from the base of the obelisk, it was hollowed out. In its core resided a crystal the size of a human's head. This was the center point of all the light it shone brightly enough to illuminate the entire chamber, all but the high-reaching ceiling, anyways.

As Brodea swept her gaze across the room, she again saw more of the human effigies. They were all facing inward towards the strange monument. She noticed that these were not worn down like the others outside and she marveled at the intricate detailing of each of them. She could make out little glyphs that danced about the robes of each one of the statues and could even see fine-cut lines in the etchings of the men's beards. Even age lines were visible on the faces of some of the statues. Again, their hands were outstretched in strange arcane positions. She counted thirteen in all of the stone wonders.

The trickling sound of water echoed throughout the hollow chamber. It didn't take long for the two of them to notice a small brook running around the outskirts of the chamber. Four individual streams ran to the center tower creating a cross within the large room.

With spears drawn, the duo approached the strange pyramid in the center of the room. It was captivating. As Brodea walked around one of the figures, she noticed that there was a large thick tome laying open at the foundation of the statue. Cautiously she approached it.

Brodea squatted down and quietly placed her spear on the floor. She hefted up the heavy volume. It was worn and aged, the leather binding faded and crumpled. There appeared to be no title or markings on the front, just plain, indescript leather binding.

As she began to turn the archaic yellow pages, she realized that there was writing on them. It was a language she didn't recognize, though to be honest she did not known many. The common language of the world outside Shalis-Fey was called

Trade Tongue, and of that she could understand only the most basic. Speaking it, she knew maybe a handful of words.

Ambit approached her, his eyes still roaming heavily across the room's horizon. He didn't like this at all. There was a great aura of wrongness about the place, not to mention the unearthly cold. He looked to see Brodea fully engrossed in a strange tome, her spear lying on the floor next to her. "What is that?" he whispered harshly.

"I'm not sure. Some sort of book. I can't read it," she answered.

"Then put it down. I like not the feel of this place," he returned.

As Ambit swept his hunter's gaze over the chamber, he suddenly began to notice things that were blind to him at his previous angle. There were baskets by two separate statues and a bunched up cloth-like object nearest one end of the obelisk. He approached the nearest basket and as he looked in he saw piles and piles of dried meats, fruits, and vegetables. A quick glance at other pile and he realized it was full of compost. Ambit hissed under his breath as he scurried to the strange pile by the base.

He didn't even get within ten feet of the object before he knew what it was; a bedroll.

Ambit ran to Brodea and grabbed her arm. She looked at him sharply; he didn't care.

"The Unbalancer didn't flee down here to try and elude you!" he barked at her. "He led you here. He's taken up residence here for weeks!"

Ambit pointed with his spear to the baskets and the bedroll. As understanding washed over Brodea, she suddenly grew very cold.

"How right you are, Wild Elf," a thick voice grumbled at them.

Ambit quickly spun around, letting go of Brodea and grabbing a javelin from his greatly depleted quiver. Brodea cradled the book to her breast and she, too, turned quickly to see him, the Unbalancer.

Where a moment before there was only darkness, suddenly a monster of a man walked into the pallid light. He stood at almost twice their height and equally as wide. Large, tattered robes that had been split and re-sewn in places more times than Brodea could even count draped his massive frame. In the cobalt glow it was impossible to distinguish its color, or colors, but it appeared marred and dirty as if the garments hadn't been washed in weeks, perhaps months.

A long, braided dark beard ran from his flat thick face and down to his twine belt that held the filthy clothing together. Long, mangy hair, dreadlocked and wild, encircled his face, sticking out sporadically from a well-worn hood. Indigo eyes glowed as fiercely as the crystal, from under thick furry eyebrows. Visible canines protruded from his lower lips.

"Wizard!" Brodea hissed.

"How very astute," the wizard replied dryly.

The wizard looked around the chamber nonchalantly, seemingly unconcerned about the armed Elf before him. "I'm sorry the accommodations are not more to your liking but rest assured there is a power here that your kind can't even begin to comprehend. I've been here for the last twelve weeks, studying . . ." he said, nodding to the book in Brodea's arms. "And exploring these archaic passageways."

Brodea's dark eyes went wide when she realized he was speaking their language. "You know our words?"

The mammoth man nodded. "And many more," he said with a chuckle. "It's amazing what you could learn if you Elves didn't live such a cloistered life."

"You're a beast and a murderer!" Ambit spat at the wizard before him, all the while trying to protect his life-mate behind him.

"You see, that's what I'm talking about," he said, pointing to Ambit. "Here we are having a civil conversation, you and I, and he jumps in all angry and full of bravado screaming beast! Murderer! How can you ever escape the trappings of your society when you cling to them like bees on honey?"

"You killed our brethren!" Brodea snapped at the wizard.

"Ah . . . that," the wizard said as he casually walked over to the obelisk in the center of the room. "Yes, well I had no intentions of even dealing with your kind, hoping to avoid your people completely. But by chance, or perhaps ill luck, I was out collecting more supplies when I had your hunters stumble across me while I was relieving myself in your woods. An embarrassing moment, I assure you. I had tried to be passive, but you Wild Elves are a tenacious lot. I was forced to kill most the first hunters, and I figured that was that. But no, you kept coming like a flood. Then I was simply hoping that you would cease after I killed, oh, I don't even know how many I killed," he said with a shrug. "But no, here you are, ever persistent."

"Wizards are a foul taint on this world!" Ambit growled at the wizard, "You are skewers of the natural balance of life, you are pestilence."

"Yes, yes," the wizard said with a bored expression as he swung his hand nonchalantly in the empty air. "I get it. I disease lands, scourge the livestock, I've heard it all before."

Brodea glanced behind her and saw her spear on the ground. If Ambit could keep the Unbalancer's attention for long enough she might have a chance to lunge for it and strike the wizard before he could cast a spell. She whispered a prayer to the spirits and silently took a step backward.

"Wizards are parasites to this world. Your taint consumes and destroys all it touches. Your filth infests the land, air, and even minds of the innocent like a festering plague. It is our duty to end your infection once and for all! The spirits demand it be so," Ambit said valiantly.

"You have no idea," the wizard returned, an evil smile taking his face. His canines expanded well over his stretched lips and dark greasy mustache. "Your kind hide from power, while I bask in it."

"This very temple you stand in now is of ancient Craetorian origin; the progenitors of the wizard. Arbiters of the magic of Destruction!" the Unbalancer boasted. "That book so ardently held upon her breast has been teaching me all I need to know about the true nature of Destruction. Did you know, Elf, that this chamber is literally a bridge into the Nether plane, where our realm and the realm of magic entwine harmoniously together? The Nether, it exists all around us, parallel to what we see. We walk through it even now, breathe it, taste it, and yet it is just out of our reach, for most of us anyway . . .

"There are creatures in there that do not sleep, moving past you as we speak, above you, beneath you, perhaps even stalking your pretty friend behind you. Ones that can consume your soul just as much as the magic you fear. There are worse things in this world than wizards."

Brodea took another step backward. She felt her bare flesh brush up against the cold shaft of her spear. She was there. Only a moment more . . .

Ambit felt Brodea's heat lessen. He knew she moved towards her spear. The time for words was over. They never should have come here alone, but what was done was done. This creature was an infection upon the world. It was his solemn duty to destroy it.

"Your words are poison," he spat.

"And your ignorance is astounding," the wizard returned flatly. "Do you really think you can contend with the likes of me?" he asked. "I have killed droves of you mongrels. What is it that you think you can really do?"

"I can have faith in the spirits!" Ambit roared as he threw his javelin and the chamber erupted into chaos.

The wizard was like a coiled snake just waiting to strike. Instantly, ancient words poured from his mouth and his hands were a blur of motion. Ambit stared in disbelief as his javelin shattered upon the wizard's robes like fragile glass thrown against a stone pillar.

Ambit reached for another javelin but was slower than the monstrosity before him. Already the wizard had invoked another spell and it was barreling his way.

Brodea dropped the heavy tome and lunged for her frost-covered spear just as the first of the wizard's horrific spells began to rain down around her. Globes of energy as black as the void hurled at the duo like little meteors of onyx.

As Brodea grabbed her spear, an icy-cold filled the core of her being like she had just been dunked in an arctic pond. It drew all breath from her body, but she didn't stop to think about it. Lungs burning for air, she rolled across the frigid surface, narrowly avoiding the bullets of obsidian.

Brodea had never seen any magic like it. As they struck the ground around her, they sizzled and dissolved the area of impact utterly. It wasn't like fire or acid, those eroded away a surface until nothing but char and refuse remained. This was different. Wherever the globes of darkness struck it simply obliterated what had been there. No scorched and tattered remains. No burning smell lingered in the air. There was nothing, just a hole where what had once been, was now gone. Brodea knew what she witnessed. It was the art of Destruction.

The raven-haired Elf looked up just in time to watch in dread as the first of the spheres of destruction connected with her life-mate. Ambit screamed in agony as Brodea watched pieces of him disappear before her eyes. The first globe connected with his upraised right arm at the elbow as he was reaching for another javelin. The suddenness of the spell's power was jolting.

As with the floor, there was no burning or rending of Ambit's flesh, just a simple absence. Where flesh, blood, and bone had been a heartbeat before, now there was nothing.

The missile sheared through his elbow like strong water through damp paper. Perfectly severed from his body, his right forearm and hand just fell lifelessly across his shoulder and onto the ground. His body, not even truly aware of the travesty that had just occurred, merely oozed its crimson cruor from the smoothly-rent stump.

The second missile connected just above his left hip. Suddenly, hardened muscle was annihilated along with the bones of his hip and lower ribs. Brodea stared, aghast as she watched her lover's entrails begin to dip out of the hole in his body.

The final umbral projectile washed across the top of his temple, instantly killing him. Brodea screamed in dismay as the powerful magic devoured bone, brain, and flesh. His long brown mane fell to the ground behind him as if he had been scalped.

Lifeless, Ambit's remains toppled to the ground, his dead amber eyes staring unmoving at his wife. Brodea watched as the shine in them fell flat.

The wizard looked at the encounter with morbid interest. Slowly his deep indigo eyes locked on to Brodea's own dark ones. She looked at him with only hate and vengeance. "Where are your spirits now?" he asked sinisterly.

Tears streaming down her face, Brodea roared at the Unbalancer as she flipped up onto her feet. Instead of reaching for her javelins she charged at the monstrous humanoid.

Unprepared for such an aggressive assault the wizard backpedaled, stumbling to bring forth another spell that would kill the troublesome Elf. He only managed get off a few ruby-red arrows of energy.

Brodea flipped, rolled, and slid under every glittering projectile that came for her. She was an unstoppable juggernaut and all of the magical missiles fell short of the deft Elf.

"Damn nimble Elf," the wizard muttered as he struggled to bring another spell to bear.

With a heart of rage, Brodea plowed into the large wizard, a flurry of motion, stabbing and slashing with her short spear. The wizard, though large, didn't have the footing to withstand her onslaught.

When Brodea barreled into the Unbalancer, it was like running shoulder-first into a tree trunk. The short spear exploded against his stone-like armor, and she felt her clavicle snap on impact. She gritted her teeth against the pain as the two of them tumbled past the obelisk and into one of the small brooks of water.

The water attacked her as savagely as any spell. So cold the crystalline liquid was, it felt like there were icy fingers that gripped at her flesh. She wailed in agony as the glacial solution drove her body numb. She tried to pry herself away from the bear of a man, but the polar water made her limbs instantly sluggish and dull.

The same didn't seem to be the case for the Unbalancer. He clambered to his feet, sloshing great swaths of water away from him with the wave of his arms. Soon the anesthetized Elf was lying upon the freezing waterbed, with no water to cover her. The beast of a man reached down and grabbed her by the throat.

His strength was immense as he ripped her from the ground as if she weighed no more than a sack of feathers. She felt herself soaring through the air and then felt her back connect hard against something behind her. Were it not for the numbness of her flesh she was sure the pain would have been overwhelming.

Struggling against the behemoth's might she kicked out, trying to find ground. Realization sunk in quicker than any of the cold had. She was held aloft in his powerful grip, the ground far beneath her feet. She could garner no perch.

Weak and sluggish, she attempted to beat upon her captor's arm, but it was as if she was trying to punch through a log. The wizard grabbed her by her jaw and forced her to stare into his evil blue eyes. "You've been quite a handful," he hissed at her. "Far more impressive than any of your brethren."

His sinister eyes, feral and hungry, began to examine the rest of her body as well. "You're also the most beautiful thing I've seen in a long time."

His evil orbs lingered long on her exposed breasts and stiff nipples. "You've even come prepared." His eyes glittered with intent.

With his free hand he reached down and twisted Brodea's nipple hard. Even through the cold, she felt the pain. She whimpered. "It's been a long time for me you know. I think you should be rewarded for your efforts."

His face was close to hers. She could smell his breath, rancid with the scent of decaying meat. His body was rank from so long without proper hygiene. He pressed his hard body against her. Brodea quivered in revulsion.

"I think you need this," he said menacingly. "I'll make it hurt."

With a final jerking twist, he removed his hand from her nipple and then began to fumble around with his own robes. Brodea squirmed and resisted him but his grip was like a vise, pinning her in place by her jawbone. Suddenly she felt him, hard and firm, by her frigid thighs and she truly knew what he was going to do.

She screamed and struggled against him, her arms flailing madly. He laughed at her as he pulled fiercely at her leather skirt with his free hand. The Unbalancer, taken by lust, drove his filthy face into the side of her neck, kissing and biting her flesh by her broken clavicle. She moaned in agony. His coarse beard began to rub her skin raw.

She felt a world of despair take her. This monster was going to ravage her body in ways that appalled her, right in front of her murdered betrothed. She screamed at the spirits for not helping her. Why would they do this! She was their most devout! Their most faithful! Tears rolled down her face in misery, she felt him tug her leather barding free as her skirt dropped to her ankles. It was going to be anguish, she knew. The next few minutes of total depreciating horror, and then he would kill her.

Brodea looked up in misery at what was about to happen. She could feel the rough fabric of the wizard's robes on her raw and frozen flesh. She bit her lower lip as she waited for the piercing pain between her legs . . .

. . . And she noticed light. The spirits had answered.

Blue and rich, it shone around her temple like the corona of a star. It was so bright that she had been surprised she hadn't noticed it sooner. She looked up above her at the smooth flat surface by her head that ran to an apex far above. The wizard had her pinned against the obelisk.

She felt his fingers against her loins, fighting for entry against the cold. She squeezed her thighs tight against his hand. His rough hands forced them brutally open again as if she offered no more resistance than a limp sack.

Quickly Brodea reached up behind her head, stretching her arms as far as they would go. If the light was this bright, it had to be close. Her shoulders screamed with fire as she contorted her arms back further past her head, bending them in ways her frame wasn't meant to do. She swallowed back the revulsion against what the Unbalancer was doing to her body with his thick hands.

Her fingers slid against stone, and then emptiness, and suddenly she touched something so *alien* that she gasped at its power against her flesh. She fumbled with it, struggling to get a grip on it, just as she felt the tip of him press against her loins.

The crystal wobbled, slipping in her frozen and torn fingers as she stretched her arms to the point of breaking, and then it was in her hand.

He pressed against her, she felt him pushing hard to enter. With all her might, she drove the crystal down on the back of his head. His attention diverted, his stone-like armored skin couldn't protect him against the magical crystal. It broke through his barrier as if it had all the consistency of pudding. The Unbalancer roared in pain as the crystal shattered into a thousand pieces against his skull.

Brilliant blue light exploded all around Brodea, momentarily blinding her. She screamed against the painful radiance, and then felt herself falling.

She hit the ground, unbalanced, and toppled over on her side. Above her, the wizard wailed in horror and agony. He staggered back and forth, unable to see her. "Bitch! Elf Bitch! Do you know what you've done?!"

An aberrant darkness engulfed them. And with it a presence she couldn't even begin to comprehend. Brodea didn't know how, but it became so cold then, that it actually pierced her soul. She could barely breathe.

The wizard continued to mutter a litany of curses at the raven-haired Elf, but she didn't care. Quickly kicking off the torn remains of her skirt, she scrambled to her feet and back-pedaled away from screaming wizard.

Brodea wondered if perhaps the light blinded her, when slowly she once again saw a pallid cobalt glow. She looked in its direction. A single shard of the crystal lay next to the tome she had dropped.

She scurried towards it, and grabbed it in her icy hands. Numb, it took her a moment to firmly hold the small two-inch sliver of crystal. She brought it around to face the wizard.

When the light hit him, he looked up and stared at her with bitter menace. Black ichor was running freely down his neck and shoulders and soaking his filthy robes. He took a step towards her and abruptly they both felt the ground tremble. A strange sound followed a high-pitched wail that came from the wizard's left. From his right came the answer . . . in the same off-tone melody.

"No. No!" The wizard hissed.

Brodea saw something indistinct and large swarm the wizard, and he screamed. She turned around and looked one last time at the ruined form of her life-mate. His amber gaze was dead and broken. A brief moment of despair overtook her when she realized he would not be there to see the birth of their child together. That despair turned to anger for the one who caused it, and it galvanized into something stronger . . .

Hate.

"I love you," she whispered, looking into his glassy eyes. "I will kill them . . . all of them I promise you. By the spirits, I promise you will have retribution."

She would see that he was avenged. This Unbalancer wasn't enough; they all needed to pay. Brodea saw the tome lying near his prone form. It had a great many answers in it about wizards, about Destruction. She heard a schlurping sound and a wail as one of the creatures burrowed into the wizard's flesh. Brodea grabbed the tome lying against the ground and ran.

Behind her she could hear the wizard scream one last time as the creatures ripped him apart. Soon it was drown out by the beasts themselves as they sang their melancholy song.

~ ~ ~

The shard illuminated her path and before she knew it she was out of temple. She looked around in the bright light, suddenly shocked by the heat. Then almost magically, Vooken was in front of her.

"Brodea. By the spirits!" he said, looking at her naked and battered form.

She didn't try to explain, she didn't have time . . .

The singing came.

Brodea looked back into the temple in horror as the off-tone melody came out of the darkened portal before them. In moments, it became louder and stronger, and she knew that they were getting closer.

"Run," she whispered. "We have to run!"

No one questioned the nude Councilor and they ran, all of the Elves, as fast and hard as they could. Within an hour, they were by a cliff side, but they didn't cease. The song seemed to follow them as they ran and even now, perhaps three miles distant from the temple, the horrible sonnet was still clear. They scaled up the crease in the land until they were finally well above the verdant woods below.

Or verdant no longer . . .

"Spirits save us all," Vooken whispered as he looked at the horizon beyond.

Where a canopy of strong-leaved oaks had once created an impenetrable ceiling of green, now only darkness remained. A grey and withering stain began to spread across the treetops, plaguing and infesting all it touched. They watched as it spread further and further from its flashpoint until it corrupted everything they saw. They didn't need to be told where it had begun. They all knew it was the temple. The singing continued the entire time. To their weary relief the pestilence ceased at the base of the cliff side.

In mere moments, an entire section of the Shalis-Fey woods had withered and died.

Vooken looked to the druids who stared at their deadened land, mortified and confused. None of them had any answers.

Brodea, still clutching the shard and tome, stared icily at the place where Ambit had died, where the father of her children had died. "Such is the work of the wizard," she said darkly. "That is why we must hunt them."

Vooken looked panic-stricken towards Brodea and immediately she knew something else was wrong. "What?" she asked.

"First Councilor Tehirs has declared that due to the extreme loss of life caused by the wizard, all balancing of their kind is to cease immediately," one of the druids instructed her.

Vooken looked at her sadly. "We weren't coming to purge the wizard, Brodea. We were sent to retrieve you."

Anger flashed across her dark eyes like sunlight against chips of onyx. "Get me!" she said, outraged.

"Look at that!" she roared as she pointed with the shard down to the deadened forest that was their home. "Ambit is down there. Dead! Brutally murdered by a wizard who has done this! Look at that desecration! Look at it!"

"I see it," Vooken said quietly.

"They need to die, Vooken!" she growled. "They all need to die!"

Vooken looked pleadingly at her, and though she wanted to tear his throat out for his seeming cowardice, she understood. He had been her friend for centuries, and Ambit had been like a brother to him. It wasn't lack of will on his part. She knew that he would stand by her every step of the way. It was the First Councilor.

"There's nothing we can do," he told her. And she knew he was right. When the First Councilor speaks, it is as if the words had come from the spirits themselves.

Brodea felt lost. All her life she had fought against imbalance, fought monsters and skewers alike. Now it seemed as if it were for nothing. Angrily she looked down at the shard and tome she held cradled against her chest. She understood why she had held on to them. They were weapons, weapons that had dispatched a wizard . . . easily. Where dozens of her brethren had failed, one crystal had succeeded.

Wizards were the greatest threat to the balance of nature, of anything alive. They were nigh impossible to kill, only a few ever recorded in their reliefs. Whatever had been held in that shard had destroyed the wizard as if he was nothing more than a defenseless babe. A dawning of understanding washed over her.

"There is nothing we can do," Vooken repeated again somberly.

"Yes there is," Brodea answered, venom dripping in her voice. "We wait. The First Councilor won't live forever, and when he dies we will hunt wizards once more."

Her eyes held such icy conviction that Vooken and even a few of the other Elves backed away from her.

"And when we do, we will destroy them all once and for all," she said, and a smile took her face.

She would be patient. She would learn. And when the time finally came, she would strike.

WATCHER

Great wings buffeted the hard wind against his body. Gales of immense force assaulted his skin as he watched her come in from her descent.

He did not mind. In fact, to watch her soar through the skies had always brought him great merriment. There was something majestic about her when she took flight. The way her sleek body cut through the air. The perfect flow of her sculpted muscles as everything about her worked with precision. The rhythmic beat of her thick leathery wings as they the drummed through the air. Everything worked in absolute harmony to keep her massive frame aloft and in smooth flight even against the toughest southern winds.

He watched as her crimson scales glistened vividly in the pale orange glow of the dying sun. She landed gracefully, like that of a feline, touching down smoothly in front of him. The ground made not a tremor from her impact, only that of the wind beneath her wings causing the verdant green grass to wildly flatten beneath her beautiful form.

Her head swayed in his direction. Her large golden eyes, easily the size of watermelons, stared piercingly into him. She blinked slowly and exhaled. Small jets of fire plumed from her nostrils and rolled gracefully across the obsidian plates that formed the bridge of her snout. He stared at the inky bone as it ran along the bridge of her head to fan out in a brilliant black crest that continued for another five feet beyond the base of her skull.

His eyes continued to trek across her frame as her brilliant wings settled into her body. He followed the long dark spines that continued past her broad crest, down her neck, and across her back between her wings. They continued their journey all the way to her tail where they ended in a wickedly barbed ball of bone. Like that of a morning star. Yet he knew the power behind that tail. Where a morning star may be capable of felling a man, her bone appendage on the end of her tail could shatter boulders. Yet for all the terror her body represented, there was also an undeniable peace in her large golden eyes. A tranquility and acceptance of being that could only come from millennia of existence.

She was a dragon.

An ancient wyrm who had seen more with her golden eyes then any of the other species of Elves, dwarves, and humans dynasties combined. She was the wisest of them; she was their elder and their leader.

Xaoentramythinea looked down at his own body. His scales were only a drab red, and held nowhere near the luminescence of her glistening body. His wings were thin and scrawny, barely capable of supporting him in flight. He knew with time he would grow into a fine young dragon, but as a hatchling of only a scant two hundred and thirteen winters, he barely had the mass to startle a cow. He sighed audibly and lowered his head in reverence as she approached.

Lift your head my youngest hatchling, the ancient wyrm commanded of him. Her voice rang in his head like the sweetest of music, like wind through a meadow, or the calm serenity of a small waterfall running into a narrow basin.

Yes Mireanthia, he returned, projecting his thoughts into her mind.

For dragons, there was no need to speak, for they were able to read the thoughts of all sentient creatures. While they could speak, and even had their own dialect of draconic, such things were unnecessary. Either way, silence at this moment was necessary and he knew it would not do to have two dragons roaring at each other. It would send every sentient within a three mile radius away screaming in terror, and that is not why he was here.

You seem troubled, Xao, she said into his mind, using a nickname that he was having trouble accepting. For dragons, the appellative of their true name was never a problem. Yet for a dragon who had to be in constant contact with the other species such nicknames were often common. The reason for this was that many of the other species had difficulty using a dragon's full name to begin with. The idea that he would be known as Xao instead of Xaoentramythinea was disconcerting. If his hatch mother had wanted his name to be Xao, she should have named him that two hundred and thirteen winters earlier, not throw it on him in the last ten. It just did not feel right.

It's nothing, Mireanthia, he said to her, but refused to look into her golden eyes.

Mireanthia studied his own yellow orbs fiercely for a moment. Xao was left submissive and fidgety, but in the end, she said nothing further, turned, and began to walk down the rich green hill they were on and into the valley below. Xao had to scamper after her to keep up with her long strides.

Why must we go on foot? Are our bodies not made to fly? Xao asked his elder as he struggled to keep up with her long swift gait.

It is because of the humans, Mireanthia responded, not once looking back to her running hatchling. *We shan't fly lest our presence be known. Remember that, Xao. Your presence amongst them cannot be known.*

Xao mentally nodded, so she would feel his confirmation as they continued to journey swiftly down the hill. As they cleared one of the grassy mounds and began to ascend another, Xao could begin to see the telltale signs of human life around. Their livestock had grazed spots of the hill; footprints abound littered the ground from both the beasts of burden and the trackers. His nostrils even picked up the smell of cooking meat lingering on the southerly winds. He licked his lips in anticipation of such a meal.

Their foods are not for you, my youngest hatchling. You must remember your place, always, she berated, feeling the hunger welling excitedly within him.

Yes, Mireanthia, Xao answered dejectedly.

Within minutes they cleared another hill and could see into the open valley far below. On the outskirts of the furthest northern edge of the valley resided a human settlement lingering on the cusp of a thick dark forest. Small hay thatched domiciles dotted the ground on the horizon. Some of them were issuing forth dark plumes of smoke through their rooftops. It was from that smoke drifting lazily in Xao's direction, that he recognized the smell of cooking meat.

Xao could see the humans that made up the settlement. They were small pink fleshy creatures with varying colors of hair, and no discernable armor plating of any kind. Indeed, he was amazed such creatures could find ways of staying alive minus such natural endowments such as wings, claws, and the ability to breathe fire. They seemed to have such a handicap. *These are our betters?* he asked, shocked.

No. Humans are no better than Dragons, and we are no better than they are. It is something you must always remember little one, Mireanthia said sternly into his mind. *While these creatures may indeed seem frail by your eyes, be not fooled, for they are the very ablest of hunters. Though their skin is soft, they have learned how to armor it. Though their claws blunt, they have learned to sharpen them by constructing swords, and spears. Humans are a hardy race and amazingly adaptable. They can survive within any climate, and persevere within the worst of times.*

It is for this reason that we must watch them? Xao asked questioningly.

The elder dragon shook her head. *Of course not, Xao. I have known humans for hundreds on top of hundreds of winters. We watch someone different. Someone who is very special and, at this moment, fat with child.*

Xao craned his long scaly neck so that his large yellow orbs could better see in the ever-failing light. *Who?* he wondered to her. *Who is the woman that we seek to watch?*

Xao looked to Mireanthia, who nodded with him, and then directed with her snout to a house at the end of the town, tucked between a cornfield and the rim of the deep green forest. A small copse of elm trees encompassed the front of this modest home.

She is in there. Moreover, even as we are here talking, she has already begun the laborious process of bearing the child. I can feel its presence around us, and smell it in the air. Mireanthia told the little red dragon.

Immediately Xao began sniffing at the air, but could smell nothing but the sweet burning meat. *Are they cooking her?*

Mireanthia laughed heartily in his mind. It sounded like claws grating down glass, but it was something he was far too used to, to be annoyed with. *No, they are not cooking her,* she replied. *One day you too will be able to feel these things as I do. For now, you will just have to trust in my judgment.*

Xao snorted and looked back towards the small home in the copse of elm trees. *Why is she so important?* the diminutive dragon asked.

Mireanthia looked at the house longingly. *Because she is one of the rare ones, Xao,* the elder dragon replied. *One of the ones that I have been teaching you about.*

Xao looked out at the house with a renewed interest. She was one of the few special ones? He had been learning much of them for over the last one hundred and fifty winters. *What is her name?*

They call her Rune, the ancient wyrm responded. *Jade Rune.*

Jade Rune, Xao repeated to himself. She was someone important to remember. *And this human settlement?* Xao asked. *Does it have a name?*

Mireanthia nodded absently. *It does indeed,* she answered. *They call it Bremingham.*

Bremingham, Xao repeated as he looked back to the village. Slowly dusk began to consume the small line of houses, capturing it in the deep violets and blues of night.

On the northern edge of the town, Xao spotted a small female child sitting on a rock watching the sunset. She looked once in his direction, and for a moment he even thought she might have been looking at him, even though he knew it was impossible. Mireanthia would have sheltered them with a spell of camouflage; at most, he would appear as nothing more than another mound of grass on the hill. Yet she remained, looking in his direction and he grew a bit concerned. He looked once to Mireanthia and felt a tug in his mind.

She always looks this way when the sun sets. I know she likes to watch for the Elves.

Can she see us? Xao asked, nonplussed.

I do not think so. She has never made a move as if she has seen me. She has never once run in fear, nor has she grabbed anyone else and pointed in my direction. I think she just likes watching the horizon. Humans have large imaginations, especially the children, she replied, still looking at the little girl.

The girl on the rock turned quickly as a man exited the house by the copse of elm trees. He was waving at her excitedly and she hopped off the rock running at him with all haste.

Xao looked back to Mireanthia, and she took him with her vivid golden eyes. *Listen to me now, Xao. You are finally of age to begin your task. You have been chosen to watch this family. This Rune family, as I have done for the past few winters.*

But why me? Xao asked.

Mireanthia looked at him with a sense of sadness in her eyes. *Because I will not be around much longer, my hatchling. I am old and though I may not look it, it is true. Very soon now, the land and all magic will once again have its child back.*

You will die? Xao asked in terror.

We must all die sometime Xao. I have had a good life, long and much fulfilled. I do not shy away from what is to come, and you shouldn't either. This was my task, and now this task is meant for you.

Surely, there is another? Xao whispered into her mind, almost pleadingly. *Someone more worthy. I am so young. Even my wings haven't fully developed yet.*

As if in excuse, he held his scrawny wings up for her to see.

Mireanthia shook her large crimson head. *Though you yourself may not feel it yet, in you I sense a great compassion for all the sentient species of this world. Something your hatch brothers and hatch sisters lack. Do you not see, my young hatchling? It has to be you. There is no one else.*

But . . . Xao began weakly.

Do this for me, Mireanthia told him. *If not for me then do this for your ancestors. Do it for all the mistakes that we have made as a species, for we have let our pride keep us from doing what is right. Do this because you know that deep within yourself this is right, this is important. I know you can feel it, just as I felt it those winters ago.*

Xao nodded in agreement, and looked back to the small domicile as the door closed.

Content, Mireanthia looked back to the small house as well. *I know this may not make any sense to you yet, my young hatchling,* she spoke softly into his mind. *But there is something about this family. Something that may change the outcome of everything that we have ever known . . .*

A moment later, he heard Mireanthia gasp. *What is it?* Xao asked in worry.

It is done! Mireanthia said jubilantly. *The child has been born, and it is a boy.*

Xao stared out at the house eagerly. He was here to witness a birth amongst his new charges. If this were what he had to do, he would see it through for his ancestors. *What is the child's name?*

Mireanthia golden eyes stayed locked onto the small house on the horizon. Slowly a crystalline tear built up and ran down the rivulets of her glittering crimson scales.

Xao could feel the joy radiating off Mireanthia, and he was sure he could even feel it coming from the small house in the village down below. Without even looking at Xao, Mireanthia whispered the boy's name into his mind.

It rang there audibly and clear.

Ashyn.

SUMMER OF STORMS

66 "Come on, Ash!" Julietta said, taking his hand quickly and rushing him with her out the door. His little legs pumped swiftly in an effort to keep up with his spindly-legged sister.

"Where we goin'?" The small boy asked.

"To town center, silly. Pa says there's an Elf there," she said merrily.

Ashyn stopped in his tracks. "Elf," he repeated warily.

Julietta nodded feverishly. "Yes, now c'mon! I dunna wanna miss him."

The little boy refused to move. "Pa said we should fear the Elfs."

"That's Elves, honey," a voice called from around the copse of elm trees. As Ashyn turned to look, he saw his mother appear cradling a wicker basket full of plump red apples. "The correct way to say it is Elves."

"Ma!" He yelled merrily as he broke his grip from his sister and ran to his mother. He connected at full run and quickly embraced her right thigh. Jade laughed at her son and continued to walk, albeit at a waddle, while her little boy stayed firmly latched to her leg.

"My goodness!" She remarked. "It's only been a few hours. You act like I've been gone a life time."

"Julietta wants to take me to the Elves," he tattled on his sister, this time using the correct pronunciation.

Julietta crossed her arms and screwed up her face to show her displeasure. "He's gonna leave!" she whined.

Jade nodded at her son. "It's okay, Ash. The Elf that your sister wants to see is a High Elf."

"High Elf?" Ash repeated as his mother nodded approvingly. "What's the difference?"

"Only everything!" Julietta yelled impatiently throwing her hands high in the air, overly dramatic.

"Now, now Julietta your brother is only being cautious as your father taught him." She put the basket of apples down and pried her son off her leg, looking deep into his grey eyes. "The Elves in the woods are known as Wild Elves. They are a dangerous and savage people who paint their faces all scary and attack people with spears."

"But not a High Elf?" the boy asked.

Jade shook her head. "No darlin' they are very civilized and upstandin' folk. They are like us in a way."

"Oh . . . kay," he drawled. "If you say so."

Julietta jumped up and down vigorously. "Come on then! Come on!" she said as she quickly grabbed his hand and began to propel him towards the town center. "I don't want to miss my chance!"

Jade smiled warmly as she watched her children disappear through the cornfields. Ashyn always loved the cornfields. He was always so curious about the insects that resided within.

A few minutes later the two children erupted out of the opposite end of the cornfield, laughing and giggling, all reservations about the Elf banished from the little boy's mind. He held up his catch proudly in his sister's face, a wriggling grey worm that twisted and coiled about his hands. Small granules of dirt stuck to its clammy body, giving it a lumpy and disfigured appearance. Julietta made a disgusted look and swatted it away. "Quit it!" she said giggling, and she ran towards the other buildings, her long strides doubling the distance quickly from Ashyn's little pumping legs. He did not even notice.

They passed around the village houses, passing through the fenced-off areas of cows and goats. Once Ashyn even disrupted the swine, swinging his long dangling insect in front of them and sending them squealing. He kept running long after Farmer Bibs came out to berate him, his voice dying far behind the scurrying boy.

Ashyn laughed all the louder as he chased his sister through the stables, past Karl's tanning shop where the thick scent of cured leather hung fat in the air like sap clings to a tree. He wove nimbly around Fifa's little bakery and made his way past the slaughterhouse. Inside he could hear the chopping as Butcher Brown cleaved meat from the bone.

Soon he found himself in the center of town, surrounded by its three most prominent structures: the slaughter-house he had just passed; the holding cell, used to house those who became vagrant or drunk; and of course the town hall where the townspeople convened for everything from group education, to discussing droughts and plights, to communal worship of the Maker. Between the three structures, Ashyn saw him, the High Elf.

The Elf stood half a head taller than any other man in the town. He had long brown hair that flowed around him like brilliant russet cascading waterfalls. His pointed ears poked out minutely through his shiny hair. He had deep blue radiant eyes that drank in everything he looked at. His face was smooth and clean, unlike the scruffy men he was used to seeing every day. As he spoke to the men around him, Ashyn could not help but notice perfect white teeth. Every movement, every nuance seemed to flow from him like a choreographed dance. He was brilliant.

The Elf was dressed in rustic brown leathers. Ashyn recognized it as a hunter's garb, as his father was also a hunter. Nevertheless, this Elf's clothing was far more elaborate. Small studs of metal ran across his shoulders and biceps, slowly tapering into thickened cured leather at the elbows. His forearms were covered in gauntlets of heavy leather that were emblazoned with intricate patterns of autumn leaves and twisting vines. His right hand bore a glove that only covered his thumb and first two fingers. The last two were bare and exposed. Ashyn knew that it was an archer's glove. Its purpose was to cover the fingers that primarily pulled on the string of a strong taut bow. His left hand bore no glove at all, but instead had two silver rings, one of them like twisting ivy holding an emerald. The other one beheld twin dragons fighting over a ruby. Across the back of the Elf, he could see a quiver, with few arrows remaining, and a long bow. It was so tall that it easily dwarfed the small boy.

Ashyn's gaze lowered to examine the man's leather trousers that bore the same metal studs as his tunic. These studs however were slightly different; they were shaped like small maple leaves. They continued down to knee high doe leather boots. Ashyn saw that they were well-worn and knew that this High Elf must have journeyed long and far.

What impressed the boy the most was his sword. Up to this point Ashyn had only seen swords in his mother's books. No one owned one in the town, and the closest thing they had to weapons were farming scythes and butcher's cleavers. Aside from bows of course. Bows they had in ample supply. Bremingham was a hunting and farming community after all.

This sword was different though, even from what was in the books. It was a rapier. A thin-bladed weapon of finesse, and while it might not be able to deflect and parry incoming attacks, it made up for it with quick and precise strikes. It was an artisan's weapon, a master's weapon.

The hilt was adorned in an ornate design of swirling leaves like those caught in a small whirlwind on a late autumn day. Ashyn could see that the design meant to cover the hand of the wielder to protect them from striking blows to their fingers.

Richly engraved across the scabbard were ancient Elven symbols. In the center of it was an eye. Ashyn however was curious about the nature of the symbols on the scabbard. He knew what they meant. His mother had taught him. Ashyn was startled out of his admiration when Julietta whispered next to him, "He's beautiful."

When he looked up from the sword, he saw that the Elf was studying him curiously. The strange foreigner immediately broke off from the group of chattering men and approached them. Ashyn noticed that Julietta's cheeks instantly flared red.

"What have we here?" the strange Elf asked. His voice was elegant, and came out in almost a singsong manner. It was melodic, and had tranquility to it that Ashyn had never heard before. He continued, "Two children of quite the curious hue for these parts."

Ashyn knew he was referring to their complexion. It had always been a slight oddity amongst the people of Bremingham. He, his mother, and his sister all had deep olive skin and vibrant red hair. Most of Bremingham were a paler white with hair ranging from blonde to brown to even black. Nothing quite like the Rune's. As such, they were always studied with quiet suspicion. Ashyn had even heard whispers in his direction once of magic and demon possession. The people of Bremingham were a superstitious folk. They feared what they did not understand. Ashyn was about to issue a retort to the Elf's comment when another spoke.

"Them's the Rune youngins." Ashyn heard Old Tom Gregy say from behind the Elf. Tom Gregy was the resident village drunk. He had spent more time in the holding cell than all the other men of the village combined. Everyone only tolerated him because he was around at Bremingham's founding, and so he had outlasted almost all of them. Ashyn's mother said that he might never die, because he was pickled. Ashyn had no clue what that meant.

Tom Gregy staggered over next to the Elf; Ashyn could already smell the stale, homemade bourbon emanating from the old man's every pore. "Ere mother Jade, she's from far west as near as we can tell. She came here a score o' winters ago. Settled down with ole' Kindin Rune, she did. Good chap that one."

"Interesting," the Elf said as he squatted down to Ashyn and his sister's level. Placing a hand on his chest he pronounced, "I am not from around here as well, as you probably could have guessed."

Julietta broke out into a fit a giggling, which Ashyn found odd. Of course the Elf was not from around here, how was that funny?

"My name is Veer. Veer De'Storm. What are yours?"

Ashyn looked to his sister, and was shocked to see she was blushing almost crimson. She was looking down and away from the Elf, suddenly too shy to say anything at all. Wasn't it she who had wanted to see the Elf? He was content at home reading his mother's books after all. Girls. He merely shrugged and looked to Veer.

"My name is Ashyn. Ashyn Rune, sir," he said and then pointed to his sister. "This is my sister Julietta."

"A pleasure to meet you, Sir Ashyn Rune and Lady Julietta," Veer returned, and Julietta flared an even deeper red. Ashyn pondered for a moment if she might very well explode. "I am from the west, too." he remarked. "Tell me, do you perchance know your origins?"

"I heard tell Jade is from Gurgen, far to the west," Old Tom Gregy spoke up again.

At this Veer politely turned around. "Please, if you would, let the children speak for themselves good sir."

Ashyn was surprised to see this Elf defend him. No one ever really defended him before. Mostly they just stared at him because he was different. That was why he did not like to go outside with the others. Because they saw him as different.

"It's as he says, Sir Veer. My ma says she came from Gurgen."

"I see," he said quietly in contemplation. Ashyn watched as Sir Veer's eyes darted to the men who were watching them, and then back to Julietta and himself. Ashyn saw the looks of suspicion and even repulsion as they looked his way. Even though he was used to it, it did not mean he liked it.

There was a moment of silence that grew slightly uncomfortable between the three. Seeing as he had nothing more to say, his eyes drifted back to the ornate rapier. He could feel the Elf's eyes studying him.

"Do you like it?" Veer asked him.

Absently Ashyn nodded. "It's very pretty," he remarked, for indeed he found the sword beautiful.

Veer stood up and slowly drew the blade. A few around them grew startled and nervous. Tom Gregy was about to interject, but a glance from the blue-eyed Elf made him think better of it.

Once Veer fully drew the blade, he squatted down level with Ashyn again. He held the pommel with his right hand and laid the thin silvery blade flat across his left hand and arm. He raised it towards Ashyn so that he may see the fine engraving across the blade.

Ashyn gasped at the majesty. Etched across the glistening blade were twin lightning bolts. It was like nothing he had ever seen before.

"My foster father made this for me," Veer remarked.

Ashyn looked up.

"You see, I am like you young Sir Rune," he told the boy. Ashyn raised an eyebrow curiously. "Even though I am a High Elf, I was not raised by them. I come from the Shemma, the Great Woods, which is west of here. I was raised by Wood Elves."

Ashyn assimilated the knowledge. "Where are your parents?" he found himself asking.

"They died when I was very, very young," the Elf answered him. "Younger than you are now. I don't remember much of them. I was found by the Wood Elves and taken to their home city of Featherset deep within the Shemma. There I was taken in by a very nice couple who raised me since as their son." His voice drew to a whisper meant only for the boy. "So you see my young Ashyn, I know what it's like to be different. I know what it's like to not look like everyone else, not fit in with everyone who wants you to be the same."

"You do?" Ashyn asked.

Veer nodded. "What is important, young Rune, is that you realize that even though you may not look the same as the others of this town, there are those here that still love you. Take solace in that love and it will give you strength beyond measure."

Ashyn thought on his words for a while as he did he watched Veer slide the sword back into the scabbard. His eyes drifted across the Elven sigils once more.

"Is there a reason why those markings say your last name Sir Veer De'Storm?" he asked, pointing to the scabbard.

"Excuse me?" Veer asked, suddenly shocked by the child.

"Your scabbard," Ashyn replied. "It says 'Wild winds of the Storm.' Is that about you?"

Veer blinked at him, momentarily too perplexed to say anything.

"He does this all the time," Julietta said, finally breaking out of her captivated trance. "He always says things he's not supposed to. I'm sorry, Sir De'Storm sir."

Veer shook his head. His long amber hair swaying like a soft silk banner caught in a breeze. "No, no, it's quite alright really." He looked back into Ashyn's startling grey eyes. "You can read Wood Elven Script?" he asked the young child.

Ashyn nodded.

"Can you speak it as well?"

"Oh yes!" Julietta replied, seeing that Veer was not angry with Ashyn for saying anything out of place. Now trying to capitalize on the attention, she continued. "He can speak all kinds of languages. He reads all of the time." Her voice dropped to a loud whisper that everyone could still hear, "It really gives everyone the jitters, because you know . . ." she said pointing at him. "He's so young."

"Yes, yes," Veer mumbled. "So you're fully literate then?"

Ashyn nodded, slightly embarrassed. This was another one of those things that unnerved the people around him. The fact that he could read and write. Most of the town was largely illiterate. His mother had often times tried to train them, but the older ones were reluctant to learn. The children, however were fascinated by it and some of the parents cautiously let his mother, Jade, teach them. He was the only one in town though that could read, write, and speak a multitude of languages. Aside from his mother, anyhow.

"Just how many languages can you speak?" Veer asked.

Ashyn kicked at the dirt at his feet nervously. "Four," he mumbled.

"Four," Veer mouthed in shock. He then stood straight and began speaking fluently in a variation of Wood Elven dialect that he knew. He ended it by asking him to translate what he said.

Ashyn's ears flared red as he repeated the words, "I find it amazing that one so young has the capacity to learn so much in such a short period of time. Surely you are blessed by the gods."

That brought gasps from all around, and immediately sent Tom Gregy into a rant. "Blessed? More like cursed I'd say! No child should know what he knows! There's a demon in there! A demon I say! The Maker would never allow that kind of thing in a good, hardworking, Maker-fearing boy!"

"Now, now," Veer said suppliantly. "There's no need for that, good sir. I merely asked him to repeat what I asked."

Tom Gregy pointed angrily at the boy, swaying only slightly. "We tolerate their presence here because Kindin is a good man. A good man that has done right by us. But it doesn't mean we have to tolerate such blasphemy!"

His word brought nods of approval from the other few men around. Ashyn could see that once again he was upsetting those around him. He did it often. He stared down at his dirty little boots in shame.

"Perhaps I should take you home," Veer whispered to the Rune children. Ashyn could only nod.

The journey home took longer than it did to get to town proper. This time there was no cutting through pigpens and horses stables. The entire time none of them spoke, though Ashyn was the only somber one. Veer walked between both children, as Julietta skipped along merrily holding his hand. To Julietta this was probably her best day ever. To Ashyn this was just like every other day he interacted with people. Something always went wrong.

As they approached the house encircled by the copse of elm trees, Veer came to a stop. Julietta looked at him longingly, while Ashyn only glanced up to him through hooded eyebrows.

"I suppose this is the end then," Veer said in a melancholy tone.

Julietta's eyes went wide with horror. "No! No! You must come inside and meet our mother! She'll be so happy to meet you! Please Sir Veer? Pleeeeaaaasse?"

Ashyn could feel the Elf's blue eyes on him. He could feel the lingering question in the air that he always felt from others. One that echoed in his mind always. Why was he so different?

"I really shouldn't," Veer commented halfheartedly. "I came here for directions and more arrows. I should see to that."

If there was any way possible for Julietta to become more excited, she found it. "Oh! Oh! My mother is wonderful with maps she can help you, she can! She's the greatest!"

"Why does that not surprise me?" Veer said, and again Ashyn could feel the Elf's eyes upon him. He stared dejectedly at the dirt road wishing that Julietta would just give up, and that Sir Veer would be able to leave so he could run into the house and hide in his books. He even realized that at some point he had lost the dangly insect he had been holding before he met Veer. He sighed; he was hoping to compare it to some pictures in his mother's books. Now it was gone.

"There's still a matter of arrows," Veer told Julietta. "I must have a means of hunting, and my road is still a long one yet."

Ashyn saw out of the corner of his eyes the forlorn look on his sister's face. Already he had figured out the answer to that one. As much as he wanted to hide in his books, he had to admit that he rather liked Veer. The Elf had admitted to being like him. Different, and alone in a place where he was not accepted. However, he did not want to speak. He did not want Veer to dislike him as the town's people did. He took a step towards his house when, out of the corner of his eye, he saw his sister's eyes light up.

"Pa!" she said jubilantly. "Pa's a hunter! He makes arrows! I'm sure he'll make some for you. Please, Sir Veer, do come. Perhaps Ma might even keep you for supper."

"I wouldn't dare impose," he answered.

"Nonsense!" She answered.

Ashyn smiled to himself despite his self-pity. His sister was good at deadlocking people. Even though she looked like him with her deep tan skin, red hair, and for her, hazel eyes. She was more widely accepted within the village. He figured it was because she was more like the other children, the other girls. She could read, but chose not to. She only knew one language. She liked clothes, sitting on rocks fantasizing about Elves, and looking pretty. She was normal to them. Normal. Something Ashyn keenly knew he was not.

Ashyn heard Veer sigh and knew he was defeated. "Very well," the Elf remarked. "But I will not cause your family any undue hardship."

Julietta jumped up and down for joy, taking the poor Elf's arm roughly with her. With it decided, Ashyn dredged forward dragging his feet and kicking up plumes of dust in the process.

Julietta burst through the door merrily with Ashyn and Veer in tow. Instantly she yelled to her mother, "Ma, Ma! Guess who brought us back home!"

Her mother, hard at work over the small stove in the back of their home turned her head to regard her energetic daughter. "Oh who might that . . ." She froze in the middle of her sentence. "Oh!" she stammered when she saw the Elf.

Veer shook his head. "I'm sorry. I'm imposing, I should leave," he said as he bowed his head.

Jade shook her head in return, "No, no. Please stay," she said as she fussed with her fiery red hair trying to put the fallen strays back into her ponytail. "I just wasn't expecting company."

"All the more reason not to be a burden, my lady," he said politely.

"No really it's fine," Jade told Veer with a sincere smile. "Kindin will be home shortly; he'll be delighted to meet you. It's not often that Bremingham sees visitors, let alone we get to have guests in our home."

Veer smiled and bowed once more. "Then I would be honored."

"I hope you like stew I'm afraid it's all we have."

Veer again smiled with his dazzling white teeth. "I'm sure it will be quite delightful."

Ashyn meanwhile watched the interaction with more than a little curiosity. It was true that the Rune residence rarely saw company. Other than Karl the tanner. Karl always came over. He and his father were old friends since they were small boys. Karl was probably the only person other than his family that did not make him feel like he did not belong.

His mother's expression brought on his wonderment though. Even though her smile was warm and sincere, Ashyn saw something more in her grey eyes. Was it fear maybe?

"Why don't you two go to the well and wash up before supper?" she told Ashyn and his sister. Without objection, both of them went outside to gather water to clean up.

Ashyn's father, Kindin, came home a short time later and they all sat around their modest little table in their one room house. Ashyn sat quietly, barely touching his stew at all while he listened to both Veer and his father trading hunting techniques.

For all his father's warnings about the Wild Elves in the woods, he was treating Veer De'Storm as if he were an honored guest, not someone to be wary of.

In a way, Ashyn supposed he was. Of all the people in town, he chose the Runes to sup with that night. Ashyn was sure anyone would have offered him a hot meal. Some, like the Bibs, could have offered him a wondrous meal and a warm place to sleep. The Runes of course could not offer him a soft bed, but Veer did not make a single complaint.

Veer remained lively and cheery all through the meal, as did Julietta who stared at him amorously. Girls. Ashyn thought as he shook his head.

Ashyn just watched however, curious. Whenever Veer would ask him a question he would retreat within himself, not answering. He was afraid he would say something again. Something stupid that might anger Veer and make him go away. As much as he was uncomfortable with Veer staying, something inside of him didn't want the Elf to leave either.

Therefore, he just continued to watch. He watched as his mother continued to have a wary look in her eyes. One that could not be noticed outright. It was in the corners of her eyes in those moments when she glanced at their guest every so often. Ashyn wondered what it could be? Everyone could see that the Elf was polite, he was courteous, and he was harmless. So what was it that their mother feared from this person?

Finally night fell and with it the desire to sleep. Ashyn was exhausted; his eyes would barely stay open. He felt himself lifted by his father and placed in his bed. It was nothing more than a rough leather strip on a stack of hay but it was his, and it was warm. Shortly after, he felt his mother pull up his quilt to his shoulders and kiss his head. Within moments he heard the rhythmic breathing of his sleeping sister and then the whispering of a good night and protection of the spirits from Veer in a Wood Elven dialect. After that all Ashyn saw was darkness.

~ ~ ~

Ashyn opened his eyes early the next morning. He could just make out the subtle pink hues of light in the azure sky as the sun began to crest the horizon. He sat up quickly. The house was quiet, very quiet. He looked down to his sister in her bed next to his. She was asleep, her breath nothing more than a shallow whisper on the wind. He saw his mother across the room on his parents' bed, her breathing the same. His father was gone.

This did not surprise him of course. His father was the hunter of the family and often would go out before sunrise to capture his fare for the day. Ashyn remembered his father's idiom well: The early bird catches the worm. He looked through the rest of the house. He did not see Veer anywhere. Where was the Elf? Did he leave in the night? Was he hunting with his father?

Slowly the boy picked himself from the bed, careful not to disturb his nearby sister. Carefully he tiptoed his way across the house, around the center table and to the window. He looked outside to the rising sun. Orange and yellow rays added to the already pink pallet, casting a vivid display of color across the horizon. Still he could not see the Elf. Had he truly gone? Perhaps Ashyn had dreamed the whole experience. A desire to meet someone like him, someone who was different and had yet somehow found a way to belong. He sighed quietly, and began to make his way back towards the bed.

Another urge overcame him then. One of the basest and most primitive of all urges that all species have. Ashyn suddenly realized he had to pee. Quietly he dressed as quickly as he could hope to and still wake no one in his haste. When he was done he grabbed their refuse bucket and shovel, just in case the need to pee turned into something else, and quietly went out the door and to the back of the house.

When he was finished, he walked around the house once more. As he did, he glanced out far to the smooth rock that his sister liked to sit on, at the very far reaches of Bremingham, next to the Shalis-Fey forests. He was surprised to see that someone was on it.

Placing his shovel and bucket on the ground, he began to make his way to that smooth flat stone. No one but his sister would sit on that stone. She would do it almost every evening, as the sun set. Waiting. Watching expectantly. Hoping to catch a glimpse of the mythical and dangerous Wild Elves that lived in the woods. Ashyn figured that, to his sister, it must be some sort of game. That the threat the Elves represented could not possibly be real. When mother would tell stories of Elves, she would always tell them as beautiful and grandiose creatures; a people larger than life.

Now with meeting Veer De'Storm, Ashyn was sure that Julietta's image of Elves would become more skewed. That she would think they were all as nice and as friendly as the High Elf. He hoped it was not the case. Ashyn loved his sister, even if she may be a tad hyper. She was the only friend he had besides his parents anyway and he knew they loved him unconditionally.

As Ashyn moved closer to the flat rock, he could begin to see more features of the person on top of it. It was an adult, male, and he was shirtless. He could see lean muscles running across the person's back as they sat atop Julietta's rock. Who would do such a thing he wondered? Then a glimmer of new sunlight struck the top of the person's head. He saw the smooth glistening amber waves of long hair. A big smile took his face. It was Veer.

Quickly he ran over to the Elf, hoping excitedly to talk to him alone, before anyone was awake. As he got closer, he could see the Elf was sitting on the rock rigid. His legs were crossed beneath him, and he sat with his arms outstretched across his knees, his palms were facing up. As he came around to face him, the Elf's eyes were closed, and his mouth shut in a thin pale line. Indeed, Ashyn noticed now that all of the Elf's skin was very pale. He had not remembered that from the day before.

Cautiously Ashyn waved his hand in front of the Elf's closed eyes. Veer did not move. Confused, Ashyn leaned forward and snapped his fingers in front of the stationary figure. Nothing.

Worry began to settle like a worm in the little boy's gut. Was Veer hurt? Perhaps something had happened when he went to sit upon the rock? Maybe he had tripped and hit his head, and he sat on the rock to rest and he passed out?

That could be it, Ashyn realized. He had read it in one of his mother's books. What was it called? Concussis? No that wasn't it. Confucius? No, that didn't feel right either. Concussion? That was it! Ashyn realized he might have a concussion. He struggled to remember what it had said. Of all the books he read, the ones treating injuries and maladies he had found the most boring.

He remembered he needed to check to see if Veer was cold. If he was cold, it was not good. Cautiously he poked the Elf's meaty shoulder. Warm. Perhaps his head? Ashyn reached out with the back of his hand to touch Veer's pale forehead. It too was still quite warm. That was a good thing.

What else did the book say? He knew that sleep was not good; perhaps he needed just to wake him up. Looking back and forth to make sure no one was watching he leaned close to the Elf's ear. "Veer?"

The Elf did not move. "Veer, you need to wake up," he said slightly louder. Still the lean Elf did not move.

Nonplussed, Ashyn moved back to observe the situation. What if he never woke up? He wondered. Perhaps he should wake his mother? She would know what to do. She always knew what to do; she had that knack about her. Yes. That is what he would do.

He turned to run back to the house when another thought overcame him. The house was awfully far away. What if wolves or Wild Elves attacked Veer while he was off getting his ma? Ashyn looked around. Veer's bow and sword were nowhere in sight. He had not recalled seeing them at the house either. Then again, he had had to pee rather badly. It was possible he had just missed them. Still he did not think it would be good to leave the Elf all alone so close to the Shalis-Fey woods.

He would have to try harder.

Steeling himself, he grabbed the large Elf by the shoulders with his tiny tanned hands, and began shaking. "Wake up," he said louder. When shaking did not work, he resorted to poking him with his little fingers. "Wake up!" he said very loudly, almost to the point of yelling.

As Ashyn went to jab Veer in the ribs again with his finger, the nimble Elf swiftly grabbed the small boy's wrist. "Careful," he whispered in a monotone voice. Nothing near as melodic as he had heard the evening before. Ashyn stared at the Elf a mixture of shock and terror.

Slowly Veer's dazzling smile took his face. "That tickles." Quickly he opened his eyes and lunged forward at Ashyn, "Boo!"

Ashyn fell backwards giggling and Veer moved forward tickling the small child with his own powerful fingers. Ashyn rolled and squirmed under the onslaught, laughing all the while. Finally, after many minutes of tickling abuse, Veer sat back on the rock.

Ashyn, breathing heavily, sat up and looked at the Elf. Veer was smiling down at him, his blue eyes sparkling. "I'm glad to see you are feeling better today."

Ashyn nodded, but did not want to say anything. He did not want to upset anyone again. He could tell the Elf seemed to sense this. "Do not be afraid," Veer told the boy. "There's nothing wrong with being an intelligent little boy."

Ashyn looked away from Veer and into the town center, a slight frown on his face. "They don't seem to think so."

"That is because they fear what they don't understand," the High Elf answered.

Ashyn smiled. "That's what my Ma says."

Veer nodded. "She's right. Being different is not a bad thing. It is a good thing. If everyone were the same in this world then I think this place would be mighty boring."

"But they hate me," Ashyn returned.

Veer shook his head. "They're just scared, is all. They don't see how a child only a fraction of their age can be capable of so much knowledge. I think it's wondrous. I think you are very special."

Ashyn's eyes lit up like gems. "You do?"

Veer nodded. "I think one day you will be capable of a great many things. Nevertheless, you must be patient. Even though you are very smart, you need to also allow yourself to be a little boy, too."

Ashyn crossed his arms. "But I don't like being a little boy. None of the other boys like me."

Veer smiled a knowing smile. "When I was little none of the other Wood Elven boys liked me either. I was so different from them," he told the deeply tanned child. "Here I am, tall and pale, with light brown hair and blue eyes. And they were copper-skinned, with deep brown hair; some even black! Wood Elves have green, brown, or black eyes, none of them blue. Not to mention not a single one of them could even come near me in height. I was a head taller than they all were. Sometimes two heads! Wood Elves are notoriously short." Ashyn could not help but giggle.

"What did you do?" he asked.

"I persevered," the Elf answered. "I took one day at a time. I refused to let their persecution get to me. I was determined to be accepted. It took a long time, but you know what it paid off."

"Really?"

Veer nodded. "Because I found something I was good at. Something that everyone could respect and that no one could be afraid of."

"What?" Ashyn asked eagerly.

"I have a rather remarkable talent for the sword," Veer returned. "You see, in Wood Elven society, especially that of Featherset, all young boys must learn how to wield a sword. Even if they never become a soldier, or a hunter, they must learn the basics in case we are ever attacked."

Ashyn sighed, a pout coming to his lips. "We don't have anything like that here. No one knows how to fight like that. There is no need. We are hunters and farmers, nothing more."

"Perhaps," Veer answered. "But that is only an example. I came to find acceptance amongst my peers because I was good at something they valued amongst themselves. Something that they believed was important. I would never tell you to do anything you don't want to do, nor would I say that you have to do what others consider the norm. I only say that with time, the people, the children, will come to accept you. It may not be today, it may not be tomorrow. But eventually you will find where it is you belong. And when you do, rest assured they will value you."

Ashyn smiled. He would like to be valued.

"Do you remember what I told you yesterday?" Veer asked.

"What's that?"

"That there are those here that still love you. Take solace in that love and it will give you strength beyond measure. I have met your mother and father. They both love you very much. Even your sister loves you unconditionally. These are pillars, young Rune. Bastions of strength to lean upon as you grow into a man. Remember that and I assure you, you will not fail," he told the boy.

Ashyn nodded. He would remember.

"Now then," Veer said in all seriousness. "Let's talk about a certain young man running out before dawn to the edges of the Shalis-Fey. I'm certain you don't need to be reminded of how dangerous it is out here?"

"Me?" Ashyn asked perplexedly. "What were *you* doin' on the rock?"

"Don't try and change the subject," the Elf said, smiling. "And for your information I was meditating."

"Meditating?" the little boy repeated.

"Yes. Haven't you read about that?" Veer asked. "You seem to have read about everything else so far."

Ashyn shook his head. "I don't know this meditating?"

"Aha!" Veer suddenly replied jubilantly. "So you aren't all-knowing! I was growing worried for a moment."

Ashyn put his little hands on his hips. "I'm not as old as you."

Veer laughed. "No, certainly you are not. I think the only one closest to my age was your resident town drunk."

Ashyn did not understand what he meant by that. Veer certainly looked no older than his mother did; old Tom Gregy was triple her age, easily. However, Veer continued before he got a chance to ask.

"There is a place far north-west of here called the Order of the Sacred Fist. Have you ever read about it?"

Ashyn shook his head no.

Veer nodded. "The people there train night and day to perfect their minds and bodies as one."

"What's that mean?" the curious child asked.

"Don't interrupt and I will tell you," Veer returned. "Now where was I? Oh, yes. Training. You see, the people there call themselves monks.

"Eunuchs?"

Veer shook his head and laughed. "No, monks. Though if you asked some of them, they'd probably say they used it so little they might as well be eunuchs."

Ashyn had no idea what he meant by that, so he merely reiterated the word, "Monks."

"Very good. Anyway, these people. These monks, they trained all the time with their bodies learning how to fight without using weapons of any kind. They use their own bodies as their weapons. Their fists, their feet, and their heads. They train their bodies to do things that most people cannot do. They can stretch farther, jump higher, run longer than others think is physically possible. To do this, however, is not just making their bodies capable of the act, but their minds as well."

Ashyn listened attentively.

"You see, the mind is a very versatile thing. It is capable of much more than anyone takes for granted. If you can teach yourself to believe that something is possible, you can make it happen."

"Like magic?" Ashyn asked.

Veer nodded. "Like magic. I take it you have read about magic."

Ashyn nodded vigorously. "I have, I like it so much. I wish I could learn it too!"

Veer laughed. "Well then you know what I'm talking about. Teach the mind that anything is possible, and the sky is the limit. That's what monks do. But instead of training their minds to accept just magic, they train them to accept that their bodies can do more than they thought possible. Defy what is normal so to speak."

"And you do this?" Ashyn asked in wide-eyed wonder.

Veer shook his head. "Oh no," He said with a chuckle. "I visited there once, The Order of the Sacred Fist, some winters ago, but a monk's life was not for me. It was just there that I picked up meditation."

"What you did on the rock?"

"Precisely."

"So you sit there with your eyes closed? That's medication?"

"Meditation," Veer corrected the boy, "And no, it's more than just sitting with your eyes closed. It's hard to explain and would take a long time to teach. Basically I just clear my mind of everything and open it instead to the tranquility of the world around me."

"Sounds boring," Ashyn said with a frown.

"It is," Veer commented, laughing again. "But it's useful. You'll see when you get older. The mind becomes cluttered with so much that sometimes you just need a minute to clear yourself of everything and let it all go."

Ashyn shrugged. "If you say so."

Veer stood up quickly, stretching his long lean muscles. "Well I think I have overstayed my welcome. I suppose it is time for me to leave."

Ashyn looked at him mortified. "You're leavin'?"

Veer nodded. "I have a full quiver of arrows thanks to your father, and a general heading of where to go thanks to your mother. It is about time that I continue my journey."

Ashyn's eyes began to water. "But you just got here."

Veer looked at him kindly. "I'm afraid that this wasn't my destination, young Ashyn. I was merely passing through in the hopes of re-supplying. I didn't expect to meet anyone near as friendly as your family has been. And I certainly never expected to meet a young boy quite like you."

He didn't want the Elf to leave. Though he knew that Veer was much older than he was and had his own things to do, it felt good to have a kindred spirit around. Someone that had a similar childhood. Someone that knew what he was going through. Ashyn realized that Veer was his first true friend outside of his family.

Unable to stomach the idea of Veer leaving, he needed to look away. It did not matter where, just anywhere but at the Elf. His hazy grey eyes fell to the hillocks of the south. Long had he watched those verdant green mounds as he was sent to grab his sister from the rock. Either because she had stayed out too late long after the sunset, or for some mundane task.

The tears in his eyes obscured his vision as if he was staring through the bottom of a glass. He wiped his hand across his face, sniffling once. There was something strange about those grass-lined fields. Something was out of place. Like one of the mounds of grass that he had seen all his life was suddenly gone. Before his mind could digest what he was seeing, his concentration was shattered. There was a noise reverberating deep in the back of his head. It sounded like a voice, a warning telling him to look to Bremingham. Ashyn spun in the direction of the village, his grey eyes trying to search past his tears.

"Did you hear that?" Veer said, also looking towards the town. Both of them scrutinized the village before them in an eerie silence. "I could swear I heard someone speaking," the Elf told him.

Then they both heard a girl scream.

Their eyes shot to Ashyn's home. Even from this far away it was not hard to spot the doorway. It was open. In his curiosity, Ashyn had forgotten to shut the door when he saw Veer on the smooth stone.

They both started to run as they heard a scream issue out again. Ashyn, nowhere near Veer's height and speed or age, quickly fell behind. Seeing this Veer quickly turned around and picked up the boy, running all the while to the house.

Ashyn bounced around while Veer ran, hanging on to the Elf's strong arms for dear life. Had the situation not been so dire, he might have had fun. As it was, he only had concern for his sister.

Veer closed in on the house quickly, and as he entered their yard he dropped Ashyn roughly onto the ground and barreled into the house.

Ashyn hit the ground with a roll, kicking up dirt wildly as he tried to stop spinning. His chin hit the ground hard, and he felt the piercing pain as his teeth bit into his tongue. Immediately the hot rush of copper flooded his mouth.

He spit out the crimson mass and struggled to his feet, wobbly and dizzy. Inside he could still hear Julietta screaming, followed by yelling, and then what sounded suspiciously like growling. He shook his head trying to rid himself of the cobwebs. A strange feeling overtook him, he could sense something indiscernible, like a presence that was malicious and dangerous. He had never before been able to 'feel' anything in his life. The effect was disconcerting.

Julietta screamed again forcing him to push the unusual hyper-awareness of his body aside. Wiping the dribbling blood from his chin, he staggered into his house.

Veer was just inside. Between him and Ashyn's family was a large wolf. It was twice the size of a typical wolf and its coarse coat was the color of auburn. It was still facing his mother and sister who were now behind the overturned dining table. When they entered, his mother had her arms raised in front of her, hands contorted in a curious position.

When Ashyn's mother realized that Veer was present, her eyes went wide and she dropped hands-down, trying to hold the table between them and the creature, as if that was what she had been doing all along. Whether Veer had seen her, or had been concentrating on the great wolf, he did not know. Nevertheless, Ashyn had missed none of it.

Ashyn could immediately see that Veer planned to tackle the creature. Ashyn was glad he had not lingered outside longer. "Veer, don't!" he yelled. "It's a Bristle Wolf."

Ashyn was surprised when Veer hesitated. He was just a little boy after all, and it was not often that adults listened to him.

"What's a Bristle Wolf?" Veer asked quietly, an open sense of urgency dripping from every word.

"Their coat, it's like a porcupine's. Even though it just looks mangy, those are spines," Ashyn quickly explained. "They're solitary hunters, unlike regular wolves. They hunt small prey, like me, mostly. So the spines are a defense against creatures trying to pull them off their prey. Like parents."

"Lovely," Veer remarked dryly.

Ashyn was looking around quickly and he could tell Veer was doing likewise. He saw the Elf's sword and bow slung against the wall. It was out of the way, on the opposite side of the house. Veer had seen it as well and slowly began making his way over to the wall. Ashyn jumped when the creature lunged at the table smacking hard into it, cracking the wood. Julietta screamed in terror.

"Hurry," his mother whispered.

Ashyn looked around for some way to help. He did not know what to do. It was his fault after all. His father had always told him to shut the door in the hours of dawn and dusk. You never knew when a monster was waiting for the right opportunity to attack them in their sleep.

Then he saw his bow. It was only a few feet away to his left. It was tiny, only made for the hands of a small boy, and he knew that his little arrow would never kill the Bristle Wolf. He had only ever shot hares and young does with it. Even then, he often did not kill the does. He simply did not have the strength to put torque behind his arrows.

The Bristle Wolf crashed into the table again and the wood exploded into splinters. It lunged at Julietta. Ashyn's mother screamed as she raised her hands again, Veer raced for his sword, and Ashyn just reacted.

Before he could even register how it happened, an arrow was sailing through the air and his little bow was in his hand with another nocked and ready to loose. The arrow struck the Bristle Wolf in the meaty part of its thigh, just between the creature's spines. The impact sent the wolf's lunge past its mark and slamming into the rear wall by the stove. It recovered quickly, growling angrily at its new threat. The wolf's coat bristled out as it locked on its newest target, the child with the bow.

It barreled through the fragmented remains of the table, past Jade and Julietta and straight to Ashyn. He let his next arrow fly, striking the furious wolf in its shoulder blade. It barely even registered the effect. Ashyn attempted to nock another arrow, but the wolf was already there.

It came at him a flurry of teeth, claws, and bristles. Snapping and biting. On instinct, the little boy dropped his bow, rolled on to the ground beneath the lunging wolf. He fell just beneath the rapid animal's front paws, only catching a glancing blow across his trailing left shoulder.

With his arms tightly tucked against his chest, he continued to roll into the wolf's hind legs. With the diminutive arrow embedded in its left thigh, the large beast tripped over Ashyn and crashed down.

Ashyn could feel the animal's powerful hind legs kick into him, knocking the air out of his lungs, and causing him to see stars. His world spun around violently as the creature toppled over.

Veer was on the creature in a flash, his thin elegant blade stabbing and slashing between the wolf's vicious spurs. Thick red ichor coated his blade as the blood ran freely down the beast's flank and into pools beneath him.

Ashyn rolled and struggled frantically to keep away from the wolf's devastating, kicking paws. Though muffled underneath the weight of the beast he could hear his mother screaming for him, panic-stricken. Moving was all he could do to keep from being crushed to death by the massive beast.

Ashyn soon realized he faced another problem aside from the frantic kicks of the wolf. With the creature's weight bearing down on him, the boy realized he couldn't breathe. The belly of the animal was pushing down on him furiously, smothering his nose and mouth. It was too heavy to lift with his young underdeveloped muscles. Additionally the wolf's weight was crushing what scant air he had left from his lungs.

Gasping only brought in the bitter, salty taste of the animal's dirty fur mixed with that of its blood. It dawned on Ashyn that when he went to sleep, he might never wake up again. Never listen to his sister's pestering remarks, see his father's smile, or witness that glimmer in his mother's grey eyes that was meant only for her son.

He struggled all the more. He wanted to be there for those things. He wanted to continue being badgered by his sister to go outside. To do things other kids were supposed to do. He wanted to make his Pa proud as he shot another hare.

Still he could not stop the weight of the wolf, and as it finally stopped struggling, so did he. Stars were replaced with a dying light, and slowly all his strength began fleeing his arms and legs. He felt them hit the ground beneath the coarse furry underside of the wolf. As darkness enveloped him, he felt everything else ebb away into nothingness.

STORMWIND

Heavy hooded eyes slowly opened to the dim light of a flickering candle. Around him, he could smell the scent of freshly picked lavender and mint. He could hear crickets chirping outside, a telltale sign that the sun was far beneath them for yet another day. Was it nighttime already? Where had the day gone?

As he lay, still he could hear the slow rhythmic breathing of his sister fast asleep at his side. He turned his head and gazed at her. She was sleeping with her head down against his bed, her hand held firmly within his.

Across the room, he could hear two people talking softly, attempting not to disturb the sleeping children. In the quiet of the night, he could hear them clearly.

"I have been to Gurgen," one voice said. It was male and very familiar. There was a strange silence between them. An uncomfortable one.

He slowly raised his head to look across the room. There he could see his mother and Veer De'Storm standing by the window. Veer was looking intensely at his mother while his mother stared outside, lost in her thoughts. He could see they were holding cups, each with steam rolling out of them gingerly. Perhaps it had been his mother's tea? She made very good tea.

He watched as Veer let those words linger in the air. The Elf did not press his mother, but instead took a sip from his cup. Finally when no response was forthcoming he continued. "I have met its people, Jade."

Ashyn could see his mother turn and look at the High Elf. He could see the flickering candle light reflected in the glimmering tears in her eyes. "What do you want?" she asked.

Again, silence hung heavy in the air. Ashyn wondered why it was so threatening that Veer had been to Gurgen. Wasn't seeing where his Ma came from a good thing?

"Does the boy know?" Ashyn heard Veer ask about him. He could see his mother shaking her head no.

Veer sighed, and looked out the small portal into the night with his mother. Ashyn could see the tears rolling down her face. He had no idea what the Elf was talking about.

"I am well educated," Veer told his mother. "By a people who have been around for generations upon generations. I have heard the stories told." Veer looked back at his mother. "I have seen some of the signs that are in those stories."

Jade shook her head. "I am just a simple woman. All I want is a simple life with my family. Nothing more." Her words were stifled, broken like the tears drifting down her face.

Veer nodded. "I would never take that from you, from him," he answered.

"Thank you," Jade whispered back.

Veer looked back out to the expansive horizon beyond. "One day though, someone will come. Some one that is equally as educated and they will also see what it is I see. They will want to take him."

"I hope not," his mother answered. "Can't he just be a special little boy?"

Veer peered back at him, and Ashyn quickly laid his head back down pretending to be asleep. The moments ticked by in agonizing slowness. Did Veer see him? Did he know he was awake? Finally, he heard the Elf answer. "One can only hope."

Seeing as there was no more conversation forthcoming Ashyn once again let sleep take him. He dreamt of fighting wolves alongside Veer, a hero to the town of Bremingham, and all the people of Kuldarr.

Morning came swiftly, and when he opened his eyes, once again he was staring into the deep blue eyes of Veer looking over him. "Good morning to you, child," the Elf said with a smile.

"Mornin'," Ashyn replied in a groggy voice.

He looked over to his side to see that his sister had been moved back into her bedding, and that his mother was still fast asleep once more. Father, once again, was not home. It was no surprise to him really. Sometimes his hunts would take days, and when he came home, it would always be well worth the wait. Sometimes he would take Ashyn with, but never on the long extended hunts, just the shorter ones.

"You feel strong enough to walk with me this morning?" Veer asked him as he moved away from the boy's bedding.

"Sure," he croaked, as he struggled to get up. His body was sore beyond anything he had ever felt before. When he looked down he saw his chest and abdomen were covered in many deep green and purple bruises. As he sat up he felt tightness in his shoulder. He glanced at it warily and saw that it was tightly bandaged in some type of green leaf.

"We call that Aloe," Veer answered, seeing the puzzled look on his face. "It helps with healing."

Ashyn nodded. "I think I read that once."

Veer smiled, "I'm sure you have."

Ashyn could see that Veer was fully dressed in the same garb that he had met him in. His quiver of arrows, and longbow were equally in place on his back, and his rapier was at his side. Ashyn knew that Veer must have been finally getting ready to leave.

Glumly he went to get dressed as Veer waited patiently by the door. He was not looking forward to saying goodbye. Finally, when he was dressed he reached up, grabbed his bow, and quiver as well. It could not hurt, he figured.

Quietly the duo exited Ashyn's house. As they did, Veer looked down at him smiling. "Make sure you close the door this time. No more wolves will keep me here."

Ashyn nodded and concealed his own smile. Together they walked quietly along the trail that led further into Bremingham. The sun was up and many people were beginning to stir. Already he could see Farmer Bibs in his field tending his crops with his sons. None of them made any effort to acknowledge Ashyn. He was not surprised.

As they passed by the other neighboring houses, Ashyn glanced up at Veer curiously. The Elf had asked him to walk with him, and yet had not said a word. Whenever his sister had asked him to walk with her she would either not shut up about the latest boy she was crushing on, or they would end up playing, usually chasing one another. Veer seemed to want none of this. And so they walked on quietly.

It was not until they had reached the town center, where Ashyn had originally met the tall Elf, that Veer turned in front of him and addressed him. "This, I'm afraid, is the end of the line, young Master Rune." Ashyn nodded fretfully while staring down at his feet.

Veer squatted down in front of him and gently raised his chin so Ashyn was forced to look into the Elf's vivid blue eyes. "I want you to know that I think you are a remarkably brave little boy. I doubt anyone here would have done what you did for young Julietta."

"She's my sister," Ashyn murmured.

Veer shook his head. "Nonetheless, many lesser boys, even men, would have frozen in fear, been incapable of action. They would have witnessed their sisters or daughters, or even mothers die at the jaws of that animal; but not you. You challenged it head-on, you outsmarted it and fought something that was bigger, stronger, and more dangerous than you, and you did it for love. I told you that love would give you strength, I just didn't expect you to take it so literally."

Ashyn chuckled slightly while trying to fight the growing tears welling in the corners of his grey eyes. He watched as Veer stood up to his full height.

"There is greatness inside of you Ashyn Rune, never forget that as long as you live. It was truly an honor to have met someone like you," he told the boy and then bowed once towards Ashyn, so that all gathering out amidst the town could see and hear him. Ashyn realized that this was Veer's gift to him: Open acceptance devoid of suspicion or contempt. To him, an ostracized child who was feared just because he was different, there could be no greater gift.

"You saved your sister, and your mother," he continued, "and your knowledge even saved me from potential harm, as well. I bid you good fortunes my little friend, and a wonderful life."

Then Veer bowed curtly once more, turned, and walked away. Ashyn stood still as he watched the back of Veer's head. On impulse, he ran forward. "Veer!" he shouted.

The Elf turned once more as he watched the child bound up to him and wrap his arms around his leg in a tight hug. Tears streamed down Ashyn's cheeks as he looked up to the tall Elf. "I'm glad I met you, too, Sir Veer."

Slowly Veer pried the little boy's arms free from around his leg, and held him out at arm's length. "Stormwind," he told the small boy.

"What?" Ashyn said through sniffles.

"My friends call me Stormwind," the Elf answered him.

Ashyn smiled through the tears, "Like your sword," he said.

Stormwind nodded. "It was crafted for me because of my name." He tussled with Ashyn's mangy reddish brown hair. "You really do remember everything, don't you?"

Ashyn nodded.

"Now I must go," he said seriously. "The majestic city of Tilliatemma northeast of here eagerly awaits my arrival." Then he winked at the boy. "I don't want to be late."

Ashyn nodded once more. "Will I ever see you again?" he asked.

Stormwind shrugged. "Friends always have a habit of visiting when you least expect it," he told Ashyn lightheartedly. "If fate carries me through Bremingham once more, I will eagerly seek out my little friend Ashyn Rune. Fate always has a way of working out in my favor," he ended in a wink.

"You promise?"

Stormwind rapped his fist to his chest, right over his heart. "You have my word of honor, my friend." With that he smiled, turned his back on the young boy, and walked towards the rising sun.

Ashyn smiled widely as he realized the villagers had begun to gather around him, the small boy who seemed to hold sway with the departing exotic stranger. Stormwind had made a difference in his life, however fleeting it might seem to be, and it had made it the greatest day of young Ashyn's life.

He looked forward to the day that the Elf would once again stroll through the minute village of Bremingham, seeking out the boy he called friend.

Little did Ashyn know then that that was a promise that Veer De'Storm would never be able to keep.

THE HUNTER'S MOON

Two winters passed since that summer day when Ashyn had met the Elf known as Stormwind. In that time many things had changed, and some of them not at all.

Like all young boys, Ashyn sprouted quickly from a small child with stubby legs, to a lanky boy who was nothing but arms and legs. His face had begun to develop into a more distinctive shape, showing prominent cheekbones and a strong chin. His naturally tan skin had grown darker as he spent more time out hunting with his father, and less time engrossed indoors with books. Like his father, he now had a matching haircut of short bangs and short-cropped hair. However, he also had a single braid of long hair running down his back, between his shoulder blades.

Ashyn had begged his mother to let him grow his hair like Stormwind's. She would hear nothing of it. She had told him long hair was reserved for women, Elves, and vagrants, nothing more. Therefore, she would only tolerate his braid. It was all the rebellion he had.

A broadening was beginning to take shape at his shoulders as his thin long arms began to develop muscles from using his bow, and carrying his kill. Ashyn was developing into a fine hunter, and an even finer sharpshooter. Yet his love of studying insects never ceased. Every evening he would bring something new home to study.

Still though, the town had never really found a true acceptance of him. The Elf's proclamation towards Ashyn being special had become nothing more than a distant memory little remembered by any that chose to care. He continued to unnerve them with a growing intelligence that rivaled even their most scholarly. The boy had scantly seen eight winters come and go and already he could recount all of Bremingham's history as their resident scribe recorded it. Even something old Tom Gregy could not do in his most sober of times.

Yet it had not ended there. Studying weather patterns and using something that Ashyn called mathematics, he had an uncanny ability to tell people when it was going to rain, and when there might be a drought. While this brought some of the farmer families closer to the Runes, but not Ashyn directly, only Karl the tanner took more of a liking to the boy. His ability to predict the weather had adverse results as well, and it pushed those that were the strongest of skeptics even further away. 'Demon' and 'freak' only being more of the gentler words used against him when he would walk through town.

No one spoke of his daring escapade against the Bristle Wolf. No one seemed to care. The only ones grateful were Ashyn's parents, and of course his sister.

So even after two winters, Ashyn's only true friend was still his sister. However, even with that, spending time with her was getting almost nonexistent, as she had fallen into something that was beyond the young boy's capacity to understand. Courtship.

For Julietta had reached fourteen winters of age, and already she was blossoming into an exotic and beautiful young woman. Unlike Ashyn, whom many tried to avoid because of his awkwardness, boys flocked to get a chance to speak to Julietta, their resident star of Bremingham.

So that was life in Bremingham. Small, quiet, and peaceful.

~ ~ ~

"Ye sister is late again, Ash," his mother said to him as he studied his latest new insect find.

"Ash?" she repeated to him as he continued to examine his find. "Ashyn Rune, I'm talking to you," his mother added with an air of authority in her voice.

The little boy lazily looked up toward his mother, his grey eyes contrasting with the tan features of his skin. It had been a long day on the hunt that had turned up fruitless. There was simply nothing worth hunting that day in the hillocks. Ashyn was tired and he just wanted to study his insects.

"Go on, boy. Find ye sister. It'd do ye good," she said, this time in a tone of finality.

Ashyn Rune stood, closed his books, and replaced his little exotic creatures back in their jars. Looking once more at his mother, he sighed his defeat and headed toward the door. She smiled as he ran out the door to find his sister.

Ashyn looked around as the darkness took the small town of Bremingham. He knew where his sister was, of course. She always watched the sunset at the same rock, all this time later. Chances were that she was still on top of either the rocks, or messing in the outskirts of the forest trying to find the pointy-eared Wild Elves. After meeting, Veer De'Storm she became further infatuated with the Elves, unable to see how anything so beautiful could be so lethal.

That, or she was behind the rock with Gregiry Bib. Gregiry was two winters older than her, and the pride of Bremingham. He was a tall, broad shouldered, blonde headed boy who seemed to have the entire village wrapped around his finger even though he was still only a farmer. The Bibs, though farmers, were also Ashyn's greatest skeptics. That made it all the more awkward as Gregiry was Julietta's latest crush.

Very recently, he had been sent to fetch his sister from that same damnable rock when he had caught the two of them kissing behind it. Julietta had chased him for the better part of an hour demanding he not tell their parents. For fear that she might actually crush his bugs as she had threatened, he had finally agreed.

Lost in hesitant thoughts of what he might walk into when he found his sister, he decided to take the long route and pass through the cornfields. He carefully navigated his way through the tight bristly stalks, always watchful so that he would not be poked. They loomed high over his head making it incredibly dark to navigate through. It did not matter though; he knew the way. He had found many unusual bugs in the soft soil used to grow the corn, and he could almost navigate it blindfolded. He emerged on the other end unscathed and looked up at the moon above.

It was a curious color tonight, a reddish hue that loomed large and close. He had never seen a moon quite like it. It was massive, and dominated most of the eastern horizon. It seemed so close that he could almost touch it. He wondered idly what might cause the moon to appear the way it had. They were better thoughts than the idea of his sister smooching yet another boy.

He made his way quickly through the dimly-lit streets. Lanterns flickered from the insides of the thatch roofed houses, and as he passed them he could indistinctly hear chattering voices within. It was suppertime for the village of Bremingham. It was a time for their small families to come together for the evening and talk about their days. This was probably the most peaceful time in Bremingham that Ashyn knew of. Only people like Tom Gregy would be out, likely getting drunk, as he had no remaining family to speak of. Even then, Ashyn did not see the surly man lingering in front of his house as he normally did. It looked like it was going to be a serene night after all.

As he broke through the last of the domiciles and Julietta's large, flat brown rock came into view, she was not on top of it. "Great," Ashyn muttered under his breath. He had hoped not to witness his sister lip-locked once again, but it appears fortune did not favor him this night.

He approached as noisily as he could, hoping to get them to stop before he had to witness it. Kissing was just gross to little boys after all.

Already so close, he could hear the smacking sounds of the slobbering mess he knew he was going to find; therefore, he drug his feet loudly through the dirt. It echoed in his own head. *Surely, they must have heard me?* he thought. He waited for a moment to see if they would pop up. Instead, the squelching sounds returned. Dammit!

He searched around for some means of which to disrupt them when his eyes fell to a nice-sized rock. Perfect. He picked up the rock; it was heavy in his hand. This would work nicely, and if it did not then we would just have to say something and be all embarrassed as usual.

He threw it at the large brown stone. It connected hard with a loud crack, but then continued to bounce across its smooth surface. He watched in dismay as it bounded not once but twice along the stone, only to leap off the opposite side. He heard a whack followed by a grunt of pain. Clearly not what he had in mind to disrupt them.

Gregiry leapt up from behind the large stone, his normally bland brown eyes livid with rage. Ashyn noticed that his tunic was untied and hanging open. That was new, he thought curiously.

"You!" Gregiry Bibs hissed at him.

Ashyn saw his sister thrust her head up from the other side of the rock. She was clutching the front of her dress tightly closed. Ashyn did not have time to ponder this as he saw Gregiry moving angrily around the rock in his direction.

"I dinna mean to hit ye with the stone," Ashyn said to the boy that was twice his size and likely three times his weight.

"But you did, freak!" Gregiry barked at him angrily.

"Greg, stop!" Julietta pleaded to the teenage boy. "He was probably just coming to get me." His sister looked his way. "Is it supper time already?"

Ashyn looked up once at how dark it was, and though he obviously wanted to say 'Duh?' he merely nodded instead.

Gregiry did not stop his assault, however and kept moving forward. Ashyn took a step backward. "It doesn't matter," the blonde headed boy barked at his sister. "This little freak needs to be taught to mind his own business."

"Let it go, Greg. He meant no harm. He's just a little boy," she tried to say soothingly while buttoning the front of her dress back up. She then added, "And he's not a freak."

"Oh yes he is," Gregiry said menacingly while looking right at Ashyn. "My Pa says it ain't natural to be able to tell when it's gonna rain, or drought. Everyone in this town agrees. It's not right . . . it's unholy."

"No it isn't," Julietta replied. "He just reads a lot, is all. Big books my Ma brought with her from Gurgen. He knows things."

"Things no Maker-fearing person should," Gregiry snapped. "Only a freak knows that. And that's what he is. Aren't you . . . Freak?"

"I just. . . I just want Julietta ta come home," he stammered while looking at his feet.

Gregiry was right there looming over him. Ashyn could feel the heat radiating off the boy, his shadow casting little Ashyn in a perpetual eclipse. The blonde headed teenager laughed down at him. "Whatsa matter, freak?" he taunted. "Scared? Your books and your silly languages and your evil mathematics cannot save you now, can they?"

Ashyn glanced backward over his shoulder. He knew he could run away, he should run away. He tried to look around the broad boy towards his sister. "Please just come home," he whispered loudly to her.

Gregiry looked back once at Julietta, then back down to Ashyn, "She comes home when I say she can come home, you little freak!"

Ashyn did not see it coming, it happened so fast. Gregiry's arm lanced out, lightning quick, with a right hook that caught him squarely across the face. Pain exploded like a searing white light across his right cheek and the side of his nose. He felt himself spiral out of control as he crashed down against the hard dirt surface, his ribs smacking painfully against the smaller stones that were scattered about.

Tears welled in his grey eyes at the pain, and he coughed roughly, as he struggled to fill his lungs with air. The awful tang of copper flooded his mouth and he felt the hot rush of blood coming from where his teeth dug into his cheek. He spit out the crimson-saturated saliva.

"That's for hitting me with a rock!" Gregiry yelled at him.

Lights floated hazily in front of his eyes. He blinked away the tears, trying to stay conscious. That hit hurt so badly, he just wanted it to stop.

"Stop it!" Ashyn heard Julietta yell. "I said stop it!" she screamed at Gregiry with anguish in her own voice.

Ashyn could see Gregiry just sneering down at him. "C'mon! Get up, freak! You need to learn!"

Again, the large boy attacked swiftly. His foot lashed out and connected solidly with Ashyn's stomach. He groaned in agony as he was sent rolling backwards several feet. Stars danced before his eyes and he was sent in a violent coughing fit. Ashyn gasped roughly for air that just would not seem to come.

Everything spun before his eyes. The world seemed to be teetering out of control. He barely knew up from down. He watched, almost detached from it all, as Gregiry picked up a rock. He tossed it up in the air in a motion so slow it didn't seem real. His face beheld a twisted smile as he reveled in what he was doing to Ashyn. His eyes were soaking in everything in a perverse sense of pleasure. He caught the rock and pointed at Ashyn, letting him know what he intended to do. He cocked his hand back ready to throw with all his might. Ashyn's eyes watered heavily. He hurt so badly he just wanted it all to stop. Darkness threatened to engulf him, and he almost wanted it to come just so the pain would end.

He watched as Julietta charged at Gregiry and started smacking him futilely on shoulder to get him to stop. While Ashyn knew it did no damage, it caused Gregiry to pause from throwing the stone at him. Ashyn watched as Gregiry turned on Julietta and as the broad-shouldered boy backhanded his sister. He saw as she collapsed to the ground holding her face. He saw the pain and shock in her eyes, and then something snapped within him, an anger he felt he could not control. Everything sped up to normal in the fraction of a heartbeat.

"Shut up, wench!" he heard Gregiry yell at his sister. "You think I care what you say? What you think? You're just a girl. A stupid girl, from a stupid family of freaks! Do you think anyone in this town cares about you, about any of you? You think you're a star, just because you're pretty? In the end, you're just like your brother. You're not wanted here because you're not normal! None of you are normal! All you are to me is a plaything. Now get out of my way while I do what everyone should do to freaks! Put them down!" He turned once again to throw the stone at Ashyn and froze.

Somewhere within himself, Ashyn realized something had changed. He felt a sense of strength come over him and before he even realized he had done it he was standing. The pain, while still there, had fallen to a throbbing in the back of his mind. He felt a power surging in his core. It created a vibrating feeling within him, and a deep humming in his ears. Everything he saw burned brightly around him in a rich orange hue, like the leaves of a maple tree in the fall.

He stared venomously at Gregiry, the object of his hatred. His anger consumed him so deeply that to stare at this boy made it feel as if his eyes were on fire.

"Ash?" His sister whispered as she looked in his direction from her sprawled position on the ground.

"Go home," he said calmly, his eyes never once leaving Gregiry. Gregiry did not move.

Julietta scrambled to her feet and moved swiftly past him. She looked at him oddly, and in her eyes he could see a sense of terror. The terror was not at what Gregiry had done. It was directed at him. He didn't have time to think about it though. Something needed to be done. This boy had to pay.

Ashyn could feel Julietta's presence diminishing. It was time.

"What are you?" Gregiry whispered in both a sense of anger, and dread.

Before his mind could even process the question, Gregiry threw the large stone at him with all the force he had. Ashyn knew that the stone would hit him in the face dead on. They were too close to each other for Gregiry's aim to be astray. Yet Ashyn felt an odd serenity in his anger, a sense of indifference.

His eyes drifted to the stone. It moved towards him as if it were trying to travel through molasses. He tilted his head at it only slightly, in curiosity, and then the rock disintegrated into dust.

His eyes fell back to Gregiry who stared at where the rock had once been. Ashyn could see a growing wet spot between the teenager's legs and running down to a puddle beneath his feet. "You're such a freak!" Gregiry yelled at him as he backed up away from the boy.

Ashyn took a step forward. "You hurt my sister," he said vehemently.

Gregiry didn't know how to answer, but just kept backing up from the approaching boy.

Ashyn took another step forward. He could feel his eyes blazing. An outline of primal energy was beginning to surround the blonde-headed boy.

Gregiry backed up some more and bumped into the smooth brown stone. He looked back and forth, trapped, and then back towards Ashyn as he took another step forward.

"You can't hurt me," the teenager stammered. "The town loves me. They adore me. We Bibs own this town."

Ashyn didn't care. He took another step.

"They despise you," Gregiry spat at Ashyn. "They hate you because you're a freak. Just think of what they'll do to your family if they find out you've done anything to me."

Ashyn paused. He didn't want anything to happen to his family. He loved his family. The fire started dying in his eyes.

Gregiry, pressing his advantage, pointed directly into Ashyn's face. "Face it; you'll never be like us. You'll always be different; a reject, an outcast. My Pa calls you a pariah. Your family is nothing but freaks! You'll never fit in. You should just leave. You think it is just you but it is not! You think this town cares about your sister? Really cares? Sure, she's lovely to look at, but she's nothing but a pawn. She's a toy, a plaything to be used by us and eventually discarded. Finally when were done with her she might be a trophy for some fool to take! Face it freak, no one wants you here. Not you, your mother and father, or your little whore of a sister!"

Whore. Ashyn knew that word. He knew what it represented, what it meant. Gregiry had taken advantage of his sister, used her to satisfy his teenage needs. She meant nothing to him. The fact that he admitted this to Ashyn triggered something deep within the olive-skinned boy that not even the physical pain he had taken could match. Anger renewed in his grey eyes. Gregiry needed to pay.

An image flashed into Ashyn's mind. It was an image of pain, of suffering, of a torture so inexplicable that it brought a smile to the child's face. He grabbed onto that image, and in a brilliant flash of light, Gregiry's sleeve erupted into a blaze of fire.

Ashyn, no! A foreign voice slammed into his mind with the force of a war hammer, but by then it was too late.

THE DRUMS

It was a curious feeling, Ashyn realized, to have another voice in his head. Was something truly wrong with him? Was he sick? Why would there be someone speaking to him within his mind? It didn't make any sense. He hadn't heard any voices before.

Then the boy paused. He *had* heard a voice before. When the Bristle Wolf had attacked his house there had been a warning he had heard it in the deepest recesses of his mind. He had thought it was just his own intuition, but it now dawned on him that Stormwind had heard the voice as well. Was the Elf diseased? Had he passed something on to Ashyn? Some sort of ailment?

His mind would have continued to speculate on how the voice had entered his thoughts had it not been for the terrible screaming that was distracting him. As his mind settled onto the present, the energy of his hatred diminished. For some reason, though, everything was still glowing brightly in an orange light, and he felt an intense heat very near to his face.

His eyes came into focus and he gasped. Gregiry's arm was ablaze with wickedly hot fire, and crawling up to his elbow. He was screaming in pain and terror as he whipped his arm back and forth in front of him trying to shake off the searing, hungry conflagration.

At first, he thought that he might have been dreaming. He knew he was angry, he knew he wanted Gregiry to hurt. The first thing he had thought of was . . . burning?

Put it out! The alien voice erupted once more into his mind. It was a strange tingling sensation, sort of like when his sister would try to tickle his inner ear with a piece of grass.

Was he going insane? He did not feel insane. Did he even really know what insane was? He had read about it. Perhaps he was suffering from some kind of visions. Maybe the fire burning Gregiry's arm was not real, just some figment of Ashyn's wishful thinking.

The screams continued, as did the smell of burning cloth and putrid stench of burning hair and cooking flesh. It certainly seemed real. The heat certainly felt real.

Put it out! the same voice reiterated into his mind.

Hello? Ashyn said to himself. Then thought, *this is crazy, I must be crazy.*

Put out the fire, do you want to get your family killed! the voice blared into his mind.

Yup, I'm crazy. Ashyn thought to himself.

You're not crazy, and you are not hearing things. Listen to me. There is no time; you must put out the fire that is cooking that idiot boy alive! the foreign voice commanded.

Okay. How? It's too far for water, and he's too petrified to let me try to pat it out, he returned.

No water. Will the fire to go away.

What? Ashyn thought. He couldn't have heard that right.

*Use your **will** to make the fire diminish*, the voice told him urgently.

Riiigggghhht, he returned. Yup I'm nuts. I set the most popular person in town on fire and now I am listening to voices in my head. I'm done for.

Will you just shut up and try it! the voice snapped back.

Fine! Ashyn snapped back. If this isn't bizarre enough. He stared at Gregiry who was now violently slapping his arm against the ground in a dismal attempt to get the clinging fires to subside. He really is a moron, Ashyn thought to himself.

Make the fire go away, he tried to think. Make it go out. He stared intently at it, constantly telling it to go out. Diminish, dissolve, and go away. It remained burning, and he could tell by the screaming that it was really starting to do some damage. *It's not working,* he told ... well, himself.

Because you don't believe it, the voice returned.

Of course he didn't believe it! The whole concept was ridiculous. Put out fire with his mind! Who ever heard of such a thing? In the end, he knew what he had to do.

Ashyn rushed with all his might into Gregiry, forcing him to topple over on the ground. While the boy lay stunned against the rock and ground, Ashyn scrambled on top of him and started smothering the flaming appendage with the loose dirt that was around the smooth large stone. Within seconds, he had the blaze puttered out. Still though, Ashyn could see the damage had been done.

Even though it had only been a span of seconds that Gregiry's arm had spontaneously combusted, he could see how devastating the pyre had been. His arm was an alarmingly deep crimson hue, with the majority of it already begin to welt and grow into violent white pus-filled blisters. By his hand, where it had burned longest, he could even see some of the skin was charred and blackened.

Gregiry, who was coming out of his daze, also saw the effects of his ravaged arm. He screamed once more, and Ashyn knew that all the incessant yelling was going to bring people out of their houses very soon now.

Run, the voice told him. It didn't have to repeat itself.

Ashyn started running as fast as he could. He needed a place to take cover, a place to hide and think things through. He didn't know what to do.

People started to open up their doors as he ran past, curious as to the terrible yelling. He ducked his head down so they could not see his face. It didn't matter; he knew they would figure it out fast enough. In the background, he could hear Gregiry yelling at him, "You're dead! Do you hear me, freak! You are so dead!"

He ran. He ran along the outskirts of town. He needed to think but his brain seemed to be deadlocked. Why couldn't he think? What was going on inside of him? What was wrong with him? First the anger? Then the voices? How could he explain that to anyone? Who would even believe him? He was sure even his parents wouldn't believe it. And the fire... where had that come from? He found it inconceivable that *he* could have made it come to life. It just wasn't possible. He was only a boy. An outcast, misjudged, unaccepted little boy. He couldn't create fire with a thought. The whole concept was preposterous.

He turned and ran across the wagon trail near the tanner's shop when he heard the distinct "thwack" of an arrow connecting with wood. His young senses were immediately alert. Were they after him already? Had Gregiry Bibs told people so swiftly? Now they were out hunting him? It had only been a few minutes at most, how could he have assembled the town so quickly?

He searched for the signs of pursuers and was startled to see a shadow run past to his right. The outline of the fleeing figure resembled a young girl. Not many girls in town knew how to shoot a bow. Most were too concerned with cooking, cleaning, tending livestock, or farming. Or looking pretty. They always wanted to look pretty. What girl would shoot an arrow at him?

He decided that perhaps it might have been his sister. Maybe she had seen what he did and was following him? Maybe after Gregiry hit her she was hiding as well, crying off the hurt. The aching tightness in his cheek and ribs was enough to remind him how hard Gregiry could hit. He decided likely that was what it was. It had to be his sister. He was about to chase her down when the area darkened significantly around him. He looked up in front of him to see Karl the tanner looming large overhead.

~ ~ ~

Karl the tanner was an imposing figure. He stood at well over six feet tall, maybe nearer to seven. To the little boy Ashyn, the man was a giant. He had a large bald head with eyebrows that were dark black set upon beady little brown eyes. He had a large, wide nose which he looked down now with his small eyes.

His body was heavily muscled, with a huge bull chest and forearms. Full, thick, black chest hair sprouted out from the top of his filthy tan tunic. He had a dark apron on over his tunic and pantaloons, smeared with the smelly oils used to harden the skins of animals. He stunk of the leather musk.

Looking down at the little child, he said in a gruff voice full of bass, "Hmm, it's the young Rune boy. It's mighty late for one such as you to be out." He looked around. Ashyn did as well. He was waiting for a mob of people to assail him any second, calling him a demon and saying he was possessed. Who knows, maybe they were right?

Karl was a friend of his father's though, and he happened to like Ashyn as well. Maybe Ashyn could try to explain what happened to him. If anyone in town would side with him besides his family, it would be Karl.

The large-framed man looked into Ashyn's steel grey gaze. "You should run along to your home, boy. It is a hunter's moon tonight. Bad omen." He looked around once more. "Surely Bristle Wolves will be about."

Bristle Wolves. Ashyn had not thought about that. He already knew what they were capable of. He had already been at the receiving end of their wrath once, and that was more than enough. Perhaps Karl was right; maybe it was safest to go home. Just explain what happened to them, his parents. They would protect him. They would understand; he knew they would. His Ma always understood. She would nod and just accept that

Ashyn was telling the truth. He never had cause to lie in the past. Even his sister had been there. She knew what Gregiry did. Maybe she would defend him. They were family after all. However, if he did that, he might put his family in danger. Gregiry might send the mob there first.

It didn't matter, Ashyn realized. Even if he ran away, his family would be the ones to pay the price if they believed him or thought him crazy. He needed to return home, if nothing else so that he could warn his family.

He mentally nodded to himself. That's what he would do, he decided. He had no choice. He had to tell his family and hope for the best.

Ashyn was about to say something to Karl the tanner when the shrill whistle of an arrow caught his ear. Instinctively the boy fell to the dirt. The arrow was not intended for him, he realized. It was far too high.

Little Ashyn looked up from the ground and saw Karl with the strangest look on his face. Karl couldn't understand what had happened. Ashyn's gaze then drifted slightly downward and his eyes went wide with horror. Just below the tanner's stubbly chin protruded a sharp arrowhead that glistened syrupy in the moonlight.

Karl moved his mouth as if to speak to little Ashyn, but found that no words would come from his shattered vocal cords. Instead, there was only blood as it rushed from his mouth and out the vicious wound in his neck. He reached his arms behind his back and felt the smoothness of the shaft behind his neck.

Then Ashyn could see the pain registering for the first time in the tanner's eyes. His eyes became unfocused and he swayed momentarily as if he were about to topple over. Those few seconds seemed like an eternity to Ashyn. Ashyn jumped with fright as two more arrows slammed in Karl's massive, meaty back.

Ashyn watched it all as if he were far away. Everything moved so slowly, the motions seemed almost unnatural. There was a deep humming in his ears and he thought he even could hear the sounds of the bowstrings still thrumming after the other two arrows embedded in the large man's back.

As Karl fell to his knees, the mountain of a man didn't seem so imposing anymore. He didn't seem larger than life. His beady eyes were now wide and glazed, his face a mask of pure shock.

The goliath crumpled onto his side, his massive frame slumping into the soft dirt of the recently tilled ground. As Karl lie against the ground his face leaned heavily against the loose dirt as if it were a comforting pillow.

Blood came frothing from his mouth as a bubbling red pond. The florid rivers continued to gush from of the entry and exit wounds in his neck. His mouth moved slowly as if he were trying to speak words yet all he did was spread the soft dirt, darkening the growing pool of blood into a blackened mass of mud. He looked like a fish out of water, gasping desperately for something that would not come.

Never before had the little boy seen death so close. He had hunted game with his father, but he had never seen a person die before. He stared at Karl with a grim fascination. Karl's eyes were glossy and still, staring forevermore into the distance. Ashyn watched as the light of life flittered away from the tanner's small beady eyes.

They killed him! Just like Gregiry said. He was dead. They were going to kill anyone that held favor with the Runes, to him in any way. It didn't seem real.

Then the screaming began . . .

A guttural and savage roar came from all around. It emanated from the pockets of darkness between the trees of the Shalis-Fey Forest. The roar grew almost deafening, and then between the lancing powers of the voices he heard the pounding of drums. Boom, boom, boom!

The boy had never heard anything like it before. It was the sound of war drums. The roaring died out to almost a whisper, but the reverberation of the drums continued.

Boom, boom, boom! The beating picked up its pace, and before he knew it, little Ashyn could feel his heart pounding in unison with the deadly drums.

Boom, boom, boom! The slamming of feet began to match the rhythm of the drums. A stomping and slamming of what sounded like hundreds of creatures surrounding them in the Shalis-Fey woods. Where they here? Was it the Wild Elves?

Boom, boom, boom! The feet were now in absolute unison with the terrible drums of war. Ashyn could begin to hear the drums and feet moving faster and faster. They were quickening.

Boom, boom, boom! The sound anchored to a pivotal moment. It had reached its crescendo, sending an undeniable fear coursing through the child.

He looked up at the bright red moon, hovering so close that it felt like inches from his face. It was a Hunter's moon. This was a bad omen, Karl had said. Had he brought this on them? Was Ashyn somehow evil?

His breathing became labored, and he noticed he was panting. Sweat formed at his brow. He felt the imminent terror all around him, the impending doom from some unfathomable force. Was this another vision? Was he about to set fire to the whole town? Could there be a demon lurking deep within him about to come pouring forth?

Boom, boom, boom! His eyes darted in all directions following one shadow after another. Looking, desperately searching the woods in the moonlight. The sound was so loud. It felt like it was crashing down on top of him, crushing him underneath its oppressive weight.

Boom, boom, boom! Ashyn could take it no more. He screamed. Everything fell silent.

Where was everyone? Where were the people, where was his father? Who was going to defend the town?

Deep, thick blue clouds rolled in, eclipsing the red moon. Ashyn stood alone in a dying light as shadows dominated the small town of Bremingham. Karl lay dead at his small feet. Rivulets of blood oozed their way towards his tiny moccasins. Ashyn noticed the blood and stepped back away from the snaking river. Where there before had been only deafening noise, there was now nothing but an eerie silence.

Doors began to open and the residents of Bremingham began to emerge holding pitchforks and chopping axes. Whispers of worry floated on the breeze, and Ashyn could smell the bitter tang of everyone's fear.

Then it happened.

Fires lit up all across the Shalis-Fey border, deep within the emerald woods. Small flickering lights of amber and orange dotting the shadowed range as far as the eye could see.

All around came a guttural yelling as savage creatures came running out of the forest, weapons drawn, their feral intent burning in their eyes. Those that weren't holding weapons were holding torches. The front lines of the creatures held wicked-looking bows.

The village of Bremingham was in complete disarray. None of them were soldiers, they scattered like insects as the first of the torches started to rain down on their homes.

The archers fired volley after volley of crude arrows into the town. They didn't care whom they hit. Ashyn narrowly escaped two arrows as they came down on either side of him scant inches from his feet.

The few men that were armed were cut down like stalks of grain under a farmer's scythe. The creatures flooded forward like a tide of darkness, their bodies reeking with the need to slaughter.

Men, women, and children alike were cut down by sword, arrow, and axe. There was no robbing, plundering, or even raping. It was just cold murder. The monsters came at them and with each bloody strike their twisted visage reveled in the kill.

One ran right by Ashyn in its haste to strike down a fleeing woman. He saw that their pallid grey skin was lined with dark inky veins. He could see small beady eyes as black as the void peeking out from a heavy, overly pronounced brow. He knew what these creatures were. He had read about them. They were Orcs.

Screams of terror and suffering dominated the primal yelling of the Orcs. The monsters swarmed atop anyone trying to defend themselves like ants on sugar. Any resistance to their slaughter was met with brutal carnage.

Those that weren't killed outright lie strewn against the ground, holding stumps of body parts seeking fretfully for their amputated appendage or looking, glossy-eyed for someone to help them. Almost anyone who was not running was lying amongst the gore, most fatally and viciously wounded.

The paths and dirt were soaked in deep ruddy pools. It looked as if the entire village sat in a bloody mire. Entrails were strewn around like confetti on the burning thatch-roofed buildings. The separated organs, blackening from the flames, began crackling and popping from the searing heat. The revolting smell saturated the area, sinking down into the very core of the small boy. It was as if he could almost taste the cooked and burning flesh.

Ashyn watched as the Orcs periodically stopped by one of the dead or wounded. He stifled vomiting as he saw them bend down and grab a handful of innards. They would stand straight up and begin smearing the exposed viscera of their victims across their bodies. They had no order to their chaos; it would go on their arms, chest, and legs, even on their faces and in their mouths. It was as if the monsters were performing some weird ritual using the ichor of their victims.

As the savage creatures became covered in the blood of the fallen, their already perverse appearance manifested into something wholly unnatural. It was as if their very presence polluted everything they touched, the death they caused blighting the land in a bog of cruor and gore.

He stood petrified, as if he were a statue of stone. He couldn't move, his mind couldn't think. He was only there, watching it all as if he were a casual viewer, outside his own body, watching everything around him transpire. Something screamed in his mind for him to move, an aching need to survive this onslaught. But how could he? He was just a small boy. He didn't know how to fight in a battle against monsters like this, or look after himself. It could even be entirely his fault, for all he knew.

A body toppled in front of him. He watched it, transfixed, his emotions locked in a state of inability. The body was that of a man. Ashyn's grey eyes traveled across his dormant figure. Blood soaked his clothing and skin from head to feet, marring whatever the clothing had one time been. Ashyn saw the man's back slowly rise and fall and the boy realized that this man was still alive.

He saw the man's fingers twitch. Then his shoulders shuddered. Creeping at the pace of a snail, his head finally turned to face the boy. Ashyn felt then at the sight of the man he should scream, or gasp, or even cry, but he did not. He felt . . . nothing.

Half the man's face had been sheared away, either by sword or by axe, it didn't seem important to distinguish which. Red pustules ruptured across the torn muscle, blooming geysers of crimson blood. The dingy yellow of a shattered cheekbone protruded outwards towards Ashyn like an accusing finger. His right eye was gone, nothing but a hollow socket remaining, as was much of his nose missing. Nevertheless, Ashyn recognized the elderly man. It was old Tom Gregy.

His one remaining eye glared at him vehemently. His mouth opened, either to blame Ashyn for the blasphemy that descended upon them, or perhaps to alert the Orcs of the untouched boy. Either way, neither happened. Blood poured forth like a fountain across the man's thick fleshy tongue. It ran swiftly down his chin and into a puddle below, only adding to the ever-growing mire around him.

Suddenly a shaft lanced down in front of the boy causing him to topple backwards. Ashyn heard a sickening crack as he watched the spear tip penetrate the back of Tom Gregy's head, drive through and protrude out his mouth. Tom gagged once reflexively, his one eye wide with shock and pain. Then the eye quickly glazed over and Ashyn knew the man was dead.

Little Ashyn's eyes traveled up the shaft, just as it was being yanked free of the dead man's skull. His eyes fell on the garish grey hand holding the spear. Strong rippling forearm muscles held the heavy weapon outright, but the boy's eyes did not stop. His gaze continued to travel up the weapon and beyond to look right into the face of the Orc in front of him.

Small beady black eyes drilled into his own grey ones.

Run! the voice screamed into his mind, *Run you idiot child! Run!*

The return of the voice snapped the boy out of his paralyzing terror. On all fours he backpedaled as the lumbering grey-skinned Orc stepped forward with his gore-covered spear. Ashyn backed away until his head cracked against a rough jagged surface. He turned and looked. His back was against the cornfield. Quickly turning over he staggered to his feet and disappeared into the darkness of the high rising stalks. Directly behind him, Ashyn could hear the monstrous Orc roar with glee as he chased in after him. The hunt was on.

~ ~ ~

The sharp ridges of the corn stalks cut and pulled at his skin and clothing. He kept his head low and his hands up protectively shielding his eyes as he ran, near blind, through the maze of dark vegetation. Behind him, he could hear his savage adversary closing in. The sound of the stalks breaking and tumbling under the might of the Orc's heavy swings echoed like thunder within the confines of the flora. Ashyn stopped momentarily and glanced up. The large red moon reappeared from underneath the thick blanket of azure clouds, but was barely visible so far within the confines of the deep plants. Tiny flecks of light eked through enough to illuminate his way. It was enough. It was all he needed.

A sharp crack and the ominous sway of the rigid stalks behind him let him know that even his moment of lingering could have cost him. He quickly dove back into a sprint, ducking and weaving through the sharper points of this winter's crop, as his worn moccasins plodded against the soft, tilled soil. His movements were graceful compared to that of his hunter, and he made little sound amongst the screams, the burning pyre of his village, and the thunderous pursuit behind him.

He should be able to evade the Orc for hours, but he knew that he didn't have hours.

The sounds of terror surged through his ears while he ran. It poured horrific visions into his head. Deep in the recesses of his mind's eye, he watched as villagers continued to fall dead. He could match the screams that he heard in reality, to the brutal images of Orcs violently mauling those around them.

Someone's arm flew into the cornfield and was hung upon the coarse stalks in front of him. He had to quickly backpedal against his forward momentum, stumbling and almost crashing into the amputated appendage. Ashyn stared in morbid horror as he saw the strings of tattered tendons still swaying and slapping wetly across the glistening bone.

The severed limb jerked fitfully, as it lie embedded in the stalks. The shattered muscles of the detached arm continued to spasm their last vestiges of its swiftly declining life. Ashyn stifled the vomit that surged to his throat. He attempted not to whimper as tears flooded his eyes. He moved around the separated remnants of someone he had probably known, and ran at full speed towards the direction he knew his house laid. His head was bent low and his hands framed his eyes from the stalks, giving him a strange tunnel vision, but the route in front of him was clear. It looked clear anyway.

Ashyn collided head first into what should have been an opening between stalks. The strong bones of his hands crushed into his temple and he felt the sharp jolting pain as his two pinkies snapped back against the unseen force. His nose crunched wetly against a surface that had all the consistency and play of a boulder. He staggered to the ground, brilliant white stars dancing before his eyes. His head spun as he collapsed to the ground, the whole world going topsy-turvy.

He felt his air being poured from his nose in wheezy spurts, as liquid, salty and hot, splashed across his face with each breath. He tried to stare in the direction of his impact, as his world violently teetered on edge, but he could see nothing. Nothing other than the two-foot gap between the rows of stalks. Pain threatened to engulf him in a soothing darkness, but he knew enough to stay coherent. To stay awake. What had he hit? He forced his mind to think. Had he misjudged and ran head first into a stalk? No stalk was wide enough to crush his whole face .
. .

Ashyn flexed his fingers, sending sharp jolts of pain from his pinkies up to his elbows. He could already see the stiffening end digits turning purple and swollen at the knuckle. He knew he had broken them.

He forced his labored breathing to settle. In the process, blood from his nose poured into his mouth. He tried to ignore the vile taste as he attempted to place his spinning world back on its axis. After what felt like hours, but he knew to be merely a minute or two, the stars faded and his equilibrium returned.

Ashyn forced himself to sit up, ignoring the lancing pain of his hands. He could feel the pressure on his face as the tender skin around his eyes and nose began to swell. He feared briefly that the swelling might encumber his vision, but the sound of crashing stalks behind him made him realize he had more pressing concerns to worry about.

He reached out to grab a stalk for leverage, to pull himself to his feet, when his fingers jammed again at the unseen force blocking his path. Pain like molten fire ran through his injured pinky and dribbled down his hand. He wanted to scream, but he knew such an act would kill him. Instead, he hissed in agony.

As the sharp pain subsided to a dull throb, the boy attempted it again. Only inches from the stalk, his hand contacted flatly against a rough, granular surface. Ashyn was confused. As he looked at his dirty swollen hand, he could see it firmly planted against nothing but air. But as he pushed against it, he could feel, keenly, the pressure of dozens of what felt like pebbles against his skin.

He moved his hand across the surface of nothingness attempting to discern where it began and ended. To his ever-growing alarm there seemed to be no end as he stepped one wobbly foot after another, his hand sliding across what to him felt like the bed of a stream. Hundreds, if not thousands, of smooth pebbles.

A loud crash and an explosion of flying vegetation brought his attention away from the invisible barrier and looking right into the beady black eyes of his hunter. The Orc, still soaked in the gore of others, swaggered forward in the confidence of his upcoming kill.

Ashyn, with nowhere left to go, backed up against the unseen surface. He could feel the many ridges burrowing into his back as the Orc moved forward, spear held in front of him, closing for the kill.

Ashyn could smell the blood on him. The dirty, bitter smell of death. It carried a tart odor, like that of gas erupting from pockets in the ground. The Orc was putrid to him, vile. He could feel the heat of the Orc, like waves of a hot summer sun emanating from the beast's flesh. He could see the sweat glistening on the pallid grey skin of his brow, worked up in deeds of his butchery. It too smelled of salt and copper with the bitter musk of pine from spending so much time in the Shalis-Fey woods. Ashyn knew this was to be his death. After only a meager eight winters, this was to be his end. He survived the Bristle Wolf only to succumb to the ragged and bloody tip of an Orc's spear. Unable to watch the killing blow he looked away . . .

. . . And right into a large yellow eye. It blinked slowly, momentarily disappearing altogether and then reappearing from nothingness. Ashyn couldn't understand it, couldn't fathom what he was seeing. This floating orb, nearly the size of an apple, flicked once at him, the slit of its eye dilating as it focused on him, and then turned and focused on the Orc. The creature paused in its pursuit as it too studied this new occurrence.

Then Ashyn watched the eye rise far above him, and suddenly he found himself toppling backwards as the pressure of the indiscernible wall suddenly lifted and was gone altogether. He landed backward in a roll, smacking his head roughly against the ground. Once again, stars threatened to take his vision for the umpteenth time this evening. He came to a stop on the flat of his belly and looked up just in time to see the Orc jab his spear at the nothingness.

It shattered suddenly as it impacted what Ashyn knew was the unseen force he had felt before. Ashyn could see the confusion evident in the Orc's eyes. Then before even Ashyn could understand what was happening, the Orc's head and upper chest disappeared.

Ashyn couldn't wrap his head around what he was seeing. It was as if those parts of the Orc no longer existed. He could see clearly what lay beyond where the Orc's upper torso had been. Darkened cornfield stretched beyond him, much of it obliterated by the powerful swings of the Orc's weapon while he pursued Ashyn.

Even now the Orc's arms were pounding, pounding again some intangible element. Ashyn could see the monster's hands impacting against something. What it was he couldn't say. Then he began to see streams of blood, thick and red, running down the Orc's lower torso from where the rest of his body just simply ceased to exist. To the boy's amazement the Orc was lifted from the ground, still kicking and squirming wildly, fighting something that just wasn't there. Ashyn heard the cracking of bones breaking, saw the claret spray of hot gore, and more maddening kicking from the Orc before he turned away.

Scrambling to his feet, he ran once again with all haste to his house. Behind him, he heard the sickening snap as the Orc's bones finally collapsed and gave way to whatever had it in its invisible vise.

He ran as hard as his legs would take him. He had to get home, had to get to his family. With everything going on around him, he had to be there with them if they were to die. He didn't want to die alone. Not without his ma, and pa, and sister.

He didn't even care about blocking his eyes from the coarse corn stalks. They scratched and bit at his already wounded skin. It didn't matter; he just needed to be home. He cut through the last section of cornfield. Only a few more feet and he would be out. He would be free of the scratching fingers of flora and the death he had left behind him.

He could see through the edge of the field, the large red moon casting a crimson silhouette on the green verge leading up to his family's home. As he reached the cusp of the prickly vegetation his eyes grew wide, burning in horror, as the Orcs surrounded their next target: a small house with a handful of elm trees that grew in a semi-circle right behind it.

He growled, low and visceral like an animal, and then broke out in a run for his home. Something large, heavy and strong wrapped around his torso just as he broke free of the cornfield, ripping him violently back in. The house sailed further away as he was drug back inside the darkness.

The little boy wanted to cry out, but found he had no voice. He wanted to scream, but the words would not come. Instead, he watched as his view became slightly obscured within the mass of dark plant life.

He looked up, feeling a presence he couldn't describe, like a great weight hovering over him, but he still saw nothing. He tried to move, but found he couldn't. He was pinned down by an invisible force.

Ashyn felt as the presence lowered behind him. He could feel its breath, hot and acrid against the back of his neck. He could smell a sharp tinge of sulfur mingled with the sweet odor of cooked flesh. Was this now how he was to die?

He pushed with all his might to try to free himself from the invisible monster, but the thing just pushed right back down pinning him to the ground. He waited. Waited for his head to disappear too, just as the Orc's had, but it didn't happen. He could hear the breathing of the creature behind him, but did not feel the sting of its attack. What was it waiting for?

Ashyn's eyes instead fell to his house, just barely within view, between the stalks. Mortified, he watched as all the Orcs gathered on this remaining home, his home. From what he could see there had to be over forty. They built up around the home like a gathering tide. He knew soon they would swarm on the small house and slaughter everyone within, just as they had done with the rest of Bremingham.

Arrows pierced the darkness as they flew from the small home. Two Orcs in the front lines dropped immediately. For a moment, there was nothing but stillness in the air. No screams from the Orcs or their victims. No sounds of crickets or any other creatures of the night. Nothing. Nothing but the crackling of fire as the town behind Ashyn burned. Burned to the ground.

Two more arrows flew from the house and two more Orcs dropped. The Orcs didn't even seem to notice the diminishment of their numbers. Instead, they began slamming the butts of their bloodied spears into the ground once again. Boom, boom, boom!

Ashyn knew what was to come; this was how it had all started. The massive creatures drummed their feet into the ground in sync with their spears giving out once again to the savage cadence. Again, arrows flew from the windows of the small timber home, and again more monsters fell, but the brutal chorus of mashing feet and spears continued. Boom, boom, boom!

An Orc stepped forward. He was larger than the rest, adorned in skins and the feathers of birds, now indistinguishable amongst the gore and viscera that soaked his body. He raised his spear and let forth a howl unlike any Ashyn had ever heard before. It rang of hate, menace, and terror. But most of all it rang of promise. A savage, twisted promise of what was to come.

An arrow lanced out, striking him in the chest. The massive chief Orc staggered back a step, and then two more arrows connected after the first. Whether the Orc chief even felt it, Ashyn could not say. The Orc bellowed again in fury and charged the house.

The remaining contingent of Orcs all barreled towards the house, all the while screaming their primal screams. From Ashyn's eyes tears flowed creating raging tributaries down his cheeks as he watched, in dread, the sea of crimson-soaked monsters crash toward his home like a flood against a weak dam.

Arrows kept flying from the house, striking Orc after Orc. As one fell, another stumbled over them. Any not killed by the arrows were trampled to death by their own. As the chief reached the door with his massive muscled shoulder and it exploded open with force, wooden splinters flew everywhere. They surged through the portal like a swell of polluted waters after their chief. Though he could not see in the house, Ashyn could hear the sounds of combat inside. He heard the screams of the raiders as they fell in droves; a few even ran out of the house, terrified. Some of them smoking and singed, blackened marks adorning their claret soaked frames.

Eventually their numbers overwhelmed the defenders of the home. He heard a woman's scream above all others. It belonged to a voice he knew well. One that would sing to him, calm him when he was scared, sooth him when he was ill. A voice which had carried the weight of his entire life and with it, an everlasting love. It belonged to his mother. Ashyn closed his eyes as grief overtook him, his body shaking violently with equal parts hate and sorrow, fighting futilely against the unseen power keeping him down. He wanted to scream, he tried to scream. Nothing would leave his throat.

Then the small home exploded in a blinding flash of blue fire. Ashyn's breath was taken from him as the beryl-hued pyre crested high into the night sky illuminating everything in a searing light. His house disappeared in the blast, consumed by the ravaging conflagration that engulfed it. The savages inside were incinerated instantly, and those that were still outside were flung far away from the decimated home. Burning blue wood flew outward, attacking all in its path like fiery spears from the hand of the Maker himself. Many of the surviving Orcs were burned or lacerated by the eerily flaming shrapnel. They were now the ones running and screaming in terror. They fled from the sharp biting pain of a fire that could not seem to be quenched.

The flames burned fierce and strong for too many moments for the child to count. The Orcs fell in droves, burning, utterly swallowed by the inextinguishable cobalt inferno.

In the aftermath of the blaze, as the brilliant navy light settled once again into a deep indigo sky, Ashyn stared at what was once his home. In the center of the waning sea of flames, alone in the broken remnants of Ashyn's tiny dwelling, sitting on the ground with her face in her knees crying, sat his sister, Julietta.

Recovering from the detonation, the Orcs began to regroup and converge on her. They were fearful. Their numbers a fraction of what they had been. They moved on her, spears and bows ready. Ready to attack and kill this young woman. Julietta sat drained of all energy, all reason to fight. She merely cried in great sopping heaves against her knees, content to let them come and finish her off. Yet they didn't.

Ashyn fought with renewed strength to get at his sister. He wanted this force to let go, let him go so he could go to her, save her. There were only a few Orcs left . . . maybe ten or fifteen. He could, he would do something.

For a moment he thought he felt the uncertainty within the presence. The force on him lightened, just for a moment. He pushed and moved with all his might. He slipped forward ever so slightly, and that was all it took. With steel resolve, the invisible energy pushed down on him again, smothering him of all his remaining resistance. Ashyn collapsed underneath the pressure and stared up feebly just as the Orcs grabbed his sister.

Ashyn watched, powerless, as his sister was roughly bound with ropes. Unending tears flowed as the savage beasts struck her with their fists and the butts of spears alike. He cringed and shuddered with each blow that befell her but he refused to look away. Finally, when Julietta could take no more punishment they picked up her limp and bound form and carried her away, deep into the dark maw of the Shalis-Fey.

A minor contingent of the Orc force remained behind to finish burning what was left of the village to the ground. Routinely they would hack at the stalks of corn but little Ashyn was quiet, as was whatever was holding him in place, and they never found him. The village of Bremingham burned all around him, a brilliant orange blaze that consumed every stretch of the indigo sky. With each crackle and pop, with every sound, every smell of burning wood, thatch, and flesh, with every image that seared everlasting into his mind, he knew. Ashyn knew that everything he had ever known, everything he had ever loved was destroyed in that instant, and he watched it, helpless, as it all burned away. *I am so sorry, child,* the voice whispered into his mind. *There was nothing you could do.*

Nothing I could do. Ashyn repeated to himself, his grey eyes staring intently on the shattered remains of what was once his home. He felt the fires burning around him, reflected in not only his steel gaze, but within his very being as well. He knew right then that the voice was wrong. Dead wrong. He could have done something but he was too weak, too small. He vowed to himself at that moment, as his world came burning down around him in ash and ruin, that he would never be powerless again.

SURVIVOR

At some point in the horrible night, sleep consumed him. Whether it came from the heat and pressure of the unknown presence, the sweltering heat of the burning village around him, or his own pure exhaustion from everything that had happened to him, he didn't know. Likely, a combination of everything caused him to fall into his languid torpor.

When he awoke the next morning, the impenetrable force was gone. He lay still for a moment, fearful that whatever had bound him that night might still be lingering in the cornfield. He listened ardently for any sounds, perhaps breathing, or snoring. There was nothing, only the sounds of birds chirping in the early morn.

Bright light cut large swaths through the tall stalks around him. Small shadows danced across his prone form. He squinted against the assailing daylight, letting his eyes acclimate to the sun. From where he lay, without lifting his head, he began to look about.

Most of the corn stalks were still in place. Some were knocked down in the fray of violence, especially where he lay. He noticed that they were spread out in an almost circular pattern, and broken in multiple fractures across each individual stalk, flattened and pressed into the soft, tilled earth. Ashyn had seen this before, often while tracking game with his father. He would frequently see it with twigs though, or tall shoots of grass, that was matted down. It was a sign that something had settled here, something large. He let his mind dwell on that for only a moment before continuing to analyze his predicament.

The Orc raid had not come to steal their crops. He hadn't time to check if they had rounded livestock, he had been too busy fearing for his life at the time, but he assumed that they were probably dead as well. Crops and livestock generally went hand in hand during a raid. At least that was what he had read. It might not have applied to these particular Orcs. Equally, he knew from the slaughter he had witnessed the night before they did not seem interested in slaves either. Then his mind fell to his sister. She was taken. Everyone else that he had seen had died.

Why was she taken? Perhaps they had come for the girls? Young girls?

The stiffness of his body overwhelmed his fear of the unknown, and slowly he began to stretch his limbs. Pain wracked his body from being held down in a contorted position for so long. He gritted and ignored it as his young bones popped like that of an old man. As the waves passed through him, he decided to check and see how hurt he actually was.

His chest and abdomen still hurt from where he had been kicked by Gregiry, and from the multiple times he had fallen the evening before. He was sure there was ample bruising. His eyes fell across his hands and saw that both of his small pinky fingers were thick and pink with deep purple and green bruising at the knuckles. They throbbed with constant reminder of what had caused that injury. Gingerly he raised his wounded hands against the skin of his face. He could feel the puffy and swollen flesh, tight across his cheekbones. He did not bother touching his nose. From the wheezy sounds he was making with each breath it was clear to him that his nose was quite broken.

Gradually he worked up the nerve to stand. His ribs throbbed with every movement. He groaned slightly. His head began swimming and his vision got hazy. He fought against the vertigo, and tried to focus on something solid until his equilibrium returned. His eyes fell to some of the smashed stalks on the ground. He centered on what he thought was one, but looked more like three, and waited until the three images finally blended back together to form a single crushed shoot of corn.

Shaking off the rest of the dizziness he finally put one foot in front of the other and began to stumble towards where he remembered seeing his house. As he reached the center of the circular clearing, he paused, and turned once again to look at the damaged crop circle.

Something large enough to leave a trampled den of that size should have left a wake from its passage. He looked around the forest of corn. Nothing, each one was aligned as they had all previously been with maybe a two foot gap at most between each row. Ashyn looked back down at the diameter of the crushed vegetation. It was at least ten feet wide. He knew that there should have been something broken as it moved away. Some of the flora should have been damaged. He looked around again, making sure he didn't miss anything. The tracking skills learned from his father in full swing. Still, he could find nothing. Even the Orc had left a wake of shattered plants behind him. It was as if whatever indiscernible force had been keeping him down had merely disappeared. It was not a comforting thought.

He felt a strong urge to be gone from the field. Quickly.

As Ashyn stumbled out of the cornfield, he placed one hand against the left side, over his ribs. They hurt the most when he walked. He reached the perimeter of the sea of corn stalks and immediately he saw that the fringes had met the same scorching wrath as the rest of Bremingham. The nearest of the stalks were nothing more than darkened ash against a dry, rust colored ground. He needed no reminder of what caused the reddish brown hue across the soil. It still burned brightly in his young keen mind. Blood . . . what seemed like an endless mire of blood. As he looked slightly deeper in, the stalks remaining were blackened and baked. The greens and yellows now obsidian and blistered. It appeared as if the Orcs had tried to burn the fields as well, and the blaze had not taken. He knew he should feel fortunate, and yet he felt hollow inside.

The smell of burning wood and cooking flesh permeated the air. It reeked of death, blood, and feces. The sour tang assaulted his nostrils and left a putrid roiling in his stomach. With his free hand, he covered his mouth, and nose delicately, and tried to arrest the smell as best he could. His efforts helped little.

"Hello?" he called out, hoping that there may be a survivor. Hoping beyond hope that somehow his parents survived despite what he had witnessed the evening before. That emptiness he felt inside threatened to engulf and overcome him yet he fought it down. He needed to have hope.

He listened intently for an answer. When none was forthcoming, he called out again, louder. There were no sounds of any survivors. Birds chirped loudly as if nothing out of place had ever occurred, and Ashyn could see the morning dew glistening on the shattered blackened heaps of the ruined village.

Finally, he gathered what little resolve he had left within him and he began limping to his house. Or what was left of it anyways. Blackened wooden posts stood up here and there, and he could make out the cooking stove in what used to be the rear of the home. Debris was scattered all over the area, its original form now impossible to determine. It could have been his bed, or Julietta's, or even one of his mother's chests with her books. It was all indiscernible, from one thing to another. As his eyes surveyed the destruction, they danced across one of the massive elms in the back yard. It had deep black scorch marks running up the trunk and high into the branches. Not even the trees had escaped the wrath of the inferno.

As he stumbled through the debris, he noted glumly that the air surrounding what remained of the house stank strongly of burnt flesh. All around were the blackened husks of the dead, droves of them in fact. He knew that they were the Orcs. So many charred, shriveled corpses that he didn't even bother to count. Yet any one of them could have been his father, or his mother. He supposed that he should have felt proud of his ma and pa for fighting so hard, for so long. But as he looked around now he only felt . . . empty.

He stopped in what used to be their family area. The large wooden front door that the Orc chief had barreled into was resting on top of a dead man. Ashyn could see that a boot was roughly sticking out of the twisted wreckage of burnt flesh and debris. It had remained remarkably untouched compared to the rest of the devastation. Tan leather, about shin height, peaked through the valley of ravaged flesh. It still had the laces intact. Ashyn knew that the laces of that particular boot interconnected around the boot for added security. It was a boot unlike those the townspeople wore. It was meant for rugged terrain and to be worn for long periods in the wilderness. It was a hunter's boot.

He knew the boots well. He recalled the day he first saw them. Karl the tanner had come over with a huge sense of pride on his face; he had achieved a milestone in his leather-making career. He had successfully made more than rough leather jerkins and the moccasins they were all used to. He had crafted his first hunter's boot, modeled off of what he had seen Veer De'Storm wearing when the Elf had visited them. It was his *magnum opus*, his masterpiece, and he offered his prized achievement, those boots, to Ashyn's father . . .

Ashyn could not restrain the tears as they came flowing forth. His tiny frame crawled through the wreckage and collapsed next to the boot. Blackened bodies exploded into dust at his impact and it drifted about, covering his flesh and stinging his eyes. He didn't care . . . It was over. Everything was over. Reaching down he gently touched the beige suede. He was terrified that it would turn to dust as well, but it did not. He stroked it gently, feeling the soft material brush against his sensitive fingertips. He carefully brought the boot nearer and cradled his father's foot against his chest. He could not stop his uncontrollable sobbing, and he didn't want to. It didn't matter . . . Nothing mattered. His father was dead. His mother was dead. His sister was gone. Ashyn was all alone.

He cried long and hard, his tears running from his face and down the sides of his father's boot. Time seemed to pass without him knowing about it; morning to midday, and then midday to sundown. All the while he just lay there, embracing his father's boot. His life felt meaningless to him. He felt there was no purpose to anything any longer. He may as well just lie there and let the end come for him. He felt no hunger, nor thirst, only a void. A rend in his chest where his heart had once been, ripped open and thrown away. He was nothing now, not an outcast boy, not a loved son, nothing but a sole survivor. Dusk fell over him and then he heard the screams again.

~ ~ ~

Two Orcs came from behind the elm trees, yelling their savage guttural cry. Crude swords were drawn. They charged at the helpless boy, ready to cut him down.

Ashyn had not heard them approaching, he hadn't cared enough to be concerned if the ravagers would return a second night. Now as they came he idly wondered if they were part of another raid, or perhaps just stragglers that had followed behind. It didn't matter now anyway. There was nothing he could do, nowhere could he run. Truth be told, he didn't want to.

The leader closed the distance swiftly, swinging his weapon in an attempt to viciously decapitate the little child.

Ashyn stared at the blade with dull interest. What did it matter? Something inside of him roared that it *does* matter, and it was not the strange voice he had heard the night before. It was his own instincts screaming for survival, and something more: Vengeance!

He recalled the promise he had made to himself only an evening before. He would never be helpless again. He screamed in defiance at the assailer, his small lungs carrying an anguish and force that gave the marauder swinging his sword pause.

That hesitation, that infinitesimally small moment was just enough for Ashyn to react. His hand wrapped around something on the floor. It was coarse, and wooden, and mostly burned away. He lunged at the creature, his brazen movement causing the arcing swing of his assailant's sword to miss his head and instead glance across his shoulder blades. He didn't feel the biting pain, he was in a rage.

His small body connected with the Orc's thigh, the makeshift weapon held in his hand at the lead. He distantly heard the beast howl in pain. He felt the sharp impact as the assailer backhanded him with his sword arm. He staggered and fell backwards, landing once again at his father's foot. His vision swam and danced, but a burning orange outline still flared strong around the Orc. He could see blood gushing violently from where he collided into the leader's right thigh, just an inch or so from the creature's crotch. Embedded deep into the garish grey flesh was the end of a spear, the shaft mostly burned away, but the blade remaining.

The Orc stared at the wound, terror evident in his beady black eyes. Ashyn watched him move forward, casting him in the creature's long shadow. Angry red blood spewed forth from the wound like a fountain. Ashyn knew he must have done something right because he had never seen that much blood pouring from one of his arrow punctures. The monster staggered, raising his sword for the killing blow. The other one was next to him now and Ashyn knew his chances were grim but he was determined not to give up. Not again. He began searching quickly across the burnt, blackened floor. There had to be something else.

Ashyn looked up once more at the Orc's glossy eyes. He knew the creature had enough power to make it through his swing, and that is all it would take. He couldn't avoid the blow a second time.

Lightning crackled through the air and exploded through the chests of both beasts. Deep sear marks were left across their vein-laced skin. Static crackled off their bodies, dissipating through their animal hide-wrapped feet and into the ground.

Ashyn stared wide-eyed at as their greasy, thin black hair stood on its ends while electricity effervesced through them. The impact of the blast blew the sword from the swinger's hand. It landed far behind the young child. Both savage Orcs collapsed almost simultaneously, their lives extinguished by the strong lightning blast. Billows of dark smoke rolled from their mouths and ears. As they toppled forward, Ashyn was surprised to see that behind them stood a man. His gloved right hand was still extended, with blue lightning crackling from his thick fingertips.

Ashyn could only gawk in disbelief. The corpses of the two Orcs lay by his feet, still smoldering from the power of the wicked lightning. The man lowered his hand and the sizzling energy dissolved from his fingers. He came forward and dropped to a knee to look at the little boy.

Ashyn noticed that the man was covered in thick tan robes that were heavily layered with other fabrics. A dark orange vest overlapped the robes followed by a long brown cloak. He wore heavy leather gloves with thick fingers. Inlaid in the thick hide were iridescent sapphire lines that ran from the circles of his fingertips down his fingers and hands to his wrists. He was moderately built, but the layers of clothes made him look much larger. His face was sun- worn and tanned, with deep leathery creases that ran down his cheeks and lined his forehead. He had a broad, full nose and his deep azure eyes were partially hidden under thick brown eyebrows. His hair was pulled back into a thinning ponytail of dirty blonde hair. His face remained impassive as he studied the boy.

"What have we here?" his deep voice asked the young child. The boy merely looked up into his deep azure gaze. Ashyn could no longer see anything bordered in orange . . . strange.

When the stranger could see that no answer was forthcoming from the small boy, he continued to speak. "It appears that I have arrived in time to find at least one survivor. We should go."

The strange robed man extended his hand out to the young Rune boy, but Ashyn could only continue to stare. This man had done something with his hands. He had made lightning jump from them! Kind of like Ashyn had made fire appear on Gregiry. Was this merely coincidence? A thought, a memory of something he had read burned at the back of his mind, but he could not recall it.

Subconsciously, Ashyn hands found his father's boot once again and locked onto it in a death grip. The stranger seemed to take this in. He looked to the boy and his hand on the man's boot. "Did you know this man?" he asked softly.

Tears welled up again in Ashyn's eyes. "He was my pa," he managed in a broken voice.

The cloaked stranger shook his head. "I am sorry, my boy. I am so sorry."

Even though the man was a complete stranger, Ashyn let his emotions go. He fell into the man in a hug. The stranger held him, and he cried. Tears flowed down the tanned child's face in unending currents. The salty streams pooled into the stranger's orange vest, saturating it. Ashyn felt himself being lifted as if he weighed no more than a feather and noticed he was being carried away. Ashyn glanced behind as the horror of what remained of his house started to drift away. A strong part of him wanted to remain at that house with his mother and father. Remain in a life that was all he knew.

He felt himself slowly rocking in the stranger's arms. He could hear the man whispering to him soft words of reassurance and confidence. Ashyn watched as the house with the copse of trees disappeared from his view, gone like the sun setting on a distant horizon. What was once his old life was now gone, only a memory, along with everything that had once been called Bremingham.

Exhausted from the events that surrounded him, the young child fell into a deep sleep.

SHALIS-FEY

Ashyn awoke on a small bundle of leaves. They were soft and comfortable; it reminded him of his bed. Somewhere nearby he could feel the warm undulations of a burning fire. It coated him in its seductive warmth, licking at his senses of peace and security. The sharp popping of wood filled the nearly silent air. It was tranquil and calming, Ashyn felt safe.

He sniffed once, catching the luscious scent of cooking meat. He recognized the smell. It was a delicacy he had had often; hare.

Ashyn rolled over and looked at the small fire that burned nearby. Atop a makeshift spit a hare rotated around and around, cooking over the hungry fire. Ashyn's little stomach growled. It had been a long time since he had anything to eat. The boy found himself salivating for what spun upon the spit.

Sitting on the other side of the fire, sat the robed stranger. He was turning his finger over and over following the motion of the spit. Ashyn blinked in astonishment.

It took a second for him to realize the man's finger wasn't following the motion of the spit, but the spit was following the motion of the man's finger. There was no one turning the spit! His little grey eyes went wide... first the blue lightning, and now this.

"Awake, I see," the deep voice said to him.

Instinctively Ashyn curled back into the leaves in a tight fetal position. The motion wracked his body with pain, instantly reminding him of his injuries. He hissed against the waves of agony.

"Relax, boy. I mean you no harm," the heavily robed stranger said. He stopped turning his finger and put his hand to his chest. Ashyn noticed that the spit did not stop turning. "My name is Xexial . . . Xexial Bontain. What is yours?"

Ashyn tried curling into a smaller ball than he already was, but physics had decreed just how small he could become, and he wasn't getting any tinier.

Xexial looked at him and sighed. "Okay, have it as you wish," he said and then held up a thick-gloved finger. "But know that I do not share food with strangers."

With that, the man went back to turning the spit with his finger, all the while humming a merry tune. Ashyn noticed that his voice was deep and the hum came out in a low rumbling bass. Somehow, the sound was very soothing to him.

Ashyn tried to continue to lie in the leaves in the fetal position, but once Xexial started pulling the hare apart and eating it, hunger began to supersede his fear. His stomach moaned in protest and he was even sure that Xexial had likely heard it. Ashyn looked up at the man.

If he had heard Ashyn's hunger pains, he made no indication as he plucked apart another strip of meat from the well-cooked meal. Ashyn decided then that he was just being stupid. He had once feared Veer and the Elf had turned out to be the greatest friend he had ever had. Ashyn peered at the strange clothed figure as he ate. He knew this man had killed the two Orcs, and he had rescued him from whatever else might have come into the remains of Bremingham. All Xexial was asking from him was a name? A name and he would share some of his hare, his moist, delectable, sumptuous, roast hare.

"Ashyn," he murmured.

Xexial looked up at the boy, his eyes sparkling. "What was that?"

"Ashyn," the boy repeated as he gathered courage. "My name is Ashyn, M' Lord."

A deep rumble of laughter left the robed man's mouth. "Well met, Ashyn," he said. "There is no need to call me M' Lord. Xexial will do just fine."

"Yes M' Lord," the boy answered again. Xexial's laugh intensified.

"Well since we now know each other's names and we are no longer strangers, would you like to share part of this hare with me? I fear there is too much here for me to eat by myself and I wouldn't want any to go to waste, not with such a skinny boy laying only five feet from me," Xexial said with a smile.

Ashyn smiled back and crawled off the bed of leaves. He stood up and wiped the leaves off that dangled on his behind and thighs. He then walked over to Xexial and sat next to him.

Xexial laughed at the sight. His cheery demeanor was disarming and Ashyn couldn't help but feel at ease. Xexial tore part of the freshly cooked hare and offered it to the little boy.

The morsel was hot in his hands. He didn't mind though, he was far too hungry to complain. He raised the meat to his mouth and tore away a bit of it. It was so soft and juicy; it felt like the meat just melted in his mouth. He took another bite, and then another, and before he knew it, he had ravished his meal. Xexial seemed to laugh even more.

When they were done, Xexial leaned back on a log and lit a pipe. The tobacco held a lush intoxicating scent which mixed with the deep pine of the woods they were in. Ashyn studied the odd robed man. He was calm, at peace, content in his surroundings. The young boy cast his steely gaze about the forest. The trees loomed tall, blocking out whatever traces of sunlight there were. It wasn't dark, per se, but it definitely wasn't bright either.

The trees were a mixture of elm, maple, and pine. Each was ancient. Gargantuan compared to anything that Ashyn had ever seen. He looked at the green leaves high up above him. They formed a canopy that reminded him of the thatched roof of his house. Slivers of dying amber light leaked through the thatches of green. They created small pools of orange light in scattered pockets across the ground. "Where are we?" he asked.

"Deep is the Shalis-Fey," Xexial cryptically answered.

The boy straightened. His father had told him that the Shalis-Fey forest was very dangerous and that many people entered but never returned. Most of that fear was because of the reclusive Wild Elves.

Wild Elves were not like their more mainstream cousins. They were feral in appearance. Many wore the hides of animals and painted themselves with tree sap, mud, and the blood of their victims. It added to their intimidating appearance. Wild Elves were generally shorter than most men were, but the life of living in the dangerous Shalis-Fey made their muscles dense and reflexes quick. Ashyn remembered Karl the tanner saying that the Wild Elves were some of the most accurate hunters he had ever seen with a spear. Ashyn wondered what Xexial must have been thinking to bring them in here.

Did he know? Did he know how dangerous the Wild Elves were? Maybe he didn't, Ashyn realized. Maybe Xexial was just trying to get him away from Bremingham and had not realized the danger he had placed the both of them in. Father would never go deep into the Shalis-Fey. They had only hunted the surface of the woods, and even then he had remembered the predators there on the outskirts. He tried not to think about the Bristle Wolves.

Xexial seemed to sense the child's anxiety. "Relax. No one can hurt you while I am here."

"Why? Because ye canna shoot lightning from ye hands?" Ashyn blurted before he could catch himself. He put his hands on his mouth and looked at the robed man in wide-eyed shock. Was Xexial going to zap him now, too?

"Precisely," Xexial merely said with a nod.

Seeing that he wasn't about to be incinerated for his comment, Ashyn then looked up at the trees. "My pa always told me that the Wild Elves dinna fear anything," he continued quietly.

The man chuckled. Ashyn wasn't sure if he was making fun of his father or not. It made him angry only for a moment, until he could see that it wasn't meant to be insulting.

"Did he, now?" Xexial said politely. "Well he was right. There is very little the Ferhym fear."

Ashyn had never heard Wild Elves called by that name before. "What did ye call them?" the boy asked.

"Ferhym," Xexial repeated immediately. "That is their true name. Most people simply call them Wild Elves, and for their part they are content with that, but that has not always been the name that they were given. Long ago the Elves went by 'The Hym'."

Ashyn had never heard such stories before. People in Bremingham had only ever referred to them as Elves. He thought briefly of Stormwind and wondered how he felt about being called something different from his original ancestry?

The man continued, "The Hym were the original race of Elves a very, very long time ago but they soon evolved into the separate races that you have probably heard of or seen today. There's the Dakhym, the Dark Elves; Goldhym, High Elves; Lefhym, Wood Elves, and of course the Ferhym, the Wild Elves."

The boy sat in quiet wonder. So many different Elves! So many that he never knew before! He wondered what else there was outside of the world of Bremingham?

"What is to become of me now?" he asked.

Xexial leaned back further against the log and crossed his legs one on top of the other. "I suppose that is up to you, my boy," he told the child. "It will be a few days' journey to the other side of the Shalis-Fey. Until that time you're stuck with me, but once we reach the other side and go into a town then we'll see."

Ashyn thought about it. "Do ye live in that town?" he asked.

Xexial chuckled again and shook his head. "No I live far northeast of here. I have a tower that I live in."

"Ye live in a tower?" the boy repeated.

"Yes."

"Why?" the child asked.

"Well generally all wizards have a tower," the self-proclaimed wizard said matter-of-factly.

Nonplussed, Ashyn stared strangely at Xexial. He had never heard of that title before, even in his mother's books. "What's a wizard?" he found himself asking.

"A wizard is a very special type of person," Xexial told young Ashyn. "They can use a gift that not many in this world can."

"Or can with any real skill anyways . . .," he mumbled quietly after a puff from his pipe.

"Does this have something to do with the blue lightning?" Ashyn asked excitedly.

"Yes," Xexial answered, his eyes glittering. "It does."

Ashyn thought he knew what a wizard was then, from what he had seen: the lightning from Xexial's fingertips and later, the hare turning on the spit seemingly unassisted. Now, however, it rang clear and loud in his mind. He had read about it often from his mother's books. He had been excited about it, dreamed he could do it, and even confessed a desire for it with Stormwind only two winters earlier. He felt his heart constrict in his chest in anticipation as he asked his next question.

"Do ye use magic?"

Xexial cocked his head at the boy in wonderment. "Where have you heard that word before?"

"I . . . I read it, sir," Ashyn stammered back to him.

Ashyn watched as the wizard cupped his right hand over chin and mouth as he thought, the weathered man's hooded gaze never leaving him. Finally after many moments he spoke. "So you're literate then?"

Ashyn nodded.

"How is it a boy from a small farming community can read and write?"

Ashyn stared at his feet, fighting the swell of emotions that filled him at the thought of her. "T'was my mother, sir. She wasn't from Bremingham. She was from Gurgen."

"Gurgen . . . really?" Xexial whispered to himself, but loud enough that Ashyn could hear him. The heavily robed man looked at him. "I assume you're well-educated then?"

Ashyn still staring at his feet nodded. "For my part."

Xexial took another long draw from his pipe. Ashyn looked up and watched as the man savored the smoke in his mouth before releasing it in a light grey stream into the air. "That's good then," Xexial decided, leaning back against a fallen tree stump. "Tell me then, young Ashyn, what do you know of magic?"

Ashyn was startled to see that he did not repulse Xexial. Like Stormwind had been two winters before, the man before him seemed generally interested in him. Were it not for the grief he felt, and the swell of emptiness in his stomach, this moment would have enraptured him. Another person that was not afraid of him, not fearful that there was a demon possessing him, or that he was some aberrant creature from the bowels of the Defiler.

Ashyn thought intently on how best to answer. Finally he decided just to say bluntly what he knew. "Um. From what I've read, magic is the ability to control the elements to do ye bidding. Ye can make things move, on their own, like the spit," Ashyn said. "Or ye can fill a cup full of water without need of a well or a stream. Ye can make wind blow stronger, and fire burn hotter. Or ye canna even . . ." He looked into the man's blue eyes. "Shoot lightning from ye fingertips."

With that, Xexial burst into a deep hardy laugh, his pipe bobbing precariously from the corner of his mouth, threatening to topple its burning contents out at any moment. He leaned further back into the fallen trunk and clapped his hands. "Bravo my boy, bravo!" he said jubilantly to young Ashyn. "That does indeed make it sound very romantic and appealing."

Ashyn looked down in embarrassment. He hadn't wanted it to sound romantic, though to him the idea was very appealing. When Gregiry's arm caught on fire, had he used magic? Was it possible? In addition, the voice in his head . . . had that been magic too? He desperately wanted to ask this man, this wizard, but he was afraid. What if the fire was not normal? And the voice . . . he had never read anything before on people talking inside of their heads. Would he sound preposterous? Or possibly worse? He might well sound crazy. In the end, his silence gave Xexial the time to continue.

"There are many things magical in this world, my lad, some great, some terrible," he added solemnly. "What you must understand is that magic itself cannot be controlled, per se. Manipulated, yes, perhaps even coerced, but never controlled. You see, it is not a single entity, not just a superficial external source, it is everything." He pointed all around him. "Contrary to what you may have read, magic is life itself."

Ashyn blinked confusion, "So ye control life?" he asked.

Xexial laughed long and heartily at the boy's question. "Some seem to think so, yes. But in truth the answer is no, I no more control life than you do. You see, my boy, we don't just use magic, magic uses us. I am merely its conduit, nothing more."

Ashyn shook his head. "I . . . don't understand. I saw ye shoot lightning from ye fingertips. How can ye say that ye dinna control that?"

Xexial took a long draw from his pipe and Ashyn watched patiently as the man savored the taste in his mouth before finally blowing out a heady cloud of smoke. "You certainly are a clever boy," he said modestly. "Yes, I coerced the lightning to do what I desired, which was to strike at those two savage beasts, but you must understand I did not control it. I do not own magic or make it subservient to me. I harness it, wield it, and shape it like a farmer does with a fertile field, or livestock."

"But a farmer kills his livestock for food, or if it becomes lame. They are possessions to the farmer," Ashyn answered.

"Are they?" Xexial returned with a raised eyebrow. "Tell me, young Ashyn. If a cow is a mere possession, then why does the farmer care for it, feed it, protect it from the elements, or tend to it when it is sick and ill?"

"Because he needs the cow for its milk, and eventually it's meat," Ashyn answered automatically.

"He needs the cow . . .," Xexial repeated. "So the relationship is symbiotic then, wouldn't you say? The farmer needs the cow to survive, just as much as the cow survives off of the farmer?"

"I suppose," Ashyn agreed, shuffling his feet. He had never really been asked questions like these before; it puzzled him. "But the farmer will eventually kill the cow to use as meat."

"Yes. All things die, lad. It is an unpleasant fact. It is in fact the very meaning of life. A life without end is nothing but a hollow existence. One cannot appreciate life, without death. If you could never die, then emotions like joy, love, happiness would mean nothing. It is these small things, these little moments that we have for as long as we live that make us truly know what it is like to be alive.

"You see the cow will die at the hands of the farmer, this is true, but cannot it not be said that the farmer was also likely present for its birth as a calf, or perhaps present to raise the calf of the cow that had been slaughtered to feed the farmer, his family, and the families of others? In the end the farmer and his family are as much dependent on the cow as the cow and its progeny are on him."

"It is still a servant of the farmer," Ashyn defended. "The cow is never free to live its own existence. It is still often purchased or traded."

Xexial merely shrugged. "Perhaps. It is all truly based on your perspective of course. True, the cow does not get to live freely to feed on the wild plains, and to breed, as the species is wont to do. But the farmer provides for it all the necessities of its survival, and in return the cow provides to the farmer."

"So could be said of a slave working the farms," Ashyn returned, "A slave is fed by its master, and given shelter. Are those not the very things ye are saying about a cow?"

"Indeed you are witty," Xexial marveled. "Yes, I suppose you have a valid point. What I mean to say is more that magic works in a similar fashion to, say, a tilled field. We survive on the land, and the land is strengthened by us, if we care for it properly. We nourish the soil and the soil in turn grows the food we plant and nourishes us. It is symbiotic. It needs you just as much as you need it. Magic is that way as well. I may make gestures, and use words that call forth lightning, or that turn a spit, but it too has its costs, its needs, if you will. It requires energy on my part to do this. As each spell is cast, a little more of that energy is pulled away from me, funneled into the spell. Therefore, I must be careful, you see. Too much use and I risk hurting myself, perhaps killing myself. If magic were controlled, if it were merely a possession, a slave, I would have no fear of its retaliation, of its feedback. I could use it at will and bend it to serve me. But magic serves no man; it is *I* who am *its* servant. I depend on it, and it lets me use it willingly, for a price."

"Then why use magic if it could kill ye?"

"Why use anything at all then, my boy?" Xexial countered. "A horse could trample you, a tree may fall upon you, and water may drown you, but we use these things nonetheless. They are mandatory to our survival. Water is necessary for us to survive, without it we will surely die, but too much of it and we die. Should we cease drinking water because it can kill us? No. Like all things, moderation is necessary. Magic is my trade, it is my calling, and as such, I am dependent on its survival. Nevertheless, I respect magic, you see. I always respect magic, as much as any horseman respects his steed.

Ashyn nodded his understanding.

"You ask a lot of very smart questions for someone so young, you know that, don't you?" Xexial returned.

Again, shame forced Ashyn to look at his feet. "The people of Bremingham said that, too. They called me a freak."

"Fools," Xexial scoffed. "More like prodigy, if you ask me."

Ashyn felt a strange sense of elation. Xexial didn't judge him negatively for his knowledge, but rather commended him on it. Why was this man so different? Why did he seem so similar to Veer, and yet by the same token, not? Was everyone outside of Bremingham like this? Or perhaps these men were special as well?

"You should turn in for the evening though, boy. Those wounds will not heal themselves," Xexial said, pointing to the various bruises and swellings that assailed Ashyn's small frame.

Ashyn looked through the canopy, and indeed saw the amber light had died to a pale iridescent white light. The orange flicker of the fire was the only thing to illuminate the two of them now. The boy listened as the natural wildlife of the forest began to chatter and sing around them. This was their time.

"But I've only just awoke," Ashyn retorted.

Xexial sighed, "And at sundown, I'm afraid. You see it is not safe to travel in the Shalis-Fey at night, even for a wizard. But rest assured my boy, you will always be safe in my camp."

Ashyn wanted to deny the need to sleep; he had so many more questions to ask. Xexial seemed to sense this and waved his blue lined glove in front of the small child's face. "Sleep," he whispered.

Soon Ashyn's eyes were getting too heavy to keep open, and he felt his body falling back into the pile of leaves behind him. As a soothing darkness began to drift over him, he felt a small spark of energy within him to ask one more question. "Can anyone use magic?" he muttered softly as he felt a cool serenity encapsulate him.

"Yes, if they are trained," Xexial answered the boy after another long drag on his pipe.

"Could I?" Ashyn whispered as everything faded and slowly became muffled, as if he was collapsing into heavy layers of thick cotton.

"Perhaps," Xexial responded, "But it is a long hard road. Why would a young boy want to give up his entire childhood to wield something that equally wields him?"

"Revenge," Ashyn breathed as his world faded into the blackness.

Xexial leaned back against the fallen tree and studied the boy's quiet breathing for a long time. As he let out a final cloud of smoke from between his lips, his blue eyes followed it up into the dense green tree line. "What an interesting boy you are," he whispered.

FERHYM

Ashyn followed the wizard Xexial through the Shalis-Fey quietly for the next few days. Neither of them mentioned magic again after that first night. They had had small talk here and there, mostly Xexial asking Ashyn about his family, what they were like, what they did in Bremingham, and his upbringing. Xexial seemed extremely curious about his mother, and her time before when she was in Gurgen. It was hard for Ashyn to answer questions to which he knew so little about, but he struggled to provide any information that he could to his savior.

Ashyn had to admit that he liked the man. He was hard, callous, and a bit rough around the edges, but there was also a gentler side to him. One that he had seen on the first night, and on other consecutive nights when he would have nightmares about Bremingham, Orcs, and the death of his parents. On those nights Xexial would hold him like his father used to, act as a comforting pillar in his time of need, and for that Ashyn was grateful. During the day however, Xexial kept a rigorous pace through the woods. He expected Ashyn to keep up, if not outright demanded it at times.

Ashyn never complained though, not once. For he was serious in his desire to learn magic, and since Xexial had not yet answered one way or another, he took that as a good sign that he was going to need to prove himself worthy of the wizard's notice.

"Nothing worth having is ever given," his father had often told him on their hunts, "It is earned," he would finish. It was sort of the Rune mantra, he supposed. Every meal that they hunted was earned because of their labors. The tracking, the stalking, and eventually the lining up of their prey and releasing the arrow. Their prey would not just lie there and say kill me. Ashyn and his pa had to work for the kill, work for the right to survive. If they failed, they went hungry. And there had been more than one evening when they had not eaten.

Therefore, Ashyn knew if he were to hope to have any chance to learn magic, it would have to be earned. If he were to have any chance to be strong, he would have to work for it, for his right to survive.

Ashyn began to take solace in the thick canopy of the Shalis-Fey woods. Though the sheer height of the ancient trees was daunting, it also felt strangely protective, as if sheltering him from a greater danger beyond the verdant green ceiling. Ashyn knew it was a false feeling of security of course, since his entire life was built on defending himself from what came out of the Shalis-Fey. Fear of the Wild Elves, Bristle Wolves, and now of course the Orcs. He was surprised that a place that harbored such malicious and evil creatures could feel so serene. Maybe that was part of the forest's own magic? A false sense of protection? He pondered that for a while as he walked.

Another day and another night slipped by without incident. Ashyn marveled on how the Shalis-Fey seemed so never ending. He on occasion wondered if perhaps Xexial was merely lost, but one look at the man's sure strides always discounted any worries immediately.

On their fifth day Xexial took him down into a strange fissure between two large cliff faces. It was probably over fifty steps wide, but felt confining with the large grass and vine-covered masses of land on either side of him. He had never felt particularly claustrophobic, even when in the tight confines of the cornfield, but something about this place sent off a strange trigger of alarm.

He looked up warily at the fern-covered overhang on either side. Anything could be watching them from behind the foliage. Slowly he rotated around to check the other side. It was impossible to see within the sea of green flora no matter how hard he tried. Was he just worrying? Xexial said that no harm would come to him, as long as the wizard was around. Was it just a boast, or was Xexial truly confident that no one would attack a wizard? Ashyn did not know for sure, but he knew his feelings, and he realized he had to trust his instincts.

"Xexial," he whispered.

Since they had not talked in some time, Ashyn's breaking the silence brought with it a curious stare from the weathered man.

"Something is wrong, Sir," Ashyn whispered as he looked up at the ridges high above them.

Xexial's gaze drifted up to the cliff edges as well. He looked back down to the boy and nodded once. "It's the Ferhym," he whispered back. "They are watching us."

Ashyn stayed close to the man. "Ye knew they were there?"

Xexial nodded once again. "Oh yes, my boy," he answered still quiet, but no longer a whisper. "They have been following us for three days."

Three days! The Wild Elves had been following them for the last three days and Ashyn had been unaware the whole time! Everything his father had taught him to look for; the sights, the sounds, the tracks, and he had missed it all!

Xexial looked back up to the canopy of ferns above. "They are curious, you see. They want to know what two men are doing in their homes."

"Will they attack?" Ashyn asked.

"Given the fact that they have not yet, I take it as a good sign they won't," Xexial said to Ashyn with a twinkle in his eyes. "One, however, should always remain cautious," he added.

Ashyn nervously glanced up once more. He would have liked to share Xexial's optimism, but something deep within him was vibrating with an unerring wrongness about walking further into the ravine. As much as his senses were screaming to turn around, he continued to follow the wizard. He didn't want to seem afraid and lose any chances of learning how to use magic he might have.

As they continued deeper down into the flora-laden crevice, Ashyn began to hear the trickling of a nearby stream. They walked around a particularly wide oak that had somehow found itself able to thrive growing out at a contorted angle from the gully base. The branches hung low to the ground, covered in deep green leaves. It reminded Ashyn of an old man's beard. As they cleared the leafy mass, he could see clearly the source of the running water.

Cut into the west face of the ravine was a small sparkling waterfall. It cascaded brilliant splashes of crystal clear water into the tiny brook beneath it. For a moment, Ashyn forgot about the twisting feeling in his stomach as he stared at the majesty of nature before him. It was like thousands of tiny diamonds tumbling into a narrow channel of liquid glass.

However, it was not the waterfall that enraptured the little boy so; it was what lay beyond the shimmering waters . . . a young Elven girl. She was the source of his uneasy feeling.

Similar in age to Ashyn, the delicate Ferhym child splashed blissfully in the iridescent pool, sending a spray of the luminous clear liquid misting into the air.

Her hair was a silvery blonde that ran straight and pure down her shoulders to the small of her back. It reminded Ashyn of spun platinum. It cascaded around her body as she play in the crystalline waters, like captured sunlight. Elongated slender ears poked out of the mass of her platinum hair and rose to sharp points just above the crown of her head. She had a heart-shaped face with high cheekbones and a long, delicate nose. Her lips were so full that it seemed as if the young girl were constantly pouting. Swirls of white paint, or perhaps berries, adorned the tanned copper skin of her face, arms, stomach, and legs. She wore only two simple green garments that covered her both her chest and her nether regions. She was like no Elf that the boy had ever known.

Ashyn felt Xexial freeze next to him. He looked up to see the strong gaze staring ardently at the small Elven child in the pool of water. Ashyn even thought, for a moment, there was a glimmer of fear in those deep blue eyes.

The boy looked back at the captivating little girl before him. What was it that startled Xexial so? he wondered. Ashyn knew he was enchanted by the site of the Elf because she was so different from what he knew, but surely, the wizened man could not be so mesmerized? Perhaps Xexial felt the same aura of wrongness that he did? What was it about a little female Elf that could cause such discord within him? Ashyn was about to quietly ask Xexial when the silver-eyed girl looked up at him.

Instantly Ashyn was charmed. Her eyes danced and swam before him. Twin pools of liquid mercury that enticed and beguiled him all at once. Suddenly thoughts of his sister and Gregiry Bibs canoodling didn't seem so repulsive anymore. In fact, it seemed rather . . . okay.

He felt a tug on his shoulder, followed urgently by a more forceful pull. He looked away from the girl lazily, in an almost dreamlike daze and back up to Xexial. He could see, strangely enough, that Xexial was not looking at the Elf child anymore, but away and slightly to the ground. "Do not look into her eyes," he whispered harshly.

"But wh . . . ?" Ashyn began confoundedly.

"Just do not!" the wizard finished sharply.

Disappointed, if not a bit saddened by Xexial's decree, he decided to follow the old man's instructions and look down at the ground. As he did he felt the wave of euphoria that her quicksilver gaze gave him leave his body, clearing his mind. It felt as if he had just been struck in the head with a cudgel.

"Whooh," he muttered as his mind quickly sought to find equilibrium. He stumbled momentarily grabbing his temples as he tried to gain his balance.

"Quickly," Xexial told Ashyn as he grabbed him by the elbow. "Keep walking, and listen not to a word she says."

Ashyn nodded as they began to walk and stared fixedly at the ground. He heard the distinct splash of the Elf girl exiting the pool, quickly followed by the slapping thud of wet bare feet hitting the stony ground. They padded swiftly along the hard surface, whacking sloppily against the rough rocky outcroppings. Ashyn could tell the speedily moving feet were nearing them.

"Esse balla dui nuchada, esse en due fer stirulla?" the girl's singsong voice demanded as Xexial navigated by her.

Ashyn desperately wanted to look at her again, into her eyes, but he fought the urge.

"Esse balla dui nuchada, esse en due fer stirulla?" she repeated, this time much closer to them. Ashyn noted that her voice sounded quite ethereal, almost other worldly.

He continued to stare fixedly at the ground as Xexial led him along, but he was forced to stop quickly when he found himself staring directly at the young Elf girl's wet bare feet.

"Esse balla dui nuchada, esse en dui Shalis stirulla?" she said more quietly now that she was right in front of him.

"What is she saying?" Ashyn asked Xexial without looking up. "I can't understand her."

"Trust me, that is a good thing," Xexial returned and then added, "She basically wants to know what a human child is doing in these woods."

"Shouldn't we answer her?" Ashyn asked curiously.

"No," Xexial replied flatly.

Ashyn felt himself guided to the left so he took a step. As he did, the feet in front of him took a step, too. Xexial attempted to guide him to the right. Again the feet followed, forcing him to stop. Ashyn audibly heard Xexial sigh as his touch left Ashyn.

"Dui nuchada?" The silver-eyed Elf said again.

"She is apparently very interested you, my boy," Xexial said in a perturbed state. "Especially your eyes."

"My eyes?" Ashyn questioned. "Her eyes are far more interesting than mine," he responded.

"Be that as it may, she is concerned with your eyes, and she is calling you Nuchada," Xexial told him.

"Nuchada? That's me?" he asked the wizard. As he did he saw the platinum hair of the Elf child enter view his view, followed by her chin and nose. Quickly he turned his head away, just as she dodged with him.

"Yes, Nuchada means 'spirit eyes' in her dialect."

"But there's nothing special about my eyes. They're just . . . grey," he questioned.

Ashyn felt, more than saw, the wizard shrug at his statement. "Perhaps she sees something in your eyes that we do not. I cannot say."

Again he turned, this time in another direction, and again she followed. "Ha-ha dui Nuchada!" she said laughing, following him as if it were a game.

"What do I do?" Ashyn asked as he kept dodging and weaving her, attempting not to look at her.

"Just don't look in her eyes," Xexial returned almost blandly.

"Can't we just leave?" Ashyn said desperately, still trying to avoid making eye contact with the quick, high-spirited girl.

"I'd love to," Xexial returned, "I am hoping she will lose interest in you rather quickly so that we may do just that."

"Lose interest in me?" Ashyn was incredulous. "Canna ye scare her away or something?"

"That wouldn't be a very prudent course of action, my boy. We are being watched after all. Hurting, scaring, or even killing one of their *Exemplar* would be bad for us I'm afraid; very bad."

"Their what?"

"Nothing," Xexial said dismissing him. "Now is not the time for this discussion. Quickly, just tire her out and hopefully she'll get bored with you."

"If she doesn't?" Ashyn dared to ask.

Xexial merely shrugged.

"Great," Ashyn fumed under his breath as he continued to dart and sway back and forth trying to avoid making contact with her eyes. To the girl it was great fun and she kept up with him for several minutes, occasionally piercing through his movements to look him in the eyes. In those few moments, he felt his body grow tingly, and he felt an instinctual pull to let him be taken by her eyes. It took a lot of will for the little boy to ignore her enthralling gaze. Finally, after what felt like hours to Ashyn, the Elf turned away from him. Too tired to continue, the girl, breathing heavily, let out a great sigh of frustration and sat down on a rock.

As close as she was to Ashyn he could feel the ripples of her despair as she folded her arms across her chest and looked down at her feet, absently padding the ground. "Dui Nuchada esse bui bui mudano," her melodic voice said somberly. She began to sniffle and then eventually cry. Even after all she had put him through in those last few minutes, Ashyn still could not help but feel a little sorry for her.

Ashyn took a step forward towards her, but immediately Xexial's arm came up in front of him. "You did what you had to do, my boy. It's time for us to leave."

Ashyn could not understand anything that was going on, least of all why the young Elf girl made him feel so strange when she looked into his eyes. As much as he wanted to apologize, as much as he wanted to see those exotic silver eyes again, he only nodded at Xexial solemnly. Ashyn turned away from the girl, looked up at Xexial and froze.

There, only a few scant inches away from Xexial's face, was a spear, poised and ready to strike.

Xexial, spear tip only a thumb's length from his right eye, merely stared at the wielder of the weapon. "It appears we have lingered too long, my boy," he said dryly to Ashyn.

On the other end of the spear, holding it steady and unwavering in front of the wizard, was the creature that Ashyn's father had told him to watch out for all his life: a Wild Elf.

Compact, steely muscles ran the length of the Elf's bronze-skinned arm, as he held the weapon aloft, solidly, with only one hand. Ashyn traced his gaze to the Elf's face. Undeniably male, the Elf's rough features were mostly covered in a near black substance that coated his face, and slicked back his long hair, making its color indistinguishable. Deep brown eyes the color of tree bark stared back at Xexial through his painted face.

Ashyn glanced at the rest of the Elf. The same obsidian coating seemed to cover most of the rest of his frame with the exception of his arms, which remained free of the onyx glaze. The substance that the Elf wore gave off a slightly sweet smell, like tree sap. He wondered if that is what it was.

Ashyn noticed that this Elf's ears were very similar to the child's, sweeping high up to the crown of its head, very different from that of Veer's only slightly tapered points that he had seen two winters earlier. He also noticed that the Wild Elf wasn't particularly tall, only coming up to the shoulder of the much taller human wizard. The Elf didn't even seem to register the height difference, and seemed every bit as feral as his father had described them to be.

At first Ashyn thought the Elf to be alone, but a quick glimmer out of the boy's peripheral vision showed him that there were more lurking about in the flora. A great many more.

"What do we do?" Ashyn whispered to the wizard, his grey eyes continuing to scan the dense foliage.

"I'll negotiate, my boy, don't you worry. I've communed with the Ferhym before. It will be fine," Xexial said very confidently.

Ashyn nodded, feeling a little less anxious.

"Just do me one favor," the wizard added.

Ashyn looked away from his surroundings and back to Xexial who was looking down at him out of the corner of his eye.

"Whatever you do, do not approach the Exemplar, and do not . . . I repeat . . . do not look into her eyes," Xexial said very seriously.

Taking a deep breath, Ashyn nodded again with resolve, and stared up the Wild Elf wielding the spear. He would do as Xexial bade. He would not dare look at the silver-haired Elf child.

The spear wielder began to chatter quickly to the wizard, in a language that Ashyn could only mildly identify as something remotely similar to what the girl had been speaking. He could make out similar inflections, and the occasional word, but the spear wielder spoke so quickly that it mostly sounded to Ashyn like clicks and pops.

What surprised the boy more was not the Elf's use of the language, but the fact that Xexial answered the spear wielder in the same dialect, and as far as he could tell, with unerring accuracy.

This exchange continued for several minutes, with the spear wielder, the obvious aggressor, occasionally taking the spear away from Xexial's face and pointing it at Ashyn himself, and sometimes he pointed nonchalantly to the Exemplar who had moved herself, and was now uncomfortably near to him.

He could feel her aura radiating off her, like the heat radiating off a campfire. Her presence was smothering, sweltering, as if he were as close to a fire as he could be without burning himself.

He noticed that Xexial noted this as well, and though he could not understand the language they were speaking, he could feel the sense of urgency coming from the wizard's underlying actions.

Occasionally the mercury-eyed girl next to him would add to their growing conversation, and her manner of speaking was much slower. Each time he could distinctly make out the name she had called him, Nuchada.

Whenever she used that word, the spear wielder would eye him suspiciously, but then resume his conversation with Xexial.

Finally, after what felt like an eternity to the boy, the spear wielder lowered his weapon. Ashyn exhaled a sigh of relief, a breath he had not realized he had been holding.

Xexial bowed his head in supplication to the Wild Elf and made a motion with his right hand that Ashyn found peculiar. The wizard gently touched his own forehead, eyes, then mouth, and then placed his hand palm up in front of him. The boy then watched as the spear wielder repeated the same gesture. Conversation now over, Xexial waved the boy back over to his side.

Ashyn quickly moved away from the Exemplar, and back to the wizard's side. Just as swiftly, Xexial took his hand and they turned away from the group of Wild Elves.

"We will talk about this later," Xexial said quietly, distilling any questions Ashyn may have been about to ask.

They did not make it twenty feet deeper into the ravine, when the Exemplar called from behind them. "Nuchada!"

Xexial froze, and slowly rotated the two of them around. "Remember, do not look in her eyes," he whispered harshly.

Ashyn, once again nodded.

The girl ran up to him. As she did, he saw her feet once again enter his view. There was a moment of silence as she fiddled with something he could not see, followed by the sound of something being cut.

Immediately gasps resounded from around the three of them, as the Elf girl grabbed Ashyn's left hand and gently put a braided lock of her silver hair within his palm.

Ashyn stared at the gift, dumbfounded. Never had he received any gifts from anyone outside for his family, least of all from a girl, and never anything as sentimental as a lock of hair.

When Xexial looked down to see what she had given Ashyn, Ashyn heard him curse. Suddenly Ashyn was pulled violently away from the Exemplar. "We need to leave, right now!" he stated urgently.

Ashyn felt himself being drug, more than guided, as Xexial made swift long strides to try to separate himself from the group of Ferhym behind them.

"I don't understand . . ." Ashyn began.

"She's marked you," Xexial snapped.

"But it's just a lock of hair."

"No, it isn't," the wizard said as he moved them deeper into the ravine.

"Should I throw it away?" Ashyn asked.

"No. I'll explain later, first we need to get away before . . ."

Before Xexial could finish, he felt the small child collide fiercely with the back of his left knee. The jarring impact caused his step to falter, toppling him over, breaking his handhold, and almost trampling the small boy.

"What the hells . . . !" Xexial roared as he stumbled to find his footing. A loud crack echoed just inches from his right ear. Xexial turned to see a spear imbedded, inches away, in a tree growing from the side of the earthy trench.

Ashyn swayed with the pain of impacting the back of Xexial's knee. He looked around as he saw four of the Wild Elves charging them, all covered in the same black substance, all of them wielding spears ready to skewer the duo.

Recovering quickly, Ashyn watched as Xexial began speaking in a strange and archaic tongue. Ashyn's eyes went wide as the sapphire lined gloves sparked to light with effervescent power.

The lead Wild Elf came in high, pouncing like a great cat, with his spear stabbing forward. The young boy watched as the wizard slowly raised his right hand, humming and crackling visibly with electrical energy. Locked on target, Xexial released the coiled current. With a sharp clap that sounded like rolling thunder, cobalt blue lightning laced forth striking the airborne Wild Elf square in the chest.

The force of impact reversed the feral Elf's flight, propelling him backwards several feet. He crashed down to the earth, limply, the strange inky material covering his body igniting into flames. The body hissed and popped, as the flesh began to cook.

Ashyn blinked away the sudden blinding light, seeing its traces remain in his vision like ghostly spider webs. As he struggled to see past this new obstruction, he could see that the other Elves did not falter in the least, even after witnessing such a brutal slaying of one of their own. They charged forth mercilessly at the duo.

Xexial guided Ashyn back with his free hand, while barraging the incoming three Elves with a series of short successive bolts of lightning. Each result was the same, ignition into fire. The ones not killed outright by the fulmination of energy screamed horrendously as they suffered the last remaining moments of their lives in unspeakable agony.

Shifting, all around, made Ashyn's eyes dart in all directions. From everywhere above them, dozens of Wild Elves poured forth through the flora, armed with spears and javelins, ready to rain death down upon them. The Wild Elves chattered and hooted menacingly as they prepared to strike.

Two females appeared in front of him from the ferns, one raven haired, the other a darker brown. They too wore the black sweet essence upon their bodies, but they seemed warier than the others did. They began to fan out, trying to flank Xexial and Ashyn, so that Xexial could only choose one target at a time leaving himself open to the other one, not to mention the droves of Wild Elves above them.

Ashyn could see Xexial was at an impasse, there was no way he could defend against that many attacks at once. His azure eyes searching for a means, any means, with which to escape. As his eyes stared forward, from the direction they had come, Ashyn had a sinking feeling in his stomach that the wizard had found an edge.

His eyes followed the direction of the wizard's gaze, as they fell upon the silver haired child staring in horror at the Wild Elves lying dead around her. The smell of burning flesh was beginning to become unbearable.

"No," Ashyn whispered, shaking his head.

The cackling rose to a high-pitched frenzy when they saw Xexial, not aiming above, at them, but straight, towards their Exemplar.

"I thought you said killing an Exemplar was bad!" Ashyn yelled up at the wizard.

"That was before they attacked us," Xexial responded darkly. "Few for the many, boy. One day you may understand." Not wasting his initiative, he unleashed his raw cobalt energy at the child.

Ashyn screamed in terror as the lightning bolt coursed towards the little innocent child, very near to his own age.

Momentarily an unbridled rage filled him. Rage at the injustice of the action, from the man that had saved his life. Even if it meant his own death, he would not see harm come to the girl.

His vision shifted instantly into a vivid orange hue once more. And to his amazement he watched as the lightning suddenly bent and twisted, veering only minutely off course. The hair difference saved the Exemplar's life, as the bolt of energy crashed into a rock just right of her platinum hair, incinerating it into dust.

Eye's wide in fear, her quicksilver orbs did not swirl as they had before. Ashyn looked into her eyes, as she did into his, his world bathed in a rich, ocherous light. "Nuchada," she whispered.

Around them, Ashyn could see the others staring at him, lowering their weapons. The titian illumination sputtered and waned, and his sight began to shift back to normal. From up above he could hear the amazed whispers of Nuchada coming from the Wild Elves. The two female Elves screamed and ran to protect their Exemplar child.

Suddenly a wave of lethargy overcame Ashyn. His eyelids felt like they had great stones attached to them. His legs grew very weak and shaky bearing an impossible weight. He tumbled onto the ground, dimly aware that he had struck his head roughly against a bulging root jutting from the ground. Consciousness began flickering dimly like a candle's flame in the wind. Ashyn looked up at the tan robed wizard staring down at him, his image waning. Then everything faded to black.

Whether Xexial knew why he had missed the Exemplar or not, he took advantage of the Elves' hesitation. He scooped up the small boy lying next to him and disappeared into the deep vegetation, not once looking back at the damage in his wake.

EXEMPLAR

A s consciousness finally returned, the first thing that greeted Ashyn was overwhelming nausea. He woke with a start, quickly leaning over and vomiting all over the ground next to him. The acrid bile scorched the back of his raw throat and burned his nostrils. The smell revolted him and caused him to wretch once more, mostly just stomach convulsions, with little substance coming out. Strings of spittle clung to his suddenly dry lips, and traces of putrid fluids lingered in his nose. His senses were loitered with the foulness long after his stomach had expunged the contents of his last meal. It attached itself to everything he smelled, making the unpleasantness of his situation even worse.

Finally, as the last of the roiling in his stomach subsided, a new feeling overtook him: pain. On top of all the other injuries he had sustained in the last few days, a new one topped the list. A pounding ache pulsed at the crown of his skull. Slowly he raised his hand up to his right temple. Gingerly he felt the growing lump of knotted flesh. The touch of his salty fingers burned the abrasion. His hand came away from the wound with flaky copper grime. It was his blood, coagulated blood.

"Are you okay?" Xexial's deep voice called from behind, startling him.

As Ashyn rolled over to see the wizard, he could feel Xexial's powerful gaze staring intently upon him. "I think I'm okay," the boy croaked out in a hoarse voice.

"You gave me quite a scare, knocking your head like that," Xexial said, nodding in the direction of his most recent grievance.

"Sorry," Ashyn muttered, looking away from the wizard's scrutinizing glare. After a moment he dared to glance back to see blue eyes looking back at him.

"Do you know why they call you 'Nuchada'?" the wizard asked.

Ashyn shook his head no, realizing that was all the pity he was going to receive for his hurts.

Xexial took a deep breath as he leaned back and lit his pipe. Immediately the spicy aroma of his tobacco permeated the air. It did little to absolve the stench of the bile next to the boy.

"I've been giving it some thought while you were in torpor," the wizard began, "and I think I've come to a conclusion."

Ashyn couldn't fight the tightness growing in his chest. Was Xexial going to brand him a freak now, too? Leave him alone to fend for himself, lost in the Shalis-Fey woods? Ashyn looked deep into the wizard's gaze, but could find no answers. The wizard continued.

"You see, an Exemplar is a standard. It is someone that is a paragon to all others. The Ferhym have a different name for their people. They call them the 'Voïre dui Ceremeia'. In their tongue it roughly translates to 'The Standard of Ethos'. As you can see the names are very similar, hence why we simplify them in to the title Exemplar.

"To the Ferhym, this individual is the model of their entire philosophy, their traditions, even their society. The Exemplars are essentially their culture's very way of life."

"Why?" Ashyn asked.

Xexial took a long draw from his pipe, blowing out a large bloom of white smoke, before answering. "Well, outside of dragons, the Elves are the most in tune with magic of all sentient species still living today. Magic comes very naturally to all of them. Most are so used to it, that it is included in their everyday life. Some, however, are even more in touch with the deepest roots of magic. These are their Voïre dui Ceremeia; the Exemplars. Because of this attunement to magic, they are always born with platinum hair and eyes."

"All of them?"

"Every single one of them, without fail," Xexial returned.

"Why silver though, why not black or white, or even orange?"

The wizard merely shrugged, "They think it shows they are the purest strain of Elf. The 'perfect Hym', as it were. The closest to the original progenitor of their species. This is a major deal of course, and as you can guess, it is not a common occurrence.

"Elves, because they are longer-lived than most other species, reproduce far less often, balancing out nature. So the chances of encountering more than one Exemplar in your lifetime is an exceedingly rare occurrence" he pointed out, but then raised a finger adding, "unless they are Ferhym."

"Why does being Ferhym make a difference?" the boy questioned curiously.

Xexial shook his head, "No one knows. Even the Elves to whom it happens can only speculate its true nature, but no one has any answers. Most simply guess that it is because the Wild Elves have turned their back on advancing civilization and instead choose to be as one with nature as much as possible. Since magic is the essence of life, and nature is life itself, it only makes sense that those deepest in harmony with life would be most susceptible to currents and eddies of Creative magic."

"Okay, so they are touched by magic more than other Elves? What does this mean exactly?" Ashyn asked.

Xexial smiled between draws on his pipe, "My, you do catch on fast don't you, my boy? Sometimes it doesn't feel like I'm speaking to a child at all."

Ashyn stared at his feet, his face flushing with red.

"It all goes back to what I told you a few nights ago, when you first woke up from your ordeal. As a wizard, I am merely a conduit for magic. As I use it, it uses me. Nevertheless, it is something that I do consciously. I have to call it forth; beckon to it, as it were. That is the reason for the words, the gestures, and other materials that you see me use from time to time. Even thinking strongly about it can form, or alter, magic. That is why it is called an invocation. We are invoking the magic, calling to it. An Exemplar does not function the same way, at least not in their childhood. They cannot work with the magic, it just flows in and out of them, as it is wont to do. The magic is never dangerous in the sense of random currents of lightning bouncing off the child, so do not get any wild ideas in your head. But it is dangerous to everyone else not of the species from which the Exemplar originates."

"Why?"

"Because the magic has a way of ensnaring anyone who looks in the eyes of the Exemplar. You become bound to them in ways you don't truly yourself understand. Some say it feels like love, others ecstasy. Either way they become enraptured by the magic. The Exemplar child cannot control this, they lack the training and focus necessary to keep all their Creative magic from lashing out."

Ashyn thought about the girl now. How he had felt when he stared into her eyes. It had been like raw energy running through him. It invigorated him and excited him and he did not want to look away. The idea of it being magic he was looking into, and not the girl itself, awed him even more. Then a question came to his mind. "If she was so important, why was she alone playing by the waterfall?"

Xexial laughed, a low bass rumbling from deep within him. "She was hardly alone, if you remember. And I think she was there for you."

"Me?"

Xexial nodded.

"What's so special about me? I'm a nobody from a small village," Ashyn defended.

"Everyone is special, my boy. Never think differently, ever," Xexial reprimanded. "And I believe she was there for you because of what the Ferhym told me before they attacked."

Instantly Ashyn's ears picked up. He didn't understand what was being said at the time, and now it seemed as if Xexial was going to share a glimmer of that information.

"The Elves admitted to encountering the Orcs in the woods," Xexial started.

Immediately Ashyn interjected, without thinking, "Did they find Julietta then?"

Ashyn could tell by the sadness in the man's azure eyes alone that the answer was not good. "They did find a girl, similar to your description. They say she died from blunt force trauma. I'm sorry, son."

Tears welled up in Ashyn's grey eyes. Ashyn knew Xexial was telling him in as painless a way as he could that she had been beaten to death. Even though he had known all along that Julietta was likely dead, a small part of him had held out hope that she would have survived. That hope was now shattered. He felt the hot warmth stream down his face. "I understand," he choked out, attempting to be strong. Now he knew that it was over, he was the last Rune.

Xexial was quiet for a moment, sitting in a cloud of hazy smoke that emanated from his pipe. Ashyn was grateful for those moments, as the silence helped put to rest the dying embers of hope, and to focus on a new course, one that sparked a new fire, and began to burn hot inside of him . . . vengeance.

"If you do not wish to continue . . .," Xexial commented.

"No!" Ashyn snapped back, perhaps a little harshly. "I have to know why they think I'm this 'Nuchada'."

Xexial nodded, "Very well. As I said, they found a girl that was similar to your description, and they had declared her a

'Nuchada' as well. So when the scouts found us, I assume they returned with what they had learned and dispatched an envoy, along with their Exemplar, to confirm that you were indeed a 'Nuchada' like the deceased."

"Why a little girl though? Why not a grown up?"

Xexial sighed, "Of that I am not certain, and must only speculate. If I were to guess, I would say that it is the Exemplar that identifies who is and is not a 'Nuchada'. So it would make sense to send the one who identified the first 'Nuchada' to identify the potential second."

Ashyn shook his head; it was so much to try to understand. "Ye said 'Nuchada' means spirit eyes, right?"

Xexial nodded.

"What could that mean? Why would both Julietta and I be called such a thing?"

"Again I speculate, but I have had winters upon winters of experience in dealing with things people don't understand, and I have a conjecture or two."

"Okay," Ashyn said, trying to understand everything the wizard was saying. Sometimes Xexial used words that he was not quite used to understanding. No one in Bremingham would ever say 'conjecture', but he was sure he grasped the meaning.

"First and most simply, it could be surmised that the Ferhym worship the concept of their Voïre dui Ceremeia so fully as to believe whatever this child says, while she sends them on aimlessly pointless errands."

Ashyn nodded, but he knew that Xexial did not believe what even he had said.

"Or . . . It could be that a 'Nuchada' is someone with inherent magical ability, and Exemplars can identify them because they are so connected with Creative magic themselves that they can 'see' that spark in other people as well."

Ashyn was thunderstruck. He expected that Xexial was going to call him a freak as well, claim that demons and some such possessed 'Nuchada'. He never expected the wizard to say that he may be using magic.

Ashyn had to blink a few times and close his mouth after he realized he had had it open. Was it possible? Could he really be using magic? All those times weird things had been occurring around him, could he really have been the cause? Turning the rock to dust, catching Gregiry Bibs on fire, the Orc being consumed by thin air, could that all have been him?

Ashyn thought back earlier to when he had first met Veer and the Bristle Wolf attacked. The bow and arrow had just somehow appeared in his hands. He had loosed an arrow without any recollection of doing it. Were these events tied together? Was he truly capable of doing magic?

"Don't seem so surprised," Xexial said, breaking the boy of his astonishment. "I've being deliberating the idea for days now."

"But . . . how?" Ashyn stammered.

Xexial blew out a long stream of smoke. "Your actions," he said matter-of-factly. "When I first found you, you had just grievously injured an Orc all by yourself. Despite significant injuries, you managed to move faster than a well-muscled and battle-hardened Orc who was already committed to a felling blow. Such haste is not in the average boy, especially one faced with death."

Ashyn considered what the wizard said.

"You identified magic immediately when you saw me turning the spit, and questioned it instead of turning away in fear of the unknown. Something most folk from tiny villages tend to do," he pointed out.

"Then you demonstrated clairvoyance in identifying that we were not alone in the ravine."

Ashyn found himself starting to wonder if it was true, if he really was using magic subconsciously.

Xexial did not slow down. "Not to mention you possess remarkable will and self-discipline, especially for a child. It is not easy to turn away from being ensnared by an Exemplar, and not only did you do so, but you did so quickly.

Finally, your ability to detect danger likely saved my life, saved me the unpleasantness of being skewered by a spear. All these things add up, my boy. Do not think I didn't notice," he said with a wink.

"But wouldn't that make you a 'Nuchada' too, then? You use magic," Ashyn asked.

Xexial shook his head. "No. I think it has to be inherent, something that just flows from you like an Exemplar. I had to learn my trade over many, many grueling winters."

"Are there humans then, too? Human Exemplars?" Ashyn said, wondering if he was sort of like the Elf girl he had met. Idly he looked down to his left hand. He still had the braid of her hair clutched tightly in his dusty hands.

Xexial shrugged. "Anything is possible, I suppose," he answered. "But if you are an Exemplar like the Elves, then you are the first human one that I have ever heard of, let alone two, if the girl who died was truly your sister."

"Oh," Ashyn said realizing the absurdity of the claim. "I hadn't thought about that."

"It's okay, my boy. All ideas are good ones. Never stop thinking, never stop wondering, ever."

Ashyn nodded. "Well then, if I am using magic like you say I am, how can I be doing it without knowing?"

Xexial placed his hand on his chin in thought. "That is exactly what I have been stuck upon, while you were unconscious. While I told you that some people are born with an inclination to use magic, a special drawing to it, no race still living, outside of Elves, has ever been able to cast it without rigorous training, no matter what field of magic they choose to learn.

"You seem to be reacting on instinct. Creating spells based off of raw emotions, and the need to survive."

Dread passed through Ashyn as he thought on what Xexial told him. Could it be that he was responsible for the destruction of Bremingham? Had he found a way, based on fear and anger, to summon the Orcs to lay waste to the village, resulting in the death of his entire family? Why had he survived, when so many others had not? Even though he was gripped with fear, he needed to know the answer. "Could I have made the Orcs come?" he asked. But in his mind what he was really asking was, 'Did I kill everyone?'

"No," the wizard answered flatly. "Even if you are using magic on impulse, there is no way you have nearly enough power to beckon an entire legion of Orcs to fight and kill a town. Not even I could do that. Relax child, you are not to blame for Bremingham."

Ashyn nodded, but remained unsure. "Why spirit eyes? Why not magic hands, or something?"

Xexial cocked his head to the side. "Don't you know, my boy?"

Ashyn shook his head.

"Eyes are the windows to your soul. When you look into someone's eyes, you can read everything about them. What they are feeling, if they are happy or sad, angry or calm, when they are thinking, or when they are lost. Everything takes place in your eyes. The same is to be said with magic. That spark, that knowledge resides deep within you, deep in your soul, and your eyes are that doorway."

"But why spirit?"

"Wild Elves worship spirits over one designated deity. They believe in all the spirits of nature and how they help one get through life. Essentially, they have a spirit for every element. They believe that these spirits help guide their magic as well. Most of their practitioners of magical arts specialize in one such category, like healing, or creating water and ice, the list goes on and on.

So to be called spirit eyes, means that she sees the magic spirit deep within you, in your soul."

"So if I'm not a human Exemplar, then what am I?"

Xexial shook his head. "I don't know, but I feel whatever the reason you have this spark of magic, it's because of your mother."

Ashyn arched an eyebrow in wonderment. "My mother?" he repeated.

"Yes. Your mother's past is what you know the least about. You derived your skin hue, which is not typical for humans in this region, from her, as well as your unusual hair color. Your father, for lack of a better term, was just a commonplace man living where he was raised. If you were to find out your true heritage, I would say it lies with your mother."

Ashyn thought back to the night that he had overheard his mother speaking with Veer. "I have been to Gurgen," he had told her, "I have met its people."

Ashyn remembered her response keenly; it was not one of happiness at hearing about where she was from. It was a response of being discovered in a lie. "What do you want?" she had said.

He hadn't realized it at the time because he had thought so little of it. She was his mother, he had no reason to doubt where she had said she was from, but now he knew. She had lied. She was never from Gurgen.

"Does the boy know?" Ashyn had heard Veer ask about him. He remembered seeing his mother shake her head no. What was it that he was supposed to know? What is it that a High Elf would know, and now a Wild Elf child would know about him that he did not know about himself?

He remembered seeing his mother crying that night. Crying at being discovered, he surmised.

"I am well educated," Veer told his mother, "by a people who have been around for generations upon generations. I have heard the stories told." Veer looked back at his mother. "I have seen some of the signs that are in those stories."

What were the signs? He needed to know the signs. Why was he so different from the people of Bremingham? Why could he, if the wizard was right, harness magic like no other human could?

His ability to use magic made a lot of sense, and answered some of the questions he had had about things that happened around him, but it also added more questions. Who was the woman he loved and called mother? Who was she before she came to Bremingham?

Ashyn continued to play the memory in his mind. He remembered as Veer looked back out to the expansive horizon beyond. "One day though, someone will come," the Elf told his mother. "Someone that is equally as educated, and they will also see what it is I see. They will want to take him."

Ashyn looked up from his daze, his eyes wide. "They wanted to take me, didn't they? The Wild Elves, they wanted to take me from you?"

Xexial stared at him, reading him, through the haze of spice-scented smoke. "Yes," he answered bluntly.

"Why didn't ye let them?" Ashyn asked.

Xexial looked away from the boy and into the forest beyond. Ashyn guessed he was looking more within, than anything substantial in front of him. On the other hand, perhaps he was just looking to the North. Ashyn was not sure.

"I don't know," Xexial told him honestly. "I think it's because I would like to think I am a man of character, a man of my word. I told you that I would see you safely through these woods and to Czynsk, and I intend to fulfill that obligation."

He looked back to Ashyn. "It also could be because I am curious. I am a wizard after all, and though you do not know much about what it is I do, gathering knowledge is amongst one of the top things wizards do."

Ashyn supposed he could understand. He too loved to read, loved to learn new things, especially about insects. For a moment, he longed to be back home studying his little treasures in their jars. He blinked away his nostalgia. There would be time again, he told himself. Time to be a little boy and play with new bugs, but not now. He must not lose himself to his memories. Taking a deep breath he continued. "Why would they want to take me? And what did ye say to make them not?"

"The Ferhym are difficult to explain. Let us just say that you being this 'Nuchada' is justification enough for them to want you.

As for what I said . . . well I might have mentioned that if they took you from me I would blight their lands, ruining crops and diseasing livestock for generations."

"And they believed ye?" Ashyn asked astonished.

Xexial smiled deviously at the boy. "You have much to learn about wizards, my boy. Much to learn."

"Is that why they attacked when we turned around?"

Xexial nodded, "That, and because the Exemplar marked you."

Ashyn looked down at the braid of spun platinum in his fingers. "What does it mean?"

"It means that she has bound herself to you. Why? I cannot say," Xexial merely shrugged.

"But it's just hair."

"What you hold in your hand is a lock of hair, yes, but the act of her giving it to you was a spell. A simple and yet immensely powerful spell. You see, she has given part of herself to you. Contained within that lock of hair, in their culture, resides part of her soul for you. It is something that Ferhym do only to soul mates or those they feel are destined for something, for an Exemplar to do it to an outsider . . . is unheard of as far as I know."

"But she's just a kid like me. There must be some mistake. Maybe she just thought it was a gift?" Ashyn pleaded.

Xexial shook his head, "Sorry, my boy, as much as I would like to agree with you, Ferhym are zealously trained from birth about balance, and the nature of the spirits; Exemplar even more so. She knew exactly what she was doing the moment she met you. What we first perceived as playing was more than that, I'm afraid."

"So she's my soul mate?" Ashyn asked, slightly repulsed about the idea of kissing a girl.

Xexial laughed, "Relax my boy. While I'm sure it means much in their culture, you and I do not follow the same heritage. Your life is your own, do not worry about them."

"What will happen to her now?"

"That is not for you to concern yourself with. Ferhym have a rigorous protocol for their Exemplars. It is very likely that you will never see this child again."

"Do ye think they will come for me?"

"While you remain in this forest?" he asked, and then quickly answered, "Definitely. That is why we must make all haste to leave as quickly as possible. I thought to get us through unnoticed, but it seems the denizens of these woods are drawn to you, my boy. First the Orcs and now the Ferhym. The Ferhym are nothing if not relentless. I'm sure we will be encountering them again, and I'm sure I will have to fight them again."

"I'm sorry," the little boy said sheepishly. He did not want Xexial to have to fight on his behalf, even kill for him, especially not if it involved him possibly attacking the Exemplar again.

"Do not apologize. You did not choose this course; they did."

"I have another question," Ashyn asked, attempting to stray away from the darker thoughts of the wizard attacking the little girl.

"Ask away, my boy."

"The lightning you used this time caught the Elves on fire, but the lightning you used on the Orcs did not. Why?"

Xexial chuckled to himself and blew out a swath of smoke from his pipe. "It was their paint that caused the fire, not the spell."

"Their paint?"

Xexial nodded again. "Did you notice how they smelled rather sweet?"

Ashyn bobbed his head.

"It's because they used crude. It comes from the ground. It's the sulfur, you see, that gives it that slightly sweet smell."

"Crude?"

"It's oil, my boy. Similar to what you may have seen in a lantern, though I am sure where you are from they use corn oil for that."

Ashyn nodded, he knew how to make oil from corn. Karl the tanner had shown him and his father before. Karl used oil often.

Xexial continued. "When a flame is introduced to crude it burns hot and rich for a long time." The wizard then shrugged and added, "Well depending on the type of crude, of course. Some of it is sour, and that does not burn as well. The Dwarves are specialists at dealing with crude, and the Gnomes, for different devices. But the Ferhym? Let's just say their ignorance gave us an advantage."

"Why would they use something like that?"

"They were probably using it to sneak up on us at night as it darkened their skin fabulously, and the sweet odor would generally be offset by the rich smells of the woods, namely the pine, until they were upon us and by then it would be too late of course. They deal with fire so rarely in these parts of the woods that it probably did not dawn on them that a wizard's lightning would ignite their precious lacquer." Xexial laughed to himself, and added, "Fools," under his breath, but Ashyn still heard it clearly.

This was all so much to absorb for the young boy. Magic, Wild Elves, the Exemplar. Why did they want him so badly? Whenever he came across a problem, he often would explain it to himself aloud. His mother used to love to watch him troubleshoot problems, often interjecting useful tidbits that would help him in figuring out a solution. This was a real problem, he figured. It could not hurt to do what he had always done in the past. Therefore, he began reciting to himself the problem as he saw it.

"The Wild Elves have been following us for days; ye say they came for me. They found my sister and called her 'Nuchada', and now they found me and say the same. Then their Exemplar goes and marks me. They seem to know something about me, perhaps even about my ma." Ashyn stood up and began pacing in the small camp. "I had met an Elf before, a few winters ago. Not a Wild Elf, but a High Elf, he had passed through Bremingham. He had talked to my ma, told her things, bluntly, that I had overheard. I had not noticed at the time, I was so young."

"You're still young, very young," Xexial said, chuckling.

"Yes, but he had pretty much told her she was not from Gurgen, and her reaction all but admitted it. Why lie? Why lie about where you had come from?" he asked the wizard.

"Most people hide their origins when they are running away from something, or someone."

"Running away?" Ashyn repeated. Was it possible? Was his mother hiding from someone? He remembered her initial fear at seeing Veer. Was she hiding from Elves?

"Why would my ma hide from Elves?" Ashyn asked abruptly.

"There could be many reasons, my boy. It's impossible to figure out with all her possessions destroyed."

Ashyn continued pacing, wearing a line through the leaf-strewn ground. "But she came with books, lots and lots of books. My ma spoke many languages, most of them Elven. Why would she have so many tomes of knowledge and know so many Elven languages? Do ye think she lived among them?"

Xexial was now nodding. "It is quite possible. In fact, I would say it makes good rational sense that she did, especially if she could speak their language. Elves do not often teach humans their tongue unless they have good reason."

Ashyn rubbed his thumb against the braid the Elf girl had given him. He found it was calming and helped him think. "If she lived with them, was educated by them, and learned their language, that must mean she spent her childhood among them."

"How so?" the wizard asked. "Was she young? I thought you said your sister was older than you?"

Ashyn nodded. "Aye, she was fourteen winters."

"Then that would place your mother between thirty and forty winters unless she had your sister young. Did your family celebrate the days of your birth?" Xexial asked.

"Yes."

"Can you recall your mother's?"

"Thirty four," he answered quickly, "But I'm not sure how accurate that is anymore."

"Well did she look as old as me?" the sun-weathered man asked.

Ashyn shook his head no.

"Well let's guess that she was actually the age she said she was, and that she ran away from wherever it was she was at around eighteen to nineteen winters. So if she lived amongst the Elves long enough to become fluent in their language, I would guess she would have been close to your age when she first arrived with them. That's awfully young."

"Well my ma never spoke about her ma and pa. They may have died too, and the Elves took her in."

Xexial stroked the base of his pipe, lost in obvious thought. "What Elven language was she the most proficient in, do you know?"

Ashyn nodded, of course he knew. It was the same language that he was the most proficient in as well. "Wood Elf, Sir," he responded.

"The Lefhym. That is very curious."

Then it hit him like a sack of stones. His mother said she was from the West, and Veer claimed to be from the West, from Featherset and the great woods of the Shemma. "How close is the Shemma to Gurgen?" he asked the sun-weathered man.

Xexial's azure eyes sparkled at him. "I was just thinking the same thing, my boy! As it happens, the Shemma's borders touch the very southeastern tip of the country of Gurgen. Are you putting the pieces of the puzzle together?"

Ashyn nodded vigorously, "The High Elf that visited, he knew Featherset well, and he was very interested in Julietta and me when we went to meet him."

"And do you know why?" Xexial asked.

This, Ashyn did not know, and he shook his head no.

"It's because the Lefhym's skin color ranges from olive, like yours, to deep copper. They are generally darker that their Ferhym cousins. But what makes them stand out is the wide range of their hair color. Though the Ferhym are closer to nature than the Lefhym, the Lefhym seemed to adapt to living in the forests far more than their feral relatives. Their hair matches the seasons of the Great Woods, and so it is quite common see Lefhym with all ranges of color from a sun wheat blonde, to a coal black, or even a vivid red."

Ashyn reached up and subconsciously touched his short-cropped hair.

Xexial nodded, "Yes my boy, it makes perfect sense. Your skin, your hair, your feelings of not fitting in with the others of Bremingham, not belonging. Already I've seen that you are a natural tracker and hunter. You have far quicker reflexes than many human boys your age do, and adapt to nature very easily. I assume your mother and sister were quite beautiful? Perhaps even considered exotic?"

Ashyn nodded again. "My sister was often called exotic."

"Then I think we have our answer. You have the look, the character, and the natural inclinations of the species ingrained in you. You also can harness magic without training, something no regular human can do. I think we finally figured out where your mother was from, Ashyn Rune. The Lefhym raised her because she *was* a Lefhym. You are an Elf."

Ashyn could not believe it. An Elf? Was it possible? He felt his legs turn all soft, like they were made of porridge. He needed to sit down. His mind was reeling at the implications. All the little pieces of the puzzle were clicking into place at a maddening rate. Veer's recognition at seeing him and his sister, his mother's terror at the sight of Veer, and Julietta's overt fascination with Elves. The Wild Elves identifying him, even marking him. It was impossible and possible all at once. He **was** an Elf.

"Well, not a full Elf, anyway," Xexial said with a smile. "Just part Elf."

PART ELF?

I am an Elf! Ashyn realized, as he thought immediately of Stormwind. "But I don't have pointy ears," the olive-skinned boy said as he ran his fingers over his round ears.

Xexial erupted into a hearty laughter. The bass of his deep chuckle reverberated throughout his body, causing a cascading tremor of ruffling clothing from head to toe. Ashyn didn't see what was so amusing.

"*Half*," he emphasized. "Half your lineage is tied to Elves, possibly less than half if your mother was a half Elf first. It could very well be two or three generations past that there was an Elven ancestor in your family tree. You need not display all the characteristics of an Elf to be an Elf. Think of your father for instance? Human, with traces of both his mother and father evident in his features. I'm sure there is much of you that looks like him."

Ashyn nodded. Though he had picked up the immediately recognizable traits of his hair and skin color, the rest of his features did lean towards his father.

"Since it's presumable that your mother was partly Elven herself, she too probably lacked pointed ears."

Again, Ashyn found himself nodding in agreement. Xexial continued. "It can be sometimes hard for a human to see the Elven bloodline in those of mixed descent. While obvious things like lithe frames, almond eyes, and pointed ears stand out, they are not always passed from parent to child. Ever intriguing, the ways of nature are," the wizard finished, taking a long draw on his pipe.

"So ye are certain then?" Ashyn asked. "I am part Elf?"

The man shook his head no. "Nothing is certain," he remarked. "But many indicators do point to you being of Elven lineage. The Exemplar's recognition of you only strengthens it."

"If that's true, then why Nuchada?" the little boy wondered aloud. "If all Elves can use magic in some form, what would make Julietta and me so special? If they can use magic, and we can use magic that would make us more like kin wouldn't it?"

Ashyn was surprised to see the wizard shaking his head no. "I'm afraid not. The Ferhym don't think like that. Not at all, in fact. It is more likely that they would find you a monstrosity more than anything."

Freak, once again resounded through the boy's mind. No matter where he went it seemed he could not escape that one singular word, something that set him apart as an outcast from everyone else around him. He thought of Veer. He said he had been alone for many winters, ostracized by his upbringing. Ashyn wondered if he might have the strength that Veer had asked of him. He wondered if he could wait like the High Elf did, persevering to eventually be looked at as not only an equal, but also an idol.

The aged wizard continued, breaking him of his momentary thoughts. "Ferhym view wizards with much contempt as well, you know," he said, forcing young Ashyn to look into his hooded eyes. "It is their fear of us, however, that keeps them from assaulting us outright. It is their fear of what we might be capable of doing, versus what we actually do. It is a skewed logic of course, but one that the Ferhym often embrace."

Ashyn had a great many more questions about the Wild Elves, and it seemed to the boy that Xexial could read this in his eyes, because before Ashyn could ask another question the wizard was raising a hand to stall his query. "The Ferhym's ideologies are not relevant," he stated simply. "It does us no good at this time to brood over why they want you, or why they care that you can use magic. What is important is that we get you away from them. Once you are secure in that regard, then you can research them to your heart's content."

Ashyn closed his mouth, and forced a nod. He knew if Xexial was going to agree to train him, it would be best not to push his luck with the man. He looked down to the silvery braid in his hand, lost in thoughts of his unknown origins. Xexial was peculiar that way, Ashyn realized. Openly jumping into a discussion on the origins of the Exemplar, but closed suddenly to the reasons the Wild Elves might be after him. Ashyn pondered this long into the night.

POOL OF INFORMATION

Councilor Brodea looked down into the basin of water that resided within the center of the high chambers of the Council of Elm. A row of high-backed elm seats where the Councilors sat during their sessions were behind her and the open expanse of forest loomed wide and beautiful in front of her. For the moment, she was utterly alone.

She looked at the image before her in the cool waters. Two Elven women, both Ferhym, were kneeling above her, also looking down.

It was one of their principle ways of communication, through the waters of life. Yet it only worked within the Shalis-Fey, and it only worked when a druid could manipulate those waters. Outside in the wider world their connection was severed completely, and so they had to rely on other more magical means.

"Report," she stated to the women before her.

"Branch Commander Elumin is dead," the raven-haired, dark-eyed beauty said into the pool, "killed by the Unbalancer along with three others of our branch."

Brodea cursed at the waters. "You were instructed by the Council to observe, identify, and apprehend the dui Nuchada if possible. What part did Hunter Elumin fail to comprehend?" she demanded of the women.

"Likely all of it, Councilor," the woman replied snidely. "He endangered the Voïre dui Ceremeia, recklessly, and almost got her killed."

This again sent a wave of anger rolling through her. The Voïre dui Ceremeia was sacred to her people, and even more so to her. They were the chosen, directly handed to them from the spirits. She owed the spirits so much lately. She couldn't stand the thought of losing the Voïre, especially not that one, so young.

She composed herself quickly, "Did she at least identify the human child with the skewer?"

"She did," the raven-haired Elf answered.

"And?"

"It is so. This boy is the dui Nuchada," the dark-eyed Elf answered again.

Brodea nodded. Likely Elumin wanted to impress Brodea and return not only with the dui Nuchada, but also with the head of a great Unbalancer. He had been trying to court her for winters, ever since Ambit died. As if her heart had been free to give so quickly.

Yet it was forbidden to engage wizards, as all hunters and Councilors well knew, as commanded by the spirits through First Councilor Tehirs. Of course, if Elumin sought to goad the wizard into attacking . . . well that was different. That was defense. Now Elumin had paid the price for his foolishness.

"Are they still in the Shalis-Fey?" Brodea dared ask.

This time the dark brunette was nodding. "Yes Councilor," she answered. "I saw their camp with my own eyes, not but three miles east of our present location. We have other scouts in place as we speak, but without our Branch Commander we wanted further orders if we were clear to engage or not."

"Smart girl," Brodea replied. "Here is your directive, Shedalia, daughter of Shenalia. You are to pursue the dui Nuchada and the wizard. Harry him, test their perimeter, give them no rest, but do not engage the skewer directly. We are not permitted, as decreed by the spirits, to fight that blasphemer. I want him exhausted though, so that we can claim the dui Nuchada. Of that, we have not been restricted. I know you have hate in your heart for that evil creature because of the loss of your mother, but temper that hatred. Your time will come."

Shedalia nodded at the pool. "Yes, Councilor. We will harass the skewer to no end, but we will not engage."

"Good," she said as she nodded. "The dui Nuchada is what is important, my huntresses, the Unbalancer must be let go."

Both female Elves nodded. "Understood, Councilor."

"Very well. Whisper, you are now Branch Commander. Shedalia is your second," she told them.

They nodded solemnly, but she did not miss the smiles creeping upon their faces. "If there is nothing else?" she asked.

Suddenly their meager smiles disappeared and she watched them look at one and other with . . . was it apprehension?

"Councilor," Whisper began, "the Voïre dui Ceremeia, she did something . . . unexpected."

She was just a little girl, Brodea wanted to say, but she knew very well what was expected of their chosen. For it to bother Whísper so, it must be something important. "What is it, huntress?"

"Councilor . . . she . . . she marked the dui Nuchada," Whísper finally relented.

Brodea was certain she had not heard correctly. It couldn't be possible. Why would the child do such a thing? Perhaps the pool came in unclear. That had to be it.

"I'm not sure I understood you," she said lightly. "It sounded as if you said that our Voïre dui Ceremeia has marked a human boy; the dui Nuchada, nonetheless?"

To her horror, she watched as Whísper nodded. "This is so, Councilor."

Brodea felt the color drain from her face. How could she do this? How could their chosen mark a skewer of the balance? What did it mean?

Brodea's mind flashed back to that horrible day when she was in the temple and had smashed the crystal upon the wizard's head. Subconsciously her hand drifted to her abdomen. An aberrant darkness had engulfed her. And with it, a presence she couldn't even begin to fathom. She had felt something then, something *alien* that touched her soul.

"Councilor?" the raven-haired Elf asked through the pool worriedly. "Councilor, is everything alright?"

Brodea shook the image away, but somehow the foreign presence and the cold seemed to linger. "Get a small branch in order, and get the Voïre dui Ceremeia home," she said, almost detachedly.

She looked at the women eyeing her strangely. "Of course Councilor," they said together.

Brodea blinked away the last traces of the image and looked back at Whísper directly. "No one is to know of this, am I understood? We don't need rumors to circulate. It will only cause dissension and uncertainty in our cause."

Whísper nodded slowly. "I understand, Councilor. Of the branches that are aware already?"

"Can you keep them quiet?" Brodea asked tersely.

Whísper did smile then, boldly. "I believe I can."

Brodea nodded, "Good." She then looked to Shedalia directly. "You can go, huntress, I have words directly for the Branch Commander."

Shedalia bowed and said, "As you will, Councilor."

Brodea watched curiously as Whísper and Shedalia shared a lasting eye contact together, one often shared between people who were truly close. She had wondered for some time, but now it seemed to be confirmed.

"You are intimate with her," Brodea stated when the young Elf was gone.

Whísper immediately blushed, which appeared vividly through the basin of water. "Councilor . . . I . . .,"

Brodea held up her hand. "Listen well, Whísper. This fling you have with Shedalia right now is fine, you are at that curious age. But know that soon you are expected to try and bear a child. Unless I have missed something in my long winters of life, this is not possible with two members of the same sex."

Whísper averted her gaze from the pool. "No, Councilor."

Brodea nodded, "The female form is a beautiful thing, Branch Commander. It is soft and shapely, and often attractive to the eyes. However, alone it cannot bear fruit. For that we do need men."

Brodea almost laughed as Whísper blushed such a deep hue of red that she was sure her head might explode. "This dalliance will end when you return to Feydras' Anula. Am I understood?"

"I . . . Yes, Mother," Brodea's daughter said to her.

"Good," Brodea answered curtly. "Though that was not the reason I wanted to talk to you alone. You should know that First Councilor Tehirs has suddenly . . . taken ill."

Whísper suddenly looked up curious. "He is not so old."

Brodea eyed her darkly. "No he is not, but ill he is, and I suspect he will not live out another decade."

Whísper nodded. "I understand."

"I hope so, Whísper," Brodea returned. "The Council hasn't sanctioned this hunt for the dui Nuchada, but rest assured they will know of it if you all get yourselves killed fighting the wizard. Right now we follow the rules, but the game will change once Tehirs is gone, rest assured. Blasphemers will not be permitted to walk through our woods as they have."

Whísper smiled once again. Brodea knew that her father's death pained her just as much as it pained Brodea. Ambit would not die in vain. Then she watched as her daughter's face went impassive once more. "We are not truly alone . . .," her daughter said, as if reminded of the druid's presence.

"No," Brodea answered. "So listen very carefully to what I am about to tell you. There must be no talking about what happened with the Voïre dui Ceremeia, am I understood? You must make sure of it. If other, less driven Ferhym think that the spirits are compassionate to these skewers of balance, it could ruin everything. Those that talk must be silenced . . . completely."

Whísper nodded. "I understand. And the dui Nuchada?"

"If you can't capture him, kill him. But leave the wizard alone."

Again, her daughter nodded. "Are we done?"

"We're done," Brodea said, confident her message was received.

Whísper drew her long, arched dagger and took a step closer to the pool. There was a sudden gasp and Brodea's pool grew into a deep red hue. The image began to waver and grow hazy. "I hear the Bristle Wolves are terrible this time of season," she heard her daughter say faintly as the waters faded back to normal.

Satisfied, Brodea looked away from the basin. She loved her brothers and sisters of the Ferhym fiercely; she did not want death for any of them. However, she loved something even more than her people. The cause. Brodea believed in what they were doing more than almost any other Ferhym. They were helping nature, helping the world, by rooting out the countless evils that desecrated it.

Some Ferhym had lost the sense of their righteous quest. Elves like Tehirs, who seemed to think that the values of their people outweighed the sacred mission the spirits had bestowed upon them. Brodea knew better. The spirits had touched her. They had answered her, more than once. She knew that if there was any threat to that cause, even by her own people, it had to be neutralized. Balance had to be maintained, on all fronts, and so she must remain vigilant.

The slight echo of feet on stairs brought her gaze to the entrance platform of the Council. She saw Vooken approaching up the steps.

"Is it done?" she asked her fellow Councilor when he grew near enough. She knew like her, Vooken was dedicated to the balance.

Vooken looked to her and smiled. "I fear the Council is going to need to start preparing to voice out who they think should succeed First Councilor Tehirs much sooner than anticipated. Luckily for them, I already have someone in mind."

Brodea smiled as well, a brilliant white smile. "I thought you might."

PURSUANT

The next three days were a tense collection of running, hiding, and misdirection. Xexial did everything in his power to avoid open confrontation with the Wild Elves, but they were ardent in their desire for Ashyn. Ashyn couldn't figure out why? What was it that made him so hunted by the Elves? Sure, Xexial helped conclude that he may be related to the Elves in some distinct way, and that it may be the reason that he had such an apparent connection with magic, but Ashyn could not fathom the fervent nature of the Elves now that he had been identified as 'Nuchada'. Their hunt for him seemed to border on fanaticism. They were zealously committed to this singular task.

So Ashyn ran. Ran through the Shalis-Fey night and day, with little to eat, and little rest. His broken fingers and nose ached endlessly, his head throbbed, and now he bore multiple scratches and nicks from sharp-cornered granite and hanging branches. Not to mention his feet were blistered from the nonstop trekking through the uneven landscape of the woods.

He didn't complain though. He accepted the pain, as he knew many might not. There was no room for whining. There was only survival. Xexial did not go into details on what would happen were he caught by the Wild Elves, but Ashyn could tell by the look in the wizard's strong blue glare that none of it would be good.

The true terror of their pursuit was during the nights. The Wild Elves, still covered in crude, were invisible to them, and they were just as silent as they were impossible to see. Nevertheless, Ashyn could feel them all around him. He knew they were there hunting their prey. Ashyn could also feel stress radiating from his benefactor. It was palpable, so thick it could almost be cut with a dagger.

Wild Elves weren't their only hunters, either. The howls of wolves echoed through the stillness of the black nights. Haggard breathing of the pursuing canines resounded at every turn.

There were growls, and piercing golden eyes lighting up the darkest patches of foliage. Ashyn even once spotted the auburn coat of a Bristle Wolf stalk past in the darkness.

In those nights, Ashyn could see strain in the creases of the wizard's forehead and in the corners of his wizened eyes. There was a rigidity about him now that he had not demonstrated before, a more militant mindset. He spoke not once in those next three days and nights, merely running, hiding, pushing Ashyn to the ground when need dictated, or grabbing him by the hand and pulling him roughly along.

It was a battle, Ashyn knew, one waged within, and without. Xexial was surrounded by an unseen foe while he attempted to protect a small child. All the tan robed seer need do is walk away, leaving Ashyn to whatever his fate may be. Yet Xexial pressed on, keeping the child in tow. Fatigue saturated his every movement, but Ashyn could see he fought to keep it in check. It seemed never ending. Long seconds stretching like hours, minutes like days.

Ashyn couldn't even tell what direction they were heading any more. They'd run what he felt was south for a while, only to turn east, and then invariably back north again. It was happening so often, so quickly, he couldn't find a bearing. Finally, he was forced to give up completely. He knew everything hinged on Xexial at this point, lest the Shalis-Fey swallow him whole.

A moment of respite finally arrived on the fourth day. At the breaking of dawn, exhausted from running, and feeling he could run no more, Ashyn suddenly found himself in a clearing. The world was no longer inundated with brown pillars and emerald walls. No more was an inescapable jade canopy looming above him. There was openness so far and wide Ashyn had to blink twice before he registered it. And there was sky! A long, stretching pink horizon lay before him. He could see the majestic orange ball rising to the east. Far north, Ashyn could make out a rise of snowcapped mountains. The boy had never seen mountains before! He thought the white fluff looked like cotton sweeping over large mounds of charcoal.

The clearing dropped down steeply to which Ashyn could see the tops of the trees. These were different though, as if blight had somehow touched that section of the woods. The leaves atop the trees were not green, but mottled browns and blood reds. Beneath those diseased treetops, the pallid grey trees disappeared into darkness.

It had to be at least a three hundred foot descent to the forest floor below. It was a long way to climb. Ashyn felt a tap on his shoulder. He turned from the vista to regard the adult next to him. Xexial pointed back to the north.

Ashyn followed the elder's extended arm and saw that beyond a group of hillocks, nearer the base of the massif that swept in from the east, were plumes of rising smoke.

"Czynsk," Xexial stated wearily, but Ashyn didn't miss the inflection of hope that lie underneath.

He cast his grey gaze to the tree line once more. At the base of the incline at which they now stood, it seemed far less vast than the expanse of forest behind him. Verily, it appeared as if they might only have to travel another half a day and they would be free from the clutches of the Shalis-Fey. He looked back down.

The climb wouldn't be easy.

The snap of a branch brought them quickly to focus, glancing behind them into the darkness. Their moment of reprieve was at an end. Without even looking at each other, they both scurried over the ledge.

They weren't even forty feet beneath the ridge when the first spear crashed down by Ashyn. It came like lightning, exploding into a thousand tiny splinters against a rocky outcropping that he had scaled down only seconds before.

Ashyn hugged the near vertical surface as the sharp shrapnel cut past him, biting at his neck and back. "I thought they wanted me alive!" he screamed to the wizard some twenty feet away from him.

Xexial, looking up at the growing mass of Ferhym on the ledge, shrugged. "It appears they've recanted their decision now that freedom is so close within your grasp."

"Unbelievable," Ashyn muttered as he scurried further down the rock face.

Another spear flew by, narrowly missing the boy and striking the rigid surface right next to his left hand. He quickly jerked his hand back in reaction, staggering his footing and causing him to bang roughly against granite surface. Ashyn now knew why Karl the tanner had once said Wild Elves had unerring accuracy. Another throw like that would likely skewer him.

Ashyn looked up at the crest line above. Magic had come to him before in his moments of need. He thought of Gregiry Bib, and the conflagration that had erupted from the boy's outstretched arm. He stared hard at the Wild Elves above him. If he did it then, he reasoned he should be able to do it now. All it would take is the drive, the need to make it happen. "Fire," he muttered, summoning all of his will into that singular thought.

Nothing happened.

"Burn," he tried instead. Again nothing.

Another spear flew at him and he pinned himself tightly against the face as it whistled by, narrowly missing him by inches.

"Spark!" he screamed up at the Wild Elves, hoping for something, anything, but still nothing was happening. Not like the night in Bremingham, or with Xexial and the Exemplar girl. "Come on!" he bellowed furiously as he kicked the precipice in frustration, sending a small shower of stones tumbling down beneath him. Some magic he had!

Ashyn looked up once more at the collected Wild Elves raining their death upon him and yelled in aggravation. With no way of knowing how to access his alleged 'magic,' he continued to scale down the earthen wall hoping that Xexial could protect him.

Xexial had done just that very thing, Ashyn soon realized, as the next spear plunged down for him. The flying missile was deadly accurate as it plunged directly for the small boy. Ashyn looked up just in time to see it descending far quicker than he could hope to move. Just when Ashyn thought it was all over, and that he would never get his vengeance for the loss of his family, the soaring projectile was suddenly buffeted away by an unseen gale of wind. It spun harmlessly away as Ashyn stared up in wonder at the seemingly invisible torrent hovering above his head.

He could feel the current of air bluster across his face and pull wildly at his red hair. He looked over to the wizard that had kept him alive the last three days in amazement. Xexial's eyes sparkled keenly. A large smile took Ashyn's face as he continued to climb down the narrow precipice unhindered. The Wild Elves, still clueless to the magical windstorm, wasted their supply of javelins against an impossible-to-hit child.

Though he couldn't hear the chattering between the Elves over the howl of the gusts above him, he could clearly imagine the frustrated arguing going on between them as to why they couldn't impale a simple little boy stuck on the rock face.

While the duo reached the bottom, the Wild Elves remained high above, howling in dismay. Ashyn found the state of their pursuers curious, for surely they should be climbing down the same face in pursuit. "Why do they not follow?" he asked the wizard.

"Because we have entered a portion of the Shalis-Fey where even they fear to go," The tan robed man answered. "This place is aberrant to them. Only their most privileged, most skillful hunters, travel outside of their boundaries."

"Ye saying that those Elves we've seen weren't the most skilled they have?" Ashyn asked, astounded.

Xexial chuckled and shook his head. "Hardly," he answered simply. "They are just hunters and spearmen. I doubt a small child in their woods would even warrant the Council's notice, even if he has been marked by an Exemplar."

"Council?" Ashyn replied curiously.

As a response, Xexial turned him away from the scene of the angry Elves stomping and screaming above them. They were little more than coppery smudges against the backdrop of green. "Now is not the time to discuss such things," he stated plainly, letting Ashyn know that once again, the wizard wouldn't say any more about the Wild Elves than seemed necessary.

"Why do they fear this place so?" Ashyn asked instead, changing the subject.

"Because it is haunted."

MAZE

It was still daytime, Ashyn was certain it was. He had seen the dawn sun crest the mountainous horizon only mere hours before, and yet in the woods he was in now, there was no indication that the morning light had yet to breach the thick canopy above his head. And he seriously began to doubt the possibility that it ever might. It was dark in the woods, eerily dark.

The ground was littered with dead leaves and pine needles. Each crunching step seemed to echo in the confines of the dank wood. The air was suspiciously cold, and stank of rotting vegetation. Everything about this section of the Shalis-Fey reeked of putrefaction and rot.

Xexial walked slowly, in measured steps, next to the boy, his iridescent blue-laced gloves casting a pale light against the encroaching darkness. Ashyn looked to him, watching . . . waiting. He could see the wizard drinking in his surroundings, preparing himself for any onslaught, be it a physical confrontation from the bowels of the forest or battling the mental demons of his own trepidations within him. Even though Ashyn could see wariness in his eyes, he could see no terror in those blue orbs. Xexial did not fear these woods.

They continued in silence, constantly alert to the slightest nuances of movement or sound. Even Ashyn knew that they had entered an area of the woods that was far more unforgiving than anything else he had thus seen. Finally, after what the boy could gage as four more hours of unsure travel, he looked to his arcane savior.

"We're lost, aren't we?"

Xexial surprised him by nodding. "We have been put back a bit, yes," he admitted.

Ashyn shook his head. "Did ye plan on coming through these parts?"

"No," the aged wizard remarked sternly. "I also didn't plan on being harried by dozens of Ferhym intent capturing my charge."

Ashyn looked down at his small doeskin moccasins. "Sorry," he muttered, feeling guilty that he had somehow caused this latest travesty.

A strong hand came down reassuringly on his shoulder. When Ashyn peered upward at the man he could see none of the sternness had left his posture, but there was undeniable warmth to his eyes. "It is not your fault these things are happening, my boy. Truly, the fickle fingers of fate are at work here. You merely happen to be the latest victim in a rash of ill-timed events."

Ashyn nodded gratefully, but in the back of his mind he still wondered if that were truly the case. Too much had been happening lately. Too much pain, too much loss, it was beginning to numb him to it all. Or perhaps it was just the biting cold, he thought wearily.

Now, though, it seemed that even his all-powerful wizard benefactor was being crushed beneath the weight of all these strange consistencies.

"At least the Wild Elves are gone," Ashyn replied solemnly.

Xexial concurred. "Yes, they will no longer bother us in here, that's for sure."

"Is this place really haunted?" Ashyn asked as he looked around at the festering trees around him. Though he had never personally seen something that was allegedly haunted, the simple folk of Bremingham had constantly voiced their superstitions of 'haunted' places in the past. One particular burned-down farm that Old Tom Gregy's brother, Laurel, had previously owned, Ashyn remembered keenly. Laurel Gregy had knocked down a lamp one night in a drunken haze, after which he had subsequently passed out. Of course, his wife was sleeping at the time so she had no idea of the danger she had been in. Both died that night in the inferno.

Stories abounded throughout the small village, some saying they saw the spirit of Laurel at night, crying over the burned husk of a bed that his wife had died in. Others claimed that they heard unearthly noises coming from the farm at night, and saw spirits tilling the fields. Soon all of Bremingham, Maker-fearing men and women, one and all, kept a wide berth from the farm. After that, Old Tom Gregy took to serious drinking, perhaps unable to cope with his brother's death.

That had been before even Julietta had been born. So time, compounded with fear of the unknown, led to more and more fables about the burned husk farm on the edge of Bremingham. The farm haunted by Laurel Gregy's ghost.

Well, of course Ashyn was curious. He had read about all manners of undead creatures in myths and tales from his mother's books. He read about walking skeletons and unholy wraiths that would terrorize adventurers. Or angry spirits who would rise from their graves, bodies rotting and falling apart, and walk into villages to feast on the flesh of the living. Evil tales meant to frighten children in the darkest of nights. Therefore, Ashyn did what every self-respecting seven-winter-old boy would do, or at least he thought they would do, he went to investigate the Gregy Farm.

Well, reality often does not live up to superstition, and it didn't take the little boy long to see the ramshackle remains of the farm held nothing but false notions of paranormal activity. Sure the building creaked and groaned, but little Ashyn had deduced that it was because the wooden supports were structurally unsound after the gutting wrath of the fire. This caused the remaining building to sway in the gentle winds that would occasionally come up from the southern banks.

Then there was the eerie screeching of the ghosts that inhabited the farm. Ashyn found that the Gregy's kettle had survived the pyre, and it still resided within the hearth. At times, the winds would pick up at just the right angle and pitch itself through the top opening of the cast iron container, causing it to emit a spine-chilling whistle from the spout.

Finally, the inquisitive little boy found the scorched remains of a mannequin. Mrs. Gregy had been a seamstress, and she had often made clothes for the villagers of Bremingham. So in appreciation for her efforts the village had purchased a Cumara wood model from a wandering merchant who just happened to pass through Bremingham. Cumara wood was a type of chestnut that resembled a shade of teak. It grew deep on the southern edges of the great Shemma woods. Even though the wood was extremely valuable to the right parties, the full size of the dummy turned out to be very cumbersome and large for the merchant's small wagon. Therefore, he opted instead to sell it to a township in need, and so the rural community bought it for a steal.

Unbeknownst to the people of Bremingham, Cumara wood is extremely fire resistant, so when the Gregy farmhouse burned to the ground they merely assumed everything else burned with it. Not so, for the Cumara mannequin had survived, and anyone looking upon the estate at night would find the long shaped shadow of a man, moving ever slightly in the southern breeze.

Of course, when Ashyn even remotely tried to explain this to the people they would bark things at him like *freak*, and *demon-spawn*. So he just remained silent, as the world of Bremingham went on, ignorant to the simplest truths right under their very noses.

He looked around the dark, decrepit woods he was in once more. This was nothing like the Gregy's farm. There was something undeniably wrong with the mold-covered trees. He could feel an aura of wrongness, as if the dying trees themselves wanted to sap the life out of the two living passers-by.

A strange pallid white substance oozed off a dead grey branch to the right of the duo, and into a dark hole into the ground. Ashyn recoiled at the smell it produced. It reeked like rotting eggs. He covered a hand over his nose and mouth trying to suffocate out the befouling odor.

Ashyn had seen tree sap before. His father had taught him to survive off it after all. This resembled none of it, nor did he ever witness any of a tree's juice emanate so heavily from its branches. It always seemed to come in bulk from the trunk.

He watched in surprise as it slithered down the thick tree limb like a translucent snake, before breaking away to fall in the oblong hole. For a moment it seemed like the fluid stopped and turned to look at him. He blinked away the startling notion and stared at it again, but the fluid kept slinking down into the void in the same fashion. Ashyn realized that Xexial had never answered his question about the woods being haunted. "Ye didn't answer my question," Ashyn stated, looking up at the elder man.

Xexial looked down at him sardonically. "Look around you," he told the boy flatly. "I know you're intelligent, I know you've read much. Do you really need to ask a question to which you already know the answer?" he queried.

"In all your hunting days with your father, had you ever seen anything like this?" he asked.

Ashyn closed his mouth, and shook his head no. Of course he had not. This was very new to him. However, so were the grand trees of the western Shalis-Fey, as was the silver-haired Exemplar girl that could not seem to leave his every waking thought. All of it was new! How was he to know? Ashyn tempered his flaring anger when he realized that it was just the older man's way of venting his frustration. Ashyn knew that Xexial had not wanted any of this to happen. It was supposed to be a simple trek through the Shalis-Fey woods which the wizard had made countless times before, unimpeded. But for some unexplained reason, everywhere they went in the forest its denizens seemed to be drawn to Ashyn.

Now they were here, in a deadened part of the woods that even the fearless Wild Elves dared not go. That thought alone brought great trepidation to the young boy as they moved on.

Another day passed without incident, but Ashyn knew that they were no closer to escaping the confines of the treacherous forest than they had been that morning on the ridgeline. What looked like only half a day's travel had turned into something far longer. So night descended, and when it did it brought darkness and a cold that Ashyn had little known in all his eight winters.

As the sun set somewhere outside of the woods, for he had long ago lost all sense of direction, such a pervasive blackness covered them that he couldn't even see his own hand in front of his face, even when he touched his own nose. Ashyn had never experienced such an absolute void as that which was now around him. He felt Xexial reach down and take his hand in a death grip. Ashyn struggled to see the illumination from his strange luminescent gloves, but there was nothing.

"We mustn't stop," he whispered urgently.

"But we can't see," Ashyn returned, just as quiet, but with a tremor of worry in his voice.

Ashyn felt the wizard squeeze his hand reassuringly. "We mustn't stop," he repeated.

Now Ashyn had been experienced in winter, even in the southern part of Kuldarr it still snowed a little bit. Nothing, however, could have prepared him for the bone-chilling numbness that came with the darkness. As the light died so, too, did all semblance of warmth that the forest had offered them on the other nights. This cold had found a way to get underneath his clothing and bury itself deep within his flesh, down to the very core of him. It felt as if he had plunged into an icy lake in the middle of winter. He was that cold. It saturated the very fibers of his being and left him stunned.

They moved together in the black rather swiftly considering the dangers the tree trunks, low hanging branches, and sharp thorn-covered hedges represented. Xexial kept his pace brisk, and Ashyn kept a hand out in front of him just in case they went headlong into one of the sturdy, immovable objects.

Ashyn could not discern their direction at all. The wizard pulled him left, then right, then straight, then they turned around and backtracked where they had been. It occurred to Ashyn that the unnatural gloom they were in was more than just a dimness caused by the thick canopy above them. It was an *alien* murk, foreign and otherworldly; it was quite possibly magic.

The wizard pushed and pulled again, constantly coming across barriers be they tree, shrub, or pit. Either way their avenues were blocked wherever they went. Even though Ashyn could barely feel his toes, he realized that he was beginning to sweat. His right hand was clammy in Xexial's grip. Beads collected across his brow. They were getting nowhere. They were lost. Lost inside a magical maze.

For the first time Ashyn realized there was no sound. There was no hooting of an owl, or the squeaking of a squirrel, nor was there the single howl of a wolf, in a forest that Ashyn knew was overpopulated with the beasts. There was nothing. Not even the chirping and buzzing sounds of insects. Ashyn knew what it meant. There were predators about.

Something crashed down loudly to the left of the boy, causing him to jump. Its impact sent tremors across the ground, through Ashyn's feet and clear up his spine. His hair stood up on their ends. Another object crashed down to his right, just past the wizard. Xexial's grip tightened.

Ashyn heard the thumps of heavy footfalls as the unknown creatures were moving forward, closer. He suddenly felt colder. Then there was a strange sound, a high-pitched wail that came from his left. The creature to the right answered with the same off-tone melody. They moved closer. Ashyn could feel the cold seeping into his every nerve as he held Xexial in a death grip. The sound of the creatures' breathing reverberated in his ears as they closed the gap, sniffing out their prey. Next to him, Xexial coiled like a snake, waiting expectantly.

Ashyn felt the static building up all around him, crackling and popping electricity that caused his clothes to adhere to his body and his hair to stand on end.

The muzzle of the beast closed in. First by a foot, then within mere inches. Ashyn tensed up. The cobra struck.

Brilliant blue energy flashed into the aberrant darkness as Xexial loosed a lightning bolt at the creature by Ashyn. What

Ashyn expected to be a blinding light was nothing more than a momentary flicker as the lightning was quickly absorbed into nothingness in front of the indistinct form of the creature that stood before him.

"No!" Xexial hissed, alarmed. Then they were running.

~ ~ ~

Branches snapped and exploded behind the two as the creatures barreled in pursuit of their prey. The predators were big, very big. With each stride, Ashyn could feel the ground shudder and quake beneath him. He knew they would close the gap in seconds, and it would be over. Ashyn and Xexial were blind to everything around them; however, these creatures apparently were not.

Xexial pulled him roughly to the right and slammed him against a tree just as one of the beasts barreled past, ripping through shrubbery and branches as if they had no more viscosity than wet parchment. It wailed in protest, emitting that same eerie cadence as it had when it first approached.

Ashyn had not a moment to catch his breath before they were moving again. How Xexial was navigating through the dense forest was beyond the small boy, but he was constantly pushed, pulled, and yanked away from all obstacles be they tree, rock, or bush. It was not without cost, however.

The thorns of hedges and bushes repeatedly stabbed Ashyn. Scuffed by the rough bark of the dying trees, and scratched by the sharp tips of the low hanging limbs, he bled from dozens of small wounds, as he knew Xexial did too. Their trek was not silent as they broke through branches and had their clothing torn asunder by prickly hedges. Their breathing was labored from running, Ashyn's lungs burned with fire even though he could no longer even feel his fingers and toes from the biting cold.

Still they persevered. They would not surrender to the maze and the creatures within. Xexial kept going until he hit a dead end, then he would try another path till it led to a dead end. He never stopped, but kept moving. They were always moving.

The night raged on, terrifying and primal. Ashyn did not know how long it could last, how long he could last. It seemed never ending. Xexial was like a machine, moving them along, making all the right decisions to keep them alive. Yet he could never seem to find a way out of this magical labyrinth.

The awkward chorus continued behind them as now more than a dozen creatures were crying in their unearthly melody. Ashyn for the life of him could not figure out what their noises meant. Perhaps it was territorial, or maybe it was meant to invoke fear as the howl of a wolf often did? He just didn't know. He didn't have enough time to think clearly. He needed clarity.

The ground shook and quaked from the stampede of beasts behind them. They could hear the predators trampling everything in their path, hedges, fallen limbs, even aged trunks, in a feral attempt to capture the escaping duo. The sound of dead wood exploding echoed through the still night. Ashyn knew if just one of the monsters hit him as they did the vegetation then he would be nothing more than a broken husk of a boy.

Xexial forced him low, just as one of the creatures lunged at him. Ashyn felt a searing cold race up his spine and over his crown as the predator soared over them. The beast tumbled past and crashed into a weak hollow trunk that had been dead and deteriorating for a very long time.

The monstrous elm exploded from the force of the creature and teetered precariously on two massive limbs that had managed to become intertwined with the neighboring trees. They began a low whine of protest as all of the weight shifted into them.

"Go! Go!" Xexial hollered, forcing Ashyn along, trying to escape the inevitable catastrophe.

With a whine of agony, its western heavy supporting branch snapped and tumbled overhead. The ancient goliath bellowed under the strain and the massive trunk began to list to the south, causing the ground to tremor beneath them. It hung on its last supporting branch for only a few seconds and with a deafening crack the only remaining support of the dead tree shattered, bringing the wooded monstrosity crashing down around them.

Ashyn screamed as he was pushed through the bombarding wooden hail. Branches buckled and snapped as the gargantuan tree tore down all around them. Limbs became deadly projectiles as they collided into one and other with explosive force, turning the splintering mass into shrapnel that lanced out in all directions. Ashyn gritted his teeth as he felt the cutting blows across his back from the debris. Nearby he heard Xexial grunt in pain as he too was peppered with wood.

Ashyn knew they would never clear the collapsing giant, for the tree was ancient and far too tall, too wide. Yet they ran, as the gargantuan monstrosity cascaded downward towards them. Twigs exploded like little overripe berries. Dead leaves littered the air. The archaic shell groaned loudly in protest, filling their ears with a thunderous roar. He could feel its lumbering presence overhead, as the cacophony grew to a deafening pitch. Ashyn closed his eyes. Even though he couldn't see anything in the magical enhanced darkness, he couldn't bear the idea of what was to happen. Suddenly Ashyn found himself hurtled violently through the air.

Xexial had thrown him, Ashyn realized. At the last minute the wizard had expended some magic to get him clear of the tree as it came tumbling down. He landed roughly between two other trees, an outcropped root smashing into his solar plexus and driving all remaining wind from his lungs.

Xexial, either intentionally or not, had somehow thrown him into just enough of a niche that as the goliath collapsed downward, the world trembled around the boy, as he curled up and screamed in gasping, ragged breaths. Like a terrible earthquake, the ground shook violently.

Dust and mold exploded into the air, kicked up from the impact. A vicious fallout to the perishing of such a primeval giant. Ashyn choked and gagged in the dirty air, retching hard to excrete the unwanted filth.

As the haze slowly cleared away, a silvery light washed across the fallen boy. Ashyn blinked away the miasma and was amazed to see a pale moonlight piercing through the now torn canopy above. The unnatural darkness had been wiped away and with it the mind-numbing cold. Ashyn slowly stood, pain coursing through every fiber in his body. His broken fingers shot waves of agony through him as he used his hands to support his weight. He didn't care, he was alive! Somehow, he was alive!

Ashyn looked at the aftermath. The ancient tree had tumbled to the earth, and lay embedded against two other decaying giants. He knew it wouldn't be long before their time came as well. Branches, thick long limbs, and a floor of dead leaves were scattered across the earth, all blanketed in a grey light. It was impossible for him to traverse, and left him only one direction to go.

He looked to where it had all started, hoping to see the creature now in the light. There was no such luck. All he could see crushed beneath the base of the decimated trunk was the long-fingered hand of the beast. It bore six fingers, the last acting as an opposable thumb. All of them ended in long thick claws the color of midnight, and covered in some sort of chitin-like exoskeleton. There was no way to get near it, and even if he could, Ashyn didn't want to.

His eyes scanned the aftermath in hopes of finding the wizard, but he found that he didn't have to study it long. Ashyn saw where he had been before the wizard had propelled him. The long, wide trunk was firmly pushing deep into the earth. There was no avoiding something of that size. He searched in vain anyway, desperate to find some semblance of his savior. It proved moot for in the wreckage of the elder tree, his benefactor was nowhere to be found.

Xexial was gone.

Ashyn was all alone.

TENACIOUS

He was alone.

"Xexial!" the boy screamed into the forest. With a panicked fervor, his eyes darted all across the palely illuminated landscape unable to see his savior. "Xexial!" he yelled again, hoping to stimulate any kind of response, even a groan. There was nothing. Only the sound of moaning trees piercing the uneasy silence. Not even the predators were making their strange hooting music.

He ran to the fallen tree and searched diligently for even the smallest hints of hope. A piece of torn clothing, a shoe, anything and yet there was nothing to be found.

Stubbornly, Ashyn attempted to climb the fallen tree. He attacked the trunk, trying to scale the rough bark and heavy branches. He had made it almost ten feet when the extremely damaged bough snapped and sent him down in a tumble of limbs, his, and the fallen trees. He yelled in both frustration and pain as he scurried back to his feet. He knew there was no safe way over. He also knew he couldn't waste half the night trying to find a way around, not with those monsters out there tracking him. Yet he couldn't fathom the thought of leaving the wizard behind. With his family gone, Xexial was all he knew.

"Xexial!" he cried futilely, as he dropped to his knees in forlorn sorrow.

Ashyn felt the tears well up in his eyes. Xexial was gone, and with him, any chance Ashyn had of becoming a wizard. He sobbed heavily and began to cry against the trunk. It was not fair! The little boy screamed just as much in his own head, as he did aloud. Why did this keep happening to him? Why couldn't everyone just leave him alone?

He hated everything! He hated the Orcs, he hated the Wild Elves, and he hated everything about this place! "I hate you!" he screamed upward in a primal frenzy towards the unresponsive woods. The sheer feral nature of his scream stretched his vocal chords and made him fall into a fit of coughing.

He punched the tree trunk and yelped in pain as it hit against the bruised flesh of his broken fingers. Even the trees were against him! He sucked on the wound as the spark of pain sent a recent memory flooding into his head.

He remembered the cornfield, and of losing everything, he had held dear. The last few days of running without rest had made it feel like a lifetime ago. He fought against his emotions even as the hot water streaked down his face. He had made a vow, he reminded himself. He was never going to be weak again.

He looked at himself now. Lying on the ground with predators surrounding him, just waiting for him to give up and accept death. "Pathetic," he hissed at himself.

Ashyn pushed himself up onto his feet and stared angrily down at the spot he had last seen Xexial. *I'm still in the maze*, he screamed to himself. His focus was on survival now, not self-loathing.

"One day I will avenge you," he told the spot of the tree where he had last seen his wizard. "I will find a way to learn magic, and I will return. I promise," the boy said, holding complete conviction in every word. It wasn't an empty promise, not to him. He would learn magic.

Ashyn ran his hand across his cheeks and nose wiping away the last of his tears and sniffles. He took one last look at his surroundings, studying the markings to try to remember this very place. He wouldn't forget, he said to himself defiantly. He swore to remember this spot. He soaked up all he could in the dim light. Satisfied that he could garner no further insight from the woods, he looked up to the sky.

It was a clear night and the stars were shining brightly through the ravaged hole in the canopy of dying leaves. He knew the stars. He had read about them in books, about how sailors used them to navigate. He knew about constellations. Even his father used the stars when he went out on extended hunts. He searched for a minute until he found the brightest of the stars, the North Star. He now had his bearings, something that Xexial and he had not had since they entered the maze. He looked back down to the remains of the tree. "It was not in vain," he whispered. With one final look where he thought the body of Xexial to be, he whispered his thanks and then turned back to the alcove that had saved him. He climbed through to the other side, and then turned to the north. He ran.

~ ~ ~

It didn't take long for the beasts to recollect either. Within minutes the chase was back on. He could feel the tremors in the ground, and heard their strange off-key song to each other. They were hunting.

Ashyn was better prepared now, though. He knew at least a little of what to expect. His hunters would find their prey slightly harder to catch this time around.

He saw the layout of the forest before him from the weak dying light behind him and he memorized it. He memorized the chaos. He had seen the shadow of the root sticking out before him, so he avoided it when he closed in. He had remembered where the branches had hung low, so he ducked them as he ran past. Those first few minutes of light had helped him on his way, and more importantly, it put a better gap between him and his stalkers. Ashyn kept his bearings as he plunged once more into the darkness.

After another ten minutes though, he was fully embedded within the obsidian nightmare once more. He couldn't see anything, not even his own fingers as he waved them in front of him trying to scout ahead with touch, before running headlong into a tree or worse. He relied on that tactile sensation and his quick thinking mind to get him through it all.

Once more, he could feel the cold begin creeping its way into his limbs. His fingertips felt like icicles. His toes tingled and began to grow numb. Ashyn growled and pressed on.

Seconds continued to pass like hours. He could feel the hulking shadows moving in on him from all directions. His eyes darted back and forth expecting to see something, a glimmer in the darkness. Even though he was blinded by the magical darkness, he could still see that chitin-covered claw vividly in his mind. He was waiting for that claw to come swiping in at any moment to end his trial, but it hadn't happened, and he wasn't sure why.

He knew that he had to be close to the clearing, it was impossible for him to be stuck forever in the dead maze of corpse trees. Unless it could somehow be magic?

Ashyn knew he was woefully ignorant to the functions of magic, but he was sure that no one could alter the size of the forest to seem much larger than it actually was. At least he hoped so, anyway.

The idea of it only made him more determined. He made sure he never strayed far to the left or right, always stayed as straight as he possibly could. He would not let the beasts break him again. He wouldn't lose himself to the maze. Any tree that he encountered he simply went around, mentally counting off the steps it took to reach what he perceived was the other side. Sometimes if a tree was particularly wide he would stop after a few steps, backtrack the exact same amount and then mark it either by scratching a deep groove in it at shoulder level with a stone, or breaking off a piece of bark. Then he would circle the tree counting the amount of steps it took to go fully around until he reached the marked area. After he did, he would count half the number and determine that as close to center as possible. It was not an accurate method, but it was all he had.

His curious movements seemed to confuse the pursuers as well for they couldn't seem to capture an accurate bead of his whereabouts. Again and again, they sang to each other as they trampled through the dead woods after him.

Ashyn knew he was getting close to the edge of the forest, as suddenly the brush grew thick and dense. He knew at this point he should search for a thinner point of entry along the length of the underbrush, but he was anxious, and he didn't want to risk the possibility of getting lost again. So he lowered his head and bounded roughly into the thicket. Boughs snapped and scratched, clawing at him as he pushed through the dying flora. His progress was slowed to a crawl and he ripped at the heavy skeleton-like vegetation, trying to pry himself free of its grasp, and deeper into what he hoped would lead to his freedom.

A loud crash thundered into the brush just to his right. Suddenly his entire body was drenched in the unearthly cold. He shivered and found his teeth clattering. He tried to keep his mouth shut, but still they rattled. The cold was so overwhelming that it brought with it an overpowering drowsiness. His eyelids grew heavy and he felt his movements becoming lethargic. Still he kept going, or tried to. The bone-like foliage grabbed his wrists and ankles in a steel vise-like grip. He struggled against them, but they wouldn't relinquish their grip. Behind him, he felt the little micro-quakes as the creature moved in. Ashyn fought hard against the emaciated plants, breaking and tearing at the bindings on his arms.

All the noise around him suspiciously grew quiet. He tried to open his tired eyes, but they were growing heavier. He tried to calm the fear growing in his stomach. He could hear his own breathing coming in ragged gasps. Deep in his ears, he could hear the heavy beating of his own heart. It sounded so loud he was sure that the beasts could hear it, too.

Suddenly a beast cackled its strange cadence right into his ear, less than an inch away. He jumped at the proximity of the sound, tearing free of the undergrowth and slammed the left side of his face across a low-hanging branch. He crashed down on his back. The impact against the rough ground drove all the air from his lungs. He gasped in shock. His mind began to reel and he saw stars in front of his eyes, the first thing he had seen in a while since reentering the magical darkness.

As he groaned in pain, Ashyn became suddenly aware of the breath of the beast on his forehead. He became very still. Ice crystals formed across his brow and in his red hair as the creature hovered only inches above him. He could hear it sniffing.

Ashyn imagined a porcine snout, like that of a pig hovering right above his head. He didn't know why he thought that, but then it snorted once, as if in a strange confirmation to the image. He could hear it lumbering left and right over him. It began swaying to and fro, looking at things that Ashyn couldn't see, probably the other monsters. He realized the creature was very tall, perhaps as tall as a man, maybe larger.

The monster retracted its face from Ashyn's. The boy blinked up at the unending darkness and then flinched as a creature's fist smashed into the ground above his head. There was a loud wallop that thundered through his ears, followed by another, and then another. Each strike caused the hardened clay to crack and vibrate, which only made Ashyn's chattering teeth rattle louder. Ashyn squeezed his eyes tight. He didn't want to die.

But no attack came. The strange *alien* monster just hammered the ground repeatedly, buffeting the boy with icy winds and shards of crystallized clay. Ashyn just lay there, frozen.

Why was it not attacking? Ashyn's mind raced to find an answer as each chitin-laced fist continued to rain down inches from his head. He knew that one rogue fist not landing in the same spot would likely crush his head like an overripe melon. Every inch of his body screamed for him to move, yet something in the back of his subconscious was telling him to stay.

Was it taunting him before felling the final blow? After what felt like an eternity, the creature abruptly stopped pounding the ground. Once again it made an eerie cry, this one sounding more like a plaintive issuance of submission. Then there was nothing, only silence.

Ashyn blinked several times when he realized that it was not going to attack him, not going to kill him. Still he didn't move. Then a branch snapped off in the distance. The world erupted around him in an unearthly chorus. Terror lanced through Ashyn as he realized they were all around him. The ground quaked as the creatures began to bound away from his position. He could hear the dense foliage being crushed underneath the monsters' massive frames as they leapt away at this new possible prey in their woods. Ashyn held his breath, still in shock.

After several more minutes, he felt the exhausting cold beginning to lift. Slowly he began growing more alert. He didn't know what had happened. If they were truly were gone. It didn't take much longer before the cold had all but subsided. Only trace fragments laced themselves through his small frame in sporadic spurts, a simple reminder that not all had truly vanished.

Ashyn picked himself off the ground, pain dancing through his left cheek and temple. He delicately placed his fingertips against his eye socket and could already feel the flesh becoming swollen and inflamed. Nothing more had been broken, at least he hoped not. He didn't know how many more broken bones he could actually withstand.

Slowly he reached out to find the thicket that had bound his escape. His fingers brushed against the skeletal remains of the decayed hedge. It was thinner now, he realized. Much thinner. He could likely break his way through and be clear to the other side, though he knew the sound would more than likely bring the creatures right back to him.

Logic screamed in the back of his head to follow the flora to a thinning point and escape, but again his mind fought against the right thing to do, and went with the quick thing to do. If he could pass through then he would be free, or should be at least. He quickly worried that this clump of plants may be nothing more than an outcropping in the middle of the dead woods. Then he would be no closer to escape than he had been back at the fallen tree.

Yet he had headed mostly north, of that he was certain. There couldn't possibly be any more of the decaying forest left.

Emotion overruled reason and once again he attacked the dead bush, tearing and breaking at the hollow and fragile shrub.

Once again, the eerie melody resounded throughout the decomposing forest. He could hear the thunderous stampede as the creatures rushed back to where Ashyn was.

Ashyn pushed through the foliage frantically, trying to beat the creatures that were barreling back down on him. Fear gripped his chest tight and he screamed at the stupid thicket for blocking his way. He pushed forward one foot, snapping branches and drawing deep red lines into his own flesh.

He pushed forward another foot. He could feel the sharp deathly fingers of the shrub stabbing into him equally from all sides now. He crushed into it further with his little moccasins, gritting against the pain. He made it another foot.

The ground trembled like an earthquake as the creatures rushed towards him. He grabbed the dead spruce to maintain balance and screamed at it all in feral anger. He was tired of being so afraid. Frustrated at being on the run all of the time. He had known nothing but fear and heart-gripping terror for the last few weeks. He had known nothing but loss, and pain. He had lost his father, mother, sister, and now Xexial to these Maker-forsaken woods! He was done with it. He would run no longer. Ashyn stopped wrestling with the broken bush and turned to face his predators.

Something crashed down onto the earth in front him. He heard the strange mantra it issued. He wasn't afraid, not this time. The world slowly became bathed in amber light. Ashyn Rune was angry.

~ ~ ~

Tears rolled down his face, and his body shook with an irrevocable rage. A righteous wrath seemed to fill him. An ardent desire to make the Shalis-Fey pay, to be a harbinger of retribution to all the heartache and grief that wracked his tiny frame. There would be a reckoning.

As the orange light intensified, he could begin to see through the forest's unnatural veil of shadow. A hulking umbral form moved toward him, massive in comparison to Ashyn, and yet he did not cower. He was too tired and too angry to be afraid anymore.

Even with Ashyn's sudden vision, he could not fully make out the beast. It was still nothing more than a silhouette against a ginger backdrop. The monster appeared like a giant phantom, moving forward to claim its prey.

His fury fueled him, and once again an image flashed into Ashyn's mind. It was a focus for all of his pain and suffering, now directed at the predator before him. It was a vision of torment so inexplicable that it brought a smile to the child's face. He grabbed onto that image once more, and just as Gregiry Bib's sleeve erupted into a blaze of fire, so too did the world around him.

The creature did not recoil however, nor did the shadows seem to lessen around it. As Xexial's lightning had been absorbed, so too was Ashyn's fire; by the beast anyhow.

Yet the boy pushed forth, putting all of his ferocity, all of his passion, into the flames. He felt their sweltering heat against his flesh as they licked and bit at the thicket around him. The fires turned his vision into a searing white light. A supernal clarity seemed to reach out to the boy. *Focus on the trees,* it told him calmly, and so the boy did as it bade.

Turning his focus on the monoliths of wood nearest to him, the blaze ate viciously at the dead wood of the trees. It chewed and rent the dry rotted and decayed trunks. As the intense heat boiled the residual sap and moisture within the deadened giants, the burning husks exploded ferociously sending scorching shrapnel in all directions. Ashyn did not cower from the lethal shower. Instead, he momentarily shifted his concentration on them. The wooden projectiles were incinerated when they neared the boy.

The predator, however, was not as lucky. With no means to divert the malicious flaming missiles, the fiery daggers pierced through the deep shadows and plunged wickedly into the beast's flesh. It roared in a sinuous wail of agony.

Pockets of icy vapor plumed from where the shrapnel had struck deep, temporarily neutering the intensity of the heat he felt. The creature collapsed to the ground writhing and twisting as the natural fires eviscerated the beast from within.

Ashyn watched it burn. Watched as the cryogenic mist swirled around the felled black beast and began to rise upward and quickly evaporate. He felt an overwhelming sense of glee at his minute victory, and realized that even his own rationale questioned this obscure sense of joy he felt at seeing the creature in so much pain. I should not be like this, he reasoned.

I should not feel amused by its suffering. Yet he could not help it, he was.

The thunderous groan of the shattered tree quickly brought him out of his self-reflection, and instantly his scorching vision sizzled away. The fire burned no less, however, and the world around him was still cast in a thick, rich red light. *And it was hot!* the boy realized.

He turned around to see the thicket had been reduced to nothing more than ash, and beyond that lay violet fields underneath an indigo sky. Ashyn did not look back at what he had done, he simply escaped from the maze.

He was not a hundred feet from the confines of the dead woods when an intense lethargy instantly over took him. His limbs suddenly felt as if he were trying to carry an elephant. Every step was compounded with more and more weight. Finally, after five more grueling steps, his legs gave out on him and he collapsed into the field. Ashyn tried to move his arms and realized that they would no longer function at all.

I am merely its conduit, Ashyn heard Xexial say to him in his mind, recalling what the wizard had said about the price of magic. Feedback, he realized as another wave of exhaustion pounded into him.

"Uh-oh," Ashyn muttered to himself as he felt his jaw go slack, unable to control the long string of drool that followed. His fingers twitched against the soft grassland aimlessly, outside the realm of his control. Behind him, he could still hear the fires burning wildly, and he knew that it wouldn't be long before they stretched into the field and consumed him as well. *It had all been going so well, too,* he thought somberly.

The ground trembled beneath his prostrate form as he felt something touch down heavily beside him. Heavy winds buffeted his head and back, ruffling his hair and tattered garments. Ashyn could hardly feel it, his nerves shot from the cost of the magic he had used.

His vision began to flicker as his consciousness began to fade. Everything became blurry as a massive shape lumbered over him.

Its shape was different from the other monsters, he dimly realized. In fact, he was pretty sure that he could make out wings.

Relax, a familiar voice whispered into his mind. *You are safe now,* it told him. For some reason, Ashyn believed it. Content he could do no more, he let his consciousness ebb away.

CZYNSK

A shyn felt buoyant. He felt like an autumn leaf drifting aimlessly across a fickle stream. He was weightless, and powerless to the currents that were carrying him. He struggled to open his eyes, but something was keeping them firmly shut. It was curious, he idly thought to himself, why he couldn't open his eyes. The thoughts didn't linger long however as he fell back to the tingling sensation of drifting along; lighter than air.

Whether it was minutes, hours, or days Ashyn couldn't be sure, but eventually he felt his floating body settle onto a soft downy surface. It was like nothing he had ever felt before. Certainly not like his coarse rough leather strip on a stack of hay bed that he had back in Bremingham. This was different. It was what he imagined laying in a cloud would be like. It was silky soft, plush beyond belief, and mind-numbingly comfortable. He let his body melt into the bedding. He sighed with contentment. This was good, he decided. So good, in fact, that he never wanted to leave.

"This is not you, Nuchada," he heard a melodic voice sing to him.

"What's not me?" he replied dreamily to the suddenly new presence by him. He felt he should be alarmed, but for some reason he wasn't.

"You are a fighter, Nuchada. Not someone to surrender so easily," the singing voice told him.

"I'm just a boy," he returned. "I'm not even nine-winters-old yet."

"And that determines the merits of one's courage?" the voice questioned. "The fact that you're a child means that you can submit to another so simply, as if that be the entire answer one needs."

"Of course not," he argued, realizing that he vaguely recognized the voice.

"Then what, Nuchada? What warrants your abandonment?" the voice pressed.

"I dinna abandon anyone!" he interjected, now trying to open his eyes but feeling some unfathomable pressure keeping them shut. He struggled, but found he couldn't move in the luxurious bedding. Why did he know that voice? he wondered.

"You abandoned your vows." the voice returned sharply. "You made them so earnestly, with such a powerful conviction to yourself that there should be no way you would just throw it all away to feel comfortable in a swanky bed!"

"I dinna throw it away!" he yelled at the disembodied voice. "I dunna know how to use magic. I dinna know the demand it would require from me! It's not my fault!"

"Again you acquiesce so easily!" the voice said, as if teasing him. "You place your blames so comfortably on some unseen factor which has no tangible physical presence. It is so easy to point a finger, is it not? To cede to a power greater than yourself? The Nuchada that I have seen had more substance," the presence finished disgustedly.

Who was this person to judge him? he thought angrily. Had he not suffered enough already? He had lost so much, been hurt so badly, but apparently it was not enough. Now he had to be goaded by some unseen specter. Why couldn't he just have peace? Be accepted and happy, just once?

"Why are ye so averse to this?" he challenged the voice. He continued to fight to open his eyes. The bedding was now more like the thicket, binding him, holding him firmly in place, but there was no pain, only an intense comfort.

"Because if you surrender now as the boy, then you will never become the man that I have foreseen," the voice told him somberly.

It was at that moment that he recognized the voice. It was high in pitch, like that of a small child, or a girl, or both he realized. He readied himself for the fight to open his eyes. He prepared for the resistance and then arched his eyebrows for attempted support against whatever entity was keeping them closed. He opened his eyes.

Surprisingly there was no resistance like before and he realized, sheepishly, that he must have looked quite ridiculous to whom-ever was looking at him. Bright lights penetrated his grey eyes, blanketing everything in a brilliant ivory glow. As his eyes adjusted, he found that he was surrounded in a white fog. It covered everything for as long as he could see. Directly in front of him, he saw . . . her. He found himself staring directly into her swirling, quicksilver eyes. The eyes of the *Exemplar*. Strangely, he found those eyes did not enthrall him, as they had previously. It gave him some courage to challenge her.

"Why do ye care?" he aggressively asked the platinum-haired Elf.

"Why shouldn't I?" she countered empathetically. Her response was so simple, so full of emotion that it instantly threw him off, puttering out his steam.

"Because I'm just a boy, because I'm a freak!" he said sorrowfully.

The Exemplar shook her head, her beautiful hair dancing and glimmering in the white light. "You are my Nuchada. I am bound to you."

Ashyn shook his head. It was a lot to take in. "Why did you choose me? I don't understand," he asked her.

She smiled a perfect white smile at him. "Because it is in you, that I believe."

Ashyn suddenly realized that the world was beginning to disappear around him. He looked at the Exemplar in shock. She too was beginning to fade away.

"Wait!" he pleaded. "I have so many questions!"

"Patience," her voice echoed to him ethereally.

"But . . ."

"There's a warrior within you, Ashyn Rune. All you need is to see it."

His world disappeared.

~ ~ ~

"Boy's a' comin' around," a thickly accented young man's voice said above him.

"Nonsense. Kid's been out for days. Not taking any food. Hardly a drop o' water. No way e's gonna wake up. Maker's got 'is soul now, likely," another voice said to the right of him and slightly further away.

"I's is telling ye, Uriel, this boy's a waking up," the man with the accent said again. This was followed by a groan from the boy.

"See."

"We'll I'll be a goat's right nu . . ."

"Ahem . . ."

Ashyn opened his eyes groggily. Intense light poured in through his half-opened slits, causing him to quickly shut them again. He covered his hands over his eyes, and immediately noticed an extreme stiffness in his arms. His limbs felt weak and emaciated, and he didn't think he could hold them up much longer. What had happened to him?

"Where am I?" he croaked, over a thick dry tongue. His mouth felt as if he had recently been eating nothing but sand, and he desperately needed water.

"Czynsk," the voice above him answered. "Been 'ere fer 'bout, oh six or seven days I reckon."

"Ta," the young man named Uriel, to his right, agreed. "Some merchants found ye in a field, they did. Grand story they had of it, too. Said the field was burned to a crisp all around ye, yet ye was unscathed."

"Well I wouldna say unscathed," the voice above him said with a chuckle.

Ashyn could feel the tightness in his face and as he reached up to touch his skin he found that it was swathed in bandages. As he slowly reopened his eyes he could see that his broken fingers were taped together, and that they too had been wrapped.

"Found a bit o' the ole rough and tumble, I would reckon," Uriel agreed, laughing.

Ashyn directed his gaze around the room. It was a simple wooden structure with a hay and mud roof. It was somewhat wide, perhaps thirty or forty steps from one end to the other. It was rectangular in shape, with various cots scattered throughout the room. There were small rough wooden workstations spread amongst the cots, each containing several poultices, mortars and pestles, and plenty of gauze. There were also two buckets by each station. One with clean water, and the other for waste. A hearth glowed nearby casting him in pale warmth.

He looked back at the two men above him. They were very young he realized, perhaps not even men, but just older boys. He placed them around the same age as Gregiry Bib, perhaps a winter older at most.

The one above him had shaggy brown hair, and doe brown eyes. His skin was covered in acne, and his pointy nose was slightly crooked, as if it had been broken repeatedly. He was leaning over Ashyn, resting all his weight on the shaft of a mop.

The other boy, named Uriel, was resting against the workstation that Ashyn assumed was for him. He had coal black shoulder length hair, a full face, and a button nose. He squinted through chubby cheeks with beady dark brown eyes. He had a bored look on his face, like he would rather be anywhere but here. Ashyn saw he was picking his yellowish tinged teeth with a needle used for sewing wounds. He looked back to the acne-skinned boy above him.

"So . . . ye gotta name?" the boy asked.

"Ashyn."

The young man thrust his hand out to Ashyn, "Well met Ashyn, me name's Mactonal Turgenssen, everyone round 'ere jus calls me 'Macky'." He shrugged his head over to the raven-haired boy. "Dat's Uriel."

"Hello," Ashyn grunted as he tried to sit up. Macky quickly dropped the mop to the ground and helped little Ashyn upright. Ashyn was sore all over and to his surprise, he found that he was naked under his linens, only his ribs were tightly wrapped in gauze. He pulled the covers tightly over his lower body. "Can I have some water please?" he asked Macky.

Macky smiled a mouthful of crooked teeth. "Sure, sure," he said as he moved to the workstation Uriel leaned against, and brought forth a pitcher of drinking water. Ashyn wasted no time, gulping down the cool water as fast as he could. When he was done, he nodded his thanks and Macky took the pitcher away.

"So I 'ere that the field that they found ye in, it was one o' the ones that border the Shalis-Fey, is dat true?" Macky asked.

Ashyn nodded.

Macky's doe brown eyes grew wide, as did Uriel's little squinty ones as wide as his heavy eyebrows could lift them. "Were you in those woods?" Macky asked excitedly.

Ashyn wasn't sure how much he should explain. Should he tell them all that had transpired with Bremingham, the Wild Elves, and the creatures of the maze, or should he remain quiet? Macky seemed harmless enough, but he knew so little of the both of them, he wasn't sure how they'd react. He knew how the people of Bremingham had felt about magic. Instead, he merely nodded again.

"What were ye doin' in der?" Uriel asked.

Before Ashyn could come up with some type of explanation, the flat panel wooden door opened, shining the light of a midday sun into the sparsely lit infirmary. Only the dark silhouette of a shapely woman blotted out a little of the bright light.

As she entered the building, she quickly admonished the two young men lounging by Ashyn. "How many times do I have to tell ye's two to leave that little boy alone. He's not fer waking up now, an' tis likely he never will . . . oh," she finished, surprised to see Ashyn sitting up.

As the approaching woman eclipsed the bright light, he could see that she, too, was very young, perhaps not even out of her early teens yet. She seemed closer in age to his sister than the two boys. She was adorned in little more than a white caretaker's robes, which were cinched very tightly around her waist showing off her developing frame. Her straw blonde hair was pulled tightly in a bun, and she had bright blue eyes, a small petite nose, and freckles. Ashyn was amazed to see so many different-looking people within one room. Bremingham hadn't had nearly as much variety, unless you counted the Runes themselves.

Ashyn could see by the way that the two men were quickly recovering that they were somewhat enamored by her. Their reactions reminded him of his experience with the Exemplar.

"Avrimae, this is Ashyn," Macky said proudly to the young woman.

"Oh . . . I . . . nice to meet you . . . uhm . . . how is ye awake?" the woman stuttered.

Both boys found Avrimae's discomfort quite comical, for they broke up in a roaring laughter.

Ashyn watched Avrimae blush bright crimson looking at the two boys. "Shut it!" she yelled at them, and then looked back at Ashyn, "It's just . . . well . . . people we find in your case generally never wake up, is all," she tried explaining. "The Maker usually takes them."

"Macky says it's only been six days or so," Ashyn replied.

"Well he's right." Avrimae returned. "Six days since you been here, but . . . well, we're not sure how long it was afore the merchants found ye, and ye injuries were pretty peculiar."

"What do ye mean?" Ashyn asked curiously.

"Ye clothes," Macky replied. "Theys was all burned up. Yer skin was pretty blackened too, but when we cleaned ye up, twas just soot, there wasn't a single burn mark on ye, lotsa cuts an' bruises though."

Ashyn knew the soot was from the skeletal shrubbery he had incinerated. At the time, he hadn't thought about it, but it did seem odd that when he had summoned the flames he had been, well, fireproof. Ashyn couldn't even fathom how such a thing was possible.

"That's not all," Avrimae continued. "Ye breathing, twas very shallow, little more than a whisper on the air, really. When we sees such a thing, it usually means that one is on the verge of the afterlife. Ye haven't taken a lick of food and we had to force water down ye throat, most of which ye just spit back up anyways."

"Not to mention 'is heartbeats," Uriel said, eyeing him through his dark beady eyes. "Tell 'im 'bout 'is heart."

Avrimae nodded. "Yes, tis true. When we checked how strong ye heart was, twas very, very faint. Slow and barely there at all. By all account, ye were destined fer the Maker. Tis a miracle ye's still alive."

"Or sumtin' else," Uriel now added suspiciously.

Ashyn shifted uncomfortably under Uriel's scrutiny. It was happening already, he knew. It wouldn't be long before he was ostracized here as well.

Ashyn of course already knew why his heart had been beating so slowly. Why he had been like he was. It was the price he had paid for his uncontrollable use of magic. Feedback, Xexial had called it, and he had already fallen victim to its debilitating effects twice now.

That explanation wouldn't matter to someone like Uriel though, Ashyn realized. It would likely make matters even worse. He could see the word monster just resting on the tip of Uriel's tongue, behind his yellow-stained teeth. He knew how different he looked to all of them.

"Now calm yeself, Uriel," Macky interjected before Ashyn could say anything. "Ye as well as I 'ave seen some pretty odd tings since we come ta' Czynsk as well. I'm sure young Ashyn has a good story fer why he was at the Shalis-Fey borders?"

All eyes fell to him. Ashyn felt very small at that moment. However, something that Macky said had sparked a question of his own. "What do ye mean, since ye came to Czynsk?" he asked. "Ye weren't born here?"

"Nah," he said with his crooked smile. "We're all orphans."

"Orphans?" Ashyn said confused.

Avrimae nodded. "This is a hospice, Ashyn, provided by the Jasian Enclave; the Church of the Maker. The church takes in us orphans and ships us here mostly."

Ashyn had never heard anything like that. Bremingham had been out of touch with most of the larger society and the merchants of the south didn't speak much of orphanages. Ashyn had read about an orphanage of course, he just hadn't known it to be controlled by any church.

"Why Czynsk though?" he asked.

"Cuz twas the farthest away at the time," Avrimae returned.

"From what?"

Avrimae looked between Uriel and Macky, who looked just as confused by his question, and then back at Ashyn. "From the war, of course."

"War?" Ashyn said, bewildered.

"Yeah," Macky replied. "East of here. The nation of Fermania is gripped in a brutal civil war. Czynsk sits between the borders of Fermania and Dakoria. We're a little nowhere hub of a village that merchants use between major trading capitals, like Trinsen or Buckner."

"Technically I think it's still part of Fermania since we are a human settlement and the nation of Dakoria belongs to the Dark Elves," Uriel added.

Macky just shrugged.

Ashyn looked at Avrimae as she continued. "That's why there are so many of us here. Displaced by the war. Either our families are inaccessible, or . . ."

"Dead," Uriel finished bitterly, as he got up and moved away from the group.

"We've gotten a lot of children here lately. We're some of the first ye see," Avrimae added.

Ashyn had never heard that there was a war raging on. No merchants ever brought news of war, or if they did, he had never heard of it. You would think something like that would have been on the mouth of everyone in his village. Yet he knew that Bremingham was hardly on any trade route, and only largely got straggler merchants heading to or from Gnomesgate to the far southeast. Veer was the only person that he knew that had really ever ventured north of Bremingham, most always were heading east or west.

He supposed Bremingham was separated from many of the on-goings, being on the other side of the Shalis-Fey, but the idea of being so close to a war . . . It seemed like he was in another world.

"How long has this been going on?" Ashyn asked.

"Bout six winters, I reckon," Macky said.

"Seven," Uriel added from across the room, glumly. "Seven long winters."

"That's what happened to ye, 'innit?" Macky asked. "Running from the war."

"No," Ashyn answered.

Ashyn didn't know how much he should say. He already felt the speculation and wary eyes of Uriel on him, and Avrimae said that he was in the lodging of the Church of the Maker. Ashyn's experience with pious religious members had always been negative all his young life. He hadn't expected it to change much now. He knew how they would feel about magic, about what he had seen Xexial do, of what he had done. The Church would label him, just as much as Bremingham had labeled him. His life would be terrorized by words such as possessed, demon, and freak. Plus he was a stranger here. They might react even more drastically.

Without his family or Xexial, he didn't know how he would be able to survive under the watchful gaze of the church. If they knew he came from the south, if he came through the Shalis-Fey, well that would offer too many questions. How did a little boy make the trek through the feared woods? Why was he covered in soot? Will the Wild Elves attack in retaliation for harboring him? If they found out Bremingham was laid siege by Orcs, and he survived, they may look at him as a bad omen. He knew many in Bremingham would have.

It was better to lie, he decided. Now Ashyn had always been raised to be honest, and he knew that it was marring his mother and father to lie here and now, but he hoped that given the circumstance, between life and death, fudging of the truth wouldn't be so bad.

So how to lie? He thought, quickly. He would have to be believable of course, so to do that he would have to be familiar with what he was talking about. He would need to pull from his experiences, short though they may be. Therefore, it would be best to be from some place everyone's heard of, but no one's likely to have been to. Some place far away, but somewhere he could equally be believable in saying. Some place where his complexion could possibly be rational to an inexperienced people. Some place like . . .

"Gurgen," he answered suddenly.

Everyone looked at him oddly. "I'm from a village on the outskirts of Gurgen," he reinforced, thinking of everything his mother had used to say when people asked where she was from, because of her unusual complexion.

"But . . . Gurgen?" Avrimae began, dumbfounded. "It's so far away from here."

Ashyn nodded, "South and to the west." He thought of where Veer had said he was going when he had left Ashyn that day some two winters before. "My family and I headed east, we were heading to Tilliatemma, my father is . . . was a hunter, and he heard that the Dark Elves make the finest weapons."

"You must have been traveling forever," Avrimae, said clearly amazed. "How did you wind up covered in soot, alone in a field?"

Careful, Ashyn reasoned. If he mentioned a raid from Wild Elves, it may invoke suspicion. It would be best to use something visceral, something common to attack stragglers, something natural, primal. He thought of the day he fought the Bristle Wolf.

"Bristle Wolves," he declared. "From the woods. We ventured too near to them when we made camp. My father was wary of course, being a hunter, but he thought we would be okay. They came in the night. We tried using fire but . . ."

"Yer father was an idiot. No one goes near the Shalis-Fey," Uriel countered with an arrogant boast.

Anger flashed in Ashyn's eyes at the insult to his father. Uriel didn't know the man; he had no right to post judgment! Heat welled up within him. His eyesight starting growing red.

Patience! He screamed to himself, quickly thinking of the feedback he had already suffered twice. This is a story. It's just a story you're making up. You knew your father, knew him to be a better man! Uriel is just a fool, nothing more. Let it go, he rationalized. Just let it go. It took a breath or two and Ashyn steadied himself.

"Are ye okay, Ashyn?" Avrimae asked with a concerned look on her face.

"Fine," Ashyn muttered.

Avrimae didn't seem to think so, and to his surprise she wheeled on Uriel. "That was a horrible thing to say! This boy has just awoken from a terrible ordeal!"

"Whatever," the dark-haired boy answered. "Everyone here has lost their families. His father took them too close to the Shalis-Fey, they've paid the cost."

"Uriel!" Avrimae said, shocked by his response.

"You said you were in the Shalis-Fey though," Macky quickly added, trying to diffuse the situation by changing the subject.

Ashyn nodded. "Game hunting. We had to eat, we didn't know the dangers," he finished, directing his glare to Uriel. "As I said, we're not from here."

"Did you see them?" Macky asked excitedly.

"Who?"

Macky looked both ways, as if to make sure no one but the four of them were present, and then leaned in speaking just loud enough so that only the quartet, which happened to be the only people Ashyn noted that were present, could hear. "The Wild Elves."

Ashyn thought of the battle in the gully, the poison-tipped spears, and crude-covered bodies. Images flashed of him running for his life from the skilled hunters day and night, scaling down the side of a rock face while they hurled those deadly spears at him. He thought of their Exemplar, her proclamation of him being 'Nuchada' and her quicksilver eyes that entranced him so . . .

"No," he answered. "No Wild Elves."

Macky let out an exasperated sigh. "One day," he told them. "One day I'll see me a Wild Elf, I reckon."

"Ta," Uriel answered, his mood slightly lighter. "It'll be the last day of yer life, too!"

JASIAN ENCLAVE

As the weeks went by, Ashyn's wounds began to heal, and his life began changing in ways that were unexpected. There were dozens of orphaned children within the hospice of the Jasian Enclave. Ashyn was surprised to see many were his age and even younger, all of them displaced in some way by the Fermania Civil War.

No one within the enclave, including the clergy, had questioned his story one bit. In fact, they were pleased to have a child from Gurgen, for Ashyn learned that the capital of Gurgen, the Citadel, was in fact the heart and soul of the Jasian Enclave. Therefore, it was no surprise to them in the least that Ashyn was literate. However, it was an even bigger surprise to him that he was accepted for being so.

Ashyn learned as soon as he was able to bear burden, that life with the Jasian Enclave was not all about playing with the other children, something he had never done before, but about laboring for the toils of their graciousness. This was fine with Ashyn, for he had always been one to work, anyway.

His job functions depended on the day. It was either digging ditches for the waste of the township, helping Avrimae with injured orphans, or even reading and deciphering ledgers for the Jasian Enclave's dealings with various merchants from the other races.

Strangely enough, the clergy did not find his strong mathematical mind a heresy, but a gift from the Maker. Something that the people of Bremingham had never praised.

Still fresh in his mind was the day he was approached by a priest who told him, "Given is the gift of Creation from the Maker, and none has been given this gift greater than you, child. I have no doubt the Maker sent you to us, to help in these woeful times."

Hearing those words had filled him with such pride, to be accepted by people after all. Not one of the children questioned his complexion, not one of them cared. For the first time in his life, Ashyn Rune had real friends his age.

Uriel had been the only sore spot. While nowhere near as bad as Gregiry Bib had been, Uriel constantly eyed him warily. Ashyn's strange grasp of knowledge seemed to unnerve the boy, who as Ashyn found, was raised in a small Maker-fearing village just like Bremingham. His concept of the glories of the Maker often conflicted with the Jasian Enclave, and often he accused Ashyn of witchery, when he used his mathematical skills to predict weather patterns.

Ashyn of course often pointed out that if he were to use witchery that would make him a witch. He further pointed out that a witch was a girl, and that he clearly was not a girl, so in fact, he could not be a witch. Uriel would often grow angry, squint with his beady eyes, and storm away, while everyone laughed at him.

Macky and Avrimae fast became his friends. Macky was always there to protect him from Uriel's harsh words with a disarming joke, or word himself, and Ashyn could see that Macky and Uriel were very close friends. They both, however, had affections for Avrimae, which Ashyn knew would likely one day ruin their friendship. Luckily, Avrimae seemed not to notice their amorous gestures in the least, and went on, oblivious to the fact that both boys wanted her to be more than just friends.

Avrimae felt like a sister to him. Not like Julietta, but someone he shared a kinship with. Her parents had been brutally murdered at the beginning of the civil war, and she had had a brother that was younger than she was. He had not been killed, but she had lost him when they had been forced to flee her sacked village.

Ashyn confessed that he too had a sister, named Julietta, and that she was killed along with the rest of his family. He tried not to go into details about it, telling lies about how they died had been hard enough, and he didn't need to compound it. What he did like sharing with Avrimae, though, was his education.

Like the clergy, Avrimae loved that he could read and write, especially in different languages. She would often ask him to read her passages from the Enclave's teachings while they worked, and other times even fabled stories from the odd book or two that she could wrangle from a merchant. It wasn't long before they knew everything about each other. Well, everything that Ashyn could tell her without giving away he was from Bremingham, that he survived an Orc invasion and Wild Elf hunts, or that he could possibly wield magic. It felt good though, Ashyn knew, confiding in someone.

Soon the weeks turned into a month, then two, and Ashyn felt the cool winds of change coming as the world around him began to set into Fall Season. His wounds had healed, physically at least, and his bones had mended. He still cried at night, when he felt all alone on his cot. He cried for his family, his sister, and even Xexial. Deep down inside, he felt as if his happiness was betraying them. Yet Macky always seemed to be there as a good friend to give him strength. Macky had also lost his family when he had been around Ashyn's age. He knew Ashyn's pain.

Then one late afternoon, deep into the fall months, he was raking up the leaves that had fallen from the copse of maple trees that surrounded the outside of the church grounds. Macky was with him, talking of Wild Elves, and of how pretty Avrimae's wheat blonde hair looked in a setting sun. Ashyn as usual was barely listening. When he looked up from his duties, trying to find something to drown out Macky's love sonnet towards Avrimae, his eyes fell upon a figure that was approaching the holy grounds.

Ashyn watched as a hooded man slowly walked towards the large Jasian cathedral in the center of the church ground. He could not help but stare as he watched this moderately-built man limp ever so slightly to the great doors. He leaned heavily on a walking stick, but his staggered limp was very slight. Ashyn saw it nonetheless.

He was covered in thick tan robes that were heavily layered with other fabrics. A dark orange vest overlapped the robes followed by a long brown cloak. He wore heavy leather gloves with thick fingers.   Inlaid in the thick hide were iridescent sapphire lines that ran from the circles of his fingertips down his fingers and hands to his wrists.

Ashyn didn't even notice Macky walk up next to him.

"Oh, it's him," Macky said vehemently, as he leaned on the shaft of his rake.

"It's who?" Ashyn asked, star-struck by the man walking down the grey cobblestone road. His back was to the boys now as he walked within the grounds.

"Dunno," Macky answered. "Comes here from time to time." Macky laughed to himself, "Probably seeking forgiveness."

"For what?"

"Ye dunna know much about these parts do ye, whiz boy?"

Ashyn shook his head no.

"They say he's a wizard. A magic user of the worst kind," he said darkly.

"So magic users are bad?" Ashyn asked skeptically, fearful of what Macky may think of his own innate abilities. He was surprised when Macky shook his head no.

"Nah, magic's cool," he said excitedly. "Wish I could learn me some so I wouldn't have to mop and sweep all the time," he said tapping his rake against the ground.

"Could you imagine making a bunch of mops and buckets clean all the floors for ye while ye went and just relaxed? Ahh, that'd be great," he fantasized.

"So why's a wizard bad then? If you think magic is so wonderful," Ashyn asked, flummoxed.

"They use a different kind of magic," he said as mysteriously as he could.

"Well if ye mean magicians, yes there are a few types. I've read about sorcerers and mystics and whatnot," Ashyn said, recalling the magic he read from books.

"No, no. They use a different magic altogether. One that only wizards know," Macky replied.

"Well yes, magic is just like anything else, ye canna specialize in it, just like a blacksmith could make swords, or axes, or armor," Ashyn came back.

"No, yer not lissenin' ta me, Macky told him. "Different magic."

"I dunna understand," Ashyn fired back.

Mack let out an exasperated sigh. "Listen, the Enclave teaches us that the Maker has given us the wondrous gift of Creation. A magic that can make all kinds of things from energy, to strong winds, to levitating, all kinds of neat stuff. It creates.

"Wizards can do that stuff, but they have another magic altogether." He looked again to the man who was now climbing the stairs to the cathedral and then whispered. "It's called Destruction."

"Ye mean like fire? Fire destroys, right?" Ashyn asked fearful that he used an evil magic.

Macky shook his head. "Nah, fire creates. Ye make fire, and in return, fire performs a function. It has the potential to harm, but it also has the potential to help. It cooks our food, it keeps us warm in the winter, and without fire, we'd be doomed. At least that's what the Enclave teaches.

"No, this is bad. Destruction magic does as its title dictates. They destroy stuff: utterly. Wizards have been known to completely taint crops and livestock so the land remains unfertile for hunnerds and hunnerds of winters."

Ashyn looked at the back of the man entering the cathedral. He recalled what Xexial had told him after their first encounter with the Wild Elves. "I might have mentioned that if they took you from me I would blight their lands, ruining crops and diseasing livestock for generations," he had said.

"And they believed ye?" Ashyn had asked, astonished.

Ashyn remembered Xexial's devious smile that seemed so odd at the time, "You have much to learn about wizards, my boy. Much to learn," he had told him.

"Why do they let him here, then?" Ashyn asked.

"Because the Maker loves all of his children, even wizards."

Ashyn watched as the figure disappeared behind the doors of the cathedral, a figure that was so familiar to him. Was it really him, alive after what seemed like so long? He had never been able to climb the tree and check the other side. And if he was alive, was it true? Was Xexial evil?

~ ~ ~

"What are ye doin?" Macky called to the back of him as Ashyn dropped his rake and broke into a run towards the cathedral.

"Going to see him," Ashyn called back.

"But . . ." Macky stammered. "Ye have duties to do."

"I have to know," Ashyn muttered quietly to himself.

He ran as fast as little moccasins could take him across the bumpy cobblestone surface. Behind him, he heard the familiar thwack of the rake dropping and then Macky came running up next to him. "Just a look, okay?" he said between breaths.

"Okay," Ashyn replied.

Their feet hammered across the smooth stone walkway, and then veered left onto the well-manicured green lawn. Macky took over, leading the way, his long-legged stride taking him greater distances then Ashyn. Still Ashyn kept pace, a few feet behind.

Soon they were approaching the hedges around the west end of the crème-stoned cathedral. Ashyn marveled at its size for they had nothing of the sort in Bremingham, and this was the first time he had ever been so close to it.

The orphans held their sermons in the hospice only, and none except those chosen for special duties were allowed within the cathedral. Up to this point, Ashyn had only been able to view its ivory spires from afar.

Now, so close, he could see that the spires reached like fingers to the heavens. They were tall. Not nearly as high as the trees that grew in the Shalis-Fey, but it was the most architecturally advanced building he had ever witnessed in his life, outside of the drawings and sketches he had seen in his mother's books.

The building itself was designed like a circum, as it was a complete circle. The building's roof came together like a great dome with five brilliant spires jutting from the top. Four of the spires were pyramid-like in design, with square bases that rose upwards twenty feet, and then came together with triangular walls that sloped to a point. The four were arranged in a cruciform, one at the north, south, east, and west of the domed structure. Each one was perfectly aligned within the dome to form a directional compass.

It was a symbolic gesture to indicate that the Maker's gaze reaches all ends of the earth. Each spire was also a symbol of man's reach towards the heavens.

The fifth spire was located directly in the center of the dome. This spire was taller than the rest by another ten feet, totaling its height to thirty feet. Unlike the other four, this spire's base was cylindrical, not square, as it rose up coming to a point at its apex. This spire was the most symbolic of all.

The spire, in conjunction with the outer perimeter of the cathedral, together formed a *circumpunct,* a circle within a circle, which was their symbol for one true god. This solidified their belief in the Maker. It stood as a testament against all the other gods, which they considered pagan.

Every true Jasian Enclave cathedral was designed in this fashion. Those villages that were unable to create a cathedral in such a way had to make sure that the *circumpunct* was somewhere within their temple of worship, clearly seen by all.

At least that is what Ashyn was told by the clergy, and even then, he did remember the symbol of the Maker within the town hall of Bremingham.

Unlike the cathedral, however, no other building was designed as completely on the church grounds, or in all of Czynsk for that matter. Some of the more well-designed buildings, such as the Czynsk town hall, had clay shingles, but almost every other building, including the hospice where the orphans stayed, was thatched with straw. This of course leaked when it rained. Ashyn didn't mind though, it was how he had been raised.

Standing next to the cathedral now, though, he had never seen so complete a structure up close. "This must have taken a lifetime to build," Ashyn whispered as Macky boosted him over the hedges and onto a lip on the white brick face.

"Only four winters actually," Macky whispered back, climbing up after him.

Ashyn stared at him nonplussed.

Macky smiled. "The orphans," he explained. "We built it. Been done now for a little over a winter or so. I mean, there was a group of builders who 'built' it, but the orphans handled the labor."

As if to show proof, he lifted up his shirt and showed Ashyn a long pink scar that ran from his right collarbone down to just under his right pectoral. "Sliced meself open on the edge of one of the sharp bricks for the spire when I fell off the roof two winters past," he whispered. "Hurt like a dickens but Avrimae took care o' me. First time I really talked ta her," he finished, beginning once again to fantasize about the girl.

"Children built this place?" Ashyn asked, appalled.

Macky looked at him confused. "Of course," he answered. "We have to pay the Enclave back somehow. Often it's labor."

"But . . . but . . . you could have been killed!" he whispered sharply.

Macky shrugged, "Sure, few of us were actually, but what are we to do, huh? We're orphans. Without the Enclave we would have no place to sleep, no food to eat, we would starve. Where could we go, huh? What could a bunch of war-torn children do in this land? They feed us, cloth us, give us water to bathe, and in return we provide them cheap labor."

"Wait, what?"

Macky nodded. "Yup. Good deal for us kids iffin' you ask me. It's worked for me and a bunch of the others, too. It even saved ye life!"

Ashyn thought about it suddenly. "So wait. Did the merchants that dropped me off get any money for what they did?"

"Sure," Macky answered. "The Enclave calls it a charity reward for saving another child's life from the hardships of this civil war. Tis usually the same nice merchants that come in all the time with us kids. Priests have a nickname for 'em, too. Heard it once when they dinna think I was listenin'. Call 'em 'Charity Hounds'."

Macky smiled dumbly, "Now in return for the 'Charity Hounds' saving us, we work towards that charity fee that was paid by the church."

Ashyn stared at Macky wide-eyed. "Wait a minute, are ye saying I can't leave?"

Macky shook his head, "Not until ye pay off the debt for what the Enclave has determined it cost to save ye life."

"Has anyone?" Ashyn asked.

"Nope. Not to my knowledge," he answered. "Uriel and meself are some of the older ones, we's be probably be getting closest I reckon."

"But you don't know?"

"Nope."

"Has anyone ever tried running away, or refused to work?" Ashyn asked.

"Sure," Macky gloated, "Happens all the time. But the clergy knows what's best. Dey jus' rounds 'em up and gives 'em their *penance*. Normally tis just a few lashes from a whip. Keeps the rowdy ones and the slackers in check. Speaking of which, Ash, we need to be careful when we eye this wizard so they dunna see us as well. Never had *penance* an' ain't fer wantin' it now."

As the gravity of what had he had become began to sink in, Ashyn stared at his friend Macky in shock. The older boy didn't have a clue he realized. He had no idea . . .

"There's a word for us, Macky," Ashyn hissed. "It's 'slaves'."

THE CATHEDRAL

Ashyn watched Macky merely shrug at Ashyn's revelation. "Whatever you say, Ash," He replied. "I'm not fer wantin' ta argue an' be seen. We'll talk 'bout it later, after we've gotten a gander of this wizard ye want so bad."

Good enough, Ashyn realized. It was shocking to learn that he had been sold into slavery, when this whole time he had just started enjoying his life. But Macky was right. He did come here for a purpose. He had to know if that man really was Xexial Bontain.

The foundation of the cathedral, where they now stood, was raised from the ground it sat upon. When the cathedral was designed, it was created so that it sat completely within the foundation. By creating a structure that was smaller than the foundation it resided upon, it gave it a sort of lip that they could stand on. In response to this visible mar, the builders used tall hedges to hide it, and so it went unnoticed. Something only the constructors knew about, to make use for any maintenance that would be required in the future winters.

Macky knew it was there, however, and they used it now to shimmy along between the wall and the hedges. Luckily, the hedges were tall enough that should someone walk by, the two of them could duck down and not be seen.

They scooted along the wall until they came to a slight depression. Ashyn noticed that each small dip in the surface led to a window above them. Ashyn thought it was good enough, but Macky shook his head. So Ashyn continued around the rounded lip until they came to a third depression. Macky tapped him on the shoulder and pointed up.

"This one'll have a good view of the entire chamber," Macky told him.

Ashyn looked up. High above his reach, still some five feet above Ashyn's head, was the long arched window. It was meant solely for light to illuminate the interior, not for people outside to look in. Exactly something Ashyn wanted to do.

"How are we gonna see him?" Ashyn asked.

"Ye gonna stand on me shoulders, watcha think ye was gonna do?" Macky answered.

"Ye dunna wanna look to?" Ashyn replied.

"Nah, seen 'im afore. I'm good," he said with a crooked smile.

"And if someone walks by?" Ashyn questioned.

"Then ye gets a nice bruise cuz I'm gonna drop ye," Macky answered plainly. "Unless ye have a better plan."

Ashyn put his fists on his hips, "I'm eight winters, how good of a plan ye think I canna come up with?"

Macky shrugged, "Well then get up on me shoulders, ye lout."

Seeing no other alternative, Ashyn put his moccasin in Macky's cupped hands and bounded up on to the older boy's shoulders. He grabbed onto the stone sill as best he could and attempted to balance on the teen's narrow shoulders. Macky wobbled under Ashyn's weight.

"Quit moving," Ashyn hissed.

"Canna helps it," Macky added. "Dunna have good footing, an yer heavy fer a kid."

Ashyn rolled his eyes at Macky and braced himself against the sill. After a moment, Macky stopped wobbling. Ashyn began looking around inside the cathedral.

Much to the tan-skinned boy's surprise the interior of the cathedral was not as ornate as he would have imagined. Semi-circular pews aligned the western and eastern walls leaving clear paths from the north and south. In the center of the cathedral, underneath the tallest spire, was a round white marble alter. Carved directly upon the altar's top was the *circumpunct*. Ashyn realized the cathedral was designed as such so that everyone could see the priest, no matter what he was doing, at any time.

He looked to the north wall, the only truly decorated face of the cathedral. The wall was curved inward giving the room the appearance that what he saw was the entire complex. Large crème velvet runners ran from the length of the domed ceiling to the floor. They totaled five in all, and each one was decorated with the embroidery of one of the corresponding spires from atop the cathedral. The center runner was of course the largest, and it adorned the circular spire. At the tip of the spire again was another symbol of the *circumpunct*. Beneath the spire however, was something quite different.

The only true piece of artwork within the entire visible chamber, and sitting directly in front of the large runner, against the center of that wall was a statue of Jasia. Aside from the Maker himself, she was the cornerstone of the Jasian faith.

The statue was carved as a beautiful human woman, but bearing similar features to every devoted race. She had the high cheekbones, almond eyes, and slightly pointed ears of an Elf. Long flowing hair, tied into two individual thick woven braids, fell over her shoulders reaching just below her midriff. It was a staple style of the Dwarven people. She also had about a dozen or so more noticeable traits that could tie to other races, but these were the iconic three followers. Her height and physical stature were just neutral enough that should could resemble a taller lithe Dwarf, or a slightly buxom Elven woman. To accent this she wore only a simple full-length garment, but it was cinched tightly around her waist to reveal her womanly figure.

Jasia's hands were clasped together in reverence, for her father above. In her left hand, she bore a string of pearls, each engraved with a different leaf, identifying all the Elven races that followed her. On her right hand, she bore two heavy rings, one bearing a hammer, the other an anvil. This signified her attunement to the forge, a mainstay of the sturdy mountain folk.

The representation of her hands clasped together, in prayer was symbolic of humanity everywhere. Long had humans put their hands together to pray, no matter the god, and for as long as humanity could remember. Even back unto the Fifth Era of Men; the Forgotten Era.

Jasia was the mortal daughter of the Maker, the one he had chosen to show the world that Creation is the will of one god, the Maker, not the many. It was a hard road, discounting multiple civilizations' ingrained beliefs in so many different deities. She had picked up followers, disciples, who believed in her teachings, and had even performed feats that bordered on the miraculous, even in such magical times. In the end though, she was a martyr, sacrificing herself for her beliefs. That sacrifice solidified the true birth of her religion, ultimately turning her fledgling belief into one of the most influential empires on all of Kuldarr.

Other deities remained, some even still prominent, but nothing with the all-encompassing grandeur of the Jasian Enclave. Its reach was everywhere, even in the smallest pocket villages like Bremingham.

Something about the velvet runners caught his eye. As Ashyn studied them, he noticed that they swayed ever so slightly, as if they had caught a breeze. Ashyn glanced around the room, to see if any of the windows were somehow opened, or if the building had any visible ventilation. He could see none. Then he realized why.

"This isn't the only room," he whispered down at Macky.

"Nah," the boy returned, "Looks like it, but behind the runners' is a slanted hall that leads to another chamber. It's used before sermons and to hold private councils."

"I don't see the wizard," Ashyn told Macky. "He must be in those chambers."

Ashyn leaned back, gripping the ledge tightly. He couldn't see any other windows as the cathedral slanted around. "Is there any way to see inside?"

"Didn't I jus' say 'private council'?" Macky quipped. "Course there's no way ta see inside. If he's not in there we should go back ta our duties. Someone's bound ta notice we've been gone by now."

"Just another minute Macky, I wanna wait and see if someone comes out."

"Fine," Macky retorted. "Ye gots a minute, I'm countin'."

Ashyn shook his head and chuckled. Macky couldn't even read, let alone count.

It wasn't even another two minutes, before Ashyn realized that he had begun to hear mumbling. Quickly he put his ear up against the window and struggled to hear what was being said. The pane of glass was ice cold against his bare flesh. Its chill was distracting. He pushed harder, trying to focus.

". . . telling you . . . cause . . . survive . . . odds," he heard one voice say.

". . . Know it . . . has to be . . . ground," he heard a deeper one retort.

"What's they sayin'?" Macky whispered from below Ashyn.

"Shh!" Ashyn snapped back, as he pressed harder against the window.

Macky continued to shift under Ashyn's weight, disrupting his concentration. Soon the voices were all but indistinguishable, as Ashyn spent more time concentrating on balancing and less on the conversation.

Frustrated, Ashyn looked down at the shifting teen holding him aloft. "Dammit Macky I can't hear a thing with ye moving all around like ye got a squirrel in yer knickers!" he snapped.

"Me legs are getting tired, Ash," he said. Then, understanding Ashyn's comment, sputtered, "Wait a minute! I dunna wear knickers. I'm a boy!"

"Hence the insult," Ashyn shot back.

He wanted to laugh aloud at the perplexed look on Macky's face as he struggled to understand what a boy half his age had meant.

Suddenly Ashyn noticed movement out of the corner of his eyes. He looked quickly into the cathedral chamber just as the hooded figure entered through the velvet drape. His face was obscured in shadows of his low hanging hood, but Ashyn immediately noticed the man had a thick brown beard, laced with blonde and a little grey.

Before disappointment could even fully set in, Ashyn realized that the hooded figure in the secreted hallway was staring right at him.

~ ~ ~

"Oh crap!" Ashyn said, lunging away from the window.

"Wait! Ash! No!" Macky yelled, losing balance from Ashyn's sudden movement. He pitched forward, struggling against inertia, and toppled into the hedges.

Ashyn had no time to yell in surprise as he was violently thrust backwards. Expecting to crash into the hedges he stared in shock as they sailed by below him as he kept flying through the air.

Ashyn, who had been unfortunate to be higher up than Macky, now found himself airborne, well over the protective hedges, and the only reprieve would be when he impacted with the grassy turf now so seemingly far below.

He attempted to turn over, knowing that if he landed directly on his back it would likely drive all the air from his lungs if he were lucky, hurt him severely if he was not. He managed to turn half away as the ground came rushing up upon him.

Ashyn crashed hard onto the ground, shoulder first. He tried to roll through the impact as best he could to diffuse as much damage as possible, but found that he still took the brunt of it in his shoulder. He grunted in pain, gripping his injured shoulder with his free hand. Ashyn wasted no time dwelling on the pain, though. He had been seen. He quickly steadied his resolve and struggled to his feet.

Fire laced through his nerves, shooting up his neck and down past his elbow into his fingers. He gritted his teeth and willed the sting away. He could hurt later. He had begun growing accustomed to pain since Bremingham had burned.

Stars swam before his eyes. He shook his head violently trying to shake away the dancing objects. They needed to leave. Now!

Macky staggered to his feet and toppled over the trimmed bushes, landing on his backside with an "OOF!" When he got to his feet he looked down at Ashyn. "What was that all about?"

"Wizard spotted me," the red headed boy answered. "We need to go! Fast!"

They both ran as fast as they could, Macky taking the lead as they bounded through the grass towards the copse of maples where they had been raking leaves. What had he been thinking? Of course, it wasn't Xexial! Xexial had died in the Shalis-Fey against those creatures. There was absolutely no way he could have survived that tree falling down on top of him. The only reason Ashyn survived was because Xexial hurled him at the last minute to safety.

Still the garb had been so similar, so identical. Perhaps it was the standard dress of all wizards? Maybe those gloves that he saw Xexial wear, all wizards had? He didn't know. He had never seen, or even known of a wizard before Xexial had saved him.

He only hoped his actions wouldn't get Macky in trouble. The teen had gotten away for many winters without *penance*; he didn't want to be the cause for it the first time now. The guilt of Macky being whipped because of him would be unbearable.

They rounded the front of the cathedral entrance. His feet felt the hard surface of the cobbles beneath them. Just a few more feet he reasoned, a few more steps and he could grab his rake and plead ignorance. Just act as if he did not know what they were talking about. He knew Macky would play along. He had seen Macky and Uriel do it together a dozen times. Everything would be fine. He only had to make it a dozen or so feet. They were going to make it!

A heavy hand closed down around his shoulder.

THE PENITENT

A shyn's stride came to a dead halt as the steel grip ripped him backwards on his already throbbing shoulder. He yelped in pain, causing Macky to stop and turn to look. His eyes went wide, and Ashyn could see he was unsure what to do.

"Run!" Ashyn yelled to his friend.

Macky backpedalled a few more steps, with uncertainty written all over his face. Ashyn shook his head no, and Macky bit his lower lip in frustration. Finally, he turned and sprinted away. He was safe, Ashyn reasoned to himself. He wouldn't suffer the wrath of *penance*.

Ashyn was flung around violently, and forced to stare deep into the shadowed hood of the wizard. Heavy hooded azure eyes stared down at him. He felt the man's strong grip slacken, and then let go altogether as the man staggered a step backwards.

"It can't be," his deep voice rumbled.

The bishop stumbled out the great doors behind the wizard. Overweight and wheezing terribly, he shouted towards Ashyn with a deep crimson face, "Boy! Boy! When I get my hands on you there's gonna be a *penance* like no tomorrow! How dare you spy into the house of the Maker!"

The hooded figure just stared down at him, and Ashyn looked back at him. He couldn't see anything but a beard and shadows, and those deep azure eyes, but he knew those eyes . . .

The bishop waddled up next to them both, holding a switch. "You!" the fat man barked, "Of all the children, I figured you to be beyond such vagrancy!" He raised the switch, readying himself to strike the child.

The wizard, however, raised his hand to stop the bishop. The obese holy man stared at the wizard in confusion. The shrouded figure reached up with his blue luminescent gloves and pulled back his hooded.

Impossibly, Ashyn was staring into the eyes of Xexial Bontain.

"Ashyn?" he whispered.

"Xexial?" Ashyn stammered back, wide-eyed.

A big smile took the wizard's bearded face, and Ashyn knew it was true. Xexial was alive.

With tears in his eyes, Ashyn lunged at Xexial, grabbing the man's thigh in a great hug. "You're alive! You're alive!" he cheered repeatedly, hugging the man.

Gently the wizard pried him off and knelt down in front of him. "I am," he told the boy. "I thought I had lost you. I thought I had failed." He then took Ashyn in a great hug.

It was the best feeling Ashyn had in a long time. Then the man leaned back. "How long have you been here?"

"Couple months," Ashyn answered. Then he questioned, "If you've been alive all this time, why dinna ye come for me?"

Xexial stood, pain evident in his eyes. "Ashyn, I did. I searched far and wide for you for weeks, constantly entering the Shalis-Fey again in the daylight when I was able. Tracing and retracing my steps, trying to memorize that maze. Then I came across the empty blackened field at the edge of the woods. Somehow I knew it had to have been you."

Suddenly his countence turned dark as he turned to the bishop, "That was two months ago," he said starkly. "I asked you if you had found any boys from the woods, or from Bremingham. You had told me you didn't."

Terror was evident in the portly bishop's pink face. "He's not from Bremingham. He said he was from Gurgen! Bless the Maker the boy is literate! Who would be literate in that backwater village?"

"Gurgen?" he said, and looked down at Ashyn. The boy shrugged sheepishly.

"I figured they woulda been frightened of me, if they knew I came through the Shalis-Fey. Would have been questions, too many questions." What Ashyn wanted to say was; *I would have been a freak.*

A big smile took Xexial's face. "Clever boy."

"You mean this boy lied? He's not from Gurgen?" he said as he looked angrily towards Ashyn.

"I believe he did as he thought best to survive," Xexial countered, "Just as you would have done as a child, or even I."

Pride swelled through Ashyn, not just at seeing Xexial alive, but hearing the man defend him as well. It did not seem to deter the bishop in the least.

"He lied to a man of the cloth, representing the image of the Maker. He lied to the house of the Maker," he said sternly.

Xexial shrugged.

Before anyone could dispute the fact further, Macky appeared next to them, held sternly by two of the priests. "Found this one running from the cathedral," one of the priests told the bishop. "Figured he was part of the commotion."

Macky stared in horror from the bishop to the now unhooded wizard.

The bishop seemed to regain some steam in the presence of his two subordinates. "Yes, yes," he told them, before looking to Xexial, "Regardless if this *was* your boy or not, he's *our* boy *now*, and he still has violated *our* rules. As such, he will need to suffer *penance* for his actions."

Ashyn recoiled.

Xexial glowered. "I respect the Enclave, Bishop, and I will forgive the miscommunication due to Ashyn's assertions that he came from Gurgen, and not Bremingham, since all is well now that we have been reunited, even briefly," he held up an illuminating sapphire finger. "But I strongly warrant against you punishing this child."

The look in his eyes alone caused the bishop's pink face to pale.

"You wouldn't dare oppose the Enclave over a boy!"

Xexial didn't answer, but his continued stare was enough to deter the bishop.

"Fine!" the holy man barked. He then redirected is ire to Macky, "But you have no say over this boy!" he said with a vicious smile.

Macky paled significantly.

"Mactonal Turgenssen, you have directly violated your duties, showing negligence in your ability to perform said prescribed functions. Since this is your first offense you will be issued *penance* in the amount of one lash."

Macky flinched.

The bishop looked directly at Ashyn. "But, for acting as an accomplice to one attempting to spy on the interiors of this holy ground I must also issue another two lashes."

Tears welled in the boy's eyes.

"And since it now must be determined," he said, referring to Ashyn, "whether or not this boy is to remain under the guardianship of the enclave, I must then declare that all his said transgressions will be transferred to you as well. An additional three lashes," the Bishop declared proudly.

Macky was visibly shaking, and crying now.

Six lashes! Ashyn couldn't believe this was happening. Macky was going to receive six lashes because Ashyn convinced him to spy on Xexial. It wasn't fair!

"That being said, I believe everything is now in order. *Penance* shall be issued immediately," the Bishop declared.

Both priests holding Macky nodded and started to turn with him.

"Wait," the Bishop said calmly. "I almost forgot." He looked directly into Ashyn's eyes. "Lying. Lying is one of the worst sins any person can ever do. It raises fictitious claims that could be detrimental in the determination of anything from one's health to another's livelihood. Lying is iniquitous and absolutely not tolerated within the Jasian Enclave, under no conditions, even self-preservation.

"Jasia knew this. She could have saved herself from persecution and eventual death if she had just lied, if she had just denied her faith, denounced the Maker as the one true god, and embraced the pagan deities of old she would have been spared from her own execution. She only needed to lie . . .

"She chose not to. She chose to stand firm, and ultimately give her own life instead of be swayed into speaking with lies, with the Defiler's twisted tongue. That was her sacrifice for us, and a sacrifice that we, too should make willingly every time."

"Even a young child?" Xexial interjected.

The Bishop shot him a glare, "Absolutely. For if not when they are young, then when is the right time? Do we not learn our moral ethics in childhood? Is that not where our roots are put to ground?"

He looked back to Macky, "So for lying that is an addition of two lashes, which I believe to be a total of eight. Let each strike be a lesson to you of the importance of rules. Let each rending of your flesh teach you that while the Maker is merciful, he will also cast his wrath down on those that are wicked. This is your *penance*, let your blood absolve you of your sins, child. Take him away."

Ashyn looked at Macky. He was so pale Ashyn was sure he would pass out. Eight lashes! He was sure that would break the skin. He could already see the bright red lines that would run across Macky's narrow, pale back. Ashyn knew this was meant for him. This was the Bishop's way of attacking Ashyn without actually laying a hand on him. Guilt. Hate.

Macky would despise him after this. Hate him. He would once again become an object of scrutiny. He would be an outcast once more, all because the Bishop was being spiteful. It wasn't fair!

Macky's head was hung low, his feet refused to function as they pulled him away. Ashyn watched it all in anger. He felt the fires of hatred flare within him towards the injustice of it all, towards the one who warranted such an action.

He balled his fists, his anger brought heat to them. His vision began to redden. He could imagine it. So simple, so easy. Fire. It was reaching for him, calling . . . He only needed to reach out and touch it. To grab it and it would be his to wield. A righteous purge on the one Ashyn felt was truly wicked.

A calming hand touched his shoulder. "Ashyn, no," the deep voice whispered.

He felt a squeeze of reassurance. It seemed so distant, so far away. And yet Ashyn knew that Xexial felt his anger. Felt his frustration. Knew that somewhere deep down this was wrong.

The fires in his eyes died away, but not the anger of the injustice. He wanted what was right more than he wanted to inflict pain. Wrath wasn't always the path to justice, Ashyn realized. Sometimes it lay in absolution. He had caused this. It was his fault Macky was to suffer, no one else's.

Gently he broke contact from Xexial. There was a momentary hesitation from Xexial, but then he felt the callused hand slip away. He would do this on his own terms.

"Punish me," he said boldly to the Bishop.

Surprised, the two priests stopped and turned to look at the young child.

"Excuse me?" the Bishop asked, confounded.

"I said punish me," he declared more forcefully. "Macky is innocent, I forced him to help me."

The Bishop laughed, mocking him. "You forced a boy twice your age and size to help you?"

"Yes," Ashyn said bluntly.

The Bishop seemed to think on it a moment, and then looked back at Macky. "No. The *penance* stands. Eight lashes for Mactonal."

He waved the priests away, but Ashyn wouldn't relent, the justicar within him would not allow it. "Then ye are a hypocrite"

The fat man wheeled on him. "How dare you!" the Bishop said angrily. "Ungrateful little wretch! After all *this* Enclave has done for you! We nursed you from a near-dead husk back to perfect health and this is how you treat us!"

"How dare ye!" Ashyn yelled back at him. "I admit to ye blame, but ye fail to address it. I tell ye that I should be punished, but ye deny it. Ye just preached to me about sacrifice, and about how everyone in the Enclave should be willing to do it. Well here I am!" he roared at the Bishop. "I am willing to sacrifice! Give me *penance,* not Macky. Let my blood absolve me of my sins, not his!"

The Bishop didn't know how to answer. He opened and closed his mouth several times trying to formulate a response. He looked to the wizard as if to ask what to do. Ashyn wouldn't give him the opportunity, wouldn't lose his momentum.

"Don't look at him!" he shouted at the Bishop, "Look at me! I am the vagrant! I am the liar! Punish me!"

To further get his point across, Ashyn violently ripped his tunic off over his head, exposing his bare olive skin to the chill autumn air. "I demand *penance* in place of Macky! Punish me!"

Ashyn realized his yelling had drawn a crowd of passersby. He could see that the two priests had stopped with Macky, and Macky was now looking at him with wonderment. He didn't want Macky's awe, he wanted his friendship.

Ashyn turned and cast his penetrating grey eyes into the Bishop's own dull brown.

The Bishop couldn't stand looking into that fierce gaze. It was unnerving coming from a child. He broke eye contact first, backing down.

"So be it, boy." he said quietly, "*Penance* shall be yours. Maker have mercy on your soul."

FORLORN

Brodea looked at the crystal in her hands. Ice-cold radiance poured through her lithe, flawless copper fingertips. She never could get used to the cold. It always felt evil. Yet she knew it was a weapon, a weapon that would one day be used again.

She set it on the small carved-oak table next to her. Like her, the end table was naked, its pure form open for all to see. Wild Elves did not dye or stain their wooden creations. They left them pure.

Brodea lounged against her bedding and idly traced the painted markings on her belly. She still bore the family line of Ambit against her skin. She had worn it so long, she barely even remembered her own. She looked to Vooken lying soundlessly next to her, equally naked, his chest rising and falling faintly as he slumbered.

She did not love him, not as she had loved Ambit, her life mate; however, she trusted him. Trusted him with everything they endeavored to do. He had been one of Ambit's closest friends, and he had never betrayed that trust with any sort of feelings for her, even after his death, not until yesterday.

It wasn't courting, per se. Not like Elumin, or the countless dozens of others that tried to win her affections. It had just happened. They were discussing the crystal, its application, and the recent advancements the druids had made with the tome that Brodea had salvaged from the temple those winters before.

It was a momentous moment, Brodea recalled with a smile. The druids had deciphered the components and somatic gestures for the first spell of Destruction. If they could understand it, then they could find a way to end it. Brodea knew that the Council would be the first to combat the art of Destruction directly since the Forgotten Era. If they were successful, wizards would be a dying breed.

It all hinged around some ancient race called the Craetora. If they could learn more about these Craetorians, then they could bring about the end of the greatest Unbalancers of their era.

In response, Vooken had brought plum wine and honeyed cakes to celebrate their small victory over the skewers. There was laughing and merriment over this milestone, and the next thing she knew their clothes were flying off them and she was welcoming being skewered by Vooken.

It had been short, and the experience was light and hazy from too much wine, but it had been sweet. Perhaps it wasn't so much what her emotions had wanted, but what her body needed. She was a woman after all. Did she not have needs too, even though she was a widow?

Would Vooken expect more from her now, though? Would this change things between them? She needed him for what was ahead, of that there could be no doubt. However, if she wanted to end this dalliance, would he object? Did she want to end it?

She studied the markings against his flesh. *Moonspear.* It was a prestigious family line, one that had borne many Councilors, a First Councilor, and even a Voïre dui Ceremeia once.

She looked at her late husband's markings. *Windsong.* Less prestigious, but with hopes no less lofty. It too had a Voïre dui Ceremeia in its ranks, the most recent in fact.

She admired the swirling intricacies of the lines that were drawn across her slender frame. She liked them, how they suited her curves, the shape of her breasts. It felt like her body was meant for these markings, and no one else's.

She hoped Vooken could, would, understand that. He had had a wife once too, but she had perished over a hundred winters ago during a bad plague. Maybe Vooken needed this as well, Brodea thought. Maybe his body had just needed this, too. Someone he could trust.

She thought about it for some time, until she realized the sun was growing full. Rising from her doeskin bedding she quickly donned her Councilor's garb, the leather buckled strapping that covered her breasts, and her leather skirt. The druids reported that Whisper's branches would be returning today, and she was eager to see this Nuchada for herself, and if not alive, then at least hear of his demise. They had been gone far too long as it was. Two months! In Brodea's prime, she had been able to cross the Shalis-Fey in four days. That was centuries ago, though. How the generations change, she mused.

As Brodea stepped out into the antechamber of her Councilors quarters she was momentarily startled to see that Whisper was already back. Both she and Shedalia were lying upon a small wolfskin settee together, in a spoon like position. She could see by the track lines of dew and pine on the women that they had arrived not long before and had yet to receive a proper bath. She also saw that Shedalia bore a deep pink laceration across her left cheek, which would doubtless leave a scar in its wake.

She ignored the scene before her for the moment as she strode across the chamber to grab one of the few remaining honey cakes from the evening before. Brodea looked about the room as the morning light cast faint rays through the green canopy of trees overhead. It lighted her round antechamber with small pockets of golden light. At least the setting is serene, she thought for a moment.

Brodea would have thought that Whisper would have reported to her the moment she returned, would have demanded it in fact. She wondered if the duo on the couch before her had spied Vooken and herself in coitus and thought not to interrupt. Brodea sincerely hoped not.

So, biting delicately into a honeyed cake, she sat on a chaise across from the two soundlessly sleeping. She studied them both. Her daughter was a spitting image of her when she had been only a hundred and twelve winters old. Shoulder length raven hair, obsidian eyes, and sharp exotic features. Since age barely showed on the Hym, they still looked much alike, yet Brodea was a little fuller in places now, and her features bore more wisdom with age.

Shedalia, however, looked nothing like her mother had. The Elven woman was thick with hard muscle and bore small breasts. Her dirty brown hair was chin length, and her features seemed flat, though Brodea thought that perhaps she was comely in her own unique way. She could see how Whisper might be attracted to the woman.

Judging from the swollen pockets under both their eyes, they had travelled sleeplessly for days. As a mother, she would have wanted her daughter to sleep. As a Councilor though, she needed a report.

Brodea coughed loudly, and instantly the two opened their eyes. Alert, she thought. Good. They still make fine huntresses, even exhausted.

"Councilor," Shedalia said with a bow of her head. Brodea watched as she cast a wary eye to Whisper at being caught canoodling.

Brodea smiled lightly. "Before we begin the report, I would like to know how many brothers and sisters we lost both to the Shalis-Fey and the Unbalancer." *And to your hands, daughter,* she added, but didn't say aloud.

"Four to the Unbalancer, two to the Shalis-Fey, Councilor," Whísper said.

"Just two?" Brodea said surprised.

Whísper nodded, "My branches are strong, Councilor, and fiercely loyal to Windsong."

Brodea nodded proudly. "That is good. You make a fine Branch Commander then, Whísper, and to keep such loyalty your second must be equally as loyal."

"To the end," Shedalia whispered, looking into her daughter's eyes. It brought a slight discomfort to Brodea, to see such an amorous gesture. Lust was one thing, love was quite another.

Brodea withheld her scowl for the time being. "So where is this Nuchada? Our Voïre dui Ceremeia cannot seem to stop rambling about his eyes."

Brodea saw the two of them glance at each other before Whísper's dark eyes turned to stare into her own shards of onyx. "We were unable to capture the Nuchada," Whísper said bluntly.

"I see," Brodea said, slightly disappointed. "Then he is dead?"

She watched as Whísper looked to the ground in shame. "He should be, yes."

Brodea's dark eyes grew sinister. "I think 'should be' requires a good explanation."

And so they did explain. Whísper went into detail on how they did exactly as they were told. Giving the wizard no respite, no chance to break, and forcing him to what they thought was a dead end. But it hadn't been. The wizard had continued, foolishly so, into the Maze. They had tried to kill the Nuchada then, before entering of course, but the wizard had used deceitful magics to protect the boy. Either way, they entered the Maze, and Whísper explained to her that they had spent the last two months sweeping the outskirts of the Maze on every side looking for the duo.

They even went as far as the highlands, where they found the wizard limping heavily, alone and injured. But no sign of the boy. The Nuchada had completely disappeared.

"So the wizard survived the trials of the Maze," Brodea said almost to herself. "That is interesting."

"He was grievously wounded though, Councilor," Shedalia expressed. "He would have made for an easy balancing, but we followed your orders and left him be."

Brodea nodded. "As it should be," she instructed. "Even a wounded wizard is a deadly one."

Brodea was not upset, though. This was good news. Though Whísper did not actually kill the Nuchada, there was no way the boy could have survived the Maze, even with the wizard. There would be no way the Unbalancer could protect the boy *and* himself. Seeing as how the wizard escaped the Maze, it was obvious he hadn't been successful in saving the boy at all. Frankly, she would be surprised if the wizard had even tried.

"There is one more thing, Councilor," Whísper said. "We ended the search when we, too, saw the skewer of balance returning to search for the boy. That is when we knew he was lost to the maze."

A smile took Brodea's face then. "Excellent. If the vile Unbalancer couldn't keep hold of the boy in the Maze, then the Nuchada is truly lost. You may not have killed the Nuchada with spear or javelin, but you have killed him nonetheless."

Whísper and Shedalia both smiled when they realized Brodea was not upset with them. Brodea stood up. "This concludes the report then," she informed them. "Good work."

She watched as the two stood up together, sharing a look that Brodea did not like. While she did not want to punish her daughter after doing good work, she couldn't deny what was happening between the two young Elves before her.

"One last thing," she said.

The two young Elves turned to the Councilor. "This tryst between the two of you, I do not condone it."

Shedalia looked frightened, but Brodea was surprised to see that Whísper was not scared or frightened, but defiant and angry. So much like me, Brodea thought.

"I will not stop it," Brodea continued, "But know that if you continue what you are doing, it will have to be hidden and it will end up hurting each of you more."

The look in her daughter's eyes changed from anger then to questioning. Brodea continued. "Though we may be in a lapse now, we Ferhym are always at battle, for the war for balance is never ending. As such, we must try diligently to reproduce.

"Though we live longer than most of the other races, nature curtails this with a more limited chance to bear the fruits of birth.

Most females can only have one child, rarely more. Therefore, it is important that each female continue the cycle.

"Do you understand what I am telling you?"

"Mother . . .," Whisper said quietly.

Brodea held up her hand, stalling her daughter's retort. "You will have to life mate to men, both of you. And you will have to be intimate with men in the hopes of bearing children. Now you can choose these men yourselves, through courting, or I, as Councilor, can choose them for you. I will let you decide."

Brodea was surprised to see tears gather in Shedalia's eyes. She felt bad for the young lovers, but the Ferhym needed to be strong. Especially Windsong blood. "You are both the ripest right now; you will never ever be able to bear a child as easily as you can in these next twenty winters. What you do together in secrecy is not for me to control, but know, the two of you, right this moment, that you will have to be shared by another. Men will warm your beds at home, not each other. Choose, or have one chosen for you. That is my decree."

With that, Brodea left them both in the antechamber. She hated what she had done to her daughter, but she believed in the cause. And right now the cause needed Ferhym, not queers.

SHEPHERD

A s Ashyn lay on his stomach on a cot in the hospice, he truly understood the concept of pain. Every racing red gash across his back burned like a blazing sun, and even Avrimae's gentle touch with the poultice could not dilute his feelings of misery in the least. He had thought he could take the pain, he thought he could be tougher. But in the end, he had thought wrong.

The crack of the whip still echoed like thunder in his head. Each snap had brought with it another fear, and Ashyn had realized that was the device's greatest weapon. Not the sting, but the anticipation of the pain.

He had been so bold, strolling up to the post and placing his hands there to be tethered. He had at first denied the bit in his mouth until Xexial had quietly whispered that he would need it. He listened to the wizard, and now in hindsight was grateful for it.

For a child, Ashyn feared little, but the first sound of that cracking whip so close, so loud, had sent tremors of terror through his body. A second and then a third succeeded the first. Each time lances of wind would race across his neck, hair, or back, his muscles would tighten in anticipation of the blow that wouldn't come. The job of the whip was just as much psychological as it was physical, both stressing his body and fatiguing him early on with its use of dread. It was a tool. A simple, elegant, and effective tool.

By the time the first strike ripped itself across the tense, soft skin of his back, the terror had already gripped him so profoundly that he couldn't steel himself against the pain and cried out just as everyone else had before him. The whip offered no solace either, no time to regroup, once it had pounced on his will it continued to strike. This in turn caused him to wail more and more.

His *penance* had indeed done its job.

He whimpered once more as Avrimae's patted one of his long lacerations with a damp sponge, attempting to work out more of the fibers that were left behind from the cured leather whip.

He knew that whatever she couldn't pull out with the moisture would have to be done with a wire brush. He was dreading every moment that was to come.

Ashyn heard the door open behind him, and he felt a chill wind race across the open wounds on his back. For a moment it felt delicious, but then the pain set in once again. He made no effort to look to see who it was. It didn't matter. He didn't care at this point. Suddenly a lanky body came into view. Slowly the boy lowered himself so his face was level with Ashyn's.

"Hey, whiz," Macky said quietly.

"Hey," Ashyn grunted back. He could see the sadness written all over Macky's face.

"Listen, Ash," the teen began.

"Don't worry about it," Ashyn quickly interrupted.

Macky seemed unsure. "It's just, I'm older, and . . ."

"I said don't worry about it, Macky," Ashyn reinforced. "This was my decision."

After a moment Macky nodded and looked to the floor. "Sure whiz, whatever ye say." Macky reached up and took the little boy's hand. Ashyn appreciated the feel of Macky's skinny callused fingers gripping his own. It reminded him of something his sister used to do when he was sick or injured. They sat in silence together for a long time, just drinking in each other's company. It was nice to have a friend like Macky, and the pain seemed to ebb slightly because of it. Finally, after an interminable amount of time, the door opened again. Not feeling so weary, Ashyn risked a glance back. He could see the unmistakable outline of a wizard's robes in the doorway.

Macky quickly stood up, breaking his grip from Ashyn. "I'll never forget what ye did for me, Ash," he whispered. "For the rest of my life, I'll never forget. I swear it." With that, he touched Ashyn gently on the shoulder and began to walk away. He turned only once more, "Hey Ash."

Ashyn looked up curiously.

"Ye said I wear knickers. I just got it. Ye called me a girl. Priceless," he said with a cheesy crooked grin. With that, he turned and bounded past the wizard and for the door.

Ashyn could only smile, momentarily forgetting the pain.

As Ashyn heard the door close behind Macky, he suddenly felt a heavier hand on his back with the sponge. It was not delicate, but rougher. He heard the door close again, and he realized that for the first time since their reunion, Ashyn and Xexial were alone.

The wizard continued to work the damp sponge across the deep red lacerations across Ashyn's back. "That was a brave thing you did, lad." Xexial said in a soft, deep voice behind him.

"Well I don't feel brave," Ashyn replied.

"I wasn't finished," Xexial said sternly. "Brave yes, but also stupid, foolhardy, and ultimately futile."

Ashyn wasn't prepared to be berated by the wizard, and glanced back in shock. "Ye expected me to let Macky take my punishment?"

"Yes," Xexial answered matter-of-factly.

"Friend of yours though he may be, Ashyn. This Macky is ultimately nothing more than a peon. He lacks intelligence, commitment, and ultimately the drive for the endeavors that life will inevitably bring him. What you have spared him today, will no doubt happen again in the future. It may not be tomorrow, or the next day, but it will come. By taking away this life's lesson, you have perhaps doomed him to a greater suffering in the future."

"But it was my fault!" Ashyn protested. "I made him help me!"

"Did you?" Xexial countered. "Even the Bishop said it. The boy is twice your age. Should he not be able to make his own decisions? Stand his ground to a little child such as yourself?"

Ashyn thought about it. Macky had put up a little resistance, but not much.

"Even if you did force him, what does that say about Macky? That he is so weak-willed he'll bend to the desires of a little boy?"

"But he is my friend . . ."

"There are two types of people in this world Ashyn, shepherds and sheep. You have shown yourself to be the former, while Macky has proven to be the latter. Sheep will always gather, and will always need a shepherd to guide them. Shepherds, however, can function without a flock," Xexial counseled.

"Because of this, Ashyn, you now have ultimately suffered more. These wounds on your back are merely superficial, they will heal. But because of what you have done, you have stirred something amongst the orphans. They will flock to you now, pulling themselves from the Bishop."

Ashyn sighed and placed his chin against the cot. "Perhaps they need to," he replied, "We're nothing but slaves here anyhow."

Xexial dragged the sponge across Ashyn's back, pulling loose numerous leather fibers that Avrimae had been unable to brooch. Ashyn hissed in pain. "I could see where someone as intelligent as you may rationalize that course, and indeed, in a certain point of view you are correct."

"What do ye mean, point of view?" Ashyn protested. "These orphans are trapped here, doing dangerous labor and are given nothing in return."

"Nothing?" Xexial replied. "I believe you were near death when you were delivered to the Enclave? Such a nursing back to health is not cheap, Ashyn. Neither is the continued medical care it takes to keep you in fit condition. None of these orphans seems short a meal, either. They all have most of their teeth, fingers, toes, and seemed generally well-clothed. Is doing manual labor for these taskings really too much to ask of the Enclave?"

"Children have died to build the cathedral!" Ashyn argued.

"So did priests, carpenters, masons, and countless others."

"But they can't leave when they want! Not until they pay off their charity."

"Of course," Xexial said calmly. "You can't have homeless children running rampant across Czynsk. When a person is starving, they go to great lengths to stay alive. Think of all the theft, disease, and murder that would take place. Or what about all the uncontrolled, underage pregnancies, a population boom that would sweep the city as more and more parentless children find their way here, victims from the ongoing civil war in the East? These babies would need to be fed too, by unprepared parents who can't even take care of themselves. Babies could perish, en masse.

"The Enclave controls all of this by imposing a strict code of ethics upon the orphans. It eliminates the possible theft and murder by enforcing a *penance* for such actions. It controls couplings to the best of its abilities while ensuring the children's continued survival. The Enclave even educates the orphans, where it can, which is mostly in manual labor. Orphans here learn how to till fields, sow crops, even become carpenters and masons themselves. These are crucial life skills, Ashyn. Is imposing a cost such as their 'charity fee' really so unbelievable?"

"Not when ye say it like that," Ashyn answered reluctantly. He hadn't looked at it like that. He saw only children perishing and punishment with a whip. He hadn't realized what it might take to keep a growing population of children in check. Perhaps the Enclave wasn't the beast he had thought it was early that morning.

"Besides, most orphans end up becoming priests, and even bishops, after living a life under the enlightenment of the Maker. This further helps not only the Enclave, but now the orphan, turned spiritual advisor, as well," Xexial tutored.

"Okay, okay. I get it. They're not slaves," Ashyn sighed, trying not to think about it. It was making his back ache even more.

"Good." Xexial answered. "I'm glad you're such a fast learner, because now you must understand that your actions in challenging the Bishop have caused *your* charity to be cut extremely short."

Ashyn tensed, causing ripples of pain to course through his back. He knew what was coming, but found himself asking anyway. "What do ye mean?"

"As soon as your wounds have been wrapped and you can walk, you are free to leave the Enclave, and through extension of the Enclave, Czynsk."

He felt the well deep in his stomach. It rolled in nausea, as the reality of being an outcast once again set within him. "What if I choose not to leave?"

Xexial chuckled, "I thought you didn't want to be a slave?"

Tears began to well up in the boy's eyes, "It's just . . . I have friends now."

"Friends who will follow *you* more than the Enclave. You must understand that in order to maintain order, they have to impose order. You have challenged the Bishop. You have placed his teachings and his faith back in his face. This will cause unrest amongst the orphans. Some will want to follow your lead, while others will be opposed to it. It will create a rift. There cannot be two shepherds to the same flock. One must leave.

"To maintain balance, to keep the flock moving harmoniously, they must sever the head of the snake of chaos that you have created. Either they will punish you into submission repeatedly, crushing you of your fight, driving you to go from shepherd to sheep, or they will simply let you go. Since the Enclave is truly nonviolent in nature, it is easiest for them to banish you from sight. Sheep have notoriously short memories and will soon forget there was ever another shepherd."

Ashyn felt the salty water break from the dams of his eyes and stream like crystal waterfalls down his face. "Then I am alone."

Ashyn felt a reassuring hand gently touch his shoulder. "People like us, Ashyn, tend to be alone. We have only each other for company, and it has to be enough."

Ashyn shifted himself so he could look back at the wizard. Xexial appeared blurry through his watery eyes. "We?"

Xexial nodded. "I have watched you, Ashyn, while we travelled through the Shalis-Fey, and again today. You have everything needed to become a wizard. You are intelligent, determined, resourceful, adamant, and you have an incredible will to survive where many would have surrendered. You also have a rare ability to connect with magic that many do not, a boon to be sure."

"So ye will train me?" Ashyn said between sniffles.

Xexial nodded and smiled. "I will."

A warning echoed in the back of Ashyn's mind, something that Macky had told him crept across the inside of his skull like a spider in a web. The crawling thing was a question, a question that overruled even his ardent desire to learn how to control magic.

"Can I ask ye something?"

"Of course."

"Are ye evil?"

Xexial broke his grip from the boy and leaned back away from him. Ashyn could see the indecision written in the wizard's azure eyes. "That is a question, Ashyn Rune, that cannot be answered very easily."

THE NATURE OF A WIZARD

Ashyn stared at him in horror. It was not an answer he had wanted to hear. Now, with those words so plain in front of him, doubts began to percolate about his desire to learn magic. He moved quickly away from the man, his savior, yet now total stranger, that sat before him.

Fires lanced up the deep furrows in his back, but the pain of the wounds was the last thing on his mind. He slowly backed himself away from Xexial. His backside bumped up against the north wall. He had nowhere else to go.

"Do not recoil from me, Ashyn," Xexial said. "I am no brigand."

Seeing that Ashyn was not about to move back towards him, the wizard shook his head and looked to the cot that the boy had been lying upon. "You are an idyllic young boy. This world is not as black and white as you may wish it to be. It is shrouded in layers of grey. What may be one man's hero may well be another's monster. This is the way of things, it cannot be changed."

"But ye are . . . evil?"

Xexial shrugged. "In many's eyes . . . yes, I am."

"Why? Why do ye have to be evil?" Ashyn asked, tears welling in his eyes.

"Because I am a wizard, lad. It is an unfortunate stigma carried by all wizards. It is a mantle we will carry all our lives and our successors will carry as well. Our craft has taught us things, things that no one can understand, nor comprehend, unless they are wizards themselves. This has caused our actions to appear 'evil' in the eyes of others," Xexial told him solemnly. "A part of me wishes that the masses could see the beauty of what it is that I see in my art, but it is only a small part. The rest of me has come to terms with what I am a long time ago. I am 'evil' in the eyes of the ignorant and nothing I will ever do will change that. I would hope a child as special as you could see past that veil of ignorance that has clouded the greater world around you."

Ashyn looked down in guilt. "I'm sorry. It's just, ye saved my life. I look up to ye."

Xexial nodded. "Yes I have, and by all accounts many would consider that a noble action, but I have also killed others. A good many, in fact. That alone is heinous in the extreme," he returned. "Lest you have forgotten so soon about the Wild Elves in the woods."

"Of course not!"

"Though I saved you, I killed a great many of them. Likely, they too had mothers, fathers, sons, and daughters, people who loved them dearly. Do you not think that I am a monster in their eyes? Slaughtering so many for the sake of a boy?"

Ashyn shook his head. "I dinna think of it that way."

"Of course not," Xexial answered straightforwardly. "Many do not, in fact. They see things with simple eyes and simple thoughts, drawing conclusions from their perceptions, and not the greater picture.

"Take for instance a common misconception of wizard, and our plaguing of crops. It is often done during great conflicts, such as war. A wizard may see two opposing factions in conflict. One side may have overwhelming numbers, or advanced technology, that would lead to the slaughter of the opposing indigenous species. The violence would be extreme, the death toll would be catastrophic. A wizard can avert such a horrific event with one simple act, by destroying the land on which the crops are sown.

"With no way to grow their source of food, the army will starve. Many will still die, but the army will be forced to retreat and end a conflict in which a great deal more might have perished. The wizard will have spared potentially hundreds or thousands of lives, but this will not be seen. They will only remember that the wizard plagued a city's crop supply, destroying the land for winters, perhaps centuries. An 'evil' act, to be sure. They will not remember, nor care to remember, that the reason for it was so that it would ultimately save lives," he said bluntly, and then continued. "That is the stigma a wizard will forever carry."

Even though Xexial's deep voice was straightforward and monotone, Ashyn could see the painful recollection behind the wizard's eyes as he stared off in the distance. After a moment of lost contemplation, Xexial blinked away what Ashyn thought was perhaps a memory he may have recalled, and focused once again on the boy.

"That in part is why I feel you would be an ideal wizard candidate," he told Ashyn. "You understand what it is like to be apart from the rest. You have a different view on the world, greater than those that would judge something that they will never fully understand."

"What do ye mean?" Ashyn asked, now curious.

"To be a wizard is not about choosing a side, Ashyn. It is about finding balance, the most difficult kind of balance, in fact: Finding the balance of life."

"I dunna understand," Ashyn said honestly to the robed man in front of him.

Xexial patted the cot that he was sitting on. "Please sit down and permit me to explain."

Ashyn nodded, and slowly moved forward and sat back down on the cot. In a rare showing of emotion on his usually stone-hardened face, Xexial permitted himself a small smile.

"As you know, magic comes in all forms, as people do. We are varied in species and sex, male and female. Elves, Dwarves, Gnomes, and Humans, all similar yet distinctly different. Even amongst our own races, we differ. Your eyes are grey, mine are blue, and Macky's are brown. Everything about us is different, and yet we are the same. We all still feel pain, fear, love, and hate. We all still need to eat and sleep. We cry when we are sad, laugh when we are happy. Everyone does this.

"Magic is like people. It is all different. No two magic users are alike. Sorcerers pull and command the elements to answer to their will, Mystics beckon to the healing magic of the world to help those in need, so on and so forth.

"Even two Sorcerers may be different. One may specialize in drawing power from water, creating wondrous shapes out of ice, while others may pull from the essences of fire to spring flames forth from their fingertips.

"Yet in the end, they all share the same defining characteristic. They all draw from the same fountain. They all must answer to the same magic. Every spell creates something from that font. It is where each and every wielder is the same. They must all tap from the same pool. The pool of Creation."

Ashyn thought of how Xexial constantly used lightning against people, while he, himself, seemed to be drawn to fire. He found himself listening intently to the wizard, his fear now diminishing.

"Creation, by its very definition, creates. And the magic of it is that if we believe in it, then ultimately we can achieve it.

"It is all based on our beliefs, you see. Our beliefs strongly guide our hands every single day. An architect has to believe he is capable of designing a structure before he can make it so.

True, it is practice and repetition that helps his craft, but it is first the belief that sparks the action.

"The same is true for the magic that is wielded. It is your belief structure that helps sculpt your choices as a magic user. It is what guides you on your chosen path. It is the very foundation of magic."

"So yer beliefs are what cause ye to be evil?" Ashyn asked.

"Essentially, yes," Xexial agreed.

Ashyn thought about it as Xexial continued. "We are all raised into different beliefs, just as the Bishop had said early today, and in the end it guides your moral code, what is right in your eyes, and what is wrong. What one person feels is right may not be right in the eyes of another, yet this is what they believe, this is what has been ingrained into their subconscious.

"Some actions deviate from almost all societal norms, such as rape, murder, and theft. Yet think about the child that was raised by a group of hooligans his whole life? Rape and murder would seem normal to him, even right. This is what he believes in, even though the larger society sees it as vile. So who is correct? The freebooter child or society as a whole?"

"Magic functions in the same way. It doesn't care how you use it, it only has the cost it imposes on its use. To kill with lightning, or to create water for survival, has no meaning to it. It's application all resides on the wielder, and their beliefs. As such any sorcerer can be 'good' or 'evil'."

"The reason wizardry is considered so iniquitous however, is because unlike any other magic user out there, wizards not only pull from Creation, but another source of magic altogether: Destruction."

Ashyn's ears picked up on the word. Macky had mentioned it earlier that morning. "So it's true then," he whispered.

"What's true?" Xexial asked.

"The Enclave said that wizards use magic to destroy stuff utterly, removing them from all existence," Ashyn returned as he stared at the wizard before him.

"This is a very correct definition," Xexial replied. "A common misconception is that things are destroyed when they are, say, burned. Let's go back to the stigma of a wizard plaguing a field for a moment."

Ashyn nodded, now very interested. "Okay."

"Plague is a word that the ignorant often use to explain what to them is unexplainable. That or taint or curse, you get the idea."

Again, Ashyn nodded.

"You see, burning crops is a regular practice in war to create famine for the opposing armies. But generally, the crops can be resown in the same fields. This only temporarily sets back the attacking or defending force. What a wizard does is actually destroy the life-giving properties of the soil completely."

"Um, I dunna understand," Ashyn said perplexed.

Xexial assumed an instructor's pose with his hands folded over one and other in his lap. "What does the Jasian Enclave teach people about when they die?"

"That our soul goes to heaven."

"And is heaven here? Can we take a trip there to go see our departed loved ones?" Xexial asked.

"Of course not," Ashyn said shaking his head. "You can only go there if ye soul is pure when ye die."

"So it can be said that heaven does not exist to us mortals on this realm, can it not? If it can only be accessed when we die."

Ashyn shrugged. "I guess."

"Destruction functions in a similar way," Xexial said calmly. "You take something that is, and separate it absolutely from its existence in this realm. It is destroyed completely and utterly. A tree that is destroyed ceases to exist; it does not topple, wither, or become ash. It is gone forevermore with no chance of return, severed from this world."

Ashyn stared wide-eyed at the concept. Something that no longer exists. "What happens if you kill someone with this Destruction magic? Do you destroy their soul?"

Xexial shook his head. "Even a wizard is unsure. Therefore, we vow to kill only using Creation. That is why all you have seen me use is lightning. To kill with Destruction is the worst kind of death. Our predecessors may have used it in the past, but the wizards of today refuse." Then added under his breath, "Even some of the more despicable ones."

"So you don't know?"

"No one does," the wizard answered. "The only way to find out is to die by it, and no wizard is willing try, considering there is no return from death."

"Okay, so when you destroy crops . . ."

"We remove all life from the soil. All of the properties that help fuel growth. It becomes nothing but a barren land of broken and desolate clay, devoid of all forms of life."

"Can that be repaired?"

Xexial nodded. "Given time and care a wizard can 'undo' the effects by reintroducing life-giving elements, such as water, insects, compost, fresh soil. This endeavor can take many winters, and it never truly fixes the initially damaged land, it only introduces new elements and soil. It's more of a replacement, than a repair."

"Why would someone harness a magic like Destruction? And how come only wizards know it?" Ashyn asked curiously, studying Xexial's eyes for depth of knowledge.

"To answer your first question is actually very simple. Duality."

"Duality?"

Xexial nodded. "Creation is birth, the creation of something new. A wizard devotes his life to balance, and the counter to birth is death, the taking away of something. These are the very tenets of the Circle of Life that are so important to our world. For all life there needs to be death. For every beginning, there must be an end. For if we did not die, how could we truly appreciate the precious few moments we have been given in this world?

"This is fundamental in duality. Everything necessary in this world comes in pairs, male and female; night and day; earth and water; birth and death. The counter to Creation therefore, is Destruction, and wizards are the heralds of this art. We are a necessity, Ashyn. We bring to this world the counter of all the other magicians out there. We maintain the balance so necessary in magic."

Ashyn stared at Xexial as a slow comprehension dawned on him. "So for everything that is good . . ."

Xexial nodded. "There must be evil as well, yes. This is why wizards are so feared, lad. This is why Destruction is viewed the way it is. In the end, Destruction performs only one function. It takes away.

"Everyone fears the unknown, and death is the greatest of the unknowns. To take something away permanently is the same as death. To them Destruction is *death*. In the eyes of the whole, wizards are the harbingers of death. And in a way, they are not wrong. This inevitably makes us . . ."

"Evil," Ashyn answered.

Xexial stood up from the cot, and looked around at the vacant hospice. He then paced around the cot before continuing. "To answer your second question is a little trickier. Let us just say for now that this ancient art has been entrusted to wizards for a purpose, and that is why there are so few of us. You see, a wizard can only have a single pupil in their lifetime, unlike any of the Creation-wielders. This limits the knowledge of Destruction from spreading, and also limits the number of wielders of such an awesome power. We feel it helps with the balance."

Ashyn glared at him, realizing he was navigating around the question. He could see Xexial immediately knew that Ashyn had caught on.

"I do not guard these secrets of power to be malicious or power-mongering. I do this because it is the way of the wizard. It is our tenet, our ethos, and I will only teach you more if you believe you want to follow this calling."

"So I do not have to choose to be a wizard, to use magic?" Ashyn asked.

"No," Xexial answered. "If you desire to seek another art, then I will try and help you find a tutor in such a craft. But never in my lifetime have I met someone whom I have felt is capable of learning the secrets of wizardry such as you.

"I have always held strong to my convictions. They guided me to my destiny as a wizard, just as I believe they guided me to you to be my pupil. Yet it is ultimately your belief that will determine if wizardry is a task you wish to attempt."

Ashyn digested everything he was being told. It was his opportunity, he realized, to learn magic and avenge his family and village. That hatred and anger burned deep within the core of him, and despite the past two months in the Enclave, it was something he had not forgotten. Yet it also came with a great sadness, for now that he had finally made friends, he would have to leave them. He had made a vow though, a vow never to be weak again. This was his chance to live true to his word.

"I know this is not an easy decision for you to make, Ashyn, and I wouldn't expect you to answer me right this moment. It will take a few days for your wounds to heal sufficiently to the point where you can travel without endangering yourself. I will leave you as you mend to think on what I have said. Just know that if you accept my offer, young Ashyn, it is a road that you will not be able to turn away from. Each acolyte must make an oath known as the Wizard's Covenant to his master. This oath binds you to the completion of your training no matter the cost to yourself, even death, for the art of Destruction is too powerful to let an untrained wizard 'quit'.

"This could, and likely will, take winters to complete, lad, taking away the rest of your childhood and possibly teenage winters. It will forever separate you from the rest of the world. You will never be the same. You will never *fit in*. If you thought you were different before, you will find you were wrong. After your training, you will view the world in a completely new perspective, one that others constantly feel is aberrant, even *alien*. This is a choice you must think heavily on."

Ashyn stared at the floor as the reality of what he would possibly become, began to set in. He too would be considered evil for the rest of his life. He would forever be a pariah in the eyes of others.

"Should you choose not to accept my invitation, I will not take it as an insult, and I will be good to my word in finding you another village to live in, perhaps even another mentor in other magical arts. You have a gift, young Ashyn Rune, and I wouldn't want you to squander it."

Ashyn's eyes lifted from the floor as they stared off into the distance. He didn't see his surroundings much, his vision introverted towards his thoughts. He was already an outcast, did it really matter? True, he had made friends here in Czynsk, but what was his hold on that? Already the Enclave had branded him too different to remain because he challenged the Bishop. Would his life always be like this if he choose not to go with the wizard?

And even if he decided not to go and Xexial took him to another town where he trained to be a Sorcerer or a Mystic, or any of the other myriads of magicians in the world, how long would it be before he had an episode again like he did with Gregiry Bib? How would his mentor feel then about the innate magic that Ashyn seemed to carry inside of him? Would he react the same way as the people of Bremingham or would he accept it like Xexial did? Even though Macky and Avrimae were his friends, they didn't know about his secret. How would they feel when they found out? Would they accept it, or react in terror like everyone else?

Xexial was the only one besides Veer that had ever embraced who he was. Except for his family of course, and they were dead. He didn't notice as Xexial left the hospice, or as Avrimae re-entered and once again put a soft damp sponge against the thick red lacerations on his back.

Suddenly thinking about his family sent a rush of pain in his chest. All he could think about at that moment were his parents and sister. If he had known how to control his magic, they might not have died. He might have saved everyone. Something that Xexial could offer him that perhaps no other could. So what if the price was being evil? He could live with that, couldn't he?

"Don't do it, Ashyn," he vaguely heard Avrimae whisper as if reading his mind. "Please don't do it," she said with a sob.

Lost in his haze of thoughts, he glanced emptily in her direction. She must have heard them talking from outside, heard Xexial's confession of being 'evil'. The dim flickering firelight reflected off the tears rolling down her face.

He didn't see her though, not really. He only dimly registered that she was crying, for his mind was somewhere else. It was back in Bremingham. He watched through the twisted, gnarled cornfields, as his mind replayed that horrid night in exact detail. His chest grew tight replacing pain with fear as the Orcs ripped through his village and converged on his home. He could feel the heat as his home exploded in a brilliant blue gulf of fire, stealing all the air from his lungs. He could smell the blood, the feces, and the cooked flesh all around him. As the blaze subsided, he saw his sister being carried off into the woods by the beasts, his house lie in a burning ruin. He could see the boot of his father jutting from the wreckage.

Xexial's voice echoed in his head, drowning out Avrimae's sobbing pleas. "They did find a girl, similar to your description. They say she died from blunt force trauma."

Rage gripped him tight in its vice, an unbridled anger that needed an outlet. He would make the beasts pay as he had vowed. He would destroy them all. Now was his opportunity. Now was his chance. He was barely aware of Avrimae's gasp as his world was bathed in deep crimson light.

~ ~ ~

Ashyn turned back and looked once more at the motley town of Czynsk now little more than a dot on the verdant horizon. He could see the cathedral spires reaching up to the sky. Spires that Macky had helped build.

"We mustn't dally," Xexial called ahead of him.

Ashyn nodded without looking back at the man. He had said his goodbyes to his friends. Avrimae, Macky, and even Uriel were all sad to see him go, but the Bishop had declared his 'charity' paid in full. He had had to leave.

His muscles were tight across his back, as the lacerations had begun to scab over and heal. It wouldn't be long before he was in full health once more.

Readjusting the heavy pack of provisions, and forget-me-nots his friends had given him, he slid his shoulder to a more comfortable position. He knew he had to be careful not to re-open the wounds on his back, and Xexial wouldn't be offering him any pity or help anymore. He was on his own now, proving his worth.

He whispered a silent goodbye once more to the friends he had made, and promised he would try to see them again. He then glanced back to Xexial who was already himself beginning to shrink on the horizon. He had made his choice. He had given Xexial the covenant. There was no turning back. He flexed his right hand in response to his thoughts. The gauze was still bound tight around the fresh wound in his palm. The covenant had called for blood, and blood he had given. Even now, he could feel the vial resting against his chest.

Xexial too had bled for the covenant. It was the rule. Now Ashyn was to carry with him his master's blood, as Xexial would do the same of his. Through his blood, Xexial would always be able to find him, no matter where he might be.

To Ashyn the act was superficial. He would stand by his oath. He would be a wizard, or he was going to die trying.

PART
II

TOME II

I was there that day. I watched a boy enter the ominous Onyx Tower, a tall umbral monolith that reached high into the sky. Like a spear of obsidian that pierced the very heavens themselves. There seemed to be nothing good of this tower, only evil, and as I watched this child disappear into its dark maw a sense of failure had over taken me.

To watch him had been my charge, and I knew that I would not see him again for a great many winters, if ever.

Yet I did not surrender, I held vigil day and night upon the same flat stone overlooking the horizon on which this pillar of darkness resided. *What would become of the child?* I wondered as I glimpsed for the occasional flicker of candle light from the hundreds of windows that dotted the labyrinthine structure.

Would this boy emerge an evil tyrant ready to conquer the face of Kuldarr? Or would that anger I had seen in him become tempered as he learned more and more about the wider world of magic around him?

Wizards often proclaim that they are the keepers of balance in magic, much as druids are the keepers of balance in nature. But all too often in my long winters have I seen wizard after wizard fall unto the dark arts, using their magic of Destruction as a tool to wrestle control of anything their eventual lustful greed desires.

Only the Seven keep their own loosely in line. And by 'loosely' it seems that they are more concerned with guarding the secrets of their Art then they are the facilitation of that gift. For even amongst that core group, their moral alignment seems to differ in the extreme.

Therefore, to find a wizard like Xexial Bontain, who seems almost humble to his nature, may be a fortuitous thing for the boy. It may also lead to his very fall, for often humble beginnings lead to longings of great power.

When next I saw the boy emerge, child he was no longer, but a fully-grown adult. He was dreadfully skinny, with long red hair and deep olive skin. Robes of grey hung loosely from his underdeveloped body, one spent too long indoors, and not enough hunting and traversing the terrain as he and his father had done in the past. Nevertheless, I could see from my very vantage that he had lost none of the power of his steel grey eyes. In fact, the knowledge he had garnered over those winters of life seemed to make them grow in intensity. And the raw power that radiated from him was awesome and terrible all in one. Never before had I seen such unbridled force bottled up inside someone so young.

And yet for all this energy, it was obvious he had very little understanding of it. The winters that passed may have grown him in body and intellect, but did nothing to sharpen his control of his gift.

So the person I saw before me, all these winters later, may be Ashyn Rune, but he was not yet a man. A far cry from it. And that scared me more than anything did.

-Chronology of Rune's early ages,
As seen by the Watcher Xao

THE COUNCIL OF ELM

She entered the circular chamber with steady graceful strides. Humble in her nature, she had not realized how long she had awaited this day. For the last three hundred and eighty nine winters, she had been a member of the prestigious Council of Elm.

Their function had but a single purpose. They were the designers in the overall scheme of eradicating the evils of the world. To do this they held many accolades. They were called maintainers of nature and life, hunters of the skewers of balance, and decimators of the wicked. This was their charge as handed down to them from their progenitors and the spirits. It was their drive, their calling, their religion. They were the Ferhym and they would brook no passing of evil in their world.

At the rank of Councilor, she was chief of their hunters. They were feared throughout the rest of the land by not only the vile, but by all races, including the other Elves.

She was amongst the elite for those long winters. She had been merely a simple hunter for the two hundred some odd winters prior to that. Today, however, she was to become more, so much more.

The Ferhym way was supposed to know nothing of pride, only the directive. Yet she could not deny how much she felt she deserved this moment. She had achieved something that none alive had achieved in centuries . . .

Elves, even Wild Elves, had extremely low birth rates to balance their extended life spans compared to the other races. So having one child was considered a gift. To have two was considered a rare blessing from the spirits. She, however, was the mother of three daughters. This feat went beyond the Ferhym's understanding.

And if that were not accomplishment enough, her youngest daughter was a Voïre dui Ceremeia; the Exemplar, as the other races called her. She was the parent of their chosen. One of only two that were currently alive. This elevated her to a status beyond a Councilor in many of her people's eyes.

She had always tempered the accolades she received however, telling herself and others that it was simply her calling from the spirits to do as she had done, and for her part, she truly believed it. She had found love and contentment in her position as Councilor. She had purged the world of countless skewers of balance. She had brought a small measure of harmony back to Kuldarr. It provided her with the feeling that it was what she had been meant to do.

Now, as she approached the dais around which all her fellow Councilors stood in a semi-circle waiting, she realized that this was her truest calling. This was the reason the spirits had given her so many boons in her life. She was meant for this. She smiled a perfect white smile. *Was there harm in a little pride?* she pondered. Was it not well-deserved?

Her solid green dress glided across the surface of the smooth polished elm floor. She appeared to be floating, as her feet could not be seen under the long-hemmed dress.

All around her in the circular chambers inside the heart of the great elm tree stood dozens of their finest hunters. They were adorned in their most ornate and fiercest painted markings. Nothing but blood would do for this occasion, and many boars had been sacrificed this day to make their ceremonial war paint. Their spears had been sharpened and polished in pig fat so that they glittered like gems in the flickering torch light.

She drank in her surroundings. She had been here many times in her life, almost every council gathering in fact, but today she truly felt the grandeur of the chamber.

The chamber was carved into a niche within the tallest elm in the Shalis-Fey. They stood over one hundred and thirty feet above ground level. Behind her, and intermittently at points in the high arched ceiling, there were openings carved into the wood. This was to help let in sunlight from the green canopy above. Yet the few thin beams of sunlight were not enough to light the chamber, so torches aided, flickering their dancing amber luminescence from the darker recesses of the room.

There were no lifts or ladders that allowed them into the grand chamber. It was only accessible through a spiraling set of stairs that was carved into very bark of the ancient elm itself.

It was a long, dangerous walk, but one worth it for the secrecy to which it provided, for there was only one way in and the entire Council of Elm would see who joined them.

The open expanse behind her offered a view of the Ferhym city of Feydras' Anula far below them. Unlike their Wood Elf cousins, they did not naturally live in the trees, but upon the earth. They had many look out stations, emergency buildings built within the trees, and every Ferhym was trained from birth to be able to move within the trees, as well upon the land. But they still were a people after all, and like the trees they lived around, they only felt at home if their roots were firmly planted in the ground.

She looked upon the walls behind the masses of peers around her. Long familiar were the ornate carvings of their insular societies' greatest honors. They were monuments of the smiting of the chief enemies of balance. Dragons, sentient monsters, and creatures of darkness and death were all carved in dazzling displays, each viciously slaughtered by the ever-relentless Councilors. There were even a few reliefs of their greatest adversaries, wizards, victoriously defeated.

But the walls were only a quarter of the way full and she hoped to add to it many more winters' worth of artistry and accomplishment.

She let her dark-eyed gaze drift to every hunter in the room. Each one was there for her and it was only right for her to be modest, and offer each one the thanks of recognition. She was quick, making eye contact briefly, but acknowledging them all. She paused only for a moment on one of her daughters. Whisper had become a reputable huntress herself, leading branch after branch over the last eleven winters, successfully purging this world of the skewers of balance. Next to her stood her hunter and husband, Suneris, a simple Ferhym with low intelligence but a thickly-muscled body. He stared at her vacantly, but Whisper did not hide her satisfaction and let a smile play about her lips as she nodded.

This is my truest daughter, she thought. Whisper was far more aggressive in pursuing goals. It wouldn't be long before she too called her daughter Councilor. She returned the smallest of nods to her daughter and then broke eye contact. It was time to address those in front of her.

There stood her true peers, the Councilors, and they were all wearing the same green robes as she. Twenty in all, these were the best that the Ferhym had to offer. They were the crème of the crop.

In the center of these selected few, holding a necklace of pure amber beads, was her dearest friend Councilor Vooken.Vooken had his dark brown hair pulled back into a long ponytail today, so that it rested in the center of his back. His deep brown eyes glittered as he looked to her. His face was still smooth and young looking, belaying the fact that he was almost seven hundred winters of age. He was her senior by maybe ninety winters or so as a Councilor, yet he harbored no jealousy. Instead, he merely smiled knowingly, as if he had been expecting this moment his entire life.

As she walked up to him, she stopped so close that they were almost touching. They said nothing to each other, but instead she lowered her head gracefully, her raven hair parting flawlessly, to expose her long, slender copper tanned neck.

Vooken lifted the amber beaded necklace and placed it over her head, careful not to be caught on her long pointed ears. As he placed the string of tawny globes against her breast, she saw the names of her eight predecessors carved into each individual bead of amber. Her name was carved in the ninth bead in the center of the necklace.

"Raise your head, and address your followers," Vooken said in a melodic voice.

She did as she was bid and turned to address the group before her. As one, they all dropped to their left knee, her daughter included. Only rows of immaculate spears hovered level with her line of sight. They stood, unwaveringly, like lines of trees amid a great forest of life.

Behind her, Vooken began to chant, "Spirits grant her the right to smite evil, wherever it may lie."

"Spirits grant her the right to smite evil, wherever it may lie," the collection around her repeated as one.

"Spirits guide her hand as she guides ours to help purify this land from the plagues of Unbalancers that desecrate it," Vooken continued.

The gathering followed suit.

"And spirits charge her to follow your unwavering edicts, as we follow her edicts unwaveringly, for it is her decree that will guide this world to balance."

Again the masses around her repeated Vooken's chant.

As one they all stood, and both Voïre dui Ceremeia came from around the Councilors and whispered the blessings of the spirits upon her.

"And now the spirits' test," he whispered to the crowd.

Both chosen dipped their fingers in crimson paint and began to trace the markings amongst her face. She made eye contact with neither of them, for even though one was her daughter, the Voïre dui Ceremeia were not to be looked upon now that they were adults.

She felt Vooken unlatching her dress from behind, and as she felt it loosen, she raised her arms and the dress fell away, revealing nothing underneath.

The two Voïre dui Ceremeia continued to sketch the interconnecting lines across her nude flesh. They touched her breasts and genitalia indiscriminately, only focusing on completing their tasks. She paid the act no attention. When the Voïre dui Ceremeia finished they stepped away.

For a moment, her head swooned. She knew deep within that paint were toxins extracted from over a dozen various flora and fauna throughout Shalis-Fey. Alone they were not fatal, but together the effects were greatly compounded. The poison acted fast as it contaminated her body. Briefly, nausea filled her, and then she momentarily went blind. As her vision returned, she felt a clarity that she had never experienced before. It was almost as if she could now hear the spirits communing with her. It was done. She had survived the trial.

From head to toe, she was covered in the strokes of red paint that had sent the waves of near-fatal toxins into her system. Their purpose was to act as a thread, a cord to the spirits around them. She was one with them now, the first line of communication with the great spirits of nature. She was the lead spear in the campaign. Soon the paint would burn into her flesh, forever marking her as it had the eight predecessors before her. Never in life would the concoction fade, but remain brightly scored into her flesh. Only in her death would the spiritual cover vanish, because when she died, she too would be one with the spirits, and would no longer have need of the thread with which to commune with them. She had lived, the spirits had accepted her, and now she stood before her peers naked and unafraid.

Vooken then called out so loudly that it echoed into their village below. "The spirits have chosen! A new First Councilor has been accepted! Let Lady Brodea Windsong be our Spear Maiden and charge us fearlessly on our spiritual quest!"

He roared fiercely and hundreds of spears hammered the ground both in the chamber, and down far below in their city. It echoed throughout all of the greater Shalis-Fey.

Vooken's voice grew dark and quiet so that only those in the chamber could barely hear. "And let those who would be dissonant feel her wrath!"

Brodea smiled wickedly. Long had they suffered the impudence of letting their greatest Unbalancers walk near to their very doorstep. Long had they tolerated their unnatural abilities in this world, manipulators in areas most abominable. It was only for fear of what their retaliation would bring that had caused the Ferhym to linger. Their kind was contemptible and depraved, and Brodea would fear them no longer. Harborers and protectors of their ilk would all suffer the great balancing, for their wickedness too needed to be expunged. It would be a wondrous new beginning for the Ferhym, and a brutal end for the world of wizards. *I have done it, Ambit*, she thought to herself. I have begun to plant the seeds of your retribution.

It would begin with Czynsk.

A Watcher Alone

Xao craned his long neck over the horizon to look back to the deep long treeline of the Shalis-Fey, miles away. He could hear what sounded like a faint roll of thunder coming from within those woods. Something had happened with the Ferhym, he reasoned. Something big.

He turned his deep crimson head to look back upon the shadowy obelisk before him. As he watched that long dark spire, he placed his head upon his forelimbs. It appeared even more impossibly black than usual as a new dawning sun had slowly began its long journey into the skyline.

His claws idly traced the ground. He enjoyed watching the sunrise. It gave him something to look forward to every day while he waited vainly for some sign of his charge. It had been so long since he watched the little one enter that monstrosity with his wizard mentor.

In that time, he had grown a lot. In the last eleven winters his size expanded more than in the first hundred of his life. He went from the size of an elephant, to the size of a small barn. It was an unanticipated growth spurt. Nevertheless, a very welcome one.

His long sinewy leather wings were fuller and brighter, and his muscles were thick. Even his deep red coating had begun to glisten under the growing sunlight. He smiled a toothy smile. His black plating was hardening on his snout and he measured the spines on his back to almost the length of a short sword! He was beginning to look like a proper dragon.

Xao blew out a small jetty of fire from between his nostrils. Like little squalls of flame, they arched themselves into the sky. There was no reason for the outburst, he only did it because he could. The pyrotechnic display ended as suddenly as it began, leaving in its place a thick grey haze. As the smoke rolled from his nose, he reached up one of his claws and traced the dark rising cloud in the air, creating great furrows in the murk.

Really, is that how a great Watcher spends their days? A distinctly feminine voice entered his mind. Xao quickly spun his head around, sweeping his yellow eyes across the horizon looking for the source of the voice. Yet he could see nothing. *Where are you?* he demanded of the voice.

A grating hiss of laughter entered his mind as the massive form of an elder red dragon materialized only half a dozen feet away. She was about one-and-a-half times his size. She used to be far larger and more intimidating, but his sudden growth had narrowed that gap exponentially. He watched as her crimson scales glistened vividly in the pale pink glow of the rising sun. She moved towards him gracefully, like a lioness, touching each clawed limb down smoothly on the rich wheat brown earth. The ground made not a tremor from her impact.

Her head swayed away from his direction and to the tower. Her large ginger eyes, stared piercingly at the spire blotting a beautiful horizon. She blinked slowly and exhaled. *Really, I would think a Watcher would be more attentive to his surroundings,* she chided him.

That's not the purpose of Watchers and you know it, Dremathiatius, Xao retorted, as he too cast his pale yellow gaze upon the landscape.

The female dragon snorted her contempt. Small jets of fire plumed from her nostrils and rolled gracefully across the obsidian plates that ran along the bridge of her snout. *Whatever, hatch-brother. Mireanthia is long dead; why do you continue to perform this wasted effort?*

Xao turned his head back to his hatch-sister. Though not born in the same 'hatch' it was more a term of endearment since they had both came from the same mother. Indeed, Dremathiatius looked much like their mother. His eyes continued to trek across her frame as her brilliant wings shifted lightly against her body. Her scales glistened with the same luminescence. She, however, like their mother had warned him, did not share the tranquility and acceptance of other sentient species as he did.

Because this was the task appointed to me, he told her mentally, looking away from her and back to the tall lithe structure that hid his charge.

Only because no one else wanted it, Dremathiatius shot back defensively. They sat in silence a moment before she continued. *Really, Xao, the family you were charged with watching is dead. Let it go, come back to **your** family. We are too few in number as it is to remain separated.*

Is that why you came? he asked without looking at her.

Dremathiatius nodded, and Xao felt it more than saw it. *You have been here for over a decade, just staring at nothing. Is it really worth it?*

Yes, he answered immediately. *I do this for our ancestors. I do it for Mireanthia, because this is what she wanted. Ashyn Rune is special; you know this. I must see his fate.*

Again, his sister snorted. *His fate would have been sealed, had you not interjected that night*, she snapped bitterly. *Mireanthia wouldn't have.*

Xao flinched at the intended insult. Mireanthia had meant the world to him and Dremathiatius knew it. He wanted to tell Dremathiatius that she was wrong, that their mother would have helped. That she too had admitted how important it was that at least one member of the Rune family had survived that night. Xao had had to make a choice. He had hoped it was the right one, but honestly, he didn't know. His duty after all was to watch the ongoings of the Rune family, not protect them.

You belong with your own kind, Xao.

I cannot forsake my duty, he said defiantly, even though his gut twisted with doubt. Eleven winters may not be a long time in his life span, but it was a long time of not seeing the boy. Perhaps it was time to go and he was delaying the inevitable?

Then that is your choice, Dremathiatius told him angrily. *Spend your remaining days watching these lessers, for we will not be near to you any longer.*

Xao quickly turned to look at his sister. *What do you mean?*

Her ginger eyes bore into his yellow. *We are leaving this land, Xao. Kuldarr is no longer a welcoming place. Something evil is brewing on the horizon, a great darkness that will engulf this land in the foreseeable future. The time of the dragons is at an end. We must depart.*

Xao knew by her tone that she was serious. The red dragons were going to leave. He cast his glance at the tower. Did he really want to be alone, unsure if the boy even survived?

Dremathiatius pressed him. *This is your last chance, Xao. After I leave there will be no one else. And you will not survive the journey independently. Come with your family, or stay behind to die alone.*

Xao looked at the Onyx Tower longingly. He had made a promise to his mother. He had sworn to watch the family, as she had before him. But what if his sister was right? What if Ashyn had been meant to die that night in the cornfield? What if he was dead now? Was he really failing Mireanthia staying behind to watch a tall dark tower? He had too many questions, he was too unsure.

Finally, Xao nodded. Immediately an air of superiority filled Dremathiatius. *Good. It is about time you have come to your senses and left these cattle to their fate. Let us go.*

She spread her wings widely in anticipation of lifting off, when suddenly both of them heard a click echo throughout the valley beneath them. Both turned and looked to the tower, and then down below to its courtyard. The two large obsidian doors were opening! After nearly a decade, not one, but two figures emerged.

The lead figure was covered in thick tan robes that were heavily layered with other fabrics. He wore heavy leather gloves with thick fingers, and inlaid in the thick hide were iridescent sapphire lines that ran from the circles of his fingertips up his fingers and hands to his wrists. After all this time he remained moderately built, though age had stooped him, and he now relied on the use of a long ebony staff to help him walk. He hobbled out slowly, favoring his right leg. A dirty blonde beard streaked with grey ran down to the center of his chest, wisps of hair covered the top of his near bald pate.

Behind him followed a young man. The man was tall, immensely tall for a human, standing almost a full head and a half above the elder in front of him. He stood straight, with broad shoulders, but there was a frailty about him. Underneath his plain grey robes seemed to be nothing more than skin and bones. The clothing hung limply across his atrophied frame. A far cry from the developing muscles of the boy who had entered over a decade earlier.

Vivid red hair glittered in the morning light. It was slightly past shoulder length. His deep olive skin now contrasted starkly with his long flowing hair.

Yet even from their distance, Xao could make out the young man's piercing grey eyes. His eyes took in his surroundings with the intensity of a hawk. He seemed to miss nothing. Then he did something that caused both dragons to gasp. He looked up, right at them.

Xao knew that both he and Dremathiatius were camouflaged, but the man continued to stare. It was as if he knew that they were there. Those eyes shot a memory through Xao of when he had been at Mireanthia's side all those winters before. He remembered when the little girl on the rock had looked at him and his mother.

Though Xao couldn't hear it, he saw the elder man's mouth move. He then saw the young man look down at his master in response, mumbling something as well.

The duo then began heading west across the horizon.

Mireanthia's voice echoed in Xao's head as he remembered his first day in the field, the day Ashyn had been born. *Though you yourself may not feel it yet, in you I sense a great compassion for all the sentient species of this world. Something your hatch-brothers and hatch-sisters lack. Don't you see, my young hatchling? It has to be you. There is no one else.*

Do this because you know that deep within yourself this is right, this is important. I know you can feel it, just as I felt it those winters ago. Mireanthia had told him.

At that moment, he did feel it. It was right, it was important. Mireanthia had been right. This was what he was meant to do.

I'm staying, he told Dremathiatius.

Her ginger eyes went wide with shock as she looked to him. Xao was determined, his cause renewed. He stared defiantly back at her.

So be it, hatch-brother, she hissed venomously.

Her wings already extended, she flapped them heavily, casting great gusts upon the younger dragon. He took the buffeting blows as he watched her rise from the ground.

No one will remember you when you perish. You are truly alone, Watcher.

Good-bye, Dremathiatius, he told her as he looked away from her and to his charge.

In a greater thundering of her wings, she pushed off. Then with a speed that defied what her form could do, she shot across the tree line. Xao distantly watched her leave, knowing that it would be the last time he ever saw his hatch-sister. Soon she appeared as nothing more than a glistening red speck on the horizon, and then she was gone.

Xao looked back down at the duo, which was moving deftly. Surprising, for the older man seemed far more frail than he actually was.

Climbing off his perch, he began to follow them. Ashyn Rune had finally emerged.

CZYNSK REVISITED

Ashyn stared intently at the crested ridge that overlooked the valley he currently resided in. Eleven winters had passed since he had been able to exit these double doors. A world he had left behind was now revealed to him once more. He wanted to gaze upon the horizon, to catch the scent of the green prairies that stretched out before his eyes. Or perhaps to feel the freedom of the wild grasslands beneath his feet. These were all things he had ardently desired when Master Bontain had told him only days before that an urgent call had come from Czynsk, one that demanded their immediate attention.

It was a massive moment for Ashyn, he knew. Master Bontain had said 'their' attention, not his. He knew that the wizard had finally felt Ashyn was ready to experience the wider world once more.

Ashyn of course had been outside the tower on numerous occasions, through the rear servant's entrances, which were now only used by he and Xexial. It had always been under the tight scrutiny of his master, however, and always away from any prying eyes. The secrets of wizards were well guarded. He remembered the first time his master had told him that the rear gardens behind the tower were actually under a concealment spell. To any prying eyes, they were effectively invisible, but like all things, there were limits. He could never pass the fourth line of junipers, for these evergreen shrubs with their small berrylike cones marked the end of the spell.

Xexial had explained that the entire arrangement of the garden itself formed two distinctly different glyphs, one that acted as a form of concealment and one that was used as a line of defense. Ashyn's master never went into exact details on the latter, only letting him know what would happen if he crossed the edge of the ward. Should anyone, including himself, attempt to cross the threshold of the garden unwanted, they would receive a jolt of energy that they would soon not forget.

And should that one be persistent and attempt to continue through the glyphed area and into the garden they would find the result to be quite fatal.

The jolt was merely a warning system so the intruder, or attempted escapee, wouldn't go further. Attempting to step through the ward was like trying to push through water, and if one were persistent, they would be rewarded by having the flesh rent from their bones.

After what Ashyn had seen, and learned, he did not question the reality of those wards in the least. And even the curious child never dared challenge them. He liked his flesh exactly where it was, attached to him.

He blinked away the memory and continued to stare at the rise above. He could have sworn he saw something move up there. Something large.

He gazed to that little rocky outcropping not even a quarter mile away. Something primal within him demanded he look there, but all he could see were a few fir trees growing at haphazard angles, one even dangerously close to toppling, all amidst a chunk of moss-covered granite. There was nothing there. Nothing watching him. He continued to stare, unable to shake the feeling of some tangible presence above him.

"Does this sudden freedom trouble you, lad? Perhaps I acted too soon?" Xexial's deep voice thrummed, breaking the silence.

Breaking his stare from the earthen rim, he look down to his master, who was beginning to slump with age. "Of course not, master. I am elated that you feel I am ready for this endeavor." Though Xexial did not turn to look at him, he nodded. Over a decade away from simple southern villages had taken away the improper etiquettes and slang he had learned as a child. Through his continued education, his linguistics had further improved and even surpassed that of his mentor. Ashyn now spoke fourteen separate dialects, and could comprehend, read and write almost another dozen more.

Of course, one of the first languages he had strived to learn had been the Ferhym. He now counted that language as his second most fluent, with only Lefhym holding the reigns as the leader.

Time had even altered his parlance. He spoke clearly and precisely, with little use of any slang, something that had likely developed due to the absence of contact with the outside world. His only source of companionship had been his master, and

Xexial firmly believed that everyone should use the proper vernacular. This left Ashyn with no way to adapt to the current lingos.

Finding that Ashyn's answer had been sufficient, the tan-robed man stepped forth off the tower and began to walk steadily, and at a strong pace towards Czynsk.

As Ashyn followed, he heard the double doors of the great Onyx Tower click shut. There would be no entering the place until Xexial returned. Not even Ashyn could get back in, without being next to the wizard. Some form of contact with his master was necessary for him to enter the sealed doors.

Hours passed and the sun climbed high into the sky to indicate that midday had arrived. Nature sang its tune all around him. Birds tweeted to one and other, chipmunks squeaked their interest at the strangers passing, and insects chirped in threats against the mammoth intruders to their domains.

To Ashyn it seemed exactly as he had left it. It was a clear spring day with only a slightly biting cold wind drifting down from the north, a lingering reminder that winter had passed by only a short time ago. Traces of the thaw could be seen distantly on parts of the horizon, but the immediate area around him was green and lush, full of a new season's life.

Ashyn couldn't help but let his mind drift as he followed Master Bontain across the verdant hills back to a town he had not seen in many, many winters. He thought of his core group of friends, Macky, Avrimae, and even Uriel. He wondered if they were still in Czynsk. How long after he left had it taken before their 'charities' had been paid off?

Avrimae probably was married by now, and with children of her own. He wondered if Macky and Uriel were still best friends, or if that inevitable rift had formed between them because of Avrimae? These thoughts carried him through the day, and Xexial was polite enough to give him the space necessary to daydream about what it was that they might find.

As night set in and the two of them set camp, Ashyn reached down into the freshly-arranged logs. He muttered gently the one phrase he had caught on to quicker then any of the others. The wood instantly blazed to life.

Xexial moved close to the campfire, his aging joints creaking and popping almost as loud as the burning wood. "Well at least that's one spell you will always get right," he muttered as Ashyn watched the warmth wash over his elder.

Ashyn tried not to let the jab affect him, but he knew it was true. As quick-witted as Ashyn was and as much as he had learned, his ability to take hold of the arcane had seemed to be slightly beyond his grasp. He knew all the formulas, the incantations, and the spells by heart. He could even recite them better than Xexial could. His inflection of the words was perfect. Somehow, he just couldn't connect the dots to make the magic answer him. He could handle cantrips well enough, and even a few minor protection spells, but that was it. In fact, the only thing he could do without a problem was call to fire, and to say he could do it well was an understatement. He seemed inexorably drawn to the element, able to harness it at will, at almost all times.

He felt Xexial's hooded eyes watching him in the flickering orange light. "Don't fret it, lad," he tried to reassure the boy. "We both knew this would take time."

Ashyn sighed, he couldn't help it. "I know," he answered as he reached out towards the blazing campfire. Mentally, he pulled to the fire, calling it like one would call a beloved pet. Within a fraction of a second the fire answered, dancing away from the pyre and fluttering to his outstretched hand. It rolled in his hand like a living creature, slithering and undulating in circles like a serpent.

He pulled from the cool air around him feeding the fire in his hand. The flickering flames answered merrily as they began to expand from the size of a moth into something more substantial. In seconds the blaze solidified and soon a ball of golden flame the size of a cantaloupe was hovering just above the palm of his outstretched hand. The blaze did not burn his olive skin in any way, but began to darken the frayed ends of his grey robes.

Xexial just watched the display in silence.

With another defeated sigh, Ashyn closed his hand and the fire dissipated. "I just wish I knew why I can't harness all magic like I can fire."

He looked up at his master, searching his eyes for answers that neither of them had figured out in the last few winters. Xexial took his dark staff and poked it at the burning pitch.

"This is one of those few areas that even I must plead ignorance, my boy," his deep rich voice tried to say soothingly. "You have a strong connection to the element of fire. Why that is, I cannot say for sure.

You know my speculations on the matter, though. Fire is the most primal of the elements. It is aggressive, it is merciless, and it is hungry. No other element acts as fire does.

You are equally as hungry. You yearn for knowledge, for more power; nothing is ever enough. You also have an angry streak in you, lad. I have seen it countless times. When you are angry, you become like the element. You too are aggressive, and often merciless. You draw to fire, just as the magic of it draws to you. That is why I feel you can accept it so easily."

"But it doesn't explain why I cannot do other things," he whined, looking back down at the growing campfire.

"Even I cannot do everything, Ashyn. We take things in stride, and we move in steps. That is all we can ever do. My patience for your understanding of magic goes a long way. True, it may wane occasionally," Xexial said with a gruff laugh. "But I myself know the nature of what it is a wizard deals with."

"It didn't take you this long to learn magic," Ashyn retorted.

Xexial merely shrugged, and reached into the folds of his robe to remove his long-stemmed pipe. After a few moments, he had a strong burn going and the rich smell of tobacco filled the air. "I also couldn't call on magic before I had learned its concepts, something you still can do, that even I cannot. That in itself is strength, and a weakness. Your ability to do one thing easily only adds frustration to your inability to do others. You must learn patience, young man. Eventually you will find your focus."

Xexial withdrew into sucking on his pipe and blowing out long fine lines of smoke. Ashyn knew his council had ended. It had been like this over the last few winters. Moments of compassion coupled with sudden endings in conversation. Xexial was stern, especially in use of magic, but he was also fatherly, and never wanted Ashyn to give up because he felt he couldn't do it. Ashyn respected that. It was part of what made him keep going to learn the magic. It was what made him sure that nothing in this world would ever cause him to betray his master.

Twenty minutes later, Ashyn heard a rhythmic snoring coming from across the fire. He looked over to see is mentor slumped over asleep, his pipe dangling out of the left corner of his mouth. Quietly Ashyn stood up and moved over to the aging man. Gently he pulled the pipe away from Xexial and dumped the remaining tobacco into the campfire. A small waft of sweet smelling smoke filled the air and then was gone.

He rolled the long-stemmed pipe back up in its protective cloth and then tucked it back into the breast pocket within the folds of

Xexial's robes. Once he was sure Xexial wouldn't accidently break his beloved pipe, he tenderly laid his master on his side and covered him in his sleeping blanket.

Ashyn looked to his father figure kindly. Xexial had deep grey streaks running through his long beard, and peppering his shaggy blonde wisps of hair on his bald head. Ashyn was keenly aware of the deep creases on the man's forehead and cheeks. As much as he didn't want to admit it, Ashyn knew the truth of it. Xexial was getting old.

He had already been well past middle-aged when Ashyn had met him as a child. Now Ashyn was nineteen winters, an adult by many standards. Xexial was hitting the twilight age of his life. He was becoming elderly.

The young redheaded man sat down once again on the opposite end of the flames. Pulling up his own sleeping blanket, he continued to stare across the sputtering amber light at his master's pale features. Slowly he felt a single tear build up and stream out of the corner of his eye. It wouldn't be long before Xexial would leave this world.

~ ~ ~

The morning sun came quickly, cresting over the horizon and casting the world in a soft pink glow. Ashyn was already awake, barely able to sleep from the night before. Too many thoughts were running amok through his mind. Was his apparent failing health really why Xexial was bringing him with to Czynsk? Did the elder man know his time was fast coming, and he wanted to prepare the boy for when he was gone? When Ashyn had stepped out the doors yesterday he hadn't thought of that at the time, but seeing Xexial in the light of the fire had made him question if that really were the case?

What bothered Ashyn the most wasn't so much the loss of Xexial. The wizard was aged. He could accept that. No, Ashyn knew, it was something far more integral and selfish. It had chewed at him all night long. Was he truly ready to be a wizard in the world?

Ashyn arose swiftly and cleaned up the camp long before his mentor stirred. It was something that had become common practice over the winters in the tower. Even though Ashyn had developed a somewhat messy demeanor as he entered and passed through his teens, his master was fiercely anal. Xexial kept the tower meticulous and demanded as much from his pupil, as well. So detailed was the elder wizard in nature that the man not only arranged his spell components symmetrically and with equal spacing between each, but he did the same with his eating utensils as well. This forced Ashyn to be equally as vigilant when maintaining an utterly clean environment. So by the time Xexial finally awoke, Ashyn had cleaned the camp spotless and had been ready to leave for almost twenty minutes.

Xexial said nothing, of course. He rarely praised Ashyn when the boy was tidy, only chastised when it wasn't within his usual lofty standards. Instead, the man merely reached into his travel pack to remove his morning rations. The senior ate quietly while Ashyn sat with his back turned on the man, facing west where he knew Czynsk to be. Somewhere to his south near the Shalis-Fey, he thought he heard thunder, but when he glanced at the sky, he saw it to be clear in every direction. *Odd*, Ashyn thought, but didn't consider it long. Soon the lanky young man saw Xexial's long black staff next to him, and he knew it was time to continue their journey to Czynsk.

Again, the journey proceeded at a good pace, Xexial making surprisingly adept time considering he was no longer as spritely as he had once been. By midday on the second day of their journey, Ashyn once again saw the familiar spires of Jasian Enclave's Cathedral. In only an hour more at most, he would once again be stepping foot in the town.

The thunder from the south had continued all morning, but now as they approached Czynsk, so close to the Shalis-Fey, Ashyn found it suspiciously absent, but it wasn't something he considered for long.

As the village loomed closer, Ashyn could no longer deny his growing excitement. After all this time without any social interaction, he would see people once again! He hadn't realized how much he had missed such a thing. Being an outcast in Bremingham, he had thought it would be easy not to have to deal with people anymore, and in the beginning, it had been. He had been so overwhelmed with studies that he hadn't noticed those early winters come and go. Eventually though, as he entered his teenage winters, he had been keenly aware of the absence of something in his life. Now he knew it was to be filled again, however short it may be.

It also brought with it a certain apprehension. He had always been different in the eyes of others, but now there would be more. Now he knew he would possibly be feared. How would

Macky react to him? Their last interaction had been one of awe. How would Avrimae? She had been terrified of Ashyn's visage the night he decided to be a wizard. Would she be even more so now that he was? As doubt began to fill his thoughts, he began to wonder if he really should consider entering the village at all.

"Come on, lad!" Xexial barked without turning to look at him.

Ashyn hadn't even realized that in his inner reflections he had stopped walking. Quickly shaken from his worrisome thoughts, he ran to catch up. It didn't take long. Ashyn had long legs and an equally long stride. When Xexial looked at him, the elder couldn't help but laugh jovially.

"Just keep that mouth shut, let me do all the talking and you'll be fine," Xexial informed him.

Ashyn nodded once and looked straight ahead. "I never bothered to ask you why we were coming here," he told him as they now entered the farming outskirts of the town.

"Nope, you did not," Xexial answered. "Maybe in the future you'll show a little more sagacity."

Ashyn took the discipline with a scowl, knowing that his ignorance was now going to cost him. He knew Xexial wouldn't do anything to endanger him outright of course, but humble him? That was something he did often. Ashyn attempted to piece together any ideas he could formulate as to why the town would request a wizard. Drawing a blank, he only hoped he might somehow garner clairvoyance as they continued through the farmsteads. As it stood, he was acutely aware of people now watching them from inside the windows of their homes. The very first lesson Ashyn had learned was always, **always**, be alert for danger. Ashyn looked around warily as they entered the township borders.

Finally he heard Xexial chuckle to himself. Ashyn looked down to see the older man smiling. "Fine, fine," he said. "Wipe that dour look off your face. It won't do any good meeting the Bishop like you've just been sucking on a lemon."

"Bishop," Ashyn muttered to himself.

Xexial nodded. "The Jasian Enclave has called upon us to aid Czynsk in some way. Most likely refugees from the civil war or resistance groups refusing to accept the victor have been harrying the outlying towns. The Enclave is hoping that our presence will act as a deterrent."

Ashyn nodded, he remembered the civil war well. It was the reason so many orphans had found their way to Czynsk.

Though he had never witnessed a bit of the fighting, the Onyx Tower did reside squarely within the borders of Fermania. Almost all the fighting had taken place on the far eastern side of the territory, closest to the larger cities. After seventeen winters of brutal fighting, Buckner, the capital of Fermania had won out. In the remaining aftermath, dissident groups not content with the way things played out had continued to raise skirmishes against the Fermania military. This of course required resources, and forced the skirmishers to become little more than brigands robbing their own people. They often preyed on the towns furthest from the immediate reach of the military. Towns like Czynsk.

The Enclave's call for their wizard neighbor made sense. The Bishop and Xexial had never been at odds with each other. There was never any real animosity. The Enclave may teach Destruction as a dark and corrupt magic, but the Bishop was a practical man. He knew when not to make an enemy of a potential boon. Ashyn had been the only thorn at the time, and now with so many winters passed, it was likely that wound had long healed.

Minutes later, they cleared the outlying farms. The Enclave grounds loomed high in the background, with the remaining town spread out before them.

The first thing Ashyn noticed was that little had actually changed. The bakery was still in the same spot, with the same tulips sitting at the entrance, though now only young sprouts. Across from the bakery was a slaughterhouse, and so on and so forth down the main expanse of the village. To the east and west were the housing districts, all of them were designed helter-skelter so the town could grow and expand without ever affecting the commercial district in the center. To the far north were the Jasian Enclave church grounds. There housed the Cathedral, two smaller churches, the priory where the priests lived, and of course the hospice for the orphan children.

The second thing he noticed was that nobody was in the streets. No merchants hawking their wares, no passersby, not even the orphans cleaning the town, as they normally did. There was no one. It was a ghost town.

Ashyn quickly looked down at this mentor. He needn't ask the question. He saw that Xexial missed none of it either. Xexial swept his head back and forth as they walked, never stopping or slowing, but maintaining a steady pace towards the cathedral looming tall in the background. For some reason, Ashyn suddenly felt the place was more ominous than holy.

Still he proceeded forward. Even then, he whispered an incantation he had learned early on, one of the few he had actually gotten right. Small wisps of smoke leaked from his fingertips very faintly, slowly rising up to coat his body as he walked through it. Out of the corner of his eye, he saw Xexial nodding in approval, and soon the small cloud of murky air drifted up him as well.

"There is a dissonance here that I just can't place," he whispered to his mentor.

"All the more reason that we may have been summoned. Perhaps the threat is closer than we realized?" Xexial calmly returned. "Be mindful, these people are here, but they are hiding. It's not the usual fear of magic that keeps them at bay either. There is something malefic afoot."

"How do you know?" Ashyn asked.

"This old man can sense it," Xexial returned flatly, ending the topic.

As they entered the heart of the commercial district, Ashyn began looking for some signs that may indicate such a wariness of the town folk. Perhaps a raid had already transpired? Maybe the call for a wizard had come too late? The damage had been done and the town was now fearful of strangers.

Yet as he walked by the buildings, he saw no signs of any kind of hostility. There were no burn marks to indicate fires, no shattered or re-mended doorways. He could see no fresh indications on the wind-worn wood of any of the structures of scuffing, knicks, or anything else that may have indicated a conflict.

Ashyn searched the ground for any kind of long furrows that could indicate potential raider caravans. Often, such trails tended to be wilder than a merchant caravan's was, and deeper. For a travelling merchant often loaded to lighter loads and stuck to well-known pathways. Raiders, on the other hand, always overloaded their wagons with as much as could be carried, causing far deeper ruts in the ground, and chose terrain not as well-worn by militia patrols.

Ashyn also looked for the signs of dragging. Generally, if bodies were drug for means of torture there would be a long, wide, shallow depression on the ground, far wider than the standard wagon wheel.

He could see neither of these however, just the usual patterns on the hard ground indicating the well-worn daily life going on about it. So many feet traversed the earth here it was hard to make out anything distinguishing from the rest.

When he looked up from the ground again, they were much closer to the cathedral, already entering the enclave grounds. Idly he looked to the trees where he and Macky used to rake leaves. It was unchanged. It was as perfectly manicured as it always had been. This raised another question to Ashyn.

Where were the orphans? If the grounds were so well-kept, they would have to be about, too. Were they all hiding in the hospice, fearful for their lives? He looked around for any indications that they had fled to safety. Abandoned chores, equipment, clothing and the like, but he found nothing. Everything was normal. It was as if they had all just disappeared, or at least entered their homes and then never left.

It was then that he began to notice something different about the footprints that disturbed the verdant lawn.

There were multiple smaller depressions at the front of the tracks than what he was used to seeing with prints. Five of them in fact, per print. That meant only one thing: they were barefoot. These were smaller feet, however, not the feet of human adults. Thinner, delicate feet with graceful arches and slender toes. Ashyn knew that all the orphans had some sort of booting when he had been there. Either that meant that the Enclave had to have made some budget cuts or there were . . .

"Elves," Xexial said aloud as if answering his very thoughts.

"How did you . . .?" Ashyn began as he looked up, and froze.

Standing in the doorway of the cathedral was a Wild Elf. She, like most of her race, was shorter than the humans by almost a foot. Dark raven hair ran down past her hard-muscled shoulders. She glared at them both with deep brown eyes that were almost as dark as her hair. Her face would have been exquisitely beautiful if not for the blood that was smeared across it, leaving a crimson trail of cruor across her otherwise flawless features.

She was nearly naked, like the other Ferhym he had seen a decade before. Every curve of her lithe, muscled frame was visible, with only a loincloth and a tightly-wrapped cloth across her breasts covering her body. The gory war paint was also laced across her hardened body in no discernable patterns that he could recognize.

She held a long spear, angled downwards. Its flat, wide head gleamed in the early afternoon light. Tightly fastened across her back was a satchel of javelins, each one having a jagged edge at the base of its piercing head. He knew that they would do just as much damage to someone's flesh coming out, as they had going in. Ashyn keenly remembered how accurate those javelins tended to be in the hands of the Ferhym.

Ashyn knew then that the dissonance he had felt entering the town had been much like the feeling he had known back in the ravine. It was a sixth sense, an understanding that something unseen was watching him. He had felt it in his gut, but had not truly acted on it. That meant that they were surrounded. He looked all around, and even though he could not see them, he could now feel them, all about. He cursed to himself.

Ashyn looked back at the female Elf on the steps. He was drawn into her dark eyes. They glistened at him with an unrequited hate that he couldn't fathom. She wanted to kill him. Instinctually he felt it, down to his very core. He could see deep in her orbs her ardent desire to plunge her weapon into his chest.

When she spoke, her voice floated through the air like a sonnet. It was strange to hear such a melodious voice come from someone that was dripping with such detestation and odium. What surprised him however, was when she spoke it was in the common Trade tongue and not her native language.

"Be you the dwellers of the piceous spear that taints the sky?" she asked.

For a moment Ashyn didn't understand what she was asking. Was it a code perhaps that Xexial knew? He had spoken to them in the past, maybe it was a form of greeting. Yet Ashyn knew that couldn't be the case. The people of the town were hidden, or worse. And the Elf that stood before him radiated such abhorrence that there was no way she would be greeting them in any sort of formal way. From tomes and even from Xexial, he knew they were a deeply tribal people. Perhaps she referred to something else, something more modern. Then it dawned on him that she wasn't speaking any phrase. It was merely her translation of the Onyx Tower. She was there for them.

"Have you harmed any of these people?" Xexial asked, almost nonchalantly, ignoring her initial question.

"Some, yes," she responded, just as nonchalantly, as if causing pain and ailment to others meant nothing to her. "There are 'skewers' here. This town needed to be purged of them."

"The Council's arm will have extended far indeed, if they think to administer balance to a human town," Xexial replied darkly.

"Humans mean nothing," she scoffed at him. "It is the Council of Elm's duty to keep balance in this world. Human, Hym -it matters not- only balance matters," she told him with a zealotry that Xexial had warned Ashyn about.

Xexial had ardently tutored him on the belief structure of the Ferhym, and of their system of government known as the Council of Elm. He knew that they sought to preserve the balance of nature in all things, which included the balancing of powers between the races, that they trained night and day as warriors to lead their crusade of balance.

At some point over the centuries that noble goal, however, became an obsession. And slowly their view of what power really was became horribly contorted. Now they hunted, killed, or enslaved anything that they felt disrupted the harmony of nature, which in their eyes was just about everything. Large numbers were what kept them at bay. They were like predators stalking prey, looking for the weakest and most infirm. They would hit a straggler, but never a large pack. Generally, a town as large as Czynsk would have been enough to keep the Ferhym at bay . . ., yet as Ashyn looked around the grounds it seemed as if that was no longer the case.

"Yet you endanger the others here. There are regular people whom do not skew the balance here; simple folk living simple lives," Xexial countered once more.

"Harborers of the wicked should have known better. They put their lot in with the iniquitous; they brought this fate unto themselves," she argued defiantly.

Still tight-lipped, Ashyn watched as Xexial's gaze never moved from the Wild Elf. Ashyn knew Xexial had encountered the Elves often enough to know he couldn't break them from their course. "What do you intend to do with the purged?" the elder wizard asked.

"That is for the Councilors to decide," she answered sinisterly. "Reclamation is an option."

Ashyn realized then that the people she was talking about, the 'skewers', had not been killed. They had surely been hurt. He could tell that from the Elf's countenance alone. But if the councilors were to decide their fate, that meant they were detained. If they were detained then they could possibly be saved.

Ashyn knew Xexial realized the same thing. The question was how would the wizard act on it knowing they faced such overwhelming numbers?

The Elf capitalized on the momentary indecision of the senior wizard. "You did not answer my question, strangers," she hissed in her melodic way. "Be you from the stygian spire to the east?"

Ashyn was sure she already knew the answer. If the Elves had been responsible for the summons then it was likely that they had been following them from the moment they left the tower. The Ferhym were relentless in their crusade.

He thought of the presence he had felt on the precipice the morning before. If it were the Elves, why didn't they strike outside the tower? Or in the highlands? Why would they wait until they got to Czynsk? Perhaps it was possible she didn't know the answer.

Apparently it was a gamble that Xexial was willing to take. "No, I am a humble man seeking worship from my deity," he told the Elf, and then added, "The boy next to me is merely an aide and of no consequence."

The Elf's posture stiffened. Ashyn knew it was not an answer she wanted. "Since when does a humble man need an aid?" she demanded.

Xexial shrugged. "I am venerable," he answered. "I have not the vitality I used to."

The Elf studied them both in silence for a long while. Ashyn could feel the tension mounting between them, and he was sure there were javelins already targeted on them that were just awaiting the moment to be released. The spell he had cast on himself had been a warning of incoming projectiles, the tension of its effect already beginning to hum in his ears. There was no way he would be able to dodge more than one, two if he was lucky. It was likely that he'd have a volley of no less than a dozen soaring his way, and he would be pierced like a wild boar.

Finally the Elf broke her vehement gaze from them, "You will find no respite here, old man. Seek your god elsewhere."

Xexial bowed his head and turned away from the Elf. Ashyn stared in wide-eyed horror. They were just going to leave? They were going to leave Czynsk to its fate at the hands of the Wild Elves?

"Come lad, it is time to go," Xexial told him distantly.

Outrage built within him. Images of burning buildings and blood-soaked roads flashed before his eyes. His vision flared to life with vivid heat. His world was bathed in a rich orange light. He would have acted on it immediately, incinerated everything he saw before going down in a fiery blaze of glory. But the look in his master's eyes quelled it. Ashyn saw sadness. The light died.

"You cannot win this fight, Ashyn," he whispered solemnly. "Let it go."

Ashyn could feel the Elves all around waiting for him to strike. They were anticipating it, hoping for it. They wanted him to show power, prove he was what they sought. They wanted his violence.

Worse than that though, Ashyn realized he wanted the violence, too. This startled him, even scared him; this wanton desire for another's death. So with anger seething in every step, he turned away from the enticing battle before him, and followed his master out of the Enclave's grounds, through the commercial district, and out of Czynsk.

Slowly he left it all behind him, people he had once called friends, who were probably depending on him for a rescue. He knew that they would suffer untold atrocities at the hands of the Wild Elves. His mind tried to rationalize how what his master was doing was right, but he couldn't. Even though Xexial was right in front of him, he didn't see him at all. All he saw was the image of his village ablaze all around him. All he heard were their screams of agony. It would be Bremingham all over again, and he was powerless to stop it.

BRANCH COMMANDER

Whísper knew that the wizard had been in front of her all along. Though the man was older than she remembered, his unique gloves and his intimate knowledge of the Ferhym had given away his perfidious nature. The huntress would have killed him on sight, but she had been given explicit instructions from her mother, the First Councilor. The other hunters had to see the magic if they were to hate it. They had to feel it. To be devoted to the cause they needed to first taste the wrath of evil. She needed to goad him into attacking them, just as he had all those winters before in the ravine.

The introduction of the young man had been an unanticipated complication. By all accounts, she had been told the wizard was alone. Was this redheaded man also a wizard? If so, she would need to be wary. One wizard was deadly enough on his own, but two? She would need more hunters.

Yet she couldn't help feeling that she knew this young human. His appearance seemed so familiar to her, as if she had seen him before. As she watched him walk out of the Enclave grounds, he turned once more to look their way. His skin, his hair, his face sparked a lingering memory. Where had she seen this man? Then she looked into his eyes, a piercing, grey, hawk like gaze that bore into her very spirit. She understood completely. It had been a long time since she had seen those eyes in the ravine. It appeared the boy was now a man. A moment of dread took to her face. "Dui Nuchada," she whispered. He was still alive. After all this time, he had somehow escaped the Maze?

Whísper looked to the hunter standing behind her in the shadows of the cathedral entryway. He was a thin-muscled Elf only a few decades her junior and well-developed.

"Gather the wicked ones for the council to judge. Also, gather more hunters for the added threat of the young man. We cannot rule out the possibility that he, too, is a wizard. For no one but a wizard would be vile enough not to even care for his own kind," she told the younger hunter.

He nodded at her, and turned to walk away when an idea came to Whísper. "One more thing," she ordered the hunter. He turned to look at his superior. "Bring me our 'special' girl from the caravans. There's more than one way to draw the beast out."

Again, he nodded, but Whísper could tell that he didn't understand what she was planning. *Good*, she thought. Perhaps she could make this work yet. Her dread over the sight of the Nuchada quickly faded as she realized that it might be a second chance. She could still bring him to her mother . . . alive, once again.

As the hunter was leaving down the walkway, Whísper's second in command ran up through the trees to the front of the Cathedral. She was near the same height as Whísper with chin length brown hair and bland brown eyes. A thick white scar ran across her left cheek. No amount of war paint could ever hide it. It only made her more delectable in Whísper's eyes.

Whísper watched as she saluted by placing the tip of her spear against her left shoulder.

"Report, Shedalia," Whísper said.

Shedalia looked deep into her void-like eyes. "The wizard and his aide have left this human settlement completely. They are headed east. What has happened, huntress?"

"The creatures are crafty, Shedalia. Worry not. They knew of the trap before even approaching this edifice. They used their vile trade to protect themselves, slightly, but enough to discourage our open assault here in this confined area. But on the open lands they will be a greater target, now that they are not defended within that devilish tower of theirs," she replied as if the setback had not really mattered.

Shedalia nodded at her, but Whísper could tell her second wasn't finished.

"Do you have more?" the raven-haired huntress asked her subordinate.

"What of the town?" the scarred female asked. "If they have not fallen for the ruse what becomes of this place?"

Whísper casually looked at her surroundings. Almost all the town was made using natural resources. Therefore, she couldn't fault the humans for creating roofs to place above their heads. They also lived off the land, as should all races, so they had done no wrong there.

The Elves had gathered up the small rabble of usurpers before a conflict could even ensue. She had wanted to use the rebels as leverage against the wizard, but it obviously had not worked. So the rest of the town was mostly innocent.

The only thing that insulted the spirits was the very effigy she was standing upon. It was an affront to the natural order of things, and for that those guilty would pay. "Release the villagers to their lives, but gather this 'enclave' and lock them all in the cathedral."

"And then, huntress?"

"Put it to torch."

"Is that wise?" a high-pitched, melodious voice sang out from behind her, within the Cathedral itself.

Whísper turned to acknowledge the voice, bitterly. She knew who was speaking: the one the druids followed so piously. This Elf had platinum hair with deep tan skin, her posture and demeanor were the exact same as Whísper's, that of one in charge. This female Elf in front of her also bore none of the wild paint, nor lack of clothing as the others. She was adorned in a simple green flowing dress that touched all the way down to her toes. She had high, strong cheekbones and a long thin nose. Her lips were so full that she seemed to usually have a pouty expression on her face. Her raw natural beauty always astounded the Branch Commander, and for a sliver of a moment sent a pang of jealousy up her spine. It was momentary though, for Ferhym were trained to know nothing but humility, and she was nothing if not humble. Yet Whísper still grew angry as this Elf stared up at her with startling silver eyes. She averted her gaze from the Elf's eyes as she had been directed all her life.

"You were informed that I lead this expedition, my Voïre dui Ceremeia. As such, you were told to stay away from the wizards, for your protection. I will not be known as the one who lost one of our chosen to the Unbalancers," Whísper said stubbornly, and then added, "Besides, your purpose here was singular, to identify any threats within Czynsk."

"Your compassion warms me," the platinum-haired Elf answered her. "Though I feel it is uncertain, regarding the peoples here."

"This temple is a blasphemy against nature, it needs to be destroyed," Whísper retorted.

"Yet it is a place of worship to these peoples' god," the Voïre dui Ceremeia replied.

Whisper shook her head angrily, her raven locks swaying against the wind. "A sacrilegious entity. There is nothing but the spirits, and nature. These humans should look past false idols."

The Voïre nodded, and continued, "Perhaps the temple, but the people?"

"A message needs to be sent. Skewers of the balance shall never be permitted," Whisper said earnestly. She caught a glitter of approval in Shedalia's brown eyes.

Yet a shadow of displeasure crossed the silver-eyed Elf's full lips. "This will not engender these people to our cause," she argued.

Whisper smiled deviously. "That was never the intention. The wizards, they are all we care about, not turning the faith of this profane little village."

"But . . ." the Voïre dui Ceremeia tried to say, but Whisper held up her hand stalling the argument.

"The First Councilor named me Branch Commander and tasked me with this assignment, not you, Voïre dui Ceremeia."

Whisper could see that it rankled the female more than a little. Still Whisper watched as the Voïre acquiesced to her command and instead opted to change topics. "Is it true then?" The Voïre asked. "Was the Nuchada here? Alive after all this time?"

Whisper held her composure, though she would have liked to swear. She had whispered it to herself, and yet the girl still heard. If she had wanted it open knowledge, she wouldn't have whispered it! She wanted to yell, but she supposed little could stop it now. Whisper nodded, "He was."

"I would very much like to identify him," the Voïre dui Ceremeia replied.

Whisper shook her head. "Not an option. You have your task, I have mine. I will not have you endangered, so close to wizards. I risked much just keeping you in this monstrous effigy, just so you could gather the information the Council of Elm needs. I will risk no further chance on your life to sate your curiosity. If you want him identified so badly, I will have one of the druids do it for you," she said with a tone of finality, before adding, "Besides, your motives regarding the Nuchada are . . . suspect . . . to say the least."

Whether this angered the platinum beauty or not, she made no show, instead she merely shrugged and said, "Perhaps."

Shedalia stepped forward, close to Whisper, very close, drawing her attention back to her second in command.

She could feel the heat emanating from her well-muscled body. She could smell the sour smell of her sweat mingled with the rich scents of pine. It gave her longing.

Whísper fought hard to maintain her composure in front of the branches before her, and especially the Voïre dui Ceremeia. Her mother had appointed her the honor of leading this vanguard charge against the wizards.

"What are your orders?" Shedalia asked, almost seductively, teasingly.

Whísper bit back what she wanted to reply, and maintained her best composure, "Take the Voïre dui Ceremeia and a small branch, and provide her escort to the Council so that she may report all her findings to the First Councilor."

Immediately Whísper saw that it hurt Shedalia's feelings, perhaps even pride, to be relegated to escort. But Whísper knew it needed to be done. "I was hoping to be part of the Van," Shedalia said honestly.

Whísper nodded, "And I would have you," she lied, "but the appearance of a second wizard has complicated matters. Returning the Voïre dui Ceremeia is only one of two tasks I would have you perform."

"And the second?" she asked, acting the huntress she was now, all traces of romance gone.

"To gather a second branch, perhaps multiple branches, and lead them back here. Inform the Council yourself of my request if you must, but the fact is we came to eradicate one skewer of the balance, not two. We need reinforcements. Druids, if they can be spared."

Whísper saw she was honestly shocked by the order. "I am to lead a second branch?"

Whísper nodded. "Yes, you are to be the Branch Commander." *Unless my mother, the First Councilor, deems otherwise,* she thought, but decided to leave that out.

"It is an honor, Branch Commander," Shedalia said with a salute and a smile. As she turned to leave, she gave a small wink to Whísper and then began to walk down the dais.

That is why you must leave, Whísper thought with a sigh. She would be a liability when battling the wizards, not due to lack of skill on her part, but due to Whísper's emotions for her. Impulsively she called out to Shedalia once more, "Huntress, after you gather your branch come see me in private. I will help you chose the words to take to the Council."

Shedalia turned, nodded, and then was gone.

The Voïre dui Ceremeia stepped by her, they shared a brief look towards one another, violating standard tradition. Quickly Whísper looked away, lest anyone see her small mutiny against the rules. "It has been an honor as well, to have been part of this vanguard. Regardless of how short my stay was," she said in her song-like voice. "I will report all my findings, as you say." Then she too, was gone down the dais.

Whísper sighed then as she watched the two of them go. So now she needed a new second in command for the time being. She looked to her troops. None truly served like Shedalia did, and her husband Suneris was not part of the Van, but she tried not to think of that. She saw an older fit male Elf nearby, within the Cathedral. He had been with her when they first encountered the wizard as well, back in the ravine in Shalis-Fey. He would do.

"Ringea, front and center please."

The older Elf nodded and stepped forward. "Yes, Huntress."

"You are my new second in command in the absence of Huntress Shedalia," she said almost monotonously.

Ringea nodded at her. "Yes, Huntress. What are your first orders then?"

Whísper looked around once at the convoluted edifice they stood in. She didn't care who the Voïre dui Ceremeia was, or what she thought. "Burn this defilement. Burn it to the ground," she stated boldly.

"And this Enclave?" he asked, his face emotionless.

"Burn them with it."

~ ~ ~

Crashes resounded outside as her Ferhym gathered the Enclave up. She knew that her people would be occupied for a long time as they set the perimeter of the cathedral grounds ablaze. Thoughts of the Nuchada filled her head. How did the boy survive? And a wizard now? The First Councilor would be furious to say the least, and Whísper knew she had to act quickly to quell the matter. It was only luck that she had the servant girl close at hand.

A creak from the well-worn door alerted her of another's presence inside the small domicile the Enclave had called a hospice. Cots were strewn everywhere for the orphaned children, along with chamber pots and meager medical supplies.

Whisper stared at the map the Council of Elm had made for her regarding the location of the Onyx Tower and beyond, but she really didn't see it.

She felt the firm callused hands come up from behind her, sliding across her abdomen, tracing the Windsong family mark. Now that her mother was First Councilor, she had the right to keep her heritage markings, even though she was life-mated. So keep them she did.

The strong fingers tiptoed across her sensitive skin, raising gooseflesh across her body. One hand slid up and unbuckled her cloth bindings, freeing her breasts.

Violently she was spun around. She looked into the eyes of her lover, brown, and fierce with desire. Quickly she thrust the map off the meager medical table and felt herself lifted upon it by strong muscled arms. She grabbed her lover's doe brown hair, pulling it back, revealing her strong chin and long copper throat.

Whisper smashed her lips against the others. They wrestled at each other's clothing, breathing heavily between long kisses. "Quickly," she breathed. "We mustn't be seen."

Her loincloth came away, and wet salty fingers probed. She gasped. Quickly she thrust her tongue into the other Elf's mouth. She tasted the sweetness of her, and let her hands return the favor.

Minutes later they were done, spread amongst numerous cots, intertwined in each other's arms, sweat mingled together across their slick bodies. The scent of their lust remained thick and heady in the air. Whisper could still taste her lover on her lips and tongue.

She looked deep into Shedalia's eyes. "Do I really have to leave?" her second whispered.

Whisper nodded gently, and stroked Shedalia's brown mane. "This is important," Whisper answered, "We failed to kill the Nuchada winters ago and now he is a wizard. This is a threat we cannot ignore. We need the First Councilor's backing."

"Your mother's backing," Shedalia stated plainly. Quickly the well-muscled woman sat up. Whisper noticed her lover's breasts remained aroused. Shedalia folded her arms over them. "It is because of your mother that I must share you," she said bitterly.

Whisper sat up and wrapped her arms around the scarred young Elf, "You only share my body," she whispered soothingly to Shedalia, "All my love is for you, and only you."

Shedalia hugged Whísper's arms once and kissed the top of her head. "I know. I just . . . hate hiding who we are," she said somberly.

Whísper sighed. "We must hide. We must do it for the Ferhym. Balance comes before our desires," she tried to say sincerely. But deep in her heart, she too wondered why she couldn't express who she really was.

"But why would the spirits make us this way, if they didn't want us to be like this? Are we not the present image of what they once were?" Shedalia persisted.

Whísper looked down at the floor. "We can't," she said plainly. "The First Councilor forbids it."

Shedalia pulled back. "And we're back to your mother," she said angrily.

Whísper looked at her, shocked. "She's the First Councilor, what do you expect me to do?" she argued.

"Stand up to her!" Shedalia shot back. "Be who you are. Who we are! We shouldn't be hiding like this!"

Whísper cursed silently and stared again at the ground. Even if she agreed with Shedalia, what could she do? Her mother was First Councilor; she communed with the spirits directly. She knew what it was that the spirits wanted, not Whísper, not Shedalia. "Can we talk about this another time?" she asked heatedly.

"Fine," Shedalia huffed.

Whísper thought that perhaps they were going to be leaving on a bad note, when she found Shedalia staring into her dark eyes curiously. "Was that really the Nuchada?" her lover asked.

Whísper nodded. She was certain of it. "That's another reason I want our Voïre dui Ceremeia gone. She may be loyal to our people, but I question her motives."

"She is a woman grown now. Perhaps it was only a flight of fancy, being but a child?" Shedalia suggested.

Whísper though held no such illusions. "Either way it is best to separate her from him, just in case."

The fit woman then dressed quickly, and handed Whísper's garments to her. "I just wish I didn't have to escort the Voïre dui Ceremeia. Chosen or not, they give me the creeps. Something about their swirling eyes," Shedalia shivered.

Whísper laughed. "At least you don't have one as a sister."

Shedalia laughed at that too, and then they shared one last intimate embrace. Whísper was happy it had ended well after all. "Return to me swiftly with more branches," Whisper said softly, and added, "And into my arms."

Shedalia pulled away. "You'll never even know I was gone."

As the huntress left, Whisper gathered up the fallen map and looked at it more earnestly now. Her emotions had been lifted, and she could safely do her job. She saw the perfect place to plan her rouse. A brilliant white smile took her face. It was so simple, Whisper realized, if only she could have done it eleven winters earlier.

Whisper rolled up the map and stepped out into the light. Smoke was beginning to barrel out of the broken windows around the cathedral, and with it followed the screams of terror of those trapped inside; skewers of the balance being cast their rightful judgment.

It was beautiful.

THE PRICE REALIZED

Ashyn brooded as he followed his master. There was a tempest building within him, waiting to explode. In the distance, he could hear the burning crackle of wood and stone as the Jasian Cathedral burned behind him. The windows shattered as the growing heat broiling within erupted like a volcano of smoke and debris. The raging flames drowned out the screams of the terrified people within, but Ashyn thought he could still hear them in the back of his head. Or perhaps it was only his mind hearing the screams of the dead of Bremingham. The memory was nothing more than a phantom locked in the deepest recesses of his mind, lurking its way to the surface to constantly haunt him.

The smoke plumed thick and heavy, rolling from the holy effigy and drifting high into the air. It appeared as a slate grey blanket that covered the sky. To goad him even further into anger, a westerly wind picked up carrying the odor of the smoldering ruin squarely in his path. The stench of burnt stone and flesh turned his stomach as much in fury as in revulsion.

People had died. They died once again, brutally, and by an equally savage species. He had been powerless to stop it once more. He looked down to his hands. They were shaking with frustration, with a rage he could barely contain.

He held his left hand before him. His deep olive skin began to redden. He felt it grow hot beneath his skin, broiling hot down in his very bones. There was a searing blaze at the core of him that wasn't just anger. It was something more, something visceral, something primal. Waves of heat rolled off his flesh, the air wavered around it, but Ashyn's hand did not blister or blacken. He let the rage build the fire of hate inside of him. His chest vibrated with power and fury. He could feel it, feel a connection. Then he turned his anger inward, focusing on the pyrophoric emanations coming from his hand. Suddenly a spark flared to life. That was all it took to engulf his entire limb in a raging inferno of raw magical fire. *That was new*, he thought. Even calling to fire, he had never done that before.

Then he realized that he wasn't powerless, not this time. Ashyn wasn't going to stand by and let Czynsk burn, not when he could at least try to save them.

"There's nothing we can do, my boy," Xexial said to him without turning around.

Anger still fueled Ashyn, and he wasn't about to be dissuaded again. "You haven't even tried!" he spat vehemently.

Slowly the wizened sage turned around to look at his pupil. Ashyn saw a momentary glitter in his eyes when he looked at Ashyn's burning arm. Whether it was pride or shock, Ashyn wasn't sure; his wrath wasn't allowing him to think clearly. Either way it was quickly recovered. "And what are we supposed to do, hmm? Go running in there, raining death and destruction upon the Ferhym in retaliation for what they have done to Czynsk?"

"You're damn right!"

Xexial shook his head. "And about how long do you think you'd live? A minute, maybe two? How many of them would you kill to sate your bloodlust?"

"All of them," he answered darkly.

Xexial sighed. "Youth," he muttered, shaking his head. After a moment, he looked back at the ardent young man. "Do you know what the true definition of a hero is, lad?"

"Someone who does the right thing," Ashyn countered.

"No," Xexial returned. "A hero is someone who gets other people killed."

Ashyn scoffed in open disgust at his master.

Xexial turned to look at his student fully. Ashyn's anger did not wither under the elder's scrutiny. "You're mistaking the obvious choice for the right choice. That is the common failing of a hero, to do the obvious. Czynsk is held captive by the Elves. The obvious answer is to liberate them. Right now, they are likely killing the Enclave because the cathedral is an aberration in their eyes. You detest this, and you know it is wrong. However, you must understand the larger picture. You see, the villagers will be spared.

"The Council of Elm's policies are broken, surely, but they do believe in balance, no matter how convoluted it may seem. If you go in there right now, with the intent I see in your eyes, you will fight very bravely and die very quickly. Moreover, you will absolutely get a large portion of Czynsk killed as well. Women and children alike. People that will live, if you are doing precisely as we are doing right now.

"You see, my boy, you're giving the Ferhym exactly what they want: a reason for them to call you 'evil'. All the reason they need to call all of Czynsk evil."

"So your answer then is to let the clergy die?" Ashyn said, aghast at his master's reasoning.

Xexial nodded. "If you value what they believe in, yes. Though everyone fears death, few are more ready to accept it than the men and women of the clergy. They embrace the afterlife and their Maker."

"But they are dying because of us!" Ashyn argued. "This wouldn't be happening if not for us!"

"No!" Xexial snapped for the first time, causing Ashyn to falter. "You do not accept fault for this! Do you hear me, boy! This blood is on the hands of the Ferhym and their twisted Council and no one else!"

"But they wanted wizards . . .," Ashyn said somberly as he looked to the ground. The fire in his outstretched arm slowly began to wane as the blaring orange light trickled to a moderate flickering blue from his shoulder down to his elbow.

"This crusade would take place regardless, Ashyn. They are here, doing this because they want to. If not wizards, then they would have found another reason, rest assured. You must learn not to carry the burden of other's lives on your shoulders. You'll have enough of one just being a wizard," Xexial told him empathetically.

"So we walk away like cowards? It just feels so wrong."

"And that is why it is the right choice; because it is the hardest to do. Trust me lad, it is for no weakness on my part. I do not fear the Elves. I would like nothing more than to rain vengeance down upon that dark-haired bitch. I have personally known the Bishop longer than you have even been alive. Though he may not be a friend, it does not mean that I am indifferent to what is happening. I am still human."

"Sacrifice the few . . .," Xexial began.

"For the many," Ashyn finished. It was one of the primary edicts of wizardry. Sometimes the balance of magic required that something would have to give for the greater good of all.

"But shouldn't we fight? Are we to condone tyranny?" Ashyn asked.

"Politics are not for a true wizard, lad. It is the people's choice to fight, not yours to fight for them. A wizard is not meant to be a champion, regardless of your moral grounds. We are meant to keep those people alive to the best of our abilities. Sometimes that means turning your back on them. If we stay, if we fight, they will die. But if we leave, we take the fire away from the Ferhym, and the conflict away from Czynsk."

"Czynsk will hate us for this. For abandoning them," Ashyn continued.

He found Xexial nodding. "Yes they will. Nevertheless, they will live on to hate us. Would you rather they die violently, glorifying you? Or live long, fruitful lives continuing on for many generations, all of them hating your very name?"

"I . . . ," Ashyn realized he could not answer.

Xexial looked at Ashyn, and for the first time Ashyn could see an unfathomable sadness in the old man's weary eyes. "Now you realize the true price of being a wizard, *son*, and why we are so utterly alone."

"The few . . . ," he said, pointing at himself and then Ashyn. ". . . for the many," he finished opening his hand and fanning it in a broad arc in front of him.

Without another word, Xexial turned back around and continued his journey home. Ashyn stood still for a long while. He just stared down at his hand as the remaining fires ebbed away. It had seemed so easy as a child being an outcast; just ostracize the world around him, like the sacrifice would be marginal. Ashyn realized then that Avrimae's tears all those winters prior were not for what he'd become, but for what he would endure. It was then that the truth really hit home. He was to live an existence devoid of life. Ironically, the one thing he was meant to maintain. There was only one master and one apprentice, ever. Once Xexial died, he would forever be . . . alone.

A single tear ran down his face, and broke away. It connected with his open hand, and sizzled into nothingness. Just like all the hopes and dreams of his life.

LEVERAGE

The day drug on bleakly, and Ashyn couldn't help but glance back at the long thin line of deep grey that spiraled up from the horizon. It had been hours since the cathedral was put to fire, and he knew that at this point it was nothing more than a smoldering heap, with whatever remained inside nothing but an indistinguishable pile of cinders.

Like the cathedral, all his anger had been extinguished, now he felt humbled and hollow. He had made an oath to Xexial, and the elder wizard had been forthcoming in everything, quite often in fact, but only now did his choice really sink in. His life was one meant to be lived alone. Not merely an outcast, but alone.

It had seemed easy as a little boy to make that choice. He had lost everything in Bremingham already, and perhaps so driven on revenge had not thought as clearly as he should have. Yet could a young boy ever really think clearly, he wondered? Had his pain manipulated him into making such a weighty decision prematurely?

Xexial had politely left him to his thoughts, just as Ashyn had assumed the old man was in deep contemplation as well. The Elves were afoot, Ashyn knew. They were out for wizard blood and Xexial was probably pondering the why?

Would Czynsk be the first in a long line of towns assaulted and threatened for catering to a wizard's passing? How many would follow, and would their outcomes be worse?

Though the Council of Elm's rationale never made much sense to Ashyn, his research on their application always was well-strategized. If wizards were their enemy once again, then the Council would do everything in its power to make sure they had no safe harbor. Ashyn knew that meant only one thing for Xexial. He would have to notify the Seven. Xexial was probably trying to theorize all the possible reasons why the Wild Elves would be after them, so he could give the elder wizards a proper accounting.

And so it was that they both remained lost in their own contemplations long after the sun set from the sky and night settled in around them. Ashyn was staring at the flickering fire, lost in its dance, when Xexial finally spoke.

"Odium," he said quietly.

Shaken from the torpor of his deep thoughts he looked up to his master. "Excuse me?"

"It seems to be the defining characteristic of the Ferhym's lives, odium. Wizards have been at odds with the Council of Elm since its founding. There have been countless conflicts over the generations, but it's always remained small. Us versus them, as it were. Never have they expanded their hatred for us onto the widespread populace. What they have done to the Enclave cathedral, and all of Czynsk for that matter, is unprecedented. I have no choice. I have to contact the Seven," his deep voice thrummed as he quietly thought aloud.

Ashyn nodded. "I had figured you might."

Xexial chuckled, "Yes, of course you did. That means that we'll be on the move again though, and quickly. We cannot linger in the tower overlong and just wait for the Ferhym to become bold enough to strike there . . ."

Xexial droned on about the Ferhym's tactics and how soon they would rally against the Onyx tower, but Ashyn wasn't listening. He suddenly felt a wave of apprehension roll over him that had nothing to do with what Xexial was talking about. The elder mage's words fell to the back of his mind as he slowly began to look about the field they were in. Something was wrong. Something was out of place.

He looked across the tall grasses that swayed comfortably in a gentle breeze. It was a bright moonlit evening, and he could see around him quite clearly. It was wide open, offering a large view in every direction. Yet he could see nothing. All appeared fine. And even though he was out in the vast expanse, his surroundings suddenly felt enclosed, claustrophobic. As if something were crushing in on him from all sides.

Slowly he stood up, and began to scan the horizon. He had felt this before. It took a moment but then he realized what was out of place, amidst the popping fire and Xexial speaking, was silence, a complete and utter silence. No other noise in an open and bountiful land. No animal, nor insect. Ashyn knew that silence and he knew that could only mean one thing.

Instantly Ashyn called to the fire, pulling the flames away from the campfire and holding them in massive globes the size of overripe melons in front of his outstretched hands.

Xexial watched his student, suddenly alert. "What is it?" he asked defensively.

"Predators."

Xexial pulled himself to his feet next to his student, and began peering into the silver-lit night. Ashyn could see the top of his head just out of the corner of his eye. Xexial did not question the apprehension of his pupil, and instead trusted in the boy's instincts. Ashyn recognized that.

A new sound filled his ears, a deep hum, as Xexial's luminescent blue gloves began to flicker with the crackling power of electricity.

Ashyn stared keenly at the wavering grasslands. He gauged the height of the tall shoots around three to four feet. It was plenty tall enough for something to hide amidst. That raised a question to the redheaded boy as he identified the nature of what he was feeling, something from his childhood.

"Do Ferhym ever use Bristle Wolves to hunt with?" he whispered to his master.

This caused Xexial to search the area more ardently. "A few have been known to, yes. It's hard to train them, though. What is it you know?" he asked.

"They're present. I can feel them. They're stalking something, but I don't think it's us," Ashyn told his master.

"We are very far from the Shalis-Fey, lad. Are you certain of this?"

It was true; they were miles from the deep confines of the woods within which the wolves dwelled. To be out this far on the highlands was unheard of for the beasts.

Ashyn nodded. "I have encountered one before, as a child. I know what it felt like. I feel it now. That's why I asked about the Elves."

"Good deduction then, lad," Xexial commented, looking across the silver fields.

They scanned the fields for several more minutes, an apprehension growing in the pit of his stomach. He could feel the wolves stalking, but what it was he was uncertain. It wasn't a deer or any other open land animal, of that he was positive. The Bristle Wolves represented a threat, but not to him, not directly anyway. Then he saw movement out of the corner of his eye.

Ashyn quickly spun, raising his hand in the direction of the sudden stirring. The fire raced up just as quickly, following his motions only a fraction of a second slower. The ball of flames undulated and rolled mere inches from his extended fingers, a golden sphere of liquid fire. Amber light flared out, extending its illumination across the hoary-hued fields.

To his surprise, he saw a woman sprinting across the grassland some two hundred feet away. She was running opposite of their direction, her hands held up in front of her, with her palms outstretched slapping against the tops of the tall reeds of grass. Her clothes were disheveled and it appeared that there was a blindfold tied around her eyes.

Behind her, three lines were slicing through the tall shoots of grass, leaving channels in their wake. They were moving fast, and would overtake the blindfolded woman in moments.

Ashyn didn't have time to think, he just reacted. Instantly he was sprinting across the countryside himself, the orbs of fire still dancing in his hands. Trails of orange light sparkled in long lines behind him as he raced to rescue the endangered woman.

Behind him he heard Xexial yelling, but Ashyn was already gone, committed to his action. He kept his right hand out in front of him, aiming towards the three furrows that were scything their way through the prairie. The tall grass slapped hard at his knees and thighs as his long strides carried him across the gap towards the fleeing woman.

He could clearly see that she was a human woman with long burgundy hair, slightly darker than his own red. Her stature was larger than an Elf, though she appeared emaciated. What surprised him was the ease with which she ran. She was blindfolded, and yet it was as if there was nothing hindering her vision at all. Her tactile function was in complete control.

At fifty feet away, the game was up. A Bristle Wolf, only half a dozen feet away, lunged forward, cresting over the long reeds of grass. Its thick forepaws were bearing down viciously on the woman as it soared through the air. Its mangy auburn coat was now erect, revealing the long sharp rows of quills that were otherwise recumbent. It would barrel into the woman, perforating her flesh with numerous puncture wounds. Ashyn knew he was out of time.

He yelled an incantation and thrust his extended hand forward. The sphere of fire discharged at high speed, sailing through the air as quickly as an arrow. Only scant inches from colliding with the fleeing woman, the fireball impacted with the massive wolf's face with such force that its neck instantly snapped. It flew violently away from the escaping woman, spinning end over end through the air like a furry top. The beast crashed down in the field some twenty feet away, rolling through the tall grass, issuing a series of snaps and pops as its joints and bones shattered from impact. The lifeless corpse smoldered under the biting flames that began to engulf its body.

Ashyn didn't miss it as one of the channels suddenly shifted and began a high pursuit to his position. Ashyn knew he was left with a choice. He only had one ball of fire left in his hands and two targets, one threatening himself, the other about to overtake the stranger. He knew he should save the fiery globe to attack his assailer, but if he did that, he would be committing the fleeing girl to death. Yet if he used it on the girl's attacker, he would be weaponless against the Bristle Wolf barreling down on his position. His mind flashed through the repertoire of spells he knew how to cast, limited thought they were, searching for something that could help shed a glint of light on his predicament. There was nothing, he realized, nothing that he would be able to use in time to protect himself.

The ravenous creature launched from the silvery meadow towards the escaping woman's back at the same time the other beast lunged at Ashyn. In a last-ditch effort, the redheaded man reached out and fired his last shot. The blaze lanced forth, singeing his assaulter's front paws, but continuing underneath its extended forelimbs and out past the creature completely.

It wasn't a miss, though. The sweltering projectile struck true on the wolf attacking the fleeing girl, its intended target. It instantly ignited the beast into a pyrotechnic fury. The massive creature howled in agony as it was consumed by the unrelenting flames.

Ashyn knew his sacrifice would cost him, but he wasn't going to cede to fate so readily. He gaged his encounter, timed it as the Bristle Wolf soared towards him.

Like his childhood encounter before, everything seemed to slow down to a crawl. He could make out the finest details of the lunging beast. Each claret-colored quill stood erect from its back like small curved stilettos, waiting to pierce his flesh. The creature's matted face twisted in feral anger, bloodshot eyes glimmering with the venom of the impending kill. It's long, yellow-stained fangs glistened with saliva in the moon's silver glow.

The beast did not scare him, nor did the fact that in moments it would be ravaging his body. This was not due to any magical endowments, or inherent bravery on his part. It was because the details gave rise to clarity, an understanding that showed an open weakness to the creature's attack stratagem before him.

Bristle Wolves attacked smaller creatures because they could overpower them, and then use their quills defensively against oncoming attackers, much like a porcupine uses its spines to ward off a large predator.

Ashyn in contrast was not so small anymore. The Bristle Wolf would still barrel him over with its bull's rush, and was likely to do damage, but it would need to close in on his throat in order to kill him. That could buy him time; he need only sacrifice a limb.

He remembered what he had done as a child, how he had rolled beneath the beast to protect himself. He knew how soft the wolf was underneath, how vulnerable.

Just as suddenly, as the world slowed around him, so too did it end. The Bristle Wolf plowed into Ashyn, a flurry of claws, teeth, and spittle. Ashyn, unable to hold ground, flew backwards with the force of the beast. They rolled through the long grass, as the creature bit and snapped at Ashyn's face and neck. He managed to slide his right hand up between himself and the beast to cover his neck just in time as the wolf's powerful jaws clamped down around his forearm.

Ashyn screamed in pain as powerful incisors pierced through flesh and muscle. Ashyn moved with the wolf's powerful yanking motions, trying to follow his gripped arm with the beast's movements to minimize damage. The pain was incredible, and it destroyed any chance of him being able to formulate a spell, let alone call to any type of conflagration. Tears blurred his vision and dots danced before him as he grunted through each lacerating movement of the wolf's powerful jaws.

He used his momentum to push the creature's raised spines into the soft dirt beneath them, effectively pinning the beast in place. It growled through its vise-like grip, and kicked hard with its hind legs at Ashyn's midsection, driving the wind from his lungs.

Gasping, Ashyn fought hard to worm his way between the flailing legs and find respite from the wolf's unrelenting attacks. With his free left hand, he punched futilely at the canine's abdomen and ribs. Hard, constricted muscles met his strikes with each impact.

Wheezing, and fighting against unconsciousness, Ashyn finally managed to slide down between the wolf's powerful hind legs. As he did he felt his thigh connect with a weakness, possibly his only shot.

The Bristle Wolf was male.

Grunting against the agony, he pulled his right arm forward to resist against the twisting and rending of those terrible jaws. With his left fist, he leaned back as far as he could, and hammered down against the wolf, low and with all the power he could muster.

He drove his fist in hard against the wolf's thigh, missing his mark. He pulled back and hit the beast repeatedly. Nausea began to take him as blackness descended on his vision from the wracking pain. He knew he didn't have long before he'd fade to black from the agony. Franticly he punched more and more, some falling wildly against kicking legs.

Finally, as his vision was all but a pinprick of light, his fist drove home accurately. The beast wailed in shock and surprise, its grip loosening significantly.

Ashyn drove his fist down again, connecting even harder with the Bristle Wolf's testicles, smashing them hard against the creature's body. The beast's blood-soaked teeth yanked free as it howled in agony from the sudden burst of pain.

Light flooded back into Ashyn's vision as the pain suddenly disappeared and was replaced with an aching throb. He punched again for good measure, winded, and then brought his left hand to the whimpering creature's throat.

Ashyn gripped hard on the beast's larynx as it too started to recover from the reeling pain. With his right hand now free, and the mortifying pain now merely an ebbing throb, he reached out to the burning carcass only a few feet away. His mind was suddenly clear again, and with that momentary lucidity, he called to the element that was eating away at the other wolf.

It answered.

Like a lightning bolt the fire arched across the night into Ashyn's free hand. He drove his flaming fist down into the wolf's throat. Now with both hands on the beast's tender neck, he squeezed as hard as he could, expanding the fire with his mind so that it enveloped both hands completely.

The beast's bloodshot eyes were wide as it fought frantically against the pain tearing its way through its fur and flesh.

Ashyn didn't relent, he pushed harder and harder against the wolf, feeling the hair burn away and skin blister and crack underneath. Soon the beast's throat became blackened and thin, collapsing inward. Only then did he let go.

As he stood and recovered, the dying beast twitched and kicked, the last vestiges of life fleeing from its body.

Ashyn brought great gusts of air back into his lungs as he struggled to recoup from the fight. Shaking the remaining nausea from his own throat, he looked to where he had last seen the fleeing woman. She was very still now, staring at him, less than a dozen feet away.

Well not staring, Ashyn realized, as the girl was still blindfolded, but she was still facing his exact location, as if she knew exactly where he was standing. Deep shadows pocketed her gaunt features, but there was something eerily familiar about her. Something he vaguely recognized.

He pulled and reignited a ball of golden flame and lifted it up towards her to get a glimpse of her features. When the flickering amber light illuminated her skin, Ashyn felt his legs grow suddenly weak. Olive-complected skin fluttered back at him through the sputtering light. Her burgundy hair fell around high cheeks and a narrow chin. Though he could not see her eyes, he'd recognized those lips and that nose anywhere. He had been accustomed to them for eight long winters.

"Julietta?" he whispered in shock.

Curious, the woman tilted her head like a dog hearing an odd sound. "Who are you?"

BAITED

Xexial screamed, "Boy!", from behind Ashyn. Awestruck by the woman in front of him, he barely heard his master until Xexial screamed again with a hint of fear in his voice. Alarms suddenly blaring in his head, Ashyn spun around.

Ashyn's heart crashed into the pit of his stomach at the sight. In the expanse of field that separated him from his master over three dozen armed Wild Elves stood barring his way. They were arranged in two half-moon formations, both groups semi-surrounding each wizard. How had Ashyn missed that? He should have felt it. He always felt it.

He tried to see his mentor between the swarm of half-naked midnight-colored bodies that blocked his way, but their sheer numbers hampered any visual contact. He had no way of knowing Xexial's condition, other than the fact that he was in trouble. Ashyn knew his situation was no better.

Ashyn glanced down to the ball of fire swarming around his open hand. He knew that it was near useless against the Elves surrounding him. He knew he needed something . . . bigger. But he had never been able to master any such spells. He could only hope the senior mage had ideas.

"Dui Nuchada," a familiar voice said calmly behind him. Slowly he turned back to the woman who looked so like his sister before him. She stood straight, frozen, and terrified. Then he saw why. Glinting in the silver moonlight, the razor sharp tip of a spear was visible against the base of her skull.

As Ashyn followed the tip down, he once again saw the raven-haired female that had stood on the cathedral steps. She was covered from head to toe in black paint, virtually hiding her from sight. Only her eyes shone in the lunar light. As his eyes made contact with hers, she stepped around the human woman drawing the spear across her neck as she did so. A thin red line traced the weapon's movements across her neck, drawing a whimper from the terrified woman. The Elf's near black orbs reflected hatred so profound for him, that Ashyn couldn't even begin to discern its origins.

"So the boy in the ravine is all grown up and has become a wizard," she spoke slowly and confidently.

Ashyn blinked in surprise. "Do I know you?"

The Elf shook her head no. "I was there. I hunted you for three days," she hissed, ire beginning to rise in her voice. "Until you disappeared into the Maze."

Ashyn shivered as his mind went back to that haunted and deadened part of the Shalis-Fey. That place had been a waking nightmare to him, and he never wanted to return.

"Why is it you are after me?" Ashyn asked, and tried to keep the tremble of fear from his voice, knowing there were so many spears and javelins pointed at his back.

The Elf answered by laughing maniacally at him. Her head tilted back, exposing her long slender neck briefly before her hateful gaze centered on him once more. "Wizards are parasites to this world. Your taint consumes and destroys all it touches. Your filth infests the land, air, and even minds of the innocent like a festering plague. It is our duty to end your pestilence once and for all! We are *Ferhym!* And we will liberate this world of ours from you forever. The spirits demand it be so."

"Then why are we talking," Ashyn replied through gritted teeth, trying to hold the fear from eking out. Ashyn was not afraid of pain, but that did not mean he was fearless from death.

"Because, Nuchada, I wanted you to see. I wanted you to see what happens to the Nuchada before we liberate this world from your kind," she snapped back vehemently.

Slowly she lifted the spear to the corner of the blindfold. Ashyn tensed, fearing that this twisted Elf was about to kill the burgundy haired woman on the spot. Then the Elf flicked her wrist, severing the blindfold. It fell away from the woman's face, revealing what lay underneath.

The woman, still quivering, stared at Ashyn with blackened and hollow sockets.

"Behold your future, Nuchada. Look at your sister."

"Sister?" the woman whispered in shock. She turned in his direction. "But my family is dead."

Ashyn saw her, all right. Saw her with horror and unbridled anger. It was his sister! It was only a momentary elation that she was alive, because reality quickly set in at what the Elves had done to her, done to the 'Nuchada'. She had been tortured, malnourished, and brutalized. His sister!

Small, white sunburst-shaped scars traced along the black empty pits where he remembered her beautiful eyes to be. He clenched his teeth as his chest began to tremble with rage. His throat constricted with such a fury that he began to hear a hum in his ears. His world was instantly painted in a rich orange glow.

The female Elf staggered backwards, the spear temporarily dropping away from Julietta's face, her eyes looking in horror at his own; the eyes of the 'Nuchada'. He had seen that expression before, on his very own sister so many winters before. He knew that look, what it meant . . . fear.

The female Elf's sudden movement caused her to stand upwind of him. A sweet odor drifted into Ashyn's sensitive nostrils. He recognized that smell, as he gazed through his strong amber haze to admire her ink-colored flesh briefly.

Vengeance would be his. His sister was alive and mutilated. He could brook no less than annihilation. He lowered his hand towards the silver fields, the undulating sphere of flame dancing only inches above the dry grass.

"Whatever you did in our house eleven winters ago?" he whispered to his sister. "Do it again."

The Elf's terrified brown eyes went wide as she realized what was happening. "Kill him! Kill him now!" she screamed as she turned to grab at Julietta and pull her away.

Ashyn called to all the oxygen in the air around him. The air gushed to him in a fraction of a heartbeat, displacing the life-giving substance, and causing the Elves around him to begin to gasp. That was not his intent, however. He felt the crisp coldness of the pure oxygen pour into him like frosty water into a basin. He could feel the hunger of the fire in his hands as it began to feed. He was even vaguely aware of the Elves behind him releasing their javelins. It didn't matter. All that mattered was the moment, and the fire. The icy rapture ran down his body, across the core of his being and directly into his outstretched hand. He let it all out, everything he could, in a single concentrated blast.

There was a crack, as if the dam that was restraining the use of his gift inside his own mind had been just been breached, a single deafening clap of thunder that reverberated somewhere deep within Ashyn's core. His teeth chattered, his body hummed, and the ground trembled beneath his feet. He felt the magic! More now than ever before did he feel it! It was primal, and raw. Unrestrained power flowed through him and he was its conduit. It invigorated him and frightened him all at one. He felt the fire, and it was hungry. So he fed it, and when he did he was swallowed in a heat, as he had never felt before. Ashyn's world dissolved then, in a brilliant flash of blinding white light. And he realized that this time he may have gone too far . . .

COLLATERAL

Xao didn't know what to do. Here he was stuck in the same position he had been in some eleven winters prior. Except that now instead of Orcs threatening the Runes, it was the Elves.

He couldn't believe his yellow eyes either when he looked at the emaciated woman held hostage by the onyx-drenched Elf. Was it true? Could Ashyn's sister have survived the wrath of the Orc band that had mercilessly carried her away? It seemed unfathomable, and yet here this grown woman was before him, looking very much like a Rune.

With a spear to her throat no less, and Ashyn surrounded by a myriad of other black-painted Elves. Things looked grim for the boy, too grim. Yet Xao thought of Dremathiatius' words only a few days before; *His fate would have been sealed, had you not interjected that night,* she had snapped bitterly. *Mireanthia wouldn't have.*

It did seem that this boy was destined for conflict. Perhaps his sister had been right after all? Maybe the boy was meant to die? If he did, it wouldn't be too late for Xao to return to his family. There was still a chance they hadn't left yet. He was sure it would take Dremathiatius a few days to collect all his siblings spread across the southern reaches of Kuldarr. He could still go home.

Conflict swirled within him like two trees caught in a raging tornado. How many times could he save this boy before he was killed? Then what would Xao do? He would be all alone just as Dremathiatius predicted, with no one to mourn him when he was gone.

Yet by the same token, there was his oath to his hatch-mother. She sensed something in him, and him alone, that was lacking in any of her other hatchlings, something that told him his choice in watching this boy was the correct one, that it was what he was meant to do.

But what was he then, Watcher or Guardian? Mireanthia had told him to watch the boy, not save him. Yet here Xao was, saving him at every turn. If he chose this path, if he chose to be Ashyn's guardian then was it something he should remain doing hidden, or should he let his presence be known?

Surely the thought of a dragon protecting the boy would keep the Elves at bay, but how would his wizard mentor react? What would the wizard do if he realized Ashyn's true potential? With how special he actually was to the dragons? There were too many questions in Xao's mind, and no solid answers.

He looked to the elderly wizard for some hope. The dragon stared at chaotic lightning bouncing between the fingertips of his thick iridescent blue lined gloves. Could the hunched-over man really save the boy and the girl from the Elves alone? Did he still have what it would take to defeat some thirty-plus Elves? That answer he could see in the wizard's gaze as he stared hopelessly between the Elves and his apprentice.

And that answer was no.

Xao watched the Elf step around the thin woman, drawing a thin red line with her spear tip on the fearful human's neck. Instantly the sweet scent of coppery blood blossomed in the air. Xao knew he was out of time. He needed to make a decision. Let the boy control his own fate, or be his protector?

Xao saw the quick flick of the Elf's wrist, and he watched the fabric of the filthy blindfold drift to the ground. When he saw the battered hollow pockets of the woman's eyes, the choice was made for him.

Anger swelled through him like the raging waters of a flash flood through a town. What was done to her was cruel torture, and nothing more. He couldn't abide that, and he knew his charge wouldn't either.

Xao spread his great wings and launched himself from the ground. He gathered height quickly, and when he felt his distance was good, he shifted his wings so they were firmly pressed against his back. Barrel rolling over, he came forth in a dive. He let out a snort. Plumes of fire raced up and over the black bone plating on his nose.

He would strafe the Elves, creating intersecting fields of fire, he decided. Then when Ashyn and his mentor, and possibly the girl, were safely away, he would decide his course of action on whether or not he should make his presence known to the boy.

As Xao dove, he felt the air rip swiftly across his lithe aerodynamic frame. He swept in like an invisible bird of prey. The Elves would never see it coming. He gathered even more speed, and when he was but feet from the ground, he fanned out his wings braking his decent and took a deep breath.

But there was no air! He gasped and heaved trying to draw in oxygen, but there was none to be had. With no air, he had no fire! Xao panicked, unsure of what to do and then he heard a large crack and the very air seemed to thicken around him.

He couldn't see the boy. In his sweeping descent, he came out above and ahead of the boy by about twenty feet. He should have soared right past, even with the lack of air, but something was wrong.

Then Xao felt pain.

The very air around him became a searing inferno, biting and eating at the sensitive membranes of his wings. He found himself flying again, but outside of his control. He was hurtled end over end through the air, some momentous force pushing him along on its devastating path.

Xao watched in horror as the pale silver night was alight in a furious red light. As the dragon spun out of control he saw the ground soaring beneath him blacken and curl underneath the powerful blaze of the firestorm. The light switched from its intense crimson to a blinding white and then Xao saw the ground rushing up at him too fast to stop. He collided.

Xao felt pain . . . and then darkness.

~ ~ ~

The dragon awoke sometime later, his body aching in over a dozen places. He wondered how much time had passed. Judging from the heat he felt against his scales, he guessed that it was daytime. Would he be visible? Likely.

There would be no way of maintaining his illusion in unconsciousness. Would he be surrounded by angry Elves with their little short pointy sticks? Again, he reasoned that was a strong possibility. He didn't know how he would talk his way out of it. Wild Elves were leery of Dragons, but they also hated Dragons, something about being a skewer of the balance. *Whatever,* Xao thought bitterly. Dragons had been around long before the Hym had separated into different sects of Elves.

With no answers forthcoming by keeping his eyes shut, the Red Dragon slowly opened them. He gasped. It was still night, but all around him he could see flickering orange lights, like small campfires dotting a hillside.

All around him was the blackened wreckage of a destroyed field. What had once been tall grasslands was now little more than a blackened scar of scorched earth. It seemed to go on and on for thousands of feet in every direction. The devastation was immense.

He shifted his weight and immediately regretted it. An arcing pain shot through his right wing, and he realized to his horror that he had landed on it in his crash. He looked at his stretched appendage, swollen and bent near its root to his body. Likely broken, he guessed. There was no way he would be flying anytime soon. That meant he was walking.

Xao groaned as he pulled himself to his feet. He wobbled slightly and then his equilibrium set in. Shaking his hard-plated head, he looked to where he had landed. It had not been gentle. A long gorge in the earth, about seventy feet in length from the demolished and burned field, lay ripped up as if a massive plow had been pulled through. Perhaps it had, he thought bitterly.

Xao then tested his feet, fearful that they would not support his weight. Luckily they did, though his back right calf felt tight with each step. Slowly he began to make his way into the field for some sign of his charge.

All around him, he could see the shriveled and charred husks of what had used to be living and breathing Elves. Had Ashyn done this? Was it because of him?

He tried to project his thoughts into the young wizard's mind. He had done it before when the boy was but a child; however, there was nothing. He could feel nothing, not even the trace of magic that let him communicate with Ashyn telepathically. It was gone.

He looked to all of the bodies trying to make sense of them. How would he know if one of them were Ashyn? Alternatively, the old wizard? Or the girl? He had no way of knowing. All tracks were destroyed in the pyre. The boy's scent was impossible to pick up amidst the smoldered remains of the dead. Cooking flesh all smelled the same.

What if Ashyn were dead now, he thought dejectedly. There would be no way of knowing unless he went back to the tower. And what then? How many winters would it be before Ashyn stepped out of the maw of that onyx beast again? Xao was too uncertain. What if Ashyn never came back out, what if he was dead? How would he know? Was he just supposed to sit there on that ledge and wait for a hundred winters? How was he going to continue his mission without the boy? That had been his task.

Xao traced a line in the cinders with his claw. They clung to his red scales, smearing and darkening his armored skin like an infection. Even if he gave up, without his wings he wouldn't be able to get back to his family in time before they left. He truly was stuck now.

Xao hung his head low in shame. He had failed his mother. He had lost the boy. Not knowing what to do anymore, the young dragon began to head east, away from his family, away from everything. Ashyn was gone, the girl was gone, and his family was gone. Dremathiatius was right. There was nothing for him here, and now any chance at returning was as shattered as his wing. Everything he had was gone, and now he was stuck in Kuldarr to die alone. And no one would ever remember him.

THE REINFORCEMENT

Ashyn was swimming. Swimming and laughing in a great pool of water underneath crystalline falls. The water was deliciously warm, and yet with a hint of crispness that left him feeling cool and clean. He splashed and giggled like a child, happily wading along in the driftless waters.

Julietta was there suddenly, pushing him under. He took a deep breath as he felt her hands on his stomach, soft and wrinkled from too long in the water. She pushed and pushed him down deeper, but he wasn't scared, he was elated.

Ashyn grabbed her hand and kicked himself to the surface of the water. He exploded forth from the white waters, laughing as he gasped for air. Julietta was right behind him laughing and gasping.

Rubbing the water out of his grey eyes, he turned and faced his beloved sister, the only friend he had truly had growing up as a child in Bremingham. She smiled at him with her brilliant white teeth and large hazel eyes. Ashyn smiled back. He didn't know why, but at that moment he missed her, even though she was right in front of him.

They continued to play as the hours went by; first they played a little longer in the pool of radiant waters and then in brilliant green fields with grass as high as their waists. They laughed, danced, and sang, and Julietta helped him find bugs, which he found odd because she never helped him find bugs.

Then the sun set on the two and the moon took its perch in the sky, casting the fields in a silvery glow. Ashyn felt he should be getting tired, but he was not. He was full of energy. He looked to his sister to see what fun she had in store next, but as he did, he realized something was wrong.

Her face looked thinner, gaunt, like she was malnourished. Her muscles were thin and waning. She looked older, too, older than he remembered her to be. Her hair had darkened and was disheveled.

What was happening? She looked at him sadly and then began to cry. Crystalline tears streamed down her face raining glittering diamonds into the hoary fields. She covered her hands over her eyes, crying into them.

Ashyn cradled his sister, whispering words of support. She suddenly seemed so small in his arms. When had he gotten taller than she had? She seemed so thin, so weak, so lost.

He tried to console her, telling her that he was there for her, that he would always be there. She stopped crying and looked up to him.

He gasped in horror. Her eyes were gone, replaced with blackened pits that were so deep that he could see no end to the void. Clustered star-shaped scars surrounded the corners of her eyes. She faced him and screamed. Like the wail of a banshee, it pierced his defenses and stabbed at his heart.

There was something in her hands, he realized as he tried to fight off the sound of her keen. Looking down at them his eyes went wide. She was holding a poker, its tip glowing bright white. She raised it to his eyes. He tried to fight her off him, but she was suddenly too strong for him. He attempted to grab the poker but her howl intensified and he was forced to cover his ears.

She lowered the poker into his eye. He screamed as he felt the branded steel pierce his orb. He felt the heat rupture his pupil and drive down. His eyeball exploded like an overripe berry. He felt the hot remains roll down the side of his cheek and splatter against his nose and forehead.

She yanked the poker from his skull with a sickening, squelching sound, and hovered the macabre device above his other eye. Gory remains bubbled and dripped off, while the smell of cooked flesh drifted just above him.

The empty pit that had once held his eye throbbed with such pain that he welcomed unconsciousness. Unfortunately it wouldn't come.

There was a voice in his head, echoing, distant, but strangely close at the same time. "Behold your future, Nuchada," the voice said.

His blind sister's face gnarled into a vision of intense anger and hatred. With all her might, she drove the poker down. He screamed.

~ ~ ~

Ashyn screamed as he lunged out of bed. His thin bare chest heaved heavily and sweat ran down him like rivers, soaking into his sheets and bedding.

Quickly, the young wizard ran his hands up to the corners of his eyes, touching his cheekbones, temples, and eyelids to make sure everything was intact. It was all there, he realized, as he began to take in the rest of his room.

He was in his quarters in the Onyx Tower, stripped down to his small clothes and placed in his bed. He had no idea how he had come to be here. His last memories were of a field, some Elves, and . . . his sister! She was alive!

He rushed to stand and an overwhelming pain wracked his right arm. He looked down at it in shock to see it heavily gauzed and bandaged. Even then, brilliant stains of crimson dotted the off-white wrappings.

What had happened to his arm? Vivid images of the Bristle Wolf suddenly began to replay in his head. As he thought about it, everything began to flood back. His sister blind, the Elves, the raven-haired Elf in particular, and then the spell.

Ashyn looked down to the hand that had released so much power. He flexed his fingers at the memory of it. It had taken everything out of him. He should be dead. Why wasn't he dead?

Ashyn didn't dwell on it. What was done was done. Somehow, he was alive and he was grateful for it. But he couldn't linger. His sister, she was alive! He needed to go for her as soon as possible.

Swiftly the young man hurried across the room, ignoring the pain in his arm, and began to collect his things, packing for a journey. He had everything scattered about his damp bed when he heard someone call out behind him.

"Heading somewhere, are we?"

Ashyn turned around and stood face to face with Xexial. Immediately the olive skinned boy flushed red. "I . . . well . . . I was packing, yes," he stammered.

"And why were you packing? Eager to see the Seven, I presume?" Xexial asked calmly.

Ashyn shook his head. "I . . . no. I'm going to save Julietta," he said evenly.

Xexial nodded. "Very noble," he answered.

Ashyn was surprised he wasn't being scolded.

Xexial waved at his items. "You'd better finish," he told the boy. "I'll be in the dining quarters. We need to chat before you leave." With that, Xexial was gone.

Ashyn did not know what his master meant by chat, but he could see it in the elder's eyes clearly enough. Whatever it was, it wasn't going to be good. Still, thoughts of his nightmare and his sister enduring the pain that he felt in that dream kept filling his mind. He went back to packing.

~ ~ ~

Twenty minutes later, he was heading down to the dining quarters. The tower felt oddly foreign to him at that moment, even though he had been in it for eleven winters. When he rounded a final corner near two dark stone gargoyles that he never quite liked, he saw Xexial sitting at the head of their small dining table. The table could only hold four people and was made of cherry wood, which contrasted greatly with the dark stone walls and floor. The four wooden chairs were also cherry, though Ashyn knew that only two of those chairs would likely ever be occupied.

The room was very large, considering the rest of the tower, and had three long, vertical stained glass windows that ran up the west face. Each window was a depiction of a different colored Dragon, which Xexial constantly referred to as Wyrms. The left most was green, center black, and to the right was a great red Wyrm.

On the east face that he had entered were nine suits of armor. One from every human dynasty in southern Kuldarr; the oldest dated back as far as two thousand winters. They seemed, strangely, to be watching him.

The south wall was unadorned, and held only a simple oak door that led to the tower's modest kitchen. Across the narrow face of the north wall were only two paintings. One that Xexial seemed to cherish, that depicted two horses jousting, and the other he had mentioned belonged to his master before him. It was equally as strange as the horses jousting with no riders; this one had three frogs playing a game of dice. Ashyn never quite understood them.

The ceiling sat thirty feet above him, and only a large, plain cast iron chandelier hung from it. The chandelier held forty long-stemmed candles that burned brightly, fully illuminating the room. They were enchanted, of course, so that they never burned through their wicks, and never needed replacement.

On the table, Ashyn noticed a small candle burning, a couple of rolls and a bowl of stew with steam still rising from it. They were all at his end.

Xexial motioned him to sit down. Ashyn complied. The boy noticed Xexial's eyes looked worn. The man was clearly exhausted.

"Eat," his master said. "It's been long since you've had more than honey and water. You could use a good meal before your journey."

Ashyn looked curiously at his mentor and then down at the stew. When he looked back up the man motioned to the food again. "Eat."

As the aroma wafted to Ashyn's nostrils, he suddenly couldn't deny how incredibly hungry he was. He tore into the rolls then, eating them savagely. When he ate the stew, it didn't seem to be enough. He used all the rolls before him to mop up every last morsel in his bowl until the thing was spotlessly clean. Realizing the spectacle he must have made eating so ravenously, he looked up at his elder sheepishly.

"Are you full?" he asked. "If not, I can get more."

"No, Master. I'm fine, thank you," Ashyn replied embarrassed.

Xexial nodded. "Good then. Before you leave I'd like you to do me one thing."

Ashyn raised his eyebrow. This was very unlike Xexial.

Xexial saw the raised eyebrow and continued. "It's really simple, actually. One small thing and you can be on your way."

"Okay," Ashyn answered.

Xexial motioned to the flickering candle on the table.

"I'd like you to draw that flame unto your hand."

Ashyn looked at him perplexed. "Why?"

Xexial smiled weakly. Ashyn saw deep circles under his eyes. "See, I'm not asking much, am I? You've done it thousands of times. I just want you to pull the flame to your hand, I don't care which one."

"If that's all you want," Ashyn returned skeptically.

Xexial nodded. "That's all."

Ashyn obeyed. With his good arm, he reached up and beckoned the flame to his fingertips, just as he had done hundreds of times over the last eleven winters. He extended his fingers, called to the primal element of fire burning weakly against the thin wick stem. It wavered gently in the breeze of the large tower. He pulled at it with his will, nothing happened.

Ashyn stared at it confused.

Again, he reached out to the flames and, using his mind, he ordered them to dance towards his outstretched fingers. Nothing.

He stared in shock at the candle, and then at Xexial. His tired eyes saying nothing.

Ashyn looked back to the fire. He invoked the flames using the words Xexial taught him winters before. Still the flame remained atop the small flickering candle.

"What trick is this?" Ashyn asked.

"No trick," Xexial returned. "Just a test."

"You've done something to the candle, then. Like the chandelier above," Ashyn returned, angry that the fire would not answer his summons.

"I have not," Xexial returned.

"Liar," Ashyn spat angrily. Again, he reached out to the fire, calling it, coercing it to come to him, but the small light would not budge. Livid, Ashyn grabbed the flame with his bare hand, and yipped in pain when it burned his fingers.

Xexial looked very sad then.

"What have you done to me?" Ashyn accused.

"I've done nothing," the elder wizard answered.

"I've been hexed," the boy snapped. "You've taken fire from me!"

"Perhaps another test, then?"

"Yes!" Ashyn spat, unable to contain his rage at losing the only thing in magic he was good at.

Xexial stood up quickly, and Ashyn did the same. With a sweep of his hand, Xexial sent all of the contents of the table flying unceremoniously to the floor. The bowl crashed and shattered into pieces. The candle's thin wax stem broke in two, and the fire winked out into nothingness.

The wizard then held a cloth up for Ashyn to see. He laid it down on the vacant table and unrolled it. Inside were six iron forks.

"I want to you cast your Ward of Warning, to warn you of these incoming projectiles."

Ashyn nodded. Again, this was one of those spells he actually knew.

He calmed himself briefly, and then ran his fingers into the dance of somatic gestures that would call forth the plume of magical smoke that would cover his body, activating the spell. Again, like the fire, there was nothing.

Quickly, Ashyn began the gestures again. Xexial did not wait. He levitated one of the forks up into the air where Ashyn could clearly see it hovering, and hurled it his way.

Ashyn finished the gesture but there was nothing. He yelped in sudden pain as he felt the fork slam into his chest. He looked down angrily to see the little eating utensil embedded in his right breast. He ripped it out, staring fumingly at the four prongs coated thick in crimson.

"Again!" Xexial bellowed.

Ashyn began to cast his spell, and Xexial hurled another fork his way. The spell did not go off, and again Ashyn found himself impaled.

"Again!" Ashyn growled at Xexial.

The process repeated four more times.

Ashyn was panting and bleeding from half a dozen wounds. Frustrated and angry, he cried at Xexial, "What has happened?"

Xexial slowly sat back down at the table, looking very, very tired. "You have lost your connection to magic." he said wearily.

"What?" Ashyn cried. "How is that possible? Magic is in everything!"

Xexial nodded. "It's still there, lad. You just can't reach it."

"Why?"

"Because you're wounded," he replied flatly.

Ashyn raised his mauled forearm. "This? This is causing it?"

Xexial shook his head. "No," he answered, and then reached up and touched his temple. "You're wounded in here."

Exhausted, he fell into the seat in front of him. "I don't understand," he mumbled, tears streaming down his face.

"Something has happened to you, Ashyn, something that I really can't explain . . . yet. You shouldn't be breathing right now," Xexial said morosely as he looked into his pupil's eyes. "You should have died."

Ashyn looked to his master. He knew it also. When he had cast that final spell, he had gone too far. He had taken too much in.

"Why didn't I?"

"You were very close," Xexial admitted. "When I saw what you were doing, when I felt the oxygen leaving my very lungs, I had to act immediately." he told the boy.

"Quickly I covered myself in a fireproofing enchantment I had learned long ago. It almost had not been enough. What you did, lad, it . . . it was incredible. I have never seen someone so young perform such a powerful invocation."

Ashyn could tell that Xexial was truly amazed, even through the sorrow in his voice, but none of it seemed to matter. Not with the magic now gone.

"In the aftermath there was nothing. Nothing but me and the raven-haired Elf that had hidden beneath the girl."

"Julietta!" Ashyn shrieked.

Xexial nodded. "She lived. Like me, she seemed protected from the spell, but she was drained, so drained. I was, too, for that matter. There was no way I could have fought, none of us could. The Elf took the girl and fled."

"You didn't pursue?" Ashyn said, anguished.

"How could I?" Xexial snapped. "I found you lying in the barren and blackened field, barely drawing breath, just a hiss coming from your lungs every minute or so. You think I should be concerned about a single Elf and a girl? You were my concern!"

"But Julietta . . ."

"I didn't know who she was!" Xexial argued. "Not at first, anyway."

The elder man shook his head, his bald pate glittering in the candlelight. "It took almost everything I had to get you back here before the Wild Elves could regroup. I've been nursing you back to health for the last ten days. Things looked truly dire, until yesterday. Suddenly something snapped inside you, and you began turning around. Then, not even an hour ago, I went to check on you, and here you are up and packing your things like nothing was ever wrong."

Ashyn quietly stared at the table, his tears glimmering orange in the pale dancing lights.

"But the magic . . ."

I am uncertain how long it may take to heal," Xexial commented. "I have seen it before, though perhaps not as strongly as yours."

"Did that person heal?" Ashyn muttered, fearful.

"Yes . . . yes he did," Xexial said with a waning smile.

His smile brought a small measure of relief to the boy. "Did it take long?"

"Many months," Xexial answered. "He too drew more than his share. He was young, and stupid, like you. But he too was lucky."

Months, Ashyn realized. How was he going to save Julietta now?

Xexial, seeing the conundrum in Ashyn's eyes, asked the question first. "Just where were you planning on going?"

Ashyn looked to his mentor, eyes still watering. "To get Julietta."

Xexial nodded. "So it is your sister, then?"

Ashyn in turn nodded.

"I feared as much," He said with a sigh.

Ashyn's face scrunched up in horror. "You feared as much?" he said emotionally. "You feared she was alive! Did you know?" he asked accusingly.

Xexial's blue eyes shot up at Ashyn heatedly, "Of course not, lad!" he shot back. "The Ferhym said she had died, and I took them at their word. It is not often they keep a skewer of balance alive, and seeing as how they wanted you dead so eagerly I had no doubt in my mind your sister was dead, too. But this . . ." Xexial said, angrily shaking his head. "This will conflict with everything I've been teaching you! She's a liability now. She'll be on your mind every step of the way."

"Your damn right she's on my mind!" Ashyn said incredulous. "She's my sister! And she's been hurt, enslaved, and tortured. You want me to just pretend she never existed?"

"Dammit boy, no!" Xexial said, slamming his hands on the table and standing. He began to pace. After a moment, he looked down at Ashyn. "Have you ever wondered how we choose our apprentices?" the wizard asked quietly.

Ashyn looked to him, surprised by the sudden change in topic. "You said it was because I was smart and had an incredible will to survive. You also said it was because I see the world with different eyes," he told his master.

"We choose apprentices who have nothing left to live for in life." Xexial answered bluntly.

Ashyn recoiled. "But . . ."

"Everything you said was true. Those traits helped my decision," Xexial replied. "But over all a wizard chooses someone who has nothing left in life worth living for. All you had was revenge. A revenge I knew you were never going to see."

Xexial sighed as he looked through a stained glass window, lost in his memories. Memories shared by Ashyn. "Your family was murdered, your village was destroyed, and you were even cast out of the Enclave. What did you have? What would you do? You were as good as dead had I not taken you in as an apprentice. Regardless of how strong your will may be."

Ashyn was aghast, "You took me in out of pity?" he snapped angrily.

Xexial turned to him, stone-faced, "Of course not, lad. I would never take someone out of pity if I'm offered only one chance to train an apprentice," he retorted. "I wanted the one most likely to survive, to understand the real meaning of being a wizard." He returned his gaze out the window. "But we *must* choose someone whom has nothing left. The Wizard's Covenant imposes this upon us. It just makes things . . . easier."

"How? How does it make it easier?" Ashyn exclaimed.

"Because if there's anything outside of the magic you will want it, you'll desire it, think about it, *and miss* it. The life of a wizard leaves no room for error. Our mistakes are often fatal ones, not just for us, but for everyone. Any potential conflict needs to be . . . eliminated."

Tears ran down Ashyn's face. "Eliminated? So you won't help me save her, then?" he said quietly.

Xexial looked at him, his normally stone face was so very sad at that moment. "There will be no saving your sister, Ashyn, not by the two of us."

"But . . ."

Xexial raised his hand, silencing his pupil, "I hold no ire against this Julietta, nor does what I say bring me any joy whatsoever, but we cannot dare try and liberate her from the Ferhym. There's too much at stake."

Anger welled up inside of Ashyn, pushing away his pity, "Too much at stake? You value you your life above that of my sister!"

"I value all life!" Xexial snapped back, "That's what we do! Wizards value life. Don't you dare chastise me or try and lay this at my feet, boy! You think I like telling you this? You think I derive some perverse satisfaction in telling you that I want you to forget about your sister? I hate it! I hate what those blasted Ferhym have done! Them and their twisted, broken cult they call a Council."

"I cannot just forget that she's alive, not now," Ashyn whispered.

"I know!" Xexial turned and roared at him. Truly, Ashyn had never seen the wizard so flustered.

"But what can we do?" Xexial insisted.

"We can save her . . . ," Ashyn started, and as his master was about to interrupt, he raised his hand to finish, ". . . and we can take her to the Jasian Enclave, wherever the nearest might be. Just the knowledge that she is safe, that is all I beg."

Xexial closed his mouth. Ashyn could see him thinking as his blue eyes darted about the room in silent contemplation. Finally, he looked back to the boy. "Your request is sound," he responded, and Ashyn's heart lifted up twenty feet.

"Then we can go?"

Immediately Ashyn's heart crashed back to the floor when he saw the wizard shaking his head, "I said sound, I didn't say it was possible. We would be travelling into the heart of the Shalis-Fey once again. Now the Ferhym won't even try to ignore us, since they apparently are now killing wizards on sight. Even with that, we would have to find the hidden city of Feydras' Anula, home to the Council of Elm. Supposing we found their city, then there is the matter of sneaking in, saving a blind woman, and likely having to fight our way back out. Not even with a dozen wizards could you do this. And you are asking me for the two of us to go in and rescue one girl? Perhaps if you weren't lame I might humor the idea, but all that you'd be is a liability. You can't even harness magic right now."

"But I can't just leave her!" Ashyn pleaded.

"Right now you must," Xexial returned. "Though I am not deaf to your plea, we have other pressing matters of the Council's suddenly aggressive stance on wizards. We will stick to our original plan and go to see the Seven together. There you can plead your case and hopefully with both incidents combined, the Seven will act."

"The Seven?" Ashyn said in horror, "But they're so far away! There is no telling how long it will take, months likely, maybe even a winter!"

Ashyn knew the Seven's Grand Wizard's tower lay far to the northeastern coast of Kuldarr, past almost all human lands, and into the foreign lands of Oganis, where the Scales, a race of intelligent bipedal reptile men, ruled with an iron fist.

The journey could take weeks in itself, navigating through grasslands, highlands, and mountains. Even if they went east to Buckner and sailed to the mystical city of Jaës, it would still be time-consuming, not to mention the fact that Xexial hated sailing. Then there was still the matter of him pleading his case, having them come to consensus, and rallying the wizards spread out amongst the continent. It would take months. Ashyn had no doubt it would be over a winter's time, even if they agreed. For all their power, the elder wizards never did anything fast.

"That is all we can do," Xexial said, bringing Ashyn out of his dismal thoughts. "They desperately need to know what the Ferhym have done to Czynsk, and how they are using humans as bait to draw out wizards. Julietta's case is sound, lad, they would likely rally to your cause, even being an apprentice."

"But she doesn't have that kind of time," Ashyn tried to argue.

"They have let her live this long. I've reason to believe they will keep her alive."

"But tortured," Ashyn snapped.

Xexial sighed again. "I know this is hard to accept, lad. But our hands are tied."

Ashyn jumped to his feet, his anger welling in him as he thought of his sister's ravaged face, and he couldn't let it go on for another change of the seasons. He just couldn't. "Just like they were tied when they burned the Enclave down?" he spat at Xexial. "Go . . . go to the Seven. Tell them of the Elves and their games. I have to save my sister."

Xexial raised an eyebrow at Ashyn's rage. It only seemed to compound it. "Oh?" The wizard said cuttingly. "And how will you save her without your magic?"

"I'll find a way," he fired back. "I'm not without my resources."

"If for your love and determination alone, I might believe you. Son, I realize how impossibly hard to accept this is, truly I do."

"No, you don't!" Ashyn fired back at him. "How could you? For winters, I have thought that I had lost everyone. Now my sister is alive, alive and in need of her brother! Don't you see? I thought I had failed them, failed my family by being weak. Now I have another chance! A chance to save her! Even if after I do I can never see her again, the knowledge she is safe will be worth it. I have to try."

Ashyn realized that Xexial once again was done. Every ounce of emotion and pity washed away, once again leaving Xexial with a flat, stone like expression. "You have made a vow. You have sworn the Wizard's Covenant. There can be no breaking that, son."

"I only break it if I don't have your consent to leave," Ashyn returned.

"Which you don't," Xexial replied flatly. "You are wounded. And even barring that, I wouldn't let you go. You are not ready to be a wizard yet, Ashyn. It's too soon."

Ashyn was lost in thought, torn between his loyalty to Xexial and his loyalty to his own blood. Xexial saw this written in his grey eyes. The elder wizard pressed on, "The oath you made so long ago binds you to the completion of your training no matter the cost to yourself; this even means your sister, son. Acolytes have died because of things like this. That is why we take people who have lost everything. The art of Destruction is too powerful to let an untrained wizard 'quit'."

"So what will happen to me if I quit?" Ashyn returned defiantly.

"If you leave here, Ashyn, you will be hunted by every waking wizard on the face of Kuldarr."

"Including you?"

"Including me," His master said coldly. "Wizards do not brook the insult of having a recreant counted in their numbers. Aside from that, wizards who are untrained are just plain dangerous to everyone. Too many things are susceptible to you. This little taste of Destruction may seem like power, but it's not; it's more of a hindrance. Your untrained mind is simply too ignorant to understand the responsibility that comes with wielding Destruction. That is why we hunt our recreants, and that is why *I* will hunt you if you leave."

Ashyn tried to absorb what his father figure said to him; it just didn't seem real. Xexial would hunt him down if he left to save Julietta. His only choice lay in the journey to see The Seven, and the hopes that they would hear his pleas.

"The Covenant binds us, lad. If you leave, if you try and rescue her, you will break your sacred vow to being a wizard," Xexial told him as he raised the vial of Ashyn's blood that sat around his neck.

Ashyn looked sadly into Xexial's cold azure eyes. "There is no quitting this field, Ashyn. I warned you of your choice a very long time ago. If you leave, you will never be able to come back here, and if you try to . . ." Xexial said letting the words hang in the air. "I will kill you."

A Lover's Promise

P ain coursed through every fiber of her being. She screamed so hard with each movement that it felt like she was going tear out her own lungs.

"Hold her still," she heard one of the druids say to her left, as another, this one a male, tried to hold her firmly in place with his strong hands.

Again, she felt the abrasive stone against her flesh as the druid brought it down, and again she screamed in agony as he brushed it back and forth against her wounded flesh.

Tears streamed down her face unrelentingly. Sweat slicked her body and stung her wounds brutally adding to her torment. "Kill me!" she wanted to scream at them, but her ravaged vocal cords only managed another gut-wrenching keen.

The stone grated against her flesh once more, and she fought it every step of the way, squirming and writhing away from the vicious assailant. It hurt so bad . . . by the spirits it hurt so badly.

"I can do nothing with this while she's awake," the druid stated, frustrated as he put the stone down. "Cleanse the wounds with warm salted water; we'll try again when she's unconscious," he said with a sigh, and then she heard the nature's servant walk away.

The pain subsided for a moment. It felt like a gentle kiss of ecstasy, but then it returned in full force. The other druid to her right poured something warm over her tattered flesh, and instantly the fires ripped through her body again.

She convulsed and screeched against the torrent of pure suffering that washed over her body. She saw vaguely through tear-filled eyes as the water sluiced over her skin, pulling away pieces of black, deadened flesh and streams of thick yellow puss with it. The smell was awful.

Then it was all over, and she was alone once more, alone with only her thoughts, and her dull, throbbing aches that proliferated her body.

Every time the druids would leave, they bound her down in woolen gauze and leather straps so she couldn't move and aggravate her wounds further. The gauze was itchy against her sensitive wounded skin, and often would weep a pinkish fluid after a while which required constant changing.

She could barely keep down water, and was on a strict honey and lemon diet, which unfortunately cleaned out her bowels just as often as her wounds, requiring someone to be just outside to wipe her down regularly with a damp linen cloth.

How she had made it back to the branch caravan after their atrocious annihilation in the silver fields was muddled at best. She remembered a girl, black as night and crusted . . . crusted with caked flesh.

She remembered helping the girl to her feet. She should have been dead, *I should be dead*, she thought as her mind drifted. She wished she were dead. At least then the pain would be gone. At least the bitter taste of defeat would be gone. And the sorrow . . . so many had died . . .

The boy, the Nuchada, where had the power come from? She remembered that a Bristle Wolf had wounded him, that she was sure she had him defeated, but had something changed somehow? He became angry . . . his eyes.

She could barely remember the cold torrent of air that swooshed past her, or that she couldn't breathe. But she did remember the light . . . and then pain.

That was all, though. She knew that she and the girl had stumbled around for the better part of a day. But the pain had made it so hazy. She remembered the horror in her own mind when she saw the burns across her right arm, partially across her abdomen, and the right thigh. Thick, red and swollen patches of flesh poked through the 'sweet ground paint' they used to hide themselves at night. That paint . . . it had burned so fast. If not for the crusted girl that smothered her . . . she knew she would have died. Died like all the others. Died as Elumin had at the hands of the older Unbalancer. How had the girl lived? She tried to think, but the rivers of sorrow that washed through her body constantly made it impossible to think past the fog that clouded her mind.

Eventually she drifted off into a fitful sleep.

She woke intermittently over the course of the next two days, mostly when the druids would take the scouring stone to her dead flesh, or when they would drain her infected flesh and feed it to maggots, or leeches. When they did, she saw the leeches pull her blood away and it was ugly and black.

Then there was the odd feeling of the restorative magic they would chant to wash over her body and force the flesh to knit itself together. It was brutal, and foreign, and guts-wrenching, but she knew it was necessary if there was any hope she would live. After a while she wanted to live, she decided. She wanted revenge.

Her dark eyes opened once more to see a brilliant pink sunset, and with it, sitting worriedly by her side was her love, Shedalia. Was it a dream? She had sent Shedalia to the Feydras' Anula to plea to the Council of Elm for more troops. She should be miles from here. Unless she was in Feydras' Anula?

Shedalia lunged forward towards her. "You're awake!" she said, her voice thick with emotion.

"Hi," Whisper croaked back. It was her! It wasn't a dream. She felt the huntress's hand take up her own good left hand. Shedalia's rough, callused fingers felt like paradise to her. It was so good to feel her touch that for a moment she wanted to forget everyone else around her and just be with the Elf she loved.

Tears leaked out of the corners of her lover's brown eyes and it made her smile even more. To know she was so loved. Whisper reached up with her left hand and gently touched her face. "Shh," she beckoned hoarsely, "It's alright . . . I'm alright."

Shedalia nodded, her smile lighting Whisper's heart. "They . . . they say it was the boy who did this. That you and the blind girl were the only two to survive?" she asked.

Whisper nodded. That much she remembered.

"How is this possible?" Shedalia asked. "I thought the old wizard was the threat?"

Whisper felt her knitted flesh tighten on her face as she scowled. "Listen to me, Shedalia," she rasped. "The old wizard is feeble . . . he is weak. The Nuchada is the real threat now. His power was . . . unnatural. I have never seen anything like it," she said, thinking of the blinding light and the horrendous aftermath. "The wizard, what he did eleven winters ago was nothing compared to the Nuchada. We must have his head."

Shedalia stood straight and tall, an image of pure rage flitted across her face. "The First Councilor gave me four more branches for you to command. I have over eighty hunters and huntresses at your disposal and two more druids. Tell me what you want done and I shall do it, Branch Commander."

Whisper reached for Shedalia's hand. The brown-haired Elf gave it to her and she squeezed it reassuringly. "*You* are the

Branch Commander now, Shedalia. Take the branches and druids and head for the Onyx Tower. Attack them at first opportunity. Give no quarter unless your victory is certain. We wouldn't want to anger the spirits by not giving these Skewers the option of a quick death," she said as seriously as she could, knowing her rough voice likely made her difficult to understand.

Her eyes fell to the druid who had scoured her flesh constantly with that evil stone. "Take this druid, as well. Though he wasn't directly in the conflict, he controlled the Bristle Wolves. He was the only other one to have witnessed the Nuchada's attack. He will inform you of everything that he has learned henceforth."

The druid's copper skin paled. "But Branch Commander Whísper, your wounds still need tending. They are grievous. Without my care . . . I cannot say what will become of you."

"I still have two other druids to mend my hurts," she told him. "This is my order. You are to serve Branch Commander Shedalia now, am I clear?"

"I . . . yes, Branch Commander Whísper," he said dejectedly.

Whísper smiled. At least she would not feel the wrath of that damned stone any longer. She redirected her gaze to her lover. "Leave me only the necessary Ferhym to safely take this caravan back to Feydras' Anula. All the others you will take and march upon that evil spire."

Shedalia nodded. "What of the blind girl?"

Whísper blinked in surprise. "She still lives?" Whísper was sure she would have died. Her skin had been blackened and crusted far worse than Whísper's own.

The druid stepped forward. "Yes, about that. It appears the human actually suffered no burns at all."

Whísper couldn't believe it. "That's not possible. She . . . she was on top of me." Whísper didn't want to say she had used the woman as a human shield, but what was, was.

The druid looked nervous under her piercing black gaze. Or perhaps it was the red swollen flesh around the right side of her face and scalp where the hair had burned away. She couldn't be certain. "Once her flesh was soaked in . . . in the salt mixture, the caked blackness crusted on her body just melted away, leaving her skin unharmed. I can't explain it, Huntress. We have never encountered such a resistance to fire before. From those untrained in Creation, anyway," he added.

Whisper squinted her eyes. "You seem to be lacking in much knowledge lately, druid," she said angrily. "What is your name, so that I may inform the First Councilor of your vexed nature?"

"Branch Commander!" he said, shocked, "I . . . I've been trying to save your life for the last seven days!"

"It felt more like torture to me," she hissed. "Name?"

"I . . . I . . . It is Eigron, Huntress," he said as he hung his head, defeated.

Whisper felt a reassuring hand upon her naked collarbone. She looked up to see Shedalia, looking down upon her worriedly. "Huntress, perhaps this is not the best of times. Eigron here has been tirelessly tending to your needs. Perhaps when your wounds have healed and this Nuchada lay dead, we can readdress this issue. As it stands, the woman has been unconscious for a great many days. Is this not true?" she said as she looked back to Eigron.

He nodded eagerly. "This is true. She has been drained by the ordeal for many days now," he said, and then added, "There is no telling when she will awaken."

Whisper hissed. She wanted to know how the sister of the Nuchada survived. It could be crucial in helping Shedalia. It just didn't seem possible. She looked like the walking dead, her flesh had seemed so black, so brittle. For it all to just wash away and her suffer no harm when so many of Whisper's people had died?

Yet Shedalia was right, Whisper decided. Even if they couldn't glean information from the girl, to attack Eigron had been wrong. She wasn't thinking rationally. All he had been trying to do was help over the last few days, to keep her alive. She blamed the stone, she supposed. It made her judgmental against him. She hated that stone.

"Very well, Shedalia. This waits." She nodded to Eigron, who visibly relaxed in front of her.

"Nature and spirits thank you, Huntress," he said graciously.

"You are still going with Huntress Shedalia, though." she told the druid. "This changes nothing."

Nervously he nodded, "Yes, yes of course."

She glanced to the other druid that was in the room tending her. The one whose touch had been gentler. "Leave us," she told them. They seemed more than eager to comply.

When the two were finally alone, Shedalia leaned in to give Whisper a soft embrace and peck on her lips.

"Am I hideous to you now?" Whisper asked shamefully.

Shedalia's sincere smile warmed the very depths of Whisper's spirit. "You are always beautiful to me," she answered. "Scars only add to the majesty of the piece."

Whisper smiled as she felt hot liquid build at the corners of her eyes. "I want you to do something for me, when you march against the Nuchada."

Shedalia looked at her curiously, "Anything, my love."

"I want you to wear the Windsong markings upon your skin," Whisper said to her boldly.

"But your mother . . .," Shedalia began.

Whisper shook her head. "You were right, Shedalia. You are my love, not Suneris. It should be you that bears the banner of our union upon your flesh and no one else. My mother is wrong. We should not hide who we are because the Ferhym don't accept it, because they want children so badly. This is who we are. We shouldn't be ignored."

Shedalia smiled as the tears rolled ceaselessly from her doe brown eyes. "I would be honored to wear the Windsong markings, my love."

Whisper returned her smile, but added seriously, "Have no one use the sweet ground paint anymore to hide themselves. It reacts to fire," she said feeling the tightness of her skin at the thought of what it had done to her. "You will have to find another way to sneak up on the skewers. Perhaps the druids may have a way."

Shedalia's hand cradled the side of Whisper's face. It felt so good there, so right. The way it truly should always be. "Worry not, my love," Shedalia whispered to her seductively. "I shall return to your arms, openly, and when I do I shall carry with me the head of the Nuchada."

She leaned forward and kissed Whisper passionately. It hurt against her raw flesh, but she wanted it and didn't want her lover to stop. When finally the two parted, Whisper saw Shedalia's brown orbs glitter with desire. "Together we shall burn out his blasphemous eyes."

ONYX TOWER

The next four nights were riddled with nightmares, each worse than the last. Every time Ashyn woke up in a fevered sweat, he feared to close his eyes again. And when he did the nightmares returned. In each one he was being tortured in some cruel way, whether it is by branding, having his eyes gouged out, or even his entrails removed an inch at a time. However, the pain was not what brought on the horror. It was that it was his sister that was doing it to him, whispering into his mind that this is what was happening to her, to the 'dui Nuchada'. Ashyn tried to rationalize that it was just his imagination, his fear of knowing his sister was a captive of the malicious Wild Elves, but nothing would ease his edgy nerves, nor lessen the dreams. It was on the fifth day that Ashyn knew what he was going to have to do to make the dreams stop. Yet he wasn't sure he could.

He loved Julietta more than his own life. She was the only family he had left and he was not going to leave her in the hands of the Ferhym to be tortured and mauled just for their perverse sense of justice. He vowed once that he would never be weak again, and he meant it. Even if it meant his own death

But the task ahead of him wasn't so simple. Xexial had detached himself from the boy, as if he knew the conflict brewing within Ashyn. At meals, Ashyn would steal glances at Xexial's eyes, only to find them cold and ruthless. They spoke not once since that night of Ashyn's re-awakening. There was no resolution between them, just a growing unrest in their silence. There was no training either, since Ashyn's injury had all but removed his connection with magic.

So Ashyn had preoccupied himself in other ways. At first, he began reading ancient tomes and searching the obscure rooms in the tower that he never had given a second thought to in the past. He hoped to find an answer to his predicament somewhere in the wizards' ancient pasts. Nothing catalogued seemed to reference Ashyn's internal war though, and he thought he knew why.

Xexial said that wizards target people who had lost everything. Why would there be anything written about one's strife at being driven to choose between family and law?

So Ashyn tried a visual approach and decided to stray away from ancient manuscripts and search more for answers from the Onyx Tower itself. It was on this fifth day just after noon that he found himself plodding along the outskirts to the cellars of the tower. He had not come near these cellars in many winters, his curiosity as a child lost to the intensity of his studies with magic. Now, though, he was looking for answers.

Each door that led down into the pit beneath the tower's ground floor was large and uninviting, the cast iron portals hewn from the darkest metal that Ashyn had ever seen. Each one depicted an image of grotesque horror: dragons consuming men, Orcs savagely mauling men, or great lizard-like people with wings like bats impaling men on spears. In fact, on each image on every door that Ashyn came across it appeared that men were on the losing side. "Charming," he said sarcastically to himself.

When he had been a small boy, Xexial had warned him that no child had ventured into the cellars in decades, beyond decades. Not even when he was a child had he gone within. There was no telling what lived within the bowels of an ancient wizard's tower.

He flexed his injured fingers to try to get the blood flowing again. He had read that somewhere. That it was important to keep the muscles limber after injuries like an animal mauling, in case there may have been torn tendons. Therefore, he found himself constantly flexing his hand so he could have a solid grip and full mobility for somatic gestures when he could cast again. *If he could cast again*, he thought bitterly. He tried to push the idea from his mind.

He walked a circuit once more around the twenty-three doors that led to different parts of the cellars beyond. Finally he chose the door that depicted a scene which looked like the quickest and least painful way to die: a minotaur, ten feet tall with the body like a man but head and legs like a bull's, was beheading a man with a great axe.

He removed the torch from the sconce on the wall next to the door. Luckily for Ashyn, the torch was ever-burning just like the chandelier in the dining room. *At least it was something*, he thought.

Taking a deep breath, he reached out and lifted the iron doorpost. It felt like it weighed a ton, and he had to struggle for a moment before the heavy iron shaft fell aside with a ponderous clang. With the hackles raised on the back of his neck, Ashyn opened the door. It groaned in protest after being shut for so long, but otherwise it opened remarkably easy.

Ashyn's torch twinkled its yellow light down a set of spiraled onyx steps. "Everything has to be so black," he muttered to himself as he took his first step into the Tower's depths.

The young wizard counted two hundred and sixty three steps before he found the first floor that he could examine. He noted that the steps continued to spiral further into the darkness beyond his torchlight. *It's likely to take all day,* he realized. Not that it mattered. Xexial had made it seem like their journey had been imminent on that first night, but as day after day passed, the old wizard had made no immediate efforts to leave. Perhaps he was waiting for Ashyn's arm to heal more, or perhaps he was hoping that Ashyn would lose his desire to rescue his sister. Something Ashyn knew was never going to happen.

Ashyn decided to examine the first floor he was on. He brought the pale, twinkling, amber light across the hallway . . . and into the mouth of a monster.

Ashyn screamed and stumbled backwards, barely catching himself on the outstretched cold iron railing. He looked at the precipitous drop below, realizing that he almost went tumbling down the lengthy spiral stairs.

Slowly Ashyn brought the torch back up to the hall. Once again, the long, dagger-like teeth flickered and reflected its golden light. It took a moment for the boy to register what he was looking at, with its long, black-plated snout on top of a pristine white skull with empty sockets. It was a dragon's skull, and it was mounted directly at eye level to Ashyn. He grunted in displeasure of being frightened so easily. Gathering his resolve, he ducked under the skull and walked into the room.

The ceiling sat very low. Perhaps it measured at only about seventy to seventy-two inches from floor to ceiling. He wondered why anyone would build a ceiling so low, until he cast his light on the surrounding walls, and then he understood. The hallway was cylindrical in shape with pockets hollowed out on both sides of him as it wound around in a complete circle. Each hollow pocket in the walls was a cell, but not a prison cell meant for a person. There was water. Bubbling, churning, water inset in each of the alcoves. It was then that Ashyn realized how hot it was inside the room.

He studied each cove of water curiously, as it jetted upwards above him, sending its boiling contents high into the tower above. The slight smell of sulfur tingled in his nostrils. "The tower is built on a hot spring," he marveled aloud.

That was why it rarely ever was cold in the wintertime, and why he could barely ever recall burning firewood in a hearth. It was ingenious, he realized. Madly he dashed about the lower-ceilinged room examining all the portals of water and how they functioned, either sending the water, or their hot gases up above in between the walls of the tower to keep the place perpetually warm. Ashyn understood the reasoning for the black stonework that the tower was made of then. He ran his fingers across the stygian surface. "It's volcanic rock," he whispered aloud. "Onyx Tower doesn't sit in a gulley, it sits in a crater. A dead, volcanic crater."

While the sudden comprehension of Onyx Tower fascinated him, Ashyn knew he had better continue on with his task of finding anything that could help him ahead. Giving one last cursory glance at the room of bubbling cauldrons, he ducked his head once more through the dragon guardian's arch and resumed his trek down the winding stairs.

The next floor was not nearly as far down as the first, at only one hundred and three steps, and Ashyn couldn't deny how hot it was becoming. Sweat began to pepper his forehead as he stuck his torch into the next hallway. Once again, he saw another dragon skull holding vigil over the entrance. This one was slightly bigger than the last and so it was angled downwards as if its eyeless sockets were staring down its long, blue-plated snout at the entrant. Teeth the size of longswords greeted him as he walked gingerly underneath.

This time the ceiling was further above him, by almost three times his height, and the alcoves on his sides were indeed prison cells. As he stared at the ceiling, he noticed holes placed above each cell and throughout the circular hallway. As he continued around he noticed, too, that ten of the twenty-three entrances actually made their way to this floor. He would have thought that weak protection if the imprisoned escaped until he understood the nature of the holes in the ceiling. They were murder holes.

At any point in an attempted escape, the person on the floor above could flood the lower floors with boiling hot water. Ashyn quivered at the idea. Not the type of end he would wish to meet. But the construction of prison cells beneath the water supply began to make sense to him.

Each cell was made of blackened iron, and large enough to fit four or five prisoners. Mats of decayed and dilapidated hay were bundled in the corners, and Ashyn even came across a refuse bucket or two that had long since rotted away in the humid air.

He continued the journey down, choosing a different stairwell three more times, each time coming to another room full of cells. The cells were getting smaller, he realized as he descended, as was the means of accessing them. By the time he reached the fourth level of cells, he counted that overall he had found twenty-two of the twenty-three entrances into the cellars.

On this level, the humidity was so thick that Ashyn felt as if he were pushing through water. Sweat ran down his body liberally. He had noticed that each descent gave way to a new dragon skull, each with a different bone-plated design and color, be they white, green, or a copperish hue. Whoever had designed the tower either was fascinated with dragons, or loathed them. Perhaps both.

As he cast his light across the cells he noticed the now typical murder hole design in the ceiling, but the cells themselves were much different.

Each cell was maybe only four feet wide by seven feet, just large enough for someone to lie down. The door that barred the way had only one portal and that was a small sliding door at the bottom. It allowed for food and a refuse bucket to be slipped back and forth. It was obvious that the occupier would have no source of light, nor ability to tell time being so far beneath the surface, their only friend would be whatever vermin might scatter by.

The walls and ceiling were no longer stonework, and it seemed more than likely that the structure was carved directly into the volcanic stone itself. Each of the walls was rough and rigid with enough scrapes and cracks to infer that more than one person imprisoned down here had claimed their own life against the unforgiving stone.

Ashyn knew the day was beginning to wane and as he reached the stairwell, he saw that none of the steps would descend any further. He was about to adjourn when a sudden curiosity got the better of him. Twenty-two entrances, judging from the layers of cells, yet there were twenty-three entrances total. He began his long climb upward in an attempt to try to figure out his puzzle. At each floor he did a round, counting the entrances to make sure he was indeed correct. By the time he reached the water distribution floor, he knew he was right. Twenty-two of twenty-three entrances accounted for. One of the entrances went somewhere else. But which one?

He made the long climb back to the main floor and when the Minotaur door creaked open once again, he was met with the brilliant pink hues of sunset.

White salt stains crusted his grey robes under his arms and across his chest and back. He looked at himself, slightly disgusted, and then after a moment laughed. When he had been a boy, he had gotten far dirtier than this far more often. Had all his winters inside the tower really changed that?

He gave it little thought as he came about to the new task at hand: figuring out which of the twenty-three doors would take him elsewhere beneath the tower other than prison cells.

He walked by them all in sequence, studying them repeatedly. Minotaur, Orc, Bat-winged Creature, Sea Monster, Dragon, Gargoyle, and so on. He tried to map out where he had been below with the doors above, but it was just no good. It was too easy to get your bearings lost so far beneath ground. In the end, Ashyn was left with little alternative.

"I have to guess," he muttered to himself.

Theorize, he realized Xexial would say. *I have a conjecture or two,* he would tell Ashyn, when he would ask some obscure question that Xexial had no answer to. Just a fancy word for guess.

Therefore, Ashyn studied the doors repeatedly. Were there any illustrations where a man was not being killed at some point? *No,* he realized. All met some grisly end.

Were there any that didn't have man at all? He did his rounds. Nope. Ashyn watched as the pink slowly turned into a cobalt blue as the sun settled behind the horizon.

Minotaur, Orc, Bat winged Creature, Sea Monster, Dragon, Gargoyle . . . he started around again and froze. He went back two doors to the dragon devouring the man. On every floor he had journeyed there was a dragon skull at the entrance. Could it possibly be connected? Could it be that easy?

He placed his burning torch in the empty sconce, and this time used both hands to lift the doorpost up and out of the way. As it clamored to the floor with a great bang, he reached up once more to reclaim his torch. This door opened soundlessly on well-oiled hinges, and it instantly occurred to Ashyn that this particular door had been used far more frequently. *How could that be?* he wondered idly. Xexial said he never went down in the cellars *as a child,* Ashyn recalled. Xexial said nothing about when he had become a wizard. Perhaps this door led to something that Ashyn wasn't ready to deal with yet. Perhaps he shouldn't enter at all? His hesitation was momentary, however. If he weren't allowed to enter, there would be something barring his way more powerful than a doorpost. This was a wizard's tower, after all. Not to mention the hundred-some-odd other rooms within the higher levels of the tower he was never permitted to access. Those had locks and ward-like defenses placed on them to bar him from entering. This just had a post to bar those who had entered from leaving. If Xexial had not wanted him in this room, he would have placed a ward upon it.

He cast his light down the stairs and was surprised to see that they were straight, not spiraling. "This must be it."

He quickly descended the eighty-six steps, feeling the heat buildup, as he knew he was somewhere just atop the bubbling pools of superheated water. Yet when he reached the bottom, all he saw was a long, dark stone hallway. The ceiling was maybe seven feet high, if that. He reached up and touched the cut stone. Slimy moisture came off on his fingertips. *The water must channel directly through here*, he thought to himself.

Slowly he proceeded down the narrow hallway. There were no windows, no doors, alcoves, or cells like any of the other chambers beneath the tower, just one long, straight hall.

It continued for a long ways, perhaps a quarter mile or maybe even closer to a third of a mile. Ashyn knew without a doubt that he was no longer beneath the tower, but somewhere within the crater itself. The warmth continued to build and he could see moisture openly running down the walls as the flames from his torch fanned by them.

Then the long hall ended, and he found himself in front of a door unlike any he had ever seen before within the tower. Where everything else in the Onyx tower was black, this door was a solid white. A relief was carved within of a man hatching out of an egg. The detail was exquisite. It was almost as if he were staring at something real. He could see the muscular definition of the naked man, the lines and creases of his well-developed frame. A flock of curls adorned his head and made up his beard. But that wasn't what drew him in. It was the eyes. So detailed, so real, these eyes looked into the very depths of his being as if reading his soul like an open book. It was as if this carved man knew what Ashyn was thinking of doing.

There was no handle on the door, or niche with which he could grab a hold. In fact, he couldn't even see where the hinges rested upon. It was just a smooth, ivory surface completely around the relief.

Ashyn reached out and touched the door. It was smooth and hard beneath his touch, but not cool like stone or marble. It was warm and dry.

"Dragonbone," he realized aloud. It was fabled that a dragon's bones kept its magic within them when they died, and that a skilled practitioner could use that magic to create anything from magical arms and armor to magical doors.

Suddenly the door rumbled beneath the touch of his skin, and Ashyn felt his flesh grow warm, then hot. A deep thrumming filled his ears, vibrating so hard that his chest shook and his teeth chattered. Quickly he drew his hand away from the ivory portal. But the tremors coursing through his body did not subside. If anything, they intensified.

His heart beat like a hammer in his chest. What had he done? Had he set off an alarm? A ward that was going to sheer the flesh from his bones?

He wanted to turn and run away, but he found he couldn't. He was helpless before the might of the door. *Was this his great demise?* he wondered. Killed by a door?

The pulsations intensified down to his very core, he felt the blood in his body rushing to the surface of his skin, flushing him with an internal heat that was as hot as fire. Everything began to glow an intense orange before him, deeper and richer than the torch light. He recognized the hue from when he was angry, but he wasn't angry now, only scared.

Just as quickly as it started the shuddering subsided and his body began to cool. He looked at his olive-skinned hands and found steam rising from them. How hot had he become?

Then the door in front of him slid open, within a hidden recess in the wall. Ashyn gasped at the sight before him.

Within the doorway was a portico overlooking a great gallery below. As Ashyn stepped through, he took two ivory steps downward to the balustrades that would stop him from falling over thirty feet to the floor below. The curved supports were made of the same beautiful crème-colored marble as the steps he took, yet they beheld a myriad of iridescent blue-laced symbols that flowed flawlessly up and around the thick railing and supporting balusters.

The gallery was circular in shape, reminding Ashyn of the rest of the tower that he had left behind. Above him was a ceiling that rested like an apse. Painted across the majestic covering were thousands of men in battle against every known color of dragon that Ashyn had ever read about. It was a battle that was unknown to the young man.

It took many minutes before he pulled his gaze away from the massive war depiction to look below him. There, thirty feet below, were twenty-three great statues of men, all facing one another. Twelve were in poses that suggested they were casting great spells that Ashyn couldn't recognize. Ten were posed in silent contemplation, palms pressed firmly together at the center of their chest, as if in prayer. Each man was robed in traditional wizard fashion, though the style seemed to change minutely from one man to the next. All the men bore beards and long hair, except for the last. The final statue that Ashyn looked at stood at the center point of the circle. If Ashyn could guess, he would say it was the northern-most statue, though he couldn't be quite certain.

This statue was unlike any of the others. He stood in battle regalia, an intricately-carved breastplate that bore runes similar to ones Ashyn had seen dozens of times in manuscripts and tomes that Xexial had had him read. He knew they were symbolic of the wards and glyphs of various protections, many of which he had never been able to invoke yet successfully. But across the center of his breastplate was a great dragon taking flight, its wings spread from his collarbone to collarbone and its great bony tail trailing down his stomach and wrapping along the left side towards his back. Even from his vantage, he could see the majesty of the artwork.

In his hands were gauntlets adorned with runic symbols, much like his armor, and they held a large gem-like object on the back of each hand. They didn't offer much in the way of protection, Ashyn surmised, but they were amazing nonetheless.

Underneath that armor were layered robes, just like any of the other twenty-two statues around him.

Yet that alone was not the only thing that stood him apart from the others. It was his face. His head was bald, or shaven, Ashyn wasn't sure. He also had a short-cropped beard that hugged his cheeks and chin, nothing more. Nothing like the long, gangly beards he was used to seeing in the tomes about wizards of old. Above the carving of facial hair there were deep etches in the marble that was the man's flesh. These etches were swirls, and rakes, and cuts, and what Ashyn thought at first was damage to the statue quickly became obvious that it was more. They were tattoos.

Tattoos that covered over his eyes and nose, and ran across his bald palate, over his ears, and down the back of his head and neck. They were savage and barbaric, and they made him look primal.

Ashyn quickly descended the steps to the floor below. He was amazed to find that the statues were far taller, once he was on ground level, each standing at nearly twelve feet. At this point, Ashyn did not miss the connotation of the twenty-three statues and the twenty-three doors. He wondered how many other things within the tower were also twenty-three in number.

Still he felt drawn to the center point statue all in armor. Ashyn had no doubt that this was a wizard, but he was unlike any other wizard Ashyn had ever learned of. He was a king amongst wizards.

As the he approached this master wizard, he realized what this room truly was. It was a tomb, a tomb of buried wizards, perhaps the original creators of the Onyx Tower.

Ashyn felt a sort of reverence to them then. These were his peers, the progenitors of the craft before him. Carefully, he took a step towards the man in the battle armor. There was a placard at the pedestal by his sandaled feet. Ashyn read it aloud. "Magelord Rheynnaus Craëgolshien, Bastard of Ashyreus, First of his name, and last born heir of Mysticarus."

So he was a king! He certainly looked it. Yet Ashyn also noted that there were no dates on the placards, nothing to give an indication of how old they were, or of the Onyx Tower. Ashyn looked to the other statues, each containing placards: Faust the Mighty; Alred the Inept; Dilark the Diligent; Romerik Rillerion of Silversprings . . . the names went on and on.

All were the originators of their statue likeness, yet no dates. It was as if no one wanted them to know when they existed, only that they had indeed existed.

"Were these your men?" he asked the still sculpture of the Magelord. "Did they ever have doubts? Or people they loved that needed their help?"

Ashyn knew then why this room wasn't blocked off like the others. It was important to wizards. It let them know their roots, where they came from.

He walked up to the Magelord and got on his knees before the man's tattooed visage. "Tell me then?" he pleaded. "What would you have done if it were your sister? Or this Ashyreus you descended from? Would you have fought for them? Would you strive to rescue them even if you were . . . lame?" he said as he struggled with the fact that he was now unable to harness magic.

"Or would you hold to the Wizard's Covenant- even knowing that somewhere out there your sister was being mutilated, or perhaps worse- all because it was supposed to be your sacrifice?" he asked the fierce statue before him.

Standing, he started to slowly pace around the Magelord as he spoke aloud. "This isn't my sacrifice though, is it?" he questioned. "It's hers. She's a slave, a plaything to be abused."

As he walked full circle around Rheynnaus he looked up into its barbarically carved face, "And when I should be out there helping her, I'm not. How am I to value life when I'm constantly told to ignore that very thing I cherish?" he demanded, before looking to the ground.

"What would you have done?" Ashyn whispered.

The room was silent for a long time, until a deep voice said behind him, "He would endure."

Ashyn spun around to see Xexial standing in the doorway, leaning heavily against its white bone frame. The elder wizard stepped into the room. Ashyn suddenly felt very nervous. How much did Xexial overhear? How much did he know?

"I . . . I," he stammered.

Xexial merely raised his hand. "I know."

Ashyn studying his master's cold eyes, but he found them unreadable. Instead, Xexial continued.

"While we have no true details on Rheynnaus, we believe that it was he who constructed this tower to be some sort of defensive war post. We wizards believe that his life was full of pain and strife, and that he was constantly tested day after day, winter after winter, on what he believed was right. Yet he never gave up. He kept on going, and he endured whatever horrors were thrown at him.

"I cannot free your sister, Ashyn, and whether you believe me or not it tears me up inside to say it. I hate it even more to tell you that you, too, have no hope of saving her. Yet you have always been brave, and stubborn, and strong of will and I cannot tell you that you need to heed the Covenant. You already know this.

"You must choose your own path, boy, as every man must. I only ask that you truly think carefully before you do, and realize the magnitude of your decisions when that time does come."

He turned around to leave, but stopped once more to look back at the boy. "I am truly impressed you managed to enter this chamber. The door only accepts those that are worthy. It must have found something worthy within you that was not magic. What could that be, I wonder?" And with that, he was gone. Disappeared down the long hall that led up to the tower somewhere above.

Ashyn looked away from the door, lost in thought, and back up to the Magelord. "Could you endure this?" he asked the statue.

LIKE AN OLD FRIEND

Ashyn knew it was very late when he finally picked himself off the ground from Rheynnaus' feet. Xexial had left him there hours before, and Ashyn had found himself replaying his master's words in his head again and again. He had hoped that he would garner some clarity from them, and that they would have helped, but it only made it harder, he decided. Xexial knew Ashyn's conflict, and it compounded the burden on his heart even more that Xexial did not force him to stay, but gave him a choice.

He loved the man; there was no denying it. His respect for him was without peer. However, he wasn't Ashyn's family. Not in the same sense. His love for his sister . . . it was different.

Ashyn had never been one to play by the rules. It was part of what had made him so unaccepted in Bremingham. He knew that. The Wizard's Covenant though, that was final. To walk away, there was no coming back from that. Wizards would hunt him to the end of his days. He wasn't trained enough to stand up against a master wizard, especially taking into consideration the fact that he was now lame.

His life would be short if he broke the Covenant. If he did, he could only hope to free Julietta and get her to safety somewhere before the wizards came to claim him.

So, lost in thought, he paid virtually no attention to where he was going as he walked back through the long weeping hall, up the steps, and was once again roaming around within the tower. He passed row upon row of gargoyles as they stood silent sentinels in the great hall. He never noticed going up the stairs to the next floor, or the one after that. It was only after several minutes of disarray that he realized he had stopped walking altogether. When he looked up, he had to blink several times before he realized where he was.

The décor was sparse, bordering on nonexistent, in the oblong anteroom of the third floor's sparring chambers. Only a few sigils decorated the walls, most containment glyphs, lest any unfortunate wizard release spells too powerful that they might harm the rest of the tower in some way. A few pitted scars amongst the high walls and one cracked baluster were testament enough to the lack of control that some acolytes had experienced. Ashyn couldn't recall any time that he left so much as a blackened smear on a wall during his training. *What had brought him here?* he wondered. Yet before he could answer his own question, he found himself moving forward towards the heavy Cumara wood door. As he grabbed the cast iron handle and lifted the hatch, he thought of Mrs. Gregy's mannequin that had been made of the same wood. Dreadfully heavy and fireproof, it had become the specter of the burned down farm in Bremingham for many a winter.

Cumara could last, that was for certain, he marveled as the open portal gave way to numerous hideous black scars that lined the opposite side of the door, within the sparring chambers.

The sparring room was probably one of the largest rooms in the entire tower. It encompassed over three hundred feet in diameter. It was once meant to train up to twenty-three wizard acolytes with the same corresponding number of masters. The nature of its construction was one designed to be a complete circle with all the supporting balusters situated along the perimeter of the wall. The chambers themselves were decorated to a far greater degree than the anteroom, but it was more for practical purposes than aesthetic.

Within the center of the round room on the floor, there were three circles, each one a different color. The largest, which covered the borders of the room, was originally meant to be a shade of jade green. Slowly time had worn it to an emerald hue over the tower's long winters of life. It was for the newest of apprentices to work in as they learned to harness the simplest spells of their trade.

The second circle, however, was only ten feet in diameter and it was originally as red as a ruby, but now was nothing more than a mottled brown. This was for wizards who were beyond the stage of 'green' acolyte, and were now on their way to becoming a full wizard. It was here, within the small confines of the circle, that they learned combat one-on-one with another wizard, or a wizard representing another type of foe. For many wizards, this was the final step in the sparring chambers.

The final circle was nothing more than a spot, at only 3 inches in diameter on the massive floor, and it was still as bright silver as the day it was created. It represented the final ascension into wizardry, and the circle within one's self. Very few masters over the generations had ever ascended to the silver circle. And it was not something that could be taught by another wizard. It had to be learned from within. As such, most wizards today were known as Wizards of the Second Circle. Not even Xexial had achieved the mantle of First Circle.

Ashyn stared at the silver sphere on the floor for many moments. In reality, Ashyn had never left the green circle, due to his inability to cast most of the required spells taught by wizards in towers across Kuldarr. Xexial, though, had moved him to the red circle anyhow, based on his technical knowledge of the way they functioned as well as the way many other spells functioned that even confounded Xexial himself.

Ashyn knew the theory of how it was 'supposed' to be done, but when it came to actually doing it, he found he couldn't. It was kind of like riding a horse. Everyone knew how to ride one in theory, but actually doing it was a completely different matter. It was still a sore subject within him, and he was grateful that there was only one master and one apprentice within the tower at this time. He would have hated to have peers. Aggravated, he looked away from the circles on the floor.

The ceiling was the only real piece of art within the entire chamber, and it stood well over seventy feet high. It was a mural of wizards in battle over the centuries, be they fighting in great wars, or more intimate battles against one another, or beasts such as dragons and the undead.

Around the perimeter of the room were a series of Cumara dummies that were used for combat-based spells when they weren't training outright with their masters. Many were nothing more than shattered and molten stumps, as the winters of repeated use wore them away. Some newer ones were only missing limbs or portions of their heads or abdomens. They may have been made of Cumara wood, but there was more to magic than merely fire. Two dummies left still maintained all their appendages.

Against the wall where he entered there resided a single, long Cumara wood table that held candles, stones, animal bones, fire salts, and a dozen other material components that helped when crafting more complex spells.

Overcome with sudden desire, Ashyn grabbed a candle, lit it, and walked across the long chamber. He then pulled one of the whole dummies into the mottled brown circle. When he was satisfied with its position in the circle, he walked to the opposite end.

He held the candle in his wounded hand, and raised his good hand in front of the tiny glittering flame. Calmly he spoke the words that Xexial had taught him long winters past. He pulled at the flame, calling it to his will. He put all of his concentration and effort into the single flickering wisp, pleading it to come to his hand.

Nothing.

He couldn't even feel the magic within the delicate flame.

Still, Ashyn did not relent and tried it a dozen more times. By the time he gave up, the wax had run down his hand, biting and gnawing savagely at his skin. First, he had ignored the pain, now it merely frustrated him. He threw down the candle in disgust, splattering the soft black wax candle against the dingy colored stone. The flimsy light died instantly, and the wax began to harden into puddles on the floor that looked vaguely like oil.

Bitter with repugnance at his own failings, he kicked the Cumara dummy and sank to the floor against it. He was too tired for tears, he had cried enough. Instead, he only sat there quietly looking at the circles he had failed to achieve.

"Perhaps I wasn't meant to be a wizard after all," he said quietly to himself. But he knew he was only trying to delude himself. He knew the formulae too well; he knew every nuance of magic. He *loved* the magic, he couldn't deny it. Even if he couldn't apply it, he knew how it worked, its fundamentals. Xexial had even commented that he might very well be the first wizard ever to 'create' new spells in over a hundred winters. The last had been a senior member of the Seven, and he had died before even Xexial's father had been born.

Ashyn needed to do something in the meantime, though. He couldn't just brood in his depression. He needed to find something else he was good at. It had just been so long since he had done anything other than magic . . .

Slowly, understanding dawned on him. Perhaps his subconscious had indeed led him here for a reason. Maybe it had been Rheynnaus answering him from the other side, for besides the antechamber that led into the sparring chambers there were two other doors against the west wall. One was the storage room where all additional reagents were kept, and the other was the armory.

Ashyn stood and smoothed out his wrinkled grey robe as best he could. With a new idea forming in his mind, he briskly walked over to the armory door.

It was an old, indescript door that had been blackened over the winters by rogue spells. There was small script carved into the archway above the door that was simply labeled 'armory'. Strangely enough, the old blackened door was actually smaller than he was by a good six inches. Either the armory had been manned by Dwarves, or it had simply been constructed at a time when men were smaller.

It had been a proven fact that men and even High Elves, were once roughly the same size as the rest of the Hym. Somewhere in the process of evolution, humans were actually becoming taller.

Ashyn opened the portal into the unused room beyond. In his childhood days, Ashyn had thought that an armory within a wizard's tower was as worthless as a prayer room in a whorehouse. Yet learning that this had been a defensive post, and with the plethora of lodging available, the tower could comfortably host over two hundred residents. It made sense that not everyone whom lived in the tower would be wizards. There would be soldiers, scouts, knights, cooks, possibly even farmers and field hands. The expanse of the gully, or crater as Ashyn realized it, was great enough to grow crops for many people. And volcanic soil was good and rich.

Yet over the millennia, the number of wizards had greatly declined, and so the practical use of the Onyx Tower as a garrison declined as well. Now, after all this time, the once great tower only housed two: Master and Apprentice.

So as the need for troops thinned, so too did the need for a fully-stocked armory. But that did not mean it was without its resources. Xexial had shown him the armory before, and there were still rows upon rows of swords, maces, morning stars, axes, and shields. There was even platemail, though it had not been properly tended to in centuries and the wool padding inside had become rotten, and the leather cracked and brittle.

But aside from that, the armory had also become the place to store the wares of one's previous life before they became wizard acolytes. Like Ashyn, not everyone had been born into wizardry. Some had been cooks, others blacksmiths, or tanners, or even tailors. And some had been warriors.

One thing though was the same for all of them. When they donned the robes, they had no need for their old life, and so those parcels that had been tools of their past were stored in the armory.

Slowly Ashyn walked by the old weapons, many now pitted and dulled from winters of disuse, some so brittle that Ashyn was sure they'd shatter on their first strike. He continued down row after row, looking for something he could be comfortable with. Xexial had once told him that all races were wizards, not just men and so as he ventured further towards the back he began to find the weapons that wizards had relinquished: Curved swords, Dwarven axes and shields, Goldhym knives, Gnomish war picks, a set of tongs, a blacksmith's hammer. Ashyn laughed when he unrolled a fine set of silver cutlery bound tightly in oiled leather.

Further back he walked, cutting through the slivers of pale gold light that poured through the high, slatted windows above him. Was it morning again already? He hadn't realized how long he had been down there soul searching with the statue of Rheynnaus.

There were notched axes, quarterstaves, strange looking punching daggers that Ashyn had once read about called katar. He even found a whip. He shivered at the sight of it. Even after all the winters that passed, the whipping he had received at the hands of the Enclave had scarred him more in his mind than his flesh.

He turned around another set of shelves and stopped. A smile crept across his face. This is what he sought.

On his left were rows upon rows of quivers bundled with arrows; on his right, bows. He walked down the long aisle, examining each one like a child at a sweets shop. There were long bows, short bows, hunter's bows, and compound bows. He saw bows made of elm, and cherry, birch, oak, pine, maple, and even an odd Cumara wood bow, though when he lifted it, he found it was very heavy. Some were plain, others ornate with scrawling markings or artistic etches running up the length of the wood. Some even decorated with fancy stones.

He found a nice, supple elm short bow, plain in design, but light enough for his wiry arms, and flexible enough for a solid draw. The grip was rotted away, but he was sure he could find enough rawhide leather around to make a suitable replacement. He noted the pull string was waning a bit as well, but another quick search found more than ample reserves protected over the ages in sealskin.

He restrung his chosen bow, meticulously, as his father had taught him. He gave it a test pull, tightened the string, and pulled again. He went through the process rigorously until it was just taut enough to give it that perfect twang on release.

He grabbed a quiver of older arrows, no point in wasting the good stock practicing, he reasoned, and turned to leave. That was when he caught a glimmer out of the corner of his eye.

He turned and looked back at the row of bows. Many of the ornate ones had fixed gems like emeralds and rubies, but that wasn't what he saw. A glance back again, and saw it flicker once more, far back against the wall in the oldest part of the armory. It was deep, where no one had ventured in probably millennia.

Ashyn shouldered the quiver and carefully walked towards the back of the armory. Dust plumed with every step, and he had to push away layers of cobwebs as he lurked deeper within the old room. He vaguely heard the scurrying of some vermin, and was tempted to nock and draw his bow, but he withheld.

One lone ray of light pierced through the gloomy vale, casting a pallid luminescence across the chamber. Everything was cast in a dim grey hue.

As he stepped closer to the slightly shimmering object, he noticed the floor wasn't entirely stable anymore due to centuries of neglect. Carefully he stepped forward, making sure each footing was solid. He stood before a decayed weapon stand that had long since dry-rotted into little more than two jutting spikes of wood sticking up from the ground. All the weapons that were held in the lower arms had turned into brittle fragments and debris, little more than shaped dust, just like the rest of the room around him.

Yet between those two remaining timber fingers was an object covered in a heavy protective oilcloth. Some of it had fallen away to reveal a silver tip that was untarnished, even after ages of neglect.

With a shaky hand, Ashyn reached up and drew the cloth away. Thick, black dust kicked up into the air, briefly blinding him and causing him to choke and gag on the filth. As the grime settled, and Ashyn could see once more in front of him, he sucked in a sharp breath.

It was a bow unlike any he had ever seen in his life.

The bow was pristine white. It was a brilliant hue, like the antlers of a stag. Even in the light, it glistened, and Ashyn guessed it must be laminated. Silver runes danced across the shaft, clinquant in the ray of early morning light. He studied them all and recognized that they were glyphs for a spell.

Looking at its length, he could tell it was a hunter's bow; smaller than a long bow, but slightly larger than a short bow. If an archer wanted, they could use it to fire while mounted on a horse, like a short bow, but it would be cumbersome. Not that it mattered to Ashyn. It wasn't as if he had a stable of horses wantonly lying around anyways.

What he did find strange, though, was that the bow before him still held its recurve, even when unstrung. This was very atypical amongst most bows.

Awestruck, he unceremoniously dropped his old bow to the ground and reached out to the new one. His fingers touched the glistening quicksilver runes and his heart skipped a beat. There was still power in them! Even though he had no connection to magic for the moment, he could still feel the energy the symbols radiated. Quickly he hefted it from its deformed perch and the last of the rotted wood disintegrated and fell away.

It was light, Ashyn noted, and well-balanced.

He ran his fingers against the smooth, laminated shaft, turning the bow over in his hands. It was bone. That concerned him for a moment, as bone didn't often bend well over time. Yet when he tested the ends, he found that they flexed wondrously.

The handgrip was made of suede leather, still in perfect condition, and surprisingly didn't slip at all when he drew the bow.

Carefully he exited the old portion of the armory, and then restrung the bow. When he was satisfied with the pull, he eagerly went back into the sparring room and pushed the Cumara dummy out of the brown circle and into the emerald. He then walked across the expanse of the room.

He slid an arrow from the quiver across his shoulder, and felt a jitter of anticipation course through his insides. He raised the bow, nocked the arrow and pulled it back. He noted that the arrow wasn't perfectly straight, and that it would likely sail off mark, so he adjusted his shot. He held the cord back. He could feel the feathers of the arrow brushing his ear. The string bit at his fingers. It was tight and sharp. He concentrated on the target in front of him until the dummy was the only thing he saw in the entire world. He loosed the arrow.

Thwang! The bow pitched perfectly.

Crack! The dummy's right arm rocked as the weak arrow shattered against the durable Cumara wood.

Ashyn was elated. He hit it! After eleven winters, he still could hit it! He drew another arrow; this one was warped, too. He adjusted some more, and loosed. Crack! The arrow shattered across the left thigh. Quickly Ashyn burned through the remaining eighteen arrows in the quiver, one after the other. His fingers, unaccustomed to the bow, began to bleed, but he didn't care. A familiar sting was coming back to him, like a kiss from an old friend.

He ran back into the armory, jubilant as a little boy, and grabbed three more quivers. For the rest of the morning he loosed arrow after arrow at the Cumara dummies, sometimes picking multiple targets at a time. Soon arrows were no longer breaking but sticking roughly out of the dummies themselves. As the sun climbed into the afternoon sky, over a dozen dummies looked like pincushions and Ashyn had shot well over a hundred and twenty arrows. His fingers bled liberally, but he paid them no heed whatsoever. He could still use a bow. That was something he was good at. Even over the winters, his aim had barely slighted at all, and his vision was as acute as ever.

Sweat soaked through his robes and they clung to him, hanging limply like wet, dead flesh. He stripped out of them, and down to his small clothes. As he dropped the robes sloppily to the ground, he could smell the fetid aroma resonating from them. He had worn them for days, sweating in them profusely. He was likely equally as rancid, but he didn't care. He had found something, for the moment, that didn't make him feel lame.

He loosed only one more quiver at the dummies before deciding that it was time to give his fingers a well-deserved break. He was also exhausted, and hungry, and in much need of a bath.

Before deciding finally to adjourn to his quarters he wanted to grab at least three more quivers of the best arrows he could find. The search didn't take long, and soon he had sixty beautiful goose-feathered arrows. As he turned to exit, one last thing caught his eye: Armor.

Seeing as how he could no longer be protected from his usual wards, he needed a new type of protection. And so he spent the rest of the afternoon dressing up in various types of armor. Platemail was too heavy and restricting, while most of the scalemail and chainmail was too rusted to move, not to mention the brown streaks it left across his skin. Disappointingly, all the leather armor that fit him, too, had gone to rot, or had been cracked and hardened due to maltreatment.

He had hoped to come across a rare gem of a find as he did with the bow, some mystical set of armor, but there was none to be had. So with a disappointed sigh, he began to sift through all the single pieces of armor, odds and ends that didn't match, or were too big, small, warped, or damaged to go with the set any longer.

He found a black leather jerkin, that had what he guessed were likely bloodstains. It was in good enough repair to wear, but it smelled like a cow's ass. Equally, he had found some forest green leather gauntlets that were in magnificent shape, considering they were buried beneath moldy padded armor. It may not have matched, but it was something. All he needed now were greaves and boots. He moved through three more piles of armor before he came to one in a crate that was labeled 'children and Elves'. He was about to ignore it altogether, due to his height, when something compelled him to look anyway.

About halfway through the crate, rifling through mold, rat feces and urine, his fingers brushed against a series of small metal balls, against something slick and hard.

Quickly he heaved the refuse-covered armor garments out of the way. This was the first piece that felt sound out of this crate. As he shook it free of the riddled heap of wool that sat atop it, Ashyn was thrust back thirteen winters, and he found himself remembering staring up in awe at a High Elf in the middle of Bremingham.

In his hands was the rustic hunter's garb of the Lefhym, the Wood Elves, the same kind that Veer De'Storm had worn the day he entered Ashyn's life. Unlike Veer's brown leathers, these were dyed a crimson color, but still displayed the same elaborately- patterned design. Small studs of metal ran across the shoulders and biceps, slowly tapering into thickened, cured leather at the elbows. Attached by thick rawhide cording were gauntlets of heavy leather. They were emblazoned with intricate patterns of autumn leaves and twisting vines.

Eagerly, Ashyn examined the size of it. It was narrow, but long for a Wood Elf. He might get lucky. Not even thinking of what the armor had been sitting in, he eagerly suited himself up. After fifteen minutes, he marveled at himself. The gauntlets fit his thin wrists perfectly, and the thick, cured-leather elbow guards were in alignment with his own. His wide shoulder span was a slight problem with the narrower armor, but he found that he could adjust the straps across the collar and back well enough that it fit comfortably. The hard leather tunic, though long for an Elf, wasn't exactly long enough for him. Where it may run to the thighs on an Elf, it stopped level with his crotch. This didn't deter him in the slightest; he would find a way around that.

He plunged his hands into the crate hoping to find matching greaves but was disappointed when he found that they were far too small for any hope of a fit. Still, he had the tunic.

He walked to the armory fitting glass, and with a sweaty hand smeared away the dust and grime as best he could. Staring at his gaunt figure in Lefhym hunter's garb, he thought once again of Veer. *How the winters had passed,* he realized. With the intense changes in his life, he had never thought of the one person that had first forged a difference in his views on life. Ashyn had lived as an outcast, rejected and unaccepted by anyone other than his family in Bremingham, until Veer.

The High Elf had been his idol, his friend, and probably his first mentor, and how did Ashyn repay this gift? By hardly thinking of the Elf since the attack on Bremingham. Sure, he could say that with all that had happened, he had forgotten about Veer, but what kind of justice did that do his first real friend?

His slid his fingers over the ribbed plates of hard leather on his breast, thinking of the day Veer willingly went to fight a Bristle Wolf, bare-chested and without his remarkable rapier. He had done it for a family he knew virtually nothing about, because his strong sense of ethics demanded it. *Where was that person in himself,* he wondered? Sure, Ashyn had saved his sister, but that was because she was family. He loved her. Veer, though? He had risked himself because he knew it was the right thing to do, to help someone in need. Not for reward, or for their blessings and thanks, but because he believed in it.

Ashyn flexed his injured forearm beneath the gauntlet. Did Ashyn believe in it? He thought back to what Xexial had told him that day he wanted to fight the Wild Elves and save the Enclave. That it was not the right thing to do, and that the definition of a hero was someone who got others killed. Veer had tried to save his sister Julietta, and no one died. Everyone was fine. Ashyn *had* saved his sister. What were Ashyn's values? Were they like Veer's? Or like Xexial's? Or were they somewhere in between? He stared at the armor for a long time, ignoring its rank ammonia-like odor.

He thought of Rheynnaus. Xexial said his life had been one of difficult choices and yet he had endured, because he did what he thought was right. Well, Ashyn knew what he thought was right, and what he had to do. More importantly, he knew who he was. He was not a hero like Veer, nor was he as cynical as Xexial. He was his own person. He was Ashyn Rune and he knew what it was that he believed in, what in life gave him his true strength.

He thought of Veer De'Storm's parting words, his sage-like wisdom, that until now he had all but forgotten. Ashyn smiled. "And you said I never forget anything."

He ran from the room but turned once more to face the mirror, staring at the armor as if it were the Elf himself. "Thank you, Stormwind, for reminding me of what is important."

Then the boy was gone. There was still so much to be done.

ADVANCED

Ashyn was changed and bathed by the time he joined Xexial for supper. He had replaced his filthy bandages on his injured forearm with clean ones, and had even bandaged his bloodied fingertips. If Xexial noticed, he made no mention of it.

They both ate in silence a thick, heady mushroom soup with flakes of bacon soaked in hearty mead. Ashyn realized that Xexial must have been cooking all day, and that meant one thing: a full belly for a long trip. He looked into Xexial's fierce azure eyes, but could read nothing.

After they were finished, they both lingered at the table. When it was obvious that Xexial was going to say nothing, Ashyn pushed. "When do we leave?"

"On the morrow. Early," Xexial replied crisply.

Ashyn nodded.

"I trust your surface injuries have healed sufficiently?" the elder wizard asked icily.

"They have."

"Good. A trip to the Seven will not be easy. We've already tarried long enough, so I have decided we will book passage from Buckner," Xexial said.

Ashyn was actually surprised. "You hate sailing."

"Which should tell you how important I feel this is," Xexial replied. "We already know that the Ferhym are attacking wizards, and that they are using other people, even towns, to coerce us out of our protection. What we don't know is the scale. Is this centralized only to the Shalis-Fey, or has the Council of Elm enlisted all of its surrogates throughout the other woods?"

"I hadn't thought of that," Ashyn remarked, realizing the potential endeavor in front of them.

Xexial nodded. "I know, but I have. If we travelled on foot to the Seven, there is no telling how many encounters we might have. Hell, boy, it might already be too late. Maker knows the Elves have had enough time to regroup after your sufficient kick to their backside."

"Why didn't we leave sooner?" Ashyn asked, slightly agitated, as if Xexial were saying it was his fault.

"You're lame enough as it is. I couldn't risk your arm becoming infected."

"We didn't need . . ."

Xexial raised his hand to stop Ashyn cold. "It was my choice, lad," he retorted in his deep voice.

Ashyn decided to change the subject to something he rather wanted. "I would like permission to change my robes."

Xexial scrutinized him for a moment before answering. "You would like to show the Seven that you have progressed a circle. That you're close to becoming a wizard." Xexial mulled it over. "You think it may help sway their decision?"

That was not the full reason, but Ashyn nodded nonetheless.

"That is sound. So let's see. What color would it be? Fire, invocations, you're astute with shields and wards. Tan? No, too much like mine; they might think it queer. There is olive, for second circle adepts at wards, yes that would be good. Go with tradition, I think."

Ashyn shook his head no. "I want crimson," he said firmly.

"Crimson?" Xexial returned, nonplussed. "That's a Blood Wizard, son. We haven't had one of those for nearly nine hundred winters."

Ashyn stood his ground, "*That* tradition. Yes, you are correct. I was thinking of a very different tradition, honestly. You see it is a well-known fact that many warriors, mainly scouts and assassins, wear deep crimson colors to hide their wounds so their opponents can never truly realize how wounded they are."

Xexial gawked, "You are no warrior."

"I may surprise you," he returned seriously.

Xexial raised an eyebrow. "Why should I let you wear the crimson robes?"

"I am lame right now. This is no secret to either of us, but our enemy doesn't know that. Though it is likely they know a wizard's traditional colors, if they're as ardent in hunting us as you say. They will want to identify who it is they hunt."

Xexial nodded.

Ashyn continued, "A Blood Wizard would give them pause. It is said that Blood Wizards become more powerful when wounded, if I read that correctly."

He could see Xexial thinking. That was good.

"Additionally, I will not be idle while we are assaulted. I will defend myself. If I am wounded, I'd rather our enemies not know it. They have met defeat at our hands once already. Let us give them doubt if they try it again. You are not as feeble as you let on; let them not think me as frail, either."

"Misdirection," Xexial said.

Ashyn nodded.

Xexial smiled, "My, you are a clever boy. Very well; crimson it is. But when we approach the Seven, bring olive garments. Blood Wizards make all wizards uncomfortable."

"Yes, master."

"Good, now go get ready. We have a long day ahead of us tomorrow, Blood Wizard."

Ashyn suppressed his frown at the title. It would do for now. He still had a lot of work to do before he slept for the night, and he was already exhausted as it was, both mentally and physically, from the stresses and being up for the last two days.

He found the crimson robes quickly enough, alone in a wardrobe little-touched. Unlike the armor he had had to sift through, all the robes were in good repair. He selected one that fit best, and set to work on it. It was late at night when he finally sat back to marvel at his work.

While he had never been much of a tailor, he had done his best with rawhide cord and a little needle and thread to mold his outfit together. *It would do,* he reasoned.

Then he spent time packing his travel sack for a long journey. As the night wore on, he finally drew out a parchment and quill. His eyes burned from exhaustion and he stared at the blank parchment for a long time, hoping that the words might pen themselves. Eventually he knew he would have to get on with it, and so with a deep breath he dipped the quill into the dark, blood-red ink and began to write. He tried not to think about what tomorrow was going to bring. . .

~ ~ ~

That night he slept soundly for the first time in a great many days. When he awoke the next morning, he knew that he had made the right choice.

~ ~ ~

Xexial was waiting at the front entrance when Ashyn finally came down. It was the first time in many winters that Xexial was ready before Ashyn had been. But the choice had been made, and most of his getting ready had been mentally preparing himself.

When he came down the long black stairway, he was afraid his master was going to laugh at him, but he didn't. He merely stared in his cold, disinterested way.

Ashyn was dressed in the crimson robes, as he had asked for, but he had modified them. He fitted the upper robes so that they were cinched tighter to his abdomen to act as a gambeson for the Lefhym hunter's armor he wore over it. He had spent countless hours the night before cleaning the tunic and removing all traces of infestation that had plagued it. It now looked almost as good as the armor he had once seen as a child did.

His sleeves were removed completely so he could maximize his maneuverability. He wore a crimson glove on his right hand, except that it only covered his thumb and first two fingers; the last two were bare and exposed.

He had fastened the platinum braid of the Exemplar, which he had kept with him all this time, to his right gauntlet for luck. Across his waist he wore a leather belt, also scavenged, and affixed one of his three quivers to his left hip. On the other hip, he had his skinning knife.

On his back, he had attached the remaining two quivers on both sides of his travel pack. His bedroll helped support them underneath. The whole outfit was surprisingly heavy, but he knew he would get used to it in time, and he also made sure none of his mobility was lessened, for when he could wield magic again. *If* he could wield magic again.

He had nowhere to store the rune-inlaid bone bow he had, and so he held on to it.

When he approached his master, Xexial eyed the bow. "It is said that Rheynnaus once wielded a bow of bone." He looked Ashyn in his steel grey eyes. "Two parts deadly, one part ridiculous. A Blood Wizard, indeed."

With that, Xexial turned and led him out the door.

BLOOD ON THE SUN

Xao stared as the blood-red sun broke the horizon from the east. Vaguely in the distance, he could see the sharp sliver of the Onyx tower peeking up over the highlands, the sun's pink light slowly forcing the sanguine night into submission.

Blood on the sun? Xao thought to himself. There would be death this day. Slowly, Xao's yellow orbs lifted from the growing crimson circle to the umbral spike piercing the sky. Even for a dragon, he could feel something was wrong. Something big was brewing.

Gently, he tried to extend his wings. Tight and swollen at the joint, his right wing could barely open beyond half of his wingspan. He felt the sharp sting against the sensitive membrane of his inner wing. Xao was still not able to fly. Not yet.

But he could run.

Xao didn't know why, but something compelled him to head back to that wizard's tower. The boy may be gone from his senses, but there was something . . . a sense of foreboding that he couldn't explain. He needed to be there, he decided. He needed to be at the Onyx Tower.

And so the young red dragon did the only thing he could. He ran.

IT GETS NO EASIER

shyn dismally watched as the Onyx Tower became a sliver in the background. When they had left in the morning, he saw a large red sun and the sky was a blue ocean, endless, as far as he could see. Now though, as they left the protective gully and the sun began to crawl up towards the center of the midday sky, it became surprisingly overcast.

Thick, colorless fog hugged the verdant earth of the lowlands they were now in. He could only see a score of feet in front of him, and behind. Yet when he looked up, there was the sun, brilliant and golden. Cloud cover was thick and heavy, and the sun was lost repeatedly underneath their grey cotton bodies, but it always came back just as vibrant as the moment it left.

Ashyn could still see the lip of what he now knew was a crater loom skyward like a miniature mountain range. Deep brown and craggy, the earth split and shifted like a great stone fist rising upwards, ready to slam down upon him.

The fog rolled down from its rocky grip like juice poured from a squished berry between one's fingers. To Ashyn the crater lip looked like a murky waterfall, one that poured into a sea of wool.

His crimson robes hung limply against him, cold and wet from the dense miasma. It clung to his clammy flesh like leeches, sucking the very life from his body. Ashyn tried not to let it affect his mood, but it was hard.

He turned back towards the east to watch Xexial. His master plodded forward stubbornly, and he could tell the weather was bothering him, too. Xexial was hardly a young man any longer.

The moisture clumped the thinning strands of hair on the master wizard's head, and gave a reflective sheen to the top of his bald palate. His beard was a mess of tangles and frayed at the ends. The wetness made his skin look sallow. His age-spotted hands held tightly to his staff for support as he walked across the slick grasslands.

Ashyn noticed his eyes, though, were wary and alert. What was he looking for?

Reflexively, Ashyn opened and closed his right hand several times, moving the wounded tendons in his forearm, and getting the blood flowing. He looked at his drenched bandages. They would need to be changed soon.

The boy wizard hurried up to walk next to his master. He saw Xexial looking at him out of the corners of his deep blue eyes. "What is it?" Ashyn asked.

Xexial just shook his head grumpily. Droplets of dirty water flew from his hair and splattered against Ashyn's Lefhym armor. They journeyed for another hour in silence and misery, until Xexial held up a water-wrinkled hand for them to stop.

Ashyn noticed then how tense he was. "What?"

"This blasted fog," he growled. "It should have ended hours ago. Dammit, boy!" His gaze ripped across the opaque landscape, looking for answers.

"I don't understand," Ashyn returned. "It's just a mist. It's annoying, yes, but what's unusual about it?"

Xexial eyed him angrily. "What's unusual is that it has been moving in the same direction we have been, but the clouds are going the opposite way."

Ashyn looked up at the overcast sky. Sure enough, the clouds were moving west by northwest, caught in an easterly gust. They, however, had been heading east the entire time.

Ashyn gripped his bow a little tighter. "What does it mean?"

"It means I'm a damn fool, that's what it means. I should have left you in the tower and sought the Seven myself. Old I am, old and soft," he grumbled. "We're too late."

"Too late?" Ashyn didn't understand. *Too late for what?* he was going ask, but then he saw something move south of him in the haze. He turned and squinted, trying to see more clearly against the gloom. It was so thick, so damn close, like a wet blanket pulled over his head.

A shadow lumbered in the murk, large and ponderous. It seemed to have a waddling gait, and was dome-shaped at the top. He couldn't tell its exact size, six feet, maybe seven? The shadows could be playing tricks.

Ashyn felt Xexial's hand at the crook of his elbow slowly pushing him back. Ashyn stepped away, as the smaller old man stepped forward, staff in both hands.

"I really wish you would have had that sixth sense of yours now, lad," he whispered quietly as Ashyn watched a blue electrical charge spark from his luminescent thick-fingered gloves and dance down to the tip of the staff.

Ashyn was still not very sure of what was happening. He heard large, plodding feet, a snort of disdain, and then the mist cleared from around the moving shape some twenty feet away. Ashyn's eyes went wide. It was a bear, a large brown bear.

The beast stopped and stood on its hind legs, extending to its full nine-foot height. It roared at them, spittle flying from between long, thick, yellow fangs the size of Ashyn's thumbs.

Suddenly, two more hunched shadows appeared to the bear's left and right, equally as large. Ashyn went very ashen then.

"Druids," Xexial spat, unmoved by the massive predator before him. "I hate druids."

The wizened old man looked towards Ashyn and down to the bone bow in his left hand. "I hope you're as good with that thing as you are with fire."

Xexial released his charge.

Lightning hissed across the landscape, sizzling in the wet air and lighting the area in an ethereal cerulean glow. It drilled through the brown bear's abdomen like a lance, blowing out of the creature's hindquarters with such force that pieces of its flank, meat and bone, exploded backward, adding a red plume into the pallid mist. The bear wailed in agony as it wobbled forward, its innards spilling from the hole that Xexial had just made.

The beast tripped over its own wet, noodle-like intestines and fell forward into the soft green earth, very still. Glistening pools of red seeped into the earth on each side of its body, creating a crimson moat around the dead bear.

A high-pitched cry pierced the air, and suddenly shadows were moving from all directions.

Ashyn raised his bow with a shaky hand, fumbling to grab an arrow from the quiver on his hip. It slipped and slid in his awkward grip. He knocked it against his bow, scrambling to pull the string backward as he raised the bow to eye level.

Moisture pooled on his eyebrows and ran into the corners of his eyes. He tried to blink away the distraction, his hand slipped, and the arrow flew away harmlessly.

The first mass of shadows cleared away as glossy auburn quills came into view. Ashyn saw the fangs drip with anticipation, slaver running from its hungry mouth. Intent poured from its eyes, like the water that was running down its maw. Bristle Wolf.

Ashyn felt his mauled forearm tighten reflexively at the sight.

He groped for another arrow, fumbling with the shaft as he lined up his target. The wolf lunged at him as he raised the bow hastily and shot.

The arrow flew beneath the wolf and disappeared into the mists. Ashyn tried to move from the angry wolf's path, but he knew it was too late.

The wolf bore down on him, but before it could barrel him to the ground, its head suddenly exploded into a gory mass, covering Ashyn in bits of brain and bone. The wolf's headless body was propelled away in the opposite direction from the overwhelming force of the blow.

Ashyn's hair was on end as the electrical discharge coursed down his body, from the proximity.

"Hit them, Blood Wizard!" his master yelled from beside him.

Ashyn wiped the bloody pulp from his eyes with his forearm, and quickly drew another arrow.

Everything was happening so fast. This was far different from the Cumara dummies. Those weren't moving targets! These were. Scurrying, leaping, and biting. Hiding in the mists!

There were animals everywhere. Two more brown bears came lumbering in where the first had fallen. Bristle Wolves were stalking and howling to each other, and he could hear the chattering war cries of the Ferhym behind them. There were so many . . .

Xexial was a flurry of motion beside him, discharges of cobalt light flying repeatedly in every direction. His mentor was not afraid. He was reacting. Xexial's measured calm gave him strength.

He raised his bow, concentrated on an incoming Bristle Wolf. He ignored its razor-sharp quills and its powerfully muscled legs. He didn't register the ferocity of the creature's eyes, or the strength of its bite. He only saw it as an objective. Slowly, the combat melted away around him. There was only him and the target. His bow was an extension of his arm, the arrow his claw.

The wolf growled and spit as it sprinted forward. Ashyn watched its eyes as its powerful haunches tore across the soft damp dirt. It plowed forward, mouth open, fangs exposed. He looked at its eyes, only its eyes. The creature leapt, predictable. Ashyn loosed his projectile.

The arrow took the Bristle Wolf in its left eye, slicing through the juicy sphere and penetrating deep into its brain cavity. It died instantly.

Ashyn moved his body slightly to the right as the limp, dead wolf sailed harmlessly by. It crashed somewhere behind him with bone-crushing force. He didn't have time to consider it. He drew another arrow.

Lightning fired off to his side, heating the corner of his face in its wake. He paid it no heed. He could smell the sizzling flesh cooking under the heat of Xexial's powerful spells. Burnt hair and sweet meat; like pork.

He raised the bow, saw his target, and shot. Another wolf collapsed to the ground, a long white shaft glistening with running crimson, protruded from its throat.

Ashyn took a step forward towards the swarming masses. There was a connection. He could sense it. There was something in him that identified with combat. He felt as one with the bow, as if he had never been parted from it for the last eleven winters.

Another beast came; a puma perhaps? It didn't matter. The animal died before it even closed a dozen feet. Ashyn began to feel a groove to the battle, a certain cadence to the maelstrom: Nock. Draw. Loose. Nock. Draw. Loose. Nock. Draw. Loose. Duck.

Wolves, Bears, Dogs, they all began to fall to him. It was like a dance. They moved, he followed. Arrows were spent, animals died.

The ground became a soppy mass of mush by their feet. Rivers of red flowed between the soles of his boots, soaking into their soft suede and touching his skin. Mounds of smoking flesh huddled around them, its smell tingling in his nostrils. It invigorated him.

He heard Xexial yelling behind him. Whether encouragingly, or berating, he didn't know. He just acted.

Thunder echoed all around him from the wizard's work. Blue lances soared over his shoulder, between the nook of his elbow and ribs, and once, just above his head.

Creatures roared in anger, yelped in pain, howled in misery, but between the two, it was all the same. Everything that came at them died. They were walking death, the two of them, and Ashyn was no longer afraid.

He saw movement out of the corner of his eye, something low, moving fast, he drew, nocked, spun, and shot. Right into the robes between Xexial's legs.

Xexial looked at him in wide-eyed anger for a moment. Ashyn was sure that his master had thought the arrow intended for him. Then he saw as the wizard felt the pressure on the back of his legs.

A large scorpion, the size of a coyote, lay dead against him, the arrow imbedded in the vermin's mandible, its arrowhead sticking out the back of its plated thorax, the silver blade glistening pink. The stinger twitched against the ground, yellowish venom oozing from the tip. One of its massive snappers was still around Xexial's ankle, open and lifeless.

Quickly his master withdrew his foot, snapped the shaft of the arrow, and yanked his robes through.

"It was going to hamstring you," Ashyn remarked nonchalantly, as his hawk-like gaze studied the battlefield. There were no other beasts moving in on them, and the Ferhym had fallen suspiciously quiet.

Ashyn felt something here. Not magic, that was absent, but what he had felt before with Gregiry Bibs all those winters before. As if he were again in the maze with those strange creatures, and back in Czynsk when confronted with the Elves. It was desire, he knew. He wanted this fight, this violence; something inside him could not deny it. It was a bloodlust. Only this time he wasn't afraid of it.

He felt his master's questioning eyes on him. He ignored them.

"We mustn't let them regroup this time. The beasts are easy to replace, we must take out the druids and shake their morale," Xexial commented, slightly out of breath.

Ashyn nodded and started forward.

"Where are you going?" he asked.

"To track them," Ashyn answered.

"But you're lame," Xexial stated.

"I'll do it the old fashioned way, like my father once taught me."

"You were just a boy then."

Ashyn looked down at his master, and for the first time in his life, Ashyn saw fear when the man looked into his hawk-like gaze. "I was just a boy when I last used a bow, too."

He wasted no more time in discussion and was off. He had Wild Elves to hunt.

~ ~ ~

It came easy to Ashyn after all this time, he realized. It was second nature. Like reading, he thought, once you knew it was hard to forget. It may dull over time, but like a sword all it needed was the rust cleaned off and a little sharpening and it was as good as new.

When he found the tracks in the soft dirt, he knew they needn't go far. The Elves were all around them, poised to strike. What he didn't know was why they hadn't yet.

"The druids control the fog. Without them it will vanish," Xexial whispered.

"Kill them. Got it," Ashyn whispered back.

He felt Xexial's hand tug at his gauntlet. Ashyn risked a momentary look backward. His master had a stern look on his face. "It may come to that, and if it does I don't want you to hesitate. But you must understand that killing a person is not like killing a beast, lad. I don't know what it is that I see in your eyes now: bravado, bloodlust, arrogance, it may even be tranquility. Whatever it is, when you kill one of them, it will be different. It will hurt."

Ashyn did not feel swayed. "They are giving me little choice," he said as he looked back to the barefooted tracks.

Xexial tugged on his gauntlet. "Dammit, boy, look at me!" he growled.

Ashyn looked back again.

"These are people. They have lives, loves, and children. This is life! A wizard's life is balance," Xexial berated.

"What are you saying? Let them kill me? Am I the few and they the many?" Ashyn scoffed.

"Of course not! I'm saying to minimize the damage, both on them, and on your own conscience. The act of murder is easy son, physically. It's emotionally, where your battle is truly waged. Just wait until you are holding one of them in your arms as their life bleeds away by your hand. You will see it in their eyes, their sorrows, their regrets, and it will be a pain as you have never felt, I promise you.

"Kill only those that you have no choice. Disable the others. Disarm, maim, whatever it takes to pull them from the fight, but try not to kill them."

Ashyn glared. "I killed them in the field, days past, how is this different?"

"You did not see it. Did not see what you did. It would be different if you saw the aftermath son, but you were unconscious. It's easy to justify when you don't have to suffer the outcome of your actions," Xexial whispered.

"Okay."

Xexial nodded. "It might be best to leave the killing to me if possible. I have come to better terms with it. It doesn't get easier, but the pain numbs.

"I just want you to understand that many of these Elves don't *want* to kill you, they are following orders to kill you. It is a big difference."

Ashyn looked into the overwhelming shroud. They were all around them, listening to the wizards. But could they understand them, he wondered? "So . . ."

"So we demoralize them, take out their druids, take out their leader. They'll scatter without them. They still fear us, lad. Use that fear against them. They will always fear what they don't understand. And none can understand a wizard, but a wizard."

Ashyn heard a shift in the grass, followed by a squelching of mud. Quickly he pushed the old wizard back as a javelin soared between the two of them.

Battle cries resonated all around them and suddenly there were javelins everywhere, sailing for the two of them.

Ashyn watched Xexial's hands fly up in a flurry of motion and felt the air grow dense around him. Javelins hit the thick barriers as if they were made of stone, their wood buckled and shattered against his solid air armor like it were a wall.

The young wizard did not give pause. Arrow nocked, he rushed into the mists that surrounded him, Xexial hard on his tail.

A body broke through the pale vapor, stabbing forward with his spear. Ashyn narrowly avoided the impalement and struck forward with his left fist.

The punch caught the Wild Elf in the throat, causing him to backpedal and choke. Ashyn did not stop his momentum, but continued past as Xexial swung his staff, cracking the Elf across the head. The Elf fell to the ground in a heap, unconscious.

He nocked another arrow, and kept moving. Another javelin soared through the air at his midriff. It exploded into a hundred slivers. He loosed the arrow into the murk, heard a scream of pain, and kept going.

He reached for the quiver on his back. The arrows clacked against his fingertips, but felt pathetically low. Two quivers were already empty, he was on his last, and how many had he used? Three, four? It was hard to keep count.

He felt it behind him more than saw it, and ducked at the last moment as spear glanced across the hardened leather plate on his right shoulder. Ashyn tried to punch again, but this Elf was quicker, more honed to fighting. He dodged and brought the back of his spear crashing into Ashyn's ribs. He gasped at the pain, but was grateful that the leather absorbed most of the impact.

The blade of the spear swung around again, and Ashyn barely danced away in time.

It was only a temporary respite. Already the tip was stabbing forward at his chest. On reflex, Ashyn grabbed the shaft of the spear and ran backward with the weapon as the Wild Elf, unaccustomed to such an unusual tactic, was forced to keep running forward to maintain grip.

Xexial's hand caught the Elf by the throat, and the wild man convulsed violently as electricity coursed through his body. His eyes rolled into the back of his head and he collapsed to the ground, smoking.

Ashyn still saw his chest rising and falling, but it was faint.

"How come we're sparing these Elves, but you killed the ones in the Shalis-Fey, when I was a child?"

Ashyn found himself yelling to Xexial as he stabbed another Elf in the kneecap with an arrow. He ignored the scream as he kicked the spear away from the Wild Elf's reach.

"Because it was impossible to maim them while I was trying to escape with you as a child," Xexial answered between great gusts of breath.

He's tiring, Ashyn realized.

"This is different now, how?" Ashyn asked as another javelin disintegrated under the condensed air shield around him.

Xexial didn't answer right away, and Ashyn thought he understood why. Xexial had been a different man then, younger, brasher, sort of like Ashyn was now. Killing came easy when you didn't have to think about it.

Perhaps it had been the winters that had changed Xexial's perspective on the lives of the Elves? Or maybe he was being an overprotective father to Ashyn? Maybe Xexial was just tired of death. He had been blamed for it most of his life. Perhaps his mentor was just that . . . tired.

Of course, either way, Ashyn knew Xexial was right in the fact that not every soldier had to die to win the battle. He had studied it again and again over the winters. Target the battle leaders first. If you could sever the head then the rest of the beast dies all the same.

All Ashyn's thoughts were shattered though, as he suddenly found himself flying through the air. He didn't know what had happened; only that he was on the ground one moment running, with Xexial waning at his side, and the next he was hurtling uncontrollably through the air.

Mist ripped at his face, his bow flew away, and he didn't know the sky from the ground. But it didn't matter, for soon the ground found him.

It came hurtling up at him like a meteor, and he got his arms up in just enough time to keep from breaking his neck. He crashed hard, driving all the air from his lungs, and jolting his shoulders with so much pain that spots danced across his opaque vision. He slid across the ground ripping up grass and dirt, and making a horrible screeching sound as metal studs of his tunic slid across random stones in the lowlands.

When he finally stopped, his world was spinning around violently. Nausea grabbed at his stomach and threatened to have him vomit everywhere. He tried to get his bearings, keep the ground in one place, but it was no use. The earth tilted and bobbed like the deck of a ship on a rocky sea. Finally unable to hold it anymore, he did throw up.

He wiped his mouth off, and began to sit when the ground abruptly shifted beneath him. Dozens of vines began to slither from the earth like snakes. They slid around his arms, legs, hands, and abdomen. He pulled and ripped at them but the more he tore, the more they were replaced. Rapidly they began covering all of his body and pulling him down to the ground, tightening.

A muddy foot stepped in front of him, followed by the other. He looked up at surprisingly shapely legs to see swirls of white smear across the Wild Elf's abdomen and chest. There was a strip of cloth barely covering a virtually nonexistent chest, and then the swirls of paint continued up her slender throat and face. Wild black hair stuck out in every direction with bits of bone and twig sticking out of it.

Her fingers danced and swayed to the rhythm of the tendrils swimming across his body. He grunted as she tightened them more. He knew what he was looking at. It was a druid.

ENEMY BY NATURE

A shyn keenly heard the druid jabber "I have one!", in the Ferhym tongue.

"Kill it! Kill it!" He heard from multiple responses around him in the spell-induced gloom. He tried to answer, but the druid closed her fist and began to squeeze. As she did, the vines suddenly bit viciously into his flesh and armor, crushing the little air he had regained right out of his lungs. He gasped for air, but the pressure was so tight nothing could come back in. His vision was swimming, as spots danced around him and the corners were darkening.

He fought and writhed, clutching at the vines where he could, and pulling as hard as he was able, but their grasp was indomitable. He couldn't break free. Each moment was more wrenching as the tendrils of nature slid across his chest, forcing his armor deeper into his body. He couldn't even scream.

Images of his childhood flashed before his eyes. The smothering blanket of filthy fur covering his nose and mouth. He knew this feeling of suffocation. He had felt it before from his battle with the Bristle Wolf as a child.

Of every death Ashyn could think of, asphyxiation was one of the worst. That, and drowning. He would rather be killed in a battle by a blade or spell, than suffer this grueling, immeasurably agonizing death. His lungs screamed for air that wouldn't come, he felt his eyes bulging and his face flushing as he struggled to defeat the odds and squeak in a semblance of oxygen.

Through the pain, he saw her smiling -Smiling!- as she wrung the life from his body. She twisted her hands back and forth, jeering the whole while at the victory of her kill.

Everything was dimming, he couldn't draw air, and the pain was too great. Ashyn Rune knew this was the end. One final flush of pain coursed through his body as his blood shuddered from the lack of oxygen, and then blackness closed in on him.

All of a sudden the pressure was gone! And he was breathing! He drew in each breath hastily as light flared back to life in front of him. Each breath was cold, rich, and lovely. Drinking in the air, he looked at the druid in wonder. She, too, had a curious expression on her face as the vines began to slide off his body and back into the earth, as if somehow her spell had failed her.

His eyes lowered from her astonished expression to her hands. His own eyes went wide when he saw that she did not have hands anymore. There was nothing, just an empty space where once before were twisting fists.

As comprehension dawned on the Elf, so, too, did the pain. She screamed in horror as blood began to pump profusely from her rent stubs. Then Ashyn felt a piercing cold. It was so unnatural that Ashyn couldn't come up with any explanation for it, but at that moment he knew why.

Inky black and purple tendrils ripped through the air like lunging snakes. They sliced through the druid's kneecaps utterly dissolving everything they met. Skin, blood, muscle and bone vanished in the blink of an eye.

The screaming druid collapsed to the ground, her severed legs still standing, calves twitching, not yet understanding that they were no longer part of her body. As she lay on her body, bleeding profusely from all her severed limbs, he watched a weary, tan-robed wizard walk up to her prone form.

"Hurts, don't it?" he said maliciously, and he ended her life with a lightning blast to her throat. Her head rolled away like a loose stone.

Ashyn knew what he had witnessed. Something he hadn't been ready for, for many winters. Ashyn had finally seen firsthand the nature of Destruction.

Xexial walked up to him and offered Ashyn his hand, the same hand that had just removed the druid's head from her shoulders. He reached out and took it, and the old man helped the boy up.

"You look like the hells trampled over you," he commented.

And indeed he felt like it. His shoulders were sore and throbbing, he was bleeding wickedly from a scuff against his scalp, and his wounded forearm was tight with pain. His armor and red robes, too, were a wreck. The latter was torn and frayed from his rough tumble across the ground.

"I'm fine," he lied.

A screech drew their attention away from each other as another large brown bear burst through the thick veil around them. Riding atop it was another druid, this one male, but looking very similar to the last. The druid squealed and held out his hands as the bear reared up on its hind legs to attack.

Quicker than Ashyn would have believed possible, Xexial released his grip on the boy and flattened his right hand like a blade. A sudden humming sound filled Ashyn's ears and then Xexial slashed upward vertically with the tips of his fingers.

Ashyn felt a blast of air sheer by him, and both the bear and the rider looked strangely at the seemingly feeble old man. Then they split apart from groin to head into two halves, their innards collapsing to the ground in one big heaping pile of ichor. Ashyn had to look away as he felt the bile building back in his throat.

The spell-induced fog began to lift.

Ashyn looked at his master, who was now leaning heavily on his staff. Sweat ran profusely down his face, and his eyes were sunken, with deep, bruised pockets of flesh forming beneath them. Ashyn knew the casting was taking its toll.

Magic had a price, Feedback, and it was collecting from Xexial. *We are merely its conduit*, he had often repeated to the red-headed boy.

It wasn't long before the entire veil of mist melted away into the afternoon sky. Ashyn surveyed the damage as it became visible, and let out a long whistle. Over three dozen beasts lay scattered about the fields of grass now stained red with blood and gore. There were another dozen or so Wild Elves, all incapacitated in one form or another, moaning in pain or rendered unconscious. But circling around the duo was still a score of Elves, all armed with javelins and ready to attack.

Ashyn sighed and reached for an arrow. *They're gone,* he cursed as he realized that his sliding halt had broken or loosed all the arrows remaining in his quiver. All he had left on him was his skinning knife on his belt. It felt paltry against the numbers of Elves still in front of him. He looked for his bow and found it lying about two hundred feet in front of him, though he knew it would do little good without arrows.

One Elf moved forward. She was mounted on a tan and white mare, the only one horsebound, in fact. The horse bore neither a bit nor a bridle; she rode it bareback. As the other Wild Elves parted to let her pass, Ashyn recognized her scarred face from Czynsk. They had passed, briefly, when he was forced to flee.

When she was only fifteen feet away, she stopped and looked down on them. She, too, was dressed in only a loincloth and a strip across her small breasts, and her hard, thickly-muscled body was painted with markings similar to that of the raven-haired Elf that Ashyn knew hated him beyond reproach. This one, however, had brown hair and insipid brown eyes. She was comely, in her own small way, he supposed.

"Surrender . . . we make death . . . quick," she said in a broken bastardization of the common Trade tongue.

"This one is their Branch Commander," Xexial whispered behind Ashyn's shoulder.

Ashyn gave a brief nod to his master, as the woman seemed to be speaking to him, and not to his mentor.

"You may take your wounded and leave," Ashyn returned in the Ferhym tongue. "If you leave now we will not harm a single one of you."

The she-Elf looked at him, outraged, and then was surprised when she realized he was speaking her language. She hissed at them. "Unbalancers! Skewers!"

"Oh . . . here we go," Xexial grumbled jadedly.

"Wizards are a foul taint on this world!" the horsebound Elf growled at them. "You are skewers of the natural balance of life. You are pestilence."

"Didn't we hear this before?" Ashyn whispered to Xexial behind him."

"Yes," the wizard said in a bored reply.

"Wizards are parasites to this world," she continued. "Your taint consumes and destroys all it touches. Your filth infests the land, air, and the minds of the innocent like a festering plague. It is our duty to end your infection once and for all! The spirits demand it be so."

"Maker help me. That sounds verbatim. Do you guys read this from a book every night before you sleep, just so you can preach it before you try and kill us?" Ashyn asked her, astounded. She sounded exactly like the raven-haired Elf in the field.

"You have no idea," Xexial said as he chuckled from behind. Ashyn noted how strained and exhausted his voice sounded.

"You know we seek the same thing, right?" Ashyn asked her. "The balance of life is the balance of nature."

"Your tongue spits only poison from your sinister mouth," she spat.

"You might as well give it up, boy. We've tried dealing with them for millennia. They're bent on their beliefs," Xexial told him.

"But we believe in the same thing," Ashyn answered.

"As do many religions, but that has never stopped them from warring in the past over trivial differences."

"We must be able to compromise?" Ashyn asked the Elf commander.

"Your death is the only compromise," she returned. "You can either die swiftly in surrender, or we can slaughter you."

"Your spirits really warrant the slaughter of two men, so outnumbered? That hardly seems fair."

"If the spirits thought you worthy of balance, you would have more allies. But you do not. This world hates you because you are twisted and foul," she stated absolutely. "I grow tired of your rambling. How do you choose to die, Unbalancers? In battle? Or on your knees?"

Ashyn had never seen such fanaticism before. He knew from his childhood what he had experienced from the Ferhym, and what he had read and been taught by Xexial, but now twice, these Elves wouldn't leave him be. He couldn't begin to imagine the horror of his sister's life.

That thought made him angry. "Battle," he spat.

The Elf smiled at him. "I shall enjoy killing you, dui Nuchada, for the pain you caused my Whísper."

She turned and rode back to her line of Elves.

Ashyn turned to Xexial. The old man looked at him resignedly. "I'm sorry," Ashyn said.

Xexial shook his head. "I expected no different, lad. She would never have listened, even if it were I. When the Council of Elm starts a crusade, little can sway them. The Council and wizards have had an uneasy truce for many winters. It was only a matter of time before that truce was broken. They are all the more the fools."

Ashyn surveyed the field as the female Elf on the horse barked out commands and the soldiers assumed what he supposed were battle formations.

"Ashyn," Xexial's deep voice said quietly.

The boy looked to his master, "You must listen very carefully now, son. Whatever happens next, I want you to promise me that you will continue on to the Seven, and report everything that we have seen."

"I . . . what?" Ashyn asked, not understanding.

"I want your word that you will go on to the Seven and report the activities of the Council of Elm. This is bigger than you are, bigger than I am. All wizards must be made aware. A war is coming."

No! No! Ashyn thought. This wasn't supposed to happen. This wasn't how it was supposed to be! He had planned. He had been sure of his purpose. Not like this, not now!

"Promise me," Xexial demanded.

"Master, I can't . . .," Ashyn said, water brimming in his grey eyes.

"Dammit, boy, promise me!" Xexial roared at him.

Ashyn closed his eyes and looked away. Tears rolled down his bloodied cheeks. He couldn't betray Xexial, not now, not when his master needed him most. "I promise."

Ashyn saw the relief, and pride flood into Xexial's eyes. It stabbed at the core of Ashyn's very being. "You will make a great wizard one day," he told the boy.

Ashyn, however, wasn't so sure.

But what was done, was done. The Branch Commander had rallied her battle lines, and the Wild Elves were now racing down upon them in a great mob. They weren't as organized in a large group on the empty plains as Ashyn had feared, but without a weapon or magic at his disposal, they were a formidable mass.

"Get behind me, son," Xexial said calmly. He leaned heavily on his staff, as if it were the only thing in the world holding him upright.

Ashyn, numb in his heart and soul, did as he was instructed.

The ground thundered beneath them as the flood of Wild Elves bore down upon them. It wouldn't be long now, he supposed.

"Be calm, Ashyn," Xexial said with a sense of peace that slightly unnerved the young man. "I will show you why it is that this world fears us so."

As the first line of spears lowered towards the duo, Ashyn watched Xexial close his eyes. The man began chanting in a low, deep hum. Ashyn felt a curious pressure begin to build in his chest. Through the rumbling beneath his feet, he began to feel something else, a movement deep in the ground itself. Dust and loose chips of rock and earth were bouncing around his feet. The vibrations began to gather around Xexial's fists, filling Ashyn's ears. The elder wizard's body became enclosed in a soft, blue glow like that of his luminescent gloves.

The Elven tide grew larger as they tore across the green earth, ripping up everything in their path. The ground quivered at their approach. Ashyn didn't know how Xexial could maintain such concentration in light of the mob barreling down on them. He watched as the master wizard gathered more power around himself. The faint outline of blue began thickening into a distinct ribbon of azure light around the man, then darkening to indigo, and soon black.

Ashyn watched as the wizard's iridescent gloved hands shook fiercely as if he was trying to hold a lion at bay. He figured it perhaps was literal. He had no idea what the wizard was preparing to do. The tremors were so violent that he could feel his own teeth rattling in his mouth. The hum had reached a point of deafening proportions.

The Elves swarmed in, now only fifty feet away. Impact was imminent. Ashyn knew they would be impaled if they didn't retaliate soon. Fitting, he supposed, for an alleged "Skewer of Balance".

Xexial raised his violently shaking staff in the air. It wasn't a lion, the boy decided. It looked like the old man was wrestling a giant.

The rumble grew to a roar as the Elves encompassed everything he saw. There was no earth, no sky, only angry painted flesh before him. Ashyn watched it all through the thick blackish light. Their wave was weak and disorganized, but it would trample them into the ground all the same. Thirty feet, away. Twenty. Ten. The spears were level with Xexial's chest. Ashyn felt fear deep in his abdomen, bile rising to the back of his throat. He fought to remain still, to do as his master had bade him. Stay calm, he told himself. It did little to quell the turmoil inside him, but Ashyn did not move.

With a quick motion, Xexial slammed his staff into the ground in a violent collision. Chips hurled up around the elder wood. A deafening whiplike crack followed, sounding like the thunder of an immense storm. And then silence. The Elves were here.

The spears slashed into Xexial. Ashyn expected him to be torn asunder in a myriad of red ribbons, but it did not happen. Instead, the spearheads began dissolving upon impact with the obsidian glamour that bordered around his frail body. Momentum carried the horde forward and Ashyn thought not spears, but feet, would be his death, trampled by a stampede of tree-hugging little people.

But as the mass smashed into Xexial, they melted into nothingness. Absolutely obliterated. Pieces of their body fell away like the dead leaves from a tree on a late autumn day.

Suddenly the dark light exploded forth from Xexial, drinking into the earth and then galloping along its surface like a stampede of shadowy specters. Grass, earth, and Elves were annihilated on contact. It spanned outwards like a fan, as the charge of shadow and death disintegrated everything along its path.

Long cracks ripped across the barren ground, shattering the once lush dirt into broken clay and rock. Thick bursts of indigo and violet light erupted from the long-trenched earth, casting Ashyn's entire world in a surreal twilight.

The ground, not obliterated outright, began to explode outward from the severing lines in the earth, sending chunks of rock and debris skyward. The middle lines of the approaching wave of Elves, trapped within the confines of the spell, were flung sky high. It was impossible to differentiate the Elves from the tumbling rubble.

As the pelting terrain came bounding down, it smashed hard into the remaining ranks of the Wild Elf assault. Even with everything happening, Ashyn could hear the cracking of their bodies underneath the mass of stone and scree. Ashyn briefly saw the Branch Commander's horse rear up on its hind legs, and then she was gone beneath the tumultuous cascade of earthen hail. Dust lined the skies, covering the sun in a hazy cloud of murk. And the world was changed before Ashyn Rune forever.

That was the true nature of Destruction.

BITTER

Ashyn looked around at the devastation wrought by Xexial. He had broken one of their tenets. He had killed with Destruction. Everything in front of him for perhaps a thousand feet was gone. No bodies, no blood, no grass or rocks, or sloping plains. Nothing. Only flat desolation.

Broken cracked clay stared up at him. Deep, red, angry lines rent through the flat tan surface were the only testament that something else had once been there. Beyond that were the rocky masses that remained after the earth had exploded violently skyward.

Xexial lay sprawled at his feet, his chest rising and falling faintly beneath his layered robes. Ashyn reached down, and cradled his head, in his arms.

"What have we done?" he whispered, unable to take his eyes from the wasteland before him. "Who are we to wield such power?"

Straggled survivors began to stir. All, if capable, fleeing from the might of the wizards. They had no idea that Ashyn was incapable of a similar act. All they knew from the wizards now was death by fire, and death by destruction.

The victory left a bitter taste in his mouth. Xexial was down, probably dying, and this win would do nothing to help neither his cause for his sister, nor the wizards' cause in halting this feud. So he could only sit in silence, thinking about how the Elves had changed things, once again.

He heard a shift in the rubble ahead of him. Another surviving Elf, going to flee, no doubt, back to the Shalis-Fey to warn of the monsters that rape the land, and desiccate crops. He found himself laughing. Not too far from the mark this time, though.

Slowly a shadow encapsulated him. As it blotted out the sun, Ashyn looked up from his master. The scar-faced Branch Commander loomed over him.

She was a tattered wreck, covered in blood from both her horse and that of her own. A tear of flesh ran across her forehead and down the side of her right eye. If she felt pain, he did not see it.

Violently she kicked out, knocking Ashyn sprawling onto the dead land. Chips of earth and scree shattered at his impact. He rolled around, quickly stumbling to his feet.

The ragged Elf held her short spear forward like a dagger, its long shaft broken from the collapsing shower of earth. Still, it was more than Ashyn had. He drew his skinning knife, feeling woefully inadequate.

"I will take your head, and we will burn out your eyes, dui Nuchada," she hissed at him.

Ashyn backpedaled, looking back and forth for anything to help him. There was nothing. Xexial had destroyed everything near him with the spell.

"It's over," Ashyn pleaded. "There's nothing left, your people have run."

She wasn't dissuaded. "There is still me," she spat. "And I have the protection of the Spirits. Not even the old wizard's desecration could harm me."

Ashyn wanted to argue that it was likely the horse that saved her, but he knew it was a moot point. Somehow, she would say the spirits had given her that horse, or some such thing. He was beginning to understand the extent of the Ferhym's fanaticism.

He realized the Elf was in no mood for conversation anyway, as she charged at him.

She stabbed, sliced, kicked, even tried to bite Ashyn as he scurried futilely to escape her wrath. She was smaller, quicker, and far better trained than he was. It wasn't long before she had him disarmed. A feint to the left, followed by a short jab with the spear tip in her right hand, and his pathetic skinning knife was sent spiraling away. He grabbed his weaponless hand, feeling the stinging tingle at the tips of his fingers from her thrust.

He risked a glance at his prone mentor, hoping perhaps the staff was still there, but it wasn't. It too had been consumed by the spell. Then he realized that glance was a mistake.

The Elf used his lapse in concentration and charged into him with all her might. Ashyn managed to maneuver away from her spearhead just in time but her sheer strength overwhelmed him. She barreled into him, sending him off his feet and crashing into the hard packed clay, together in a jumble of writhing limbs. They rolled across the ground, kicking up dust and chips of clay, clouding the air with debris. Ashyn gagged and spit out the grime, and he was vaguely aware that it didn't faze the Elf at all.

She stabbed repeatedly at his midsection, scoring several deadly hits. Each one cutting deep scars into the hardened leather. Ashyn was very grateful then for that armor.

Unable to get superiority over the nimble Elf, he did the only thing he could think of. He drove his fingers into the gash on her face.

She screamed in pain as his long fingertips burrowed into the vicious tear on her face, spilling slick, sticky fluid across his filthy hands. She shook her head violently, trying to dislodge his fingers, and he tried to clamp down harder. Blood flowed across his forearm liberally as he felt his fingernails claw deep under her flesh.

Finally she stabbed upwards with her broken spear, and he managed to get his hand back just in time to only catch a grazing wound against his palm. It wasn't deep, but it stung horribly.

She kicked him with all her might and the two went tumbling away from each other, granting Ashyn the distance he desperately needed. When he got to his feet, he saw the damage he had done.

The Elf was barely holding her face together with her right hand. Blood ran down her arm in great pulses, soaking her skin in a brilliant scarlet, and dripping off her elbow copiously. Her right eye was lost somewhere under a mass of gory, swollen pulp. She held the remnants of her spear in her left hand, and he could tell that she didn't have a comfortable grip with it.

She's right handed, he realized. Perhaps he still had a chance. She staggered forward towards him, swinging wildly.

Ashyn moved away from her furious motions easily. They were jerky and awkward. "It's over," he repeated to her in her own language. "Neither of us needs to die for this. Let's just end this. See to your wounds."

"Never!" she screamed as she tried to rush him again.

Ashyn side stepped away easily and saw an opening where he could wrench the weapon away from her. She stabbed weakly at his midsection, and he stepped just to the side of the thrust and grabbed her wrist with both hands, hoping to wrench the spearhead free.

He held her arms firm, his hands slick with her blood, and yanked the weapon down. That was when he realized it was all a ruse.

Her thick, muscled leg was between his in an instant, and she followed the downward motion of his pull, swinging his arms down and over, hyperextending his reach. As she did, she swept her leg up and through the back of Ashyn's knee and he suddenly found himself flipping over onto his back as she used his momentum against him.

He hit the ground hard with a crack that dazed him. The sky danced hazily above him, brilliant lights spinning before his eyes. Then there was a strange glint and he saw the spear coming down for his chest.

He barely rolled away in time as the bladed tip slid down his right breast and across his ribs, scoring a deep gouge in his armor. Close. Too close.

Near-panicked, he rolled across the ground wildly as the Elf stabbed madly behind him each time, closing the gap more and more. She was screaming in rage with each missed blow. Her blood flung wildly across the rent earth. But she had him. Ashyn knew it. She knew it.

Ashyn tried to get to his feet, but she would offer him no ground. She was right behind him, stabbing, and slashing, keeping him down. Frantic, Ashyn looked around for anything at all, but there was nothing, only desolation and clay.

And then he saw it. The sun flicker its bright reflection off something metal on the ground. He rolled again as the spear tip crashed down, narrowly missing his neck. He looked for the metal again. He saw it.

Ashyn rolled to his belly and tried to get up, but as soon as he did, he felt her knee drive hard into his kidney. Pain soared through his spine and he stumbled back to the ground.

He felt her feet again driving into his back. Agony soared down his spine, numbing his legs. He forced himself to continue; if he didn't, he was doomed. He pulled himself with his arms, aware of her proximity. She didn't stab him with her spear. Perhaps she finally realized the value of his armor. Or maybe with victory imminent she was toying with him, he thought bitterly.

He was crawling slowly, his legs barely answering him. Each shift sent a wave of nausea through him, but he didn't want to end like this. Not like this. He looked up through teary eyes. It was only six feet away.

He felt her looming above him. Five feet. She was laughing at him. Laughing at how pathetic he looked. Three feet, so close. He reached for it. Just out of his reach. He tried to get closer but his legs refused to answer. He stretched even farther, his fingers brushed against the wood.

She grabbed his hair and ripped his head back, pulling him away. Her hot blood ran down profusely from her drenched grip into his hair and down his neck. "The Spirits demand balance!" she screamed. She was going to take his head! She brought the spear down in a wide sweep.

Ashyn twisted violently at the last second and thrust upwards. He felt her spear bite across his exposed flesh, between the joints in his armor by his shoulder. The blow narrowly missing his throat, Ashyn grunted back the fire of pain that flared through him.

The Elf, however, was staring at him in confusion. And then she gasped.

Ashyn blinked in shock as he heard the spear clatter to the ground next to him. He looked at his closed hand, firmly against her breast. His skinning knife he had grabbed buried to the hilt. He looked to her face as the shock registered in her doe brown orbs. Her muscles slackened and she toppled into his arms.

Ashyn didn't know what to do. Her breaths were coming in ragged gasps, and he could hear the wound in her chest wheezing between the vent lines in the blade. She looked at him. Her dark eyes told him so much in that instant. Anger, pain, betrayal, crushed hopes, unfulfilled dreams, loves . . . lost.

"Nuch . . . nuchada," she panted. "Whísper . . . Whísper."

"Where's my sister!" he demanded as he held her. "Tell me, where is Feydras' Anula!"

Tears ran out of her good eye. "My Whísper. She will have you." She coughed blood bubbles at him.

"The blind Nuchada, where is she!" he yelled at her, frantic to know, before this Elf died. "Where is Julietta? Tell me where is the Council of Elm? Where is Feydras' Anula?"

The Elf smiled, a crimson froth oozed from her mouth and rolled down the corner to her pointed ear. "Whísper . . . my love," she whispered faintly. And then she was gone.

"No!" Ashyn roared, shaking the Elf. But it didn't matter; her brown eyes were empty and wide. "No!" he screamed as he buried his head to her breast. He cried hard then. It hurt. It hurt so badly. He had lost everything, his chance at finding Julietta, his master Xexial, his entire world. He held her close and sobbed into her broken body as he felt all his hopes crumble down around him.

A Watch Renewed

Tracks. There were so many tracks. And the scents! They were a myriad of odors. Some fresh, others old. It filled his senses copiously just like the carrion that was around him dotted the landscape.

Carcasses of all manner of forest beasts spread throughout the grassy lowland hills, some jutting with arrows, others seemingly blown asunder by some supernatural force. Scavengers were plentiful by the time he arrived. With a roar, he sent all but the most determined scattering. Those that chose to stay behind to defend their finds he sent scurrying after a nip of his dagger like teeth on their rumps or a plume of fire from his nostrils. Those left singed or bloody, or both.

Xao studied the battlefield before him. His intuition had been right: there had been blood that morning. He stared at the sun now, brilliant and yellow and beginning its inevitable descent in the West. It had taken him longer than expected to arrive. Too long. He should have never lingered around that barren field as long as he had. He had missed much. *What were the Wild Elves up to?* he wondered.

As he walked amongst the desecrated remains of animal bodies strewn throughout the field, he knew the Elves had employed druids this time. No bears and Bristle Wolves would ever act in unison as these had. They would have had to have been coaxed.

Had it not been for the strange fog heading east past the tower he would have never found this place. Yet the obscure miasma had signaled the location all too clear. It was like a giant white target on a green wall. Easy to see and to follow.

When it had disappeared so suddenly he knew something was happening. He had felt it deep in his core. That was when he had begun running again, and now here he was. At the aftermath.

He dug his inky claws into the viridian earth, ripping up moist clumps of grass and leaving deep brown furrows in its place. He had missed it again! How was he supposed to record anything about the lives of the special ones if he kept missing everything that transpired! Fire erupted from his nostrils angrily and he seared a bear carcass down to its bones. When nothing but a black husk remained he searched for another target to vent his wrath, and then he saw it. The destruction.

Slowly he trotted down to the clay wasteland that sat nestled between two small hillocks. Deep, vicious lines rent the deadened surface, cracking and separating the brittle clay. As he stepped on to its tan plain, he could already feel the heat beginning to build up on the barren ground. Xao knew in days it would become sweltering and eventually it would yellow the neighboring grass. Though he had never seen it at work, he had heard about it often enough from Mireanthia. It was Destruction. This was a scar on the land now, one that would never heal.

In the wake of destruction, Xao saw a single body. In fact, it was the only *humanoid* form left. Slowly he plodded forth, his red scales glistening in the afternoon light.

It lay on its side, almost in the fetal position. Surprisingly, the scavengers had not yet begun to feast on this body. Scared of the foreign earth, he supposed. All animals could feel when something was wrong, and Xao knew there was nothing more *alien* than a land ravaged by Destruction.

The young dragon reached out with a long claw and turned over the body so he could see its face. It rolled over easily, and he scrunched his bone-plated snout at the odor the corpse emanated. Still, he looked at it in frustration. He recognized the creature beneath him.

A dragon never forgets, Mireanthia once told him. It is our curse for what we have done to our world, she would say. No one has the right to attempt to shape the laws of magic and nature. Not even dragons. So now we are cursed. Cursed to remember that it is we that have largely brought this on our race, and on the world. And remember we do, my young hatchling. We remember . . . everything, always.

What are these Elves up to? He asked himself again. This wasn't just a spontaneous incursion against the wizards. This was more. There had been a battle, a real battle. Were the Elves starting a war against wizards?

Xao looked up to the Onyx Tower in the distance. It would likely take him the rest of the day to get back to the tower. Should he? That was the question. He still couldn't feel the presence of Ashyn, nor could he communicate with him. Yet the old wizard couldn't have fought this conflict alone.

He looked at the body beneath him once more. Could he? *No,* Xao thought at once. He remembered the silver fields that night, the look of worry in the old human's eyes. There was no way he could win such an engagement. That meant he had help. And there was only one person that would help the wizard, Xao knew.

A sense of elation coursed through his body. Ashyn was alive! He had to be!

Carefully he turned the body back over onto its side. *Sleep now,* he bid the deceased before him. *You have earned your peace.* With a great gust, he let out the most powerful blaze he had ever produced. So hot were his flames that they incinerated the body before him, and soon nothing but a blackened smear of ash remained.

No one deserves to be a feast for the crows.

Slowly he turned away from the deceased warrior, and began to search once more for tracks, any indication as to where the boy may have gone. With all the tracks from beasts and Elves alike it took him the rest of the afternoon, but as the sun finally began to set, ending another day, Xao spotted a very curious pair of tracks.

There were two sets, one smaller and stunted, showing signs of the right leg being drug across the earth, as if it was a limp; the second, just next to it and slightly behind, was very different in design and shape. This person was very light of step, like an Elf. But unlike an Elf, whose leg length was generally shorter, this one had a longer gait. That indicated someone taller, like a human. Xao could have very well considered it a High Elf's track, as they tended to be taller than humans and their other 'cousin' Elves, but Xao knew this track. He knew it well.

A dragon never forgets, he said to himself as he studied the tracks of his ward. It didn't take long before he found the tracks again, this time going in a separate direction.

Ashyn Rune was alive! He was alive and he was heading west. Xao's purpose had been renewed. He would find the boy again. He knew he would.

Xao studied the imprints of Ashyn's feet on the ground once more. There was only one set of tracks. Xao looked back to the desolate clay land behind him, and then at the tracks once more. Xao knew then what had happened. Ashyn Rune had left the battlefield, alone.

PARIAH

Ashyn could just make out the tip of the Onyx Tower in the clear morning light, a lone, dark spike stabbing upward in the distance. He had never noticed it before, from the streets of Czynsk, but there it was, a small sliver of black against a backdrop of crystalline blue.

"Sir?" the bird handler asked, bringing him back from his reverie of his old home. "You want how many again?"

"Six," Ashyn answered. "Six pigeons to make their way to the tower of the Seven. It's in northern Oganis."

The bird handler shook his head. "I ne'r heard o' the tower of the Seven," he replied, and then added, "Me birds dunna know the way."

"Jaës, then. From there, someone at Jaës could send them to the tower of the Seven. Jaës birds would know where it is."

The bird keeper scratched the dirty brown mange of hair on his chin, "Aye, I reckon tha' work well o'nough. Perhaps seven should go?" he said with a laugh. When Ashyn did not laugh in return at the jest, the man coughed nervously and averted his gaze from Ashyn's cold grey eyes.

"Six then," he agreed, but then added, "But a pigeon would ne'r make the distance, I fear. Predators an' all, plus the odd archer about lookin' fer a meal. Ye'd need a more reliable bird."

"Such as?" Ashyn asked, knowing the man was going to try to swindle him for more money.

"A raven, Sir Elf. A raven coulda do it."

Ashyn pulled the red cowl tighter over his head, masking his hair and ears. Many people in the town had taken him for an Elf because of his curious hue, lithe frame, and Lefhym armor. Not to mention the bow and ample supply of quivers he had on him.

He had known he would need a disguise when he was back at the tower. A robed, red-headed man was too easily identifiable as the wizard's acolyte, so he had figured that he might use his 'possible' Half-Elven heritage to his advantage and don the regalia of Elves, even maintaining their flawlessly hairless face and arms. Shaving his arms had felt queer at first, but he had done it nonetheless.

He also realized that a bow had its limits, and after his fight with the Branch Commander, he would need a blade. That is, until his magic returned to him. He had searched the armory for hours trying to find a likeness to Stormwind's beautiful rapier, as he had remembered it. But he had had no such luck. Instead, he had found a plain rapier with virtually no ornamentation. He didn't like the cross guard, or the fact that it seemed too small for his long fingers, but he'd hoped it would hold up well for the illusion he was constructing. Thus far, it had.

"Ravens are thieves and beggar birds," he replied darkly. He could see the man shift under his gaze.

"Even so, Sir Elf, they are large, an' strong, an' fiercely loyal. They also givem big predators pause, an' canna fly great'r distance, sir," the birdman explained.

Ashyn saw the man's logic. "Very well. Six ravens, bound for Jaës, and then to the tower of the Seven."

"Very well, sir," the birdman said as he scrolled it all down.

Ashyn had been surprised to find that the birdman had been literate, but he had explained that when he had been younger he had been an orphan and was taken in by the Enclave. They had taught him to read and write.

Ashyn glanced down to the burned-out carcass that had once been their great cathedral of the Maker. He thought of Macky, and how the boy had told him he had helped build it. Now it was gone, the entire Enclave was gone, butchered by the Wild Elves. Even the children's Hospice had not survived their scourge.

He saw the doe-eyed birdman follow his gaze. "Is not y'er kin's fault, sir," he told Ashyn.

"Excuse me?" Ashyn asked, surprised.

"Not o' yer kind to blame. Suren they came 'ere, but it was the wizards that were to blame," he spat angrily.

Ashyn stiffened, "How so?" he asked.

"They was summoned by the Enclave to parlay w' the Elves, see, an', well, words were exchanged, an' magic."

"Magic?"

"Aye," the man nodded, "What else could it be? Put the Elves in a tizzy, and brought the Enclave to torch. Then the Elves left to bother us no more, but where were the wizards? Gone. No'er came to help. Humans like us townsfolk! Er' own kin! So it is them, we say. Them that manipulated the Elves, put them in their hateful frenzy."

"Did the Wild Elves take any people?"

"Aye, jus' rebels though. The ones tha' wanted ter fight them. Serves em' all right, I says. Fight'n fer the wizards. Ta, Elves called it balance, an' who canna disagree? Canna ne'r trust a wizard. Dark magics they use. They bring death. It's all they do."

"No," Ashyn answered solemnly, "Can't trust them."

He looked back to the small black spike, so far in the sky. Xexial had warned him he would be misunderstood and hated. Here they had come to help, and instead were blamed for the destruction of the Enclave while the Wild Elves went on with slaves, home free. Ashyn was appalled at how little people actually knew, and what they were willing to believe so quickly.

"Come's ta one gold, an' thirteen silver, sir," the birdman said.

Ashyn handed him the six letters for the Seven, two gold, and bid him a good day. He then walked to the edge of town and stood there looking at the dark green horizon beyond.

Tall, ominous trees stared back at him, their maw black and uninviting. It was there he knew he had to go. It was somewhere in there he would find Feydras' Anula, and the Council of Elm. And with them he would find his sister. She was all he had left. He would do whatever it took to get her back.

"Bad things tend to happen, when a man has a look like that in his eyes," a man called out from his left.

Ashyn turned to look the man over. He was older, perhaps nearer to fifty or so winters. His hair and beard had gone grey and it was impossible to guess its original color. His skin was tanned and leathered from hard work in the sun. His clothes, too, were worn and sun-faded. He reclined on a barrel, looking Ashyn over.

"Perhaps the bad things have already happened," Ashyn remarked.

"Perhaps," the old man replied. "Or maybe they're just beginning," he countered. He stood up and sucked the air in deeply through his large, red-veined nose. "Something dark is upon us," he told Ashyn. "I can smell it in the air."

Ashyn watched him suspiciously for a moment before looking back at the woods. "I've heard a war is coming," Ashyn commented as he stared back into the shadowed expanse of the Shalis-Fey.

"Aye," the man answered, surprising Ashyn. "War's been coming for winters. Just been lucky for a while is all."

The old man then walked over to the steps of the house he was in front of. "Whatever it is yer lookin' for in those woods, son, what I see in your eyes won't bring you any peace."

And then he was gone. And Ashyn was alone. Perhaps he was always meant to be alone, he reasoned. He had been a pariah most of his youth; mistreated, and misunderstood. Now it was worse, he knew. He had betrayed the Wizard's Covenant. He was a recreant. He had forsaken his oath. He knew the rules. He knew he would be hunted.

Ashyn reached under his Lefhym tunic and drew out the vial of blood he kept around his neck at all times. He felt a stab of pain in his heart for betraying Xexial. He had promised to tell the Seven of the war. It had been Xexial's last command to him, but he couldn't go there, not after everything that had happened. He had to find *her* first. His best hope was that one of the letters would make it to them. They were all the same. He knew that they at least had to be warned, be prepared in case he failed. It was the least he could do for the man that had been like a father to him. Yet it did little to mend the hole in his heart.

He had written Xexial a letter the night before they had left to head to Buckner. He had planned on leaving the letter with Xexial while he slept, and running away in the night to seek one of the hunting parties of Wild Elves and get the Council's location. He had never had the chance.

His eyes drifted once more to the sliver of black in the sapphire sky. It had already been two weeks since he walked out those doors. He had tended to things that needed to be done, seen to his wounds, and re-outfitted. Things had seemed tense for a while, but surprisingly it worked out. When he was sure it was safe, he had left and begun his journey back to Czynsk.

On the way, he had asked every passing caravan if they had ever seen the Wild Elves city. "Wild Elves don't have cities. They live in holes, and spring from the ground," he had been told. "They live in nests in the trees!" others would say. He received no answers in the time he had left those black walls. And he knew he wouldn't. There would be no answers until he stepped back into the Shalis-Fey once more.

Idly, he wondered if he would ever walk within those black halls again. If he would dine at the small table, or read the great tomes in the circular library? Would he ever look upon the twenty-three statues of the Onyx Tower, and its founder

Magelord Rheynnaus Craëgolshien? Or feel the grass between his bare toes in the ward-laden gardens?

His life seemed to have come full circle. Once he fled those woods, running from what had seemed to be the end of all he knew. Now he was going back in, to rescue all that remained of his old life.

Ashyn took his first step forward, toward the dark labyrinth of the Shalis-Fey, and an uncertain future. *One day,* he reiterated in his head. The Onyx Tower was the only home he knew. But he couldn't go back . . . not yet. First he had a city to find, and a sister to save. "Peace was never an option for me," he said quietly into the air.

Ashyn headed toward the Shalis-Fey.

EPILOGUE

Her dark eyes absorbed the scene that was laid before her. First, there were the sightings of a young red dragon skirting the Shalis-Fey in the East, and now this. She wasn't quite sure of what to make of it all. "The wizard's body?" she asked.

"Gone," the druid answered her. Brodea looked up at the thin, young Elf before her. He had fled after Shedalia's failure, as all druids were instructed if the battle looked to be going against them. With two druids dead, three score of her hunters obliterated, and many more injured and likely to die of infection, Brodea would say the battle was a rout. She may not like the fact that he had retreated, but she knew the necessity of it. If he hadn't, she would have likely never learned the fate of her daughter's branch that had been sent after the old wizard.

The druid said the engagement took place in the lowlands. Yet this didn't look like lowlands at all. It looked like a barren wasteland. Dark tan, chipped earth surrounded the red-armored boy. It was hard to believe that this expanse of nothingness existed mere miles from the stygian spire the wizards called home. She had seen it many times over the winters when she had once been a huntress, the rolling green plains. The deep viridian gully where the tower dwelt.

She had seen evil firsthand from wizards, but to hear tell that the old, feeble human could have destroyed the very earth? It was disconcerting, to say the least.

But it was also strengthening. She had needed this very thing, and that old fool had given it to her. Her people needed to feel the pain if they were to hate them. Feel the pain like she had. Well now her pain was their pain. "Gone . . .," she whispered.

"The boy, First Councilor," the druid said respectfully, causing her to break her gaze away from the wavering image of broken desolation before her, and to focus once again on the young olive-skinned human in her tree- cousins' armor.

"What about him? He seems like no wizard to me."

"The old one called him Blood Wizard, Councilor. I know what we have been trained about them, how they become stronger when wounded."

"And?" Brodea asked impatiently. There had not been a Blood Wizard in nearly a millennia.

"It was verily so, ma'am," the young nature's servant said nervously. "It was my Bristle Wolf that had very nearly had him. When he became covered in the wolf's innards he became . . . well . . . unstoppable."

"This . . . child?" she said with a laugh.

He nodded. "I know how it sounds, Councilor, but it's what I saw. And the truth is there as well. You can see it in his eyes."

That was true, Brodea noted. There was something about his grey eyes that stole her breath when she looked at them. They were intoxicating, menacing, and powerful. Everything for which the Council stood against.

"I wish to see it again," she told the druid. He nodded in compliance. Once again, she was living the last few moments of Shedalia's life through the large basin of water before her.

That was why it was so important for a single druid to escape, so they could transfer the Branch Commander's, or next in command's, final sights back to the Council of Elm. She watched it again intently.

She saw this Blood Wizard fighting savagely, but he was untrained, uncoordinated. She saw his fingers rip into Shedalia's face. The pool of water looked thick with blood. Then he was running, on the ground, and finally Shedalia was gasping as the knife sliced through the corner of her right lung and pierced her heart.

There was a fog over the boy's initial words. Common, when pain washed over the person whose last moments they were watching. But his words next were crystal clear. "Tell me, where is Feydras' Anula!" the olive-skinned boy demanded.

"My Whisper. She will have you," Brodea heard the coughing voice of Shedalia say in a rasp.

Shedalia's incessant coughing covered what he yelled next, but then she heard, "Where is Julietta! Tell me where is the Council of Elm? Where is Feydras' Anula?" His grey eyes were a terror to behold at that moment. She could see then. Yes. Perhaps this boy could pass as a Blood Wizard? It would only fuel her campaign.

"Stop," Brodea commanded, and the druid held the last thoughts from continuing. She didn't need the Councilors to hear any more than they had already about her daughter's . . . dalliance with Shedalia. It was bad enough that they had let their relationship continue as it had, but to hear proclamations of love? No, she didn't need any more gossip spreading than necessary.

Worse, many of the stragglers returning from the battle had said that Shedalia was wearing the markings of Windsong. Would the two really be that brazen about their intimacy together? She could accept that youthful curiosity was one thing, but love? One that had gone on for many, many winters at that? Brodea knew how damaging that could be to the Windsong name, even if she was First Councilor.

Even now, Brodea was struggling hard to cover up the information. News had travelled back quickly about Shedalia's failure even before the druid brought her last thoughts. When Whisper had found out her lover was killed, she had taken it hard, screaming, wailing, and begging her mother for death. Brodea wouldn't give it of course, Whisper was her daughter. So the pain brooded and now Whisper was full of anger and sorrow, something Brodea knew herself all too well. But her burns at the hands of this wizard child had still forced her to remain in hospice. So Brodea knew that the anger would fester, and grow. Soon it would strengthen her daughter the way it had strengthened her.

Brodea stood from her carved elm highback chair, and walked around the basin, studying her enemy, this boy, this . . . Blood Wizard. She liked that title. It gave menace to the boy. Menace she could use.

His features were fair, for a human, his skin much the same color as her own. Yet it was his eyes . . . something about those eyes. *Dui Nuchada*, she reminded herself. He had first been named by the Voïre dui Ceremeia those scant few winters before. His eyes held so much power. Too much power perhaps. "What is your name, nature's servant?"

"Eigron, m'lady," the young druid answered.

"And what does the Blood Wizard know of Feydras' Anula, Eigron?" she asked.

As she feared, the young Elf shook his head, mystified. "I don't know, First Councilor."

She reached down and touched the water that displayed his face. It swirled and wavered at her touch. "You feel this boy is a threat, yes?" she asked.

Eigron coughed into his hand nervously. "First Councilor, it is not my place, you have the connection with the spirits directly . . ."

"Yes, brother, this is so, but I would like to hear it from one that witnessed his actions directly."

He nodded passively. "Yes First Councilor. I truthfully feel that this Unbalancer is the greatest threat of this Council's lifetime."

She heard the nervous murmurs of the Councilors behind her. She wanted to smile and kiss the young Elf for his words, but she kept her face impassive, and only raised a perfect dark eyebrow instead. She couldn't have asked for better words. "Elaborate."

"I witnessed this boy incinerate almost an entire mile of tall grassland within the blink of an eye, slaughtering our people instantly, and almost killing your daughter, First Councilor."

Brodea nodded.

"Then on the battlefield, this boy was unnatural. The more he fought, the stronger he became. His arrows did not seem to miss."

"But the old wizard destroyed the earth. He was the blighter, not the boy," she heard Vooken say from behind.

Eigron nodded nervously. "This is so, yes. But the scale was smaller than the boy's work from before. And where the boy was rendered unconscious from his act, there seemed to be no real repercussions to his actions. As a druid I know the affect Creation will have on me, especially if I request too much of it. A little fatigue in exchange for that ruination . . ."

Brodea watched him breathe deeply as he thought back to the horror that this young wizard must have wrought on him.

"When we engaged him again, days later, he had not waned, not like the elder Unbalancer. The Blood Wizard was in his prime on the battlefield, unstoppable. I . . . I think he relished in it," he stammered.

"When the elder skewer blighted the land, he suffered. He was dead, I think, and if not, it is likely he did not or will not recover for a long time. If this boy knows half of what that wizard knows . . .," the battle-worn Elf said as his voice trailed off.

"You think he's stronger," Vooken answered.

The druid nodded.

She looked at the boy again. She smiled then, for all to see. He would be the catalyst that started the war.

"Thank you, brother, for bringing us this information," she told him. "You are weary, and now we bade you to rest and forget the troubling woes your mind has carried to us, at least for a time. You will be rewarded of course."

"Thank you, First Councilor."

Brodea turned to their druid Cove leader, the Elder of Vines. He was wizened beyond count, and one of the most knowledgeable druids the Circle of Elm had ever had.

"Elder, would you be so kind as to transfer these last thoughts down to the great pool below, ending them at this point."

His old eyes seemed startled by the request, but he nodded, and soon the image faded. Brodea and the rest of the councilors walked to the edge of the great tree they resided in, and looked to the pond a hundred feet below.

Humans below were laboring hard at stone forges. Others were bringing stone and metal in buckets up from a quarry recently started to the south. They were paying the price for being skewers of the balance, and earning their reclamation from the spirits through manual labor. She needed weapons for the army she was building, after all.

Slowly, the image began to play. Humans, perplexed by such a sight, began to gather around the pond to watch the display. After a time she could hear them talking amongst themselves about this redheaded boy. She thought she heard recognition. Perfect.

"Skewers of the Balance," she yelled, her voice carried flawlessly down to them. "That person you see there is the Blood Wizard. The greatest Unbalancer you have ever known. See the land at his feet. See the death at his hands. He caused it all, and he will cause more. If any of you know this man, his past, tell us, and the spirits will consider it atonement for your heinous crimes against the balance of nature. Your reclamation will be at hand, if your information is sound."

Satisfied, Brodea turned and looked to her Councilors, who were shifting nervously about her. "The spirits have commanded this be done," she told them simply. "One amongst them knows this boy, and soon we, too, will know this boy."

Vooken stepped forward, his eyes glittering. "We do not doubt you, First Councilor, but many of us have still not forgotten about the tome we recovered so long ago, about its impasse."

"Yes," she said bitterly. There had been less deciphered than she had hoped over the long winters past. What had first seemed like a great weapon against the wizards was now more of a conundrum than anything. Who were Craetorians? And why were they so prevalent in the founding of Destruction?

"Elder, if you would," Vooken said as he turned it over to the Elder of Vines.

The old, venerable Elf hobbled forward. "We have no doubt of its use against the vile Unbalancers, First Councilor, but I'm afraid there is nothing more that we druids can do. The dialect is ancient, and only decipherable from someone who knows the blasphemous arts of Destruction."

"So the book is useless in our hands, then?" Brodea said angrily.

"I am sorry, First Councilor. Without actually going to that tomb again, I'm afraid we may never know," he said with a bow.

"That tomb is in the Maze!" she said angrily. "No one can survive the creatures in that place!" Anger seethed through her. She had hoped to use that book against the Unbalancers. Against *this* Unbalancer! Now she was afraid her husband may have died for nothing. She could hear the Councilors mumbling their frustrations as well behind her.

Suddenly she felt a touch at her elbow. She looked back to see Vooken had approached her. "We cannot read it," he whispered quietly to her, whilst the others were busy talking amongst themselves about this new threat in the Blood Wizard.

"But a wizard could," he finished as he redirected her gaze down to the pool below, where once again the last thought of Shedalia was replaying itself.

The Blood Wizard's voice echoed up to them. "Where is Julietta? Tell me where is the Council of Elm? Where is Feydras' Anula?"

Brodea smiled as she understood. He was coming to them. He could read the dialect of the book, and not only that, he *had* survived the Maze somehow. Where all her Ferhym had failed, this child had succeeded.

Not only were his actions now the catalyst she needed to spur the Wild Elves into action, but she would see to it that he also would be the one to unlock their greatest weapon against the wizards. All Brodea needed was leverage . . .

She was just about to ask who this Julietta was, when two hunters climbed up the stairs around the wide trunk. A fellow

Councilor began to demand to know what they were doing, interrupting a sacred council, when Brodea saw they were dragging a ragged human woman between them.

She was adorned in little more than filthy white robes that were tattered and torn around her ankles. The cinch around her waist had been ruined so often that she had to loop it around several times, yet it did nothing to mask her curvaceous frame underneath. She had straw blonde hair that hung to her shoulders and was so filthy that it was now mostly brown. Her blue eyes were worn and sunken, dark freckles danced across her sallow skin. The woman looked to be young, perhaps not many winters into being an adult. But the ordeal had worn her significantly. She looked defeated.

The hunters dropped her unceremoniously to the ground before the Councilors.

"This one says it knows the Unbalancer," one of the hunters said to Vooken.

Brodea nodded at them, and they turned and left. Once gone she got down on a knee and looked at the collapsed woman. Her breathing was raspy, and she appeared half-starved.

"Get this reclaimed one some water," she said in her best Trade tongue. She had learned much from the day Ambit had died.

The woman looked up to her, her blue eyes hopeful. Vooken came back with a tall carafe of water, from which the woman drank greedily. When she was done, Brodea continued.

"Do you know that one, my reclaimed child?" she asked in a soothingly gentle voice.

The woman nodded, and then began to cry. Between sobs, she apologized profusely, but Brodea wasn't certain it was to the Council that she was apologizing.

"It's okay," Brodea told the woman. "This man is an Unbalancer, anything you can tell us to aid us, will help put this world on a better course."

"And then I can leave?" she asked, hopeful. "I can go home to my daughter?"

"The spirits have always been good to the reclaimed, for they have found their way back to the balance, my child," Brodea answered. "This Blood Wizard, he is the great skewer. Your transgressions were minimal in comparison. The spirits always reward the most devout. Come back to the balance, child. Help us."

"I just want to do what's right," she said between sobs. "I just want to hold my baby girl again."

"And you will. You will," Brodea cooed. "What is your name, reclaimed child?"

"Avrimae, as it suits you, m'lady."

"Well, Avrimae, your daughter awaits her mother. Tell me of this Unbalancer. Return to your child's life," Brodea whispered.

Brodea watched as Avrimae looked down far below into the pool where the Blood Wizard's grey eyes reflected up at them. She saw the woman mouth the words I'm sorry.

"His name is Ashyn," she said as another tear rolled down her face. "Ashyn Rune. And I know everything about him."

"Then you know who Julietta is?" she asked, hopeful.

Avrimae nodded, "She's his sister."

Brodea smiled wickedly.

Perfect.

ABOUT THE AUTHOR

JAY ERICKSON grew up in Midwestern USA before joining the United States Air Force at the age of nineteen as an aircraft mechanic. During his active tour, he earned two Associates' degrees in Computer Applications and Aerospace Maintenance. In 2001, he separated from active service and became an Air Force Reservist.

Since that time, he has held a variety of jobs from working at a casino, to crane operation, to masonry. Even with a myriad of different careers, though, writing has been his primary interest and hobby. As an avid reader, he has always held a deep love for Fantasy and Science Fiction. It was a natural fit for his writing. Now he's taking that hobby one step further by publishing the novel, BLOOD WIZARD CHRONICLES: PARIAH for others to read.

Mr. Erickson resides in Northwest Indiana with his wife and two children.